Queen
IN EXILE

Queen
IN EXILE

DONNA HATCH

To Tom, who most definitely is not in trouble.

Walnut Springs Press, LLC
110 South 800 West
Brigham City, Utah 84302
http://walnutspringspress.blogspot.com

Copyright © 2010 by Donna Hatch

ISBN: 978-1-935217-63-3

Acknowledgments

A big thanks to my family, who are my very best cheerleaders, especially when self-doubt comes in. Also to my fellow ANWA and Desert Rose RWA sisters, who have offered immeasurable encouragement. And special thanks to Linda Prince for her tough love that helped make this story even better.

Chapter One

The thundering hoof beats of her two guards' mounts grew steadily louder behind her while Jeniah, on her own duocorn, fled Arden City as if a pack of wyrwolves pursued her. Jeniah glanced over her shoulder and willed her guards away, knowing such a wish was foolish. How she longed to truly escape Arden, her stifling role, and the terrifying new future she must soon accept. Jeniah could no more escape her destiny than she could escape her personal guards, but for a few blissful moments, she would be Jeniah. Not a princess, not a scholar, not a bride of some far-off, faceless prince. Just Jeniah.

Her duocorn, Egan, settled into a comfortable canter, his double-horned head nodding with each stride. Her guards matched her pace behind her, and she tried to forget they were there. Birds roosting in the trees scattered at their approach, fluttering deeper into the woods. Embracing the exhilaration of riding, Jeniah flung her arms out to each side, imagining how it might feel to soar unfettered into the great unknown, without a care.

Cantering over the cobblestones, Egan rounded a bend in the highway. Without warning a side path appeared, calling to Jeniah with irresistible force. She reined sharply. Egan danced against the reins, turning a full circle, and shook his head, making the bridle jingle. Jeniah's pulse galloped and her stomach quivered.

She stared down the path, irresistibly drawn, feeling the stirring whispers of destiny.

Breneg and Ciath halted their duocorns on either side and drew their swords, searching for signs of danger.

"Your Highness?" Breneg said in alarm.

Her gaze fixed on the path, Jeniah held up her hand. "Nothing's amiss, Breneg. I wish to be alone." Her voice sounded oddly distant, oddly hoarse.

"Alone? Your Highness, we cannot guard you if—"

"Only for a few moments, Breneg." Without looking at him, Jeniah knew her sternness had surprised him.

Jeniah could not explain the urgent compulsion to traverse the path alone, but the power beckoned to her very soul. Her heart skittered, and she could no longer resist the lure. Without waiting for further response, she urged Egan forward. The path seemed ordinary. It led from the highway to a shallow hollow that appeared equally mundane, yet a shiver of anticipation raised bumps on Jeniah's arms.

She dismounted, leaving Egan to graze, and walked deeper into the woods. She paused behind a tree, and the moment she knew her guards could no longer see her, she blurred. The familiar warm, tickling sensation spread over her, blending her with her surroundings. If Breneg and Ciath were to spot her now, she'd appear as nothing more than a sapling or a shrub.

A part of her feared her strange magic. Magic had been the cause of the Great Wars. In Arden, magic was shunned, feared. Not even her faithful lady-in-waiting knew Jeniah's power.

In moments of irony, Jeniah wondered why she bothered blurring. Her family acted as if she were already invisible, unless they remembered their need to forge allies.

Breneg and Ciath moved away, their duocorns' hooves rustling the dried leaves. No doubt they were following their usual pattern to sweep the area for danger, spiraling outward in opposite directions, and then tightening the spiral until they returned within visual distance of her. She would have a few minutes of solitude before they returned. Eventually, she'd have to stop blurring and reveal herself, or they'd grow frantic.

Jeniah stepped over a log peppered with mushrooms and walked deeper into the woods, following the irresistible call. Fallen leaves crunched under her riding boots. She hurried along the sun-dappled path, eager to discover the source of the compelling summons. At the rise of a hollow, she stopped. Chills of excitement tingled her spine. She held her breath.

An enormous golden-brown animal stood on four legs at the far edge of the hollow. Sunlight slanted down through the woodland trees, giving his thick pelt and mane an iridescent shimmer. Jeniah gasped. Truly, it could not be! She stared in disbelief at a sacred chayim.

He was magnificent. She felt as if she were in the presence of deity, ancient and wise beyond human comprehension. Her mouth went dry and she fell to her knees.

She'd heard the stories, of course. She'd listened, enraptured, as minstrels related accounts—legends, some said—of a chayim choosing a maiden of surpassing purity and courage, bonding with her, and guiding her as she led her people to a bright new future. In private moments of hope, Jeniah had dared to dream a chayim would choose her.

Jeniah's heart pounded as if trying to escape her chest, and her breath came in gasps. Nearly overcome, she waited for the chayim to determine her worthiness. She stood and lowered the hood of her cloak, careful to make no sudden movements lest she frighten him away.

Moving with regal grace, the chayim padded down the slope into the hollow and stopped barely out of reach. His shoulders were level with her head, and he was even longer than he was tall.

Quivering in excitement, she held out a hand. The beast took another step toward her. His long neck curved and his head dipped down while a pair of dark, intelligent eyes probed hers. She waited, trembling in anticipation, as if poised at the summit of a mountain. A step to one side would mean death. A step to the other would bring limitless freedom.

He blew gently into her face, a sign of acceptance. Her heart soared and tears of joy streamed down her cheeks. Driven by a compulsion to touch him, she raised her hand higher. When the beast opened his mouth, revealing two rows of sharp teeth, she felt no fear, only wonder, peace, and light. Her heartbeat slowed and she felt a smile curve her mouth as she spoke softly to him.

After a brief pause, the chayim answered with a low growl others might have found fearsome. Jeniah continued to extend her hand until it finally touched the long, square muzzle, finding the golden fur softer than she expected. The chayim closed his mouth and uttered a noise much like a purr.

Acceptance and an all-consuming love flowed into her as the chayim's mind gently touched hers. Through the images he sent her, she witnessed changes to the land the chayim had seen during his long life. He mentally deepened their connection, wrapping her in warmth and safety and truth.

For the first time, she saw herself as more than an annoyance, more than a pretty distraction, more than her father's pawn to forge a political alliance. She saw herself as a young woman of much greater worth. That knowledge filled her with indescribable joy and a renewed dedication to her duty. And it gave her hope.

Using her powers for others now became paramount, a realization both humbling and liberating.

Through emotion and image, the chayim assured her that her

ability to blur was not a power to fear, but merely a small part of a greater magic that would serve her, and serve her people.

Without warning, the connection shattered.

Jeniah staggered back, disoriented and empty from the sudden severance of their bond. Drained of energy, she collapsed. She raised a hand toward the chayim, desperate to renew their mental bond, but she could not reach him. His head turned toward something behind her, his tail swishing angrily. He growled.

Hoof beats approached. As she lay on her back looking up at her chayim, Jeniah's thoughts cleared, and she swallowed a growl of her own. Apparently her overprotective guards had finished their guarding pattern and returned. She could blur to prevent them from finding her, but if they had already visually marked her, blurring would not deceive them. And at the moment, she wasn't sure she had the strength.

Hoping her chayim would remain, she struggled to her feet to warn away the guards. Her weakened limbs failed her again and she crumpled.

The hoof beats grew nearer still, and an enormous silver duocorn pounded into view with a man astride him. Jeniah's chayim stood over her defensively and let out a roar that shook the ground. She pressed her hands over her ears. If she hadn't already bonded with him, she would have been terrified.

"Get back!" she tried to warn the stranger, but it came out as a weak gasp.

With a battle cry, the rider and his mount charged down the slope from the highway toward them in the hollow. Though he wore the chain mail of a knight, the rider was clearly not one of her guards.

Her chayim let out a roar more threatening than the first. He dropped to a crouch facing the intruder, and stood over her, his breath warm and moist on her face, his haunches quivering.

Drawing a sword, the stranger charged.

Jeniah gasped. Not only was the armed rider about to destroy her destined bonding with a chayim, but he planned to battle this magical beast! What brainless madman would attack a holy chayim?

And where were Breneg and Ciath? They should be alerted to the presence of another rider. Jeniah's chayim growled again, and her concern shifted to the rider. Her chayim would no doubt kill the foolish man before he could inflict any injury, yet she wished no harm upon any person. Even a fool.

"Stay away! You're in danger!" Still weakened by the aborted connection, Jeniah tried to rise but failed again.

Teeth bared at the intruder, her chayim twitched as he prepared to spring. The rider continued his charge. As her chayim leaped, he extended claws the length of daggers from his paws. The armed man and her chayim came together in a terrible clash.

Horrified by the violence, Jeniah pushed her shaking limbs to a stand. "NO!" she shouted, finally recovering her voice.

Her chayim hesitated at the sound of her frantic cry. In that moment of distraction, the warrior attacked. His sword made a graceful arc and sliced into her chayim's golden chest.

Jeniah screamed. Dread clutched at her heart, squeezing until she could barely draw a breath.

"No!" she sobbed. "No, don't hurt him!"

Her chayim fell, rolled, and jumped to his feet. Amber blood streamed from the wound. Rearing up on his back two legs, he swiped at his opponent, his claws barely missing the man's chest. The rider's duocorn danced back and then lunged, bringing the warrior and his sword in close. Man and chayim lunged, struck and parried.

Desperate to stop them from killing one another, Jeniah picked up a rock to throw at them, but halted before she let it fly. The last time she'd interfered, she'd distracted her chayim and the man had wounded him. She ground her teeth in frustration at her helplessness.

Though bleeding from multiple wounds, her chayim raked the duocorn's flank with his claws. The duocorn whinnied in pain and reared but continued circling the beast. Skillfully avoiding her chayim's teeth and claws, the man struck again. Weakened, her chayim slowed until he could no longer evade the sword. The warrior thrust his blade deep. The chayim's shriek filled Jeniah with cold dismay.

He flailed, howling in pain, his claws missing the duocorn by a breath. The swordsman severed one of her chayim's massive paws, which only threw the beast into a greater frenzy. Roaring and thrashing, her chayim came at the swordsman. Again, the warrior's blade found its mark.

Sickened and shaking, Jeniah sank to her knees.

This time, the magnificent animal collapsed. His breath labored twice, and after a spasm, he lay motionless. Amber blood flowed in a spreading stain on the leaves carpeting the woodland floor.

Silence rang out as if all nature's creatures paused to mourn.

"No," Jeniah whispered in disbelief. All strength left her limbs. Darkness drew around her, leaving her desolate and utterly lost. She felt as though she had lived all her life in darkness, then unexpectedly stepped out into the light to behold the beauty of the earth and sky, the majesty of color, the power and magnificence of the sea, only to be plunged back into darkness with naught but a taunting memory of what she had found and lost. All that remained was emptiness.

The warrior dismounted and approached the lifeless chayim. Jeniah gasped as he prodded the creature with the end of his sword. Then the swordsman turned toward Jeniah and ran to her without stirring a leaf, silent and graceful.

Through a haze of grief, it occurred to Jeniah that a man who would kill a revered creature might now harm her. At the moment, however, she was so overcome by loss that she hardly cared.

The warrior dropped to the ground in front of Jeniah. "Are you injured?"

He spoke in a foreign accent with rich, resonant tones belonging to a minstrel, not a warrior. But his violent act toward her chayim drove away any charm she might have found in his voice.

Bereft, unable to speak, she shook her head.

The warrior looked her directly in the eye as if searching for some truth he might only find there. His startlingly blue eyes burned with inner fire. Then, as if he found whatever he'd sought, he stood.

After he cleaned and put away his weapon, he removed a leather glove and held a hand toward her. "I'll help you up."

She eyed his hand, making no move. Despite his unkempt and unshaven appearance, something in his posture suggested authority. As her eyes traced his broad, muscular form, she realized no knight in the castle could match him in strength or size. While he dressed as a commoner, he had the confident, almost arrogant bearing that Jeniah associated with nobility. A simple cord held together his unadorned, travel-stained cloak instead of a metal clasp used by the wealthy. The breeches and heavily padded tunic visible underneath his chain mail had been cut from coarse fabric. That deadly sword, bane of her chayim, rested in a plain leather scabbard at his hip, almost touching worn boots caked with dirt.

His eyes fixed upon her with unnerving intensity. For an impoverished knight, this man possessed unabashed boldness. He waited, watching her, his hand extended.

"You have nothing to fear from me, my lady," he said softly in his lilting foreign accent.

Her arm moved on its own volition. Against his large, calloused hand, hers looked small and fragile. He could easily crush her bones. Instead, as if he feared injuring her, he took her hand carefully. After pulling her to her feet, he remained motionless, his fingers closed around hers, his gaze disturbingly direct.

The stranger reached out with his other hand and gently brushed away a tear lingering on Jeniah's cheek.

Shocked at the intimacy of his touch, and at the tingles that spiraled outward from it, she caught her breath. No man in Arden would touch her in such a manner. This man dared much. She snatched her hand back and stepped away to disguise the sudden awareness of her own vulnerability, and her elemental awareness of him as a man.

"You should not be out here all alone, my lady."

As his words penetrated her stunned sorrow, she pressed her lips together. Amazed at the audacity of this killer to censure her, she found her tongue. "Your permission is not required."

He blinked, clearly taken aback. His eyes narrowed. "There are many dangers to a lone girl. That beast alone—"

"I was perfectly safe. Didn't you see that the chayim had accepted me?" Her eyes were drawn to the terrible sight of her chayim lying lifeless. She choked.

"Accepted you?"

"Yes, accepted—a symbiotic lifetime of protection, of friendship." What oaf did not know the stories? "I've felt destined for this all my life." Anger and sorrow roiled in her stomach.

The warrior eyed her as if he thought her a bit insane, and glanced back at the scene of the battle. "Your life was clearly in danger, my lady."

Anger cut through her sadness. Only years of exercising

forbearance prevented her from shouting at him. "I was in no danger. He saw you as a threat, not only to himself, but to me. He never would have attacked you if you hadn't charged in brandishing your weapon. Perhaps I should be grateful you didn't turn that sword upon me in your bloodlust."

Her would-be rescuer clenched his jaw and pressed his lips into a thin line. "I would never slay an unarmed opponent, nor would I ever harm a lady. And if I had known—"

"It would behoove you to make certain of your enemies before you kill them." Grief and fury competed for dominion over of her heart, and her self-restraint slipped. She dashed aside new tears, frustrated at her loss of control.

His hands fisted at his sides. "It would behoove you to take more caution in the forest. No lady should ever be without protection. And unless you are concealing a weapon, you appear ill-equipped to defend yourself against the many dangers out here."

"How typical of a warrior, seeing danger where none exists, and leaping at any opportunity to kill."

His words came out clipped. "I do not leap at opportunities to kill."

"You did today!" She snapped her mouth closed and wiped her tears.

"By the moons," he muttered, looking upward. He raked his fingers through his dark hair, slowly let out his breath, and visibly smothered an angry retort.

Incredible. A warrior with self-control.

"If I caused you grief or placed you in danger, I apologize, my lady." His stiffly spoken words failed to bring her comfort. Then his expression softened, became earnest. "Truly, I'm sorry. I didn't mean to frighten you or cause undo harm."

For some unaccountable reason, she found that she believed him. As her eyes locked with his, she realized that as a foreigner, he probably would not know of a sacred beast unique to Arden. Her tumult faded as a new understanding came over her. He must have happened along by accident, and when he saw her lying on the ground with the large and dangerous-looking animal standing over her, naturally assumed she'd been about to be devoured. Spurred by a sense of chivalry, he'd charged in to slay the beast and rescue the maiden.

Grappling with her desire to hate him for his unforgivable actions, and her realization that she couldn't really blame him, she stared, unable to formulate a reply. Her shoulders slumped in resignation.

He grasped a crumpled leaf caught in her hair, his hands sliding down a long, dark ringlet before the leaf fell into his hand.

Startled by his familiarity, Jeniah took another step back from the stranger. Even more startling, she did not find the contact distasteful. More unsettled by her reaction to his touch than the touch itself, she began brushing leaves and bits of twigs off her gown and cloak, her actions stiff and jerky, and tried to fortify her self-control.

"Egan!"

Her duocorn came through the trees, but shied from the maimed body on the ground. The warrior's silver duocorn nickered. To her surprise, Egan answered, approaching the unknown steed. After a few huffs and flicks of their tails, they touched noses in greeting as if old friends.

The war duocorn, as heavily muscled as his master, stood several hand spans taller than Egan, and his horns had been sharpened for use as weapons. Egan's mane and featherings grew long and shinning from careful brushing, but the silver stallion's hair was clipped ruthlessly short.

The stranger extended a hand to Egan and crooned softly. Her normally shy mount came to him and nuzzled his palm.

"Traitor," Jeniah muttered.

After he stroked Egan's head, the warrior moved soundlessly upon the dried leaves to his own beast. The swordsman examined his duocorn for injuries, but to Jeniah, the wound on his flank looked superficial. The warrior appeared to agree, and he patted his duocorn and turned back to her.

"Egan, come." Jeniah glanced back at her chayim's motionless body. She hated to leave him there as food for carrion. It seemed too ignoble an end.

Approaching tentatively, she went to him, fearful of the sight. Even battered and lifeless, he exuded beauty, greatness, magic. Magic couldn't all be bad if her chayim possessed it, could it?

Kneeling next to him, Jeniah stroked his fur and whispered, "Home and sweet meat to you, my friend." She pulled a few hairs from the crown of her head, wincing slightly from the sting, and laid them over her chayim's chest. "May the god of the moons welcome you."

She ran her fingers through his mane until a few loose hairs fell into her hand. After twisting the hair into a knot, she tucked it into her bodice next to her heart. "May the god of the moons give me peace without you." She bowed her head, her heart cold and empty.

The wind gusted, bringing in the late afternoon fog. Her guards would be returning any moment. Swallowing hard, she stood. Purposely refraining from looking at the warrior standing motionless next to his duocorn, she used a rock as a step to mount Egan and settled in the saddle.

"My lady, I must insist upon accompanying you to ensure your safety." Somehow he managed to sound both deferential and condescending.

Despite his earlier plea for forgiveness and her insight into his motives, Jeniah's anger returned and gave venom to her words. She lifted her head with all the regal haughtiness of the queen mother and looked down upon him. The effect was not as dramatic as she had hoped, since, even in the saddle, she sat only slightly above eye level with him.

"You are a stranger, and you have killed a revered animal. Two very good reasons not to trust you with both my virtue and my life."

He winced. "My lady, I give you my word as a knight, I mean you no harm. I'm honor-bound to protect and defend the innocent."

"Unless they come in the form of chayims, apparently." The words were out of her mouth before she could stop them. Shame sent warmth up her neck to her face. Such petty viciousness should be beneath her, but she seemed to have lost control over her emotions.

His face grew tight and unyielding. "Be grateful I'm a man of honor, or you would already be my victim."

Jeniah's mouth dropped. "A true man of honor would not say such a thing."

"I'm trying to protect you," he ground out.

"I've but to return to the road where I left my guards and they will see me home, as they would have protected me had I been in any real danger."

He glanced about, and she could almost hear him wondering where her guards were, and why they had not intervened.

Unwilling to enlighten him, Jeniah flicked the reins and headed toward the highway.

"My lady."

Impatiently, she reined and glanced over her shoulder.

"Please, tell me your name."

She clenched her teeth, loath to give him any favor he sought, and prayed she'd never be forced to see him again. Without replying, she urged Egan into a canter.

As she rode, the wind whipped her hair and brought the scent of growing things mingled with the smells of the ocean. The woodland trees thickened, reducing the sunlight to glimmering shafts streaming through the leaves, while the duocorn deftly bounded his way around trees, mossy rocks, and fallen logs.

Her mother did not approve of her riding at such a pace. She often said it wasn't befitting a princess, especially since Jeniah would soon be of age and could no longer use youth as an excuse for a lack of decorum.

Heartache urged Jeniah to a reckless speed. She tightened her legs around Egan's sleek body and bent over his neck. She felt rather than heard Breneg and Ciath fall in with her, but they remained respectfully behind. She wanted to rail against them for failing her when she needed them, but they were blameless, since she had blurred purposely to hide from them. No doubt they wanted to chastise her for losing them. Again.

After ducking under a branch that came threateningly close to her face, she broke through the trees and out onto the wide, sandy beach. She cantered along the shore, heading farther away from the castle of Arden. At a rock formation blocking her path on the beach, she reined and absently rubbed Egan's long, curved horns. Her emotions alternated between sorrow, anger, and despair. No tutor had instructed her on how to deal with realizing, and then losing, a hope she'd nurtured all her days, or a friend she'd instantly loved above her own life. Desolation crept across her heart and settled in.

"Your Highness."

Jeniah jumped. She'd been so tightly wrapped in her cocoon of grief that she hadn't heard Breneg approach.

"Forgive me, Your Highness, but it grows late."

Jeniah drew a deep breath and wiped tears she hadn't realized she'd shed. The shadows had grown long, and darkness loomed. She pulled her cloak more tightly around her. One moon hung suspended, already high in the sky, its silvery glow dim next to the drowsy sun. The second moon hovered large and orange at the horizon.

Breneg sidled up to her, his face lined in concern as he took a long look at her. "Are you all right?"

Jeniah nodded, touched that he cared beyond his duty as her guard, and relieved that he did not demand an explanation for her absence. "Just thinking."

He didn't press her for answers, though he clearly knew she was troubled. She rode beside him, leaving the shore and climbing the rise to the highway. As they guided their mounts toward the castle, Ciath rode further ahead.

Jeniah breathed in the damp, salty air. In a long exhale, she released her turmoil, her anger, and her sadness. Fog drifted in slowly and sometimes in bursts as the wind gusted. Her heart resumed its normal rhythm and the tension in her shoulders eased. Her senses filled with the motion of riding, with Egan's warm body, the rhythm of his hooves, the crashing of the waves, the chill wind, and the smells of the ocean.

As she walked Egan, with Breneg riding next to her, she again thought of the stranger. His clothing and his accent proved he was not Ardeene, and she suspected he'd come from Govia or Darbor.

If the man were the knight of honor he claimed to be, he surely would not have killed a revered animal if he had understood the chayim's significance—unless she underestimated a warrior's need to kill. She could not hope to understand the mind of a man who trained for the express purpose of making war.

She felt Breneg's curious gaze upon her but did not meet it. With all her dreams shattered, she'd have to face her destiny. It was time to hold up her head and accept her fate. In two moon cycles, she'd be nineteen, and then she'd marry the man of her father's choosing to forge an alliance for the benefit of Arden. Duty could be a heavy burden.

Perhaps she should stop using her magic. Her ability to blur had been her secret since she discovered the ability as a young adolescent. Her chayim had assured her that she would one day reveal her power, but now that she'd lost her chayim, that time might never come.

"We must make haste, Your Highness."

Breneg was right, of course. Darkness brought danger.

They urged their mounts to a canter. The road darkened as it wound through the forest. Trees leaned across the road toward its opposite side like lovers longing for a forbidden touch. Insects sang as darkness grew. Night had nearly spread over the land when Jeniah heard a mournful howl that chilled her blood. Wyrwolves.

She had complete faith in Breneg and Ciath, but two knights against a full pack of wyrwolves would not be sufficient. If the wyrwolves attacked, blurring would only protect her from being seen; she doubted it would hide her scent from the carnivores.

Worse, her guards would pay for her carelessness. Fear coiled in her stomach. The three riders urged their mounts to a full run, their hooves clattering on the road in a cadence that kept time with Jeniah's heartbeat. As they rounded the bend in the road, Arden City and the safety of its walls came into view.

Egan's neck stretched out as he ran with all his strength. Her heart thundering in her ears, Jeniah glanced behind her. The shadowed road lay empty. Wyrwolves called again, so close that she expected to see them beside her.

Perspiration froze like droplets of ice on her face in the bitter wind. She leaned forward over Egan's neck as he somehow ran even faster. Breneg remained close and Ciath fell back to ride protectively on her other side.

With the crashing of brush, the wyrwolves came at them from the trees. She dared a glance backward.

On the road behind them, terrifyingly close, raced the nightmarish carnivores. Their oddly humanlike faces turned toward her with hideous, hungry grins. Nearly as tall as a duocorn, their shaggy bodies loped toward her with alarming speed. Leaning low over Egan's neck, Jeniah focused on Arden Castle ahead, but she feared they might not reach it in time.

Her breath came in sharp gasps. With throbbing pulse, she spoke to Egan, urging him to keep going, but he needed no more encouragement than the beasts at his heels. With the howling creatures only inches away, Egan and the other duocorns fairly flew toward the outer city gates.

The city gates opened, spitting out a full regiment of armed guards. Carrying torches, yelling and brandishing their weapons, the men charged at the hungry pursuers. A brief melee ensued while men's steel clashed with beasts' teeth. Three wyrwolves fell dead on the road. Snarling, the few remaining wyrwolves turned and slunk back into the darkness.

Safely inside the city walls with the gate firmly closed behind her, Jeniah sat frozen on her heaving duocorn. She struggled to breathe and to battle her tears. By staying out too late, she'd endangered her own life. Worse, she had endangered the lives of not only Breneg and Ciath, but the men who rushed to save her. Shame, sharper than fear, knifed through her. Afraid she might see wounded among the soldiers, she eyed them, but none appeared to be injured.

Breneg leaned over and pried her shaking hands from the reins. "Your Highness."

She dared a look at him, expecting reproach on his face, but saw only concern.

"We're safe now, Princess."

She nodded, fighting her tears. "Thank you," she said to all within hearing. "I'm sorry I put you all in danger."

Murmurs of acknowledgement, and even words brushing off her self-recrimination, came in reply. The sentries put away their weapons and melted back into the shadows.

Taking her emotions in hand, she locked them away and raised her chin. Flanked by Breneg and Ciath, she rode through Arden City toward the castle, her relief mingled with melancholy. Filled with the new self-awareness her chayim had given her, she drove away her hopelessness. She straightened her posture, lifted her chin, and rode forward to meet her destiny.

Chapter Two

*K*ai stood at attention as he faced Captain Tarvok inside the guard tower of Arden castle's wall. With the door directly behind him and a sentry posted on each side, Kai remained alert, his muscles tense, lest anyone attempt to sneak up on him. Darbor and Arden were allied countries, but Kai wouldn't be surprised if the captain of the guard staged some sort of test. If their roles had been reversed, Kai would have done so. Sweat trickled between his shoulder blades.

Captain Tarvok pinned him with an assessing, hostile stare. "You're Kai Darkwood of Darbor? I expected a Sauraii master of your reputation to be older." The clipped Ardeene accent sounded strange to Kai, but he had no trouble understanding Arden's captain of the guard.

"I hear that often," Kai replied evenly.

"I'm told you were one of the youngest students ever to have earned that title." Tarvok folded his arms and eyed him with open mistrust.

Normally, Kai did not share details of his private life, but he suspected the captain already knew and was determining if he was truly who he claimed to be. "When I completed the final task, I was fourteen."

Tarvok snorted but looked unsurprised. "Impossible."

"My father did, too."

The captain remained watchful. They stood almost the same height, and while Tarvok appeared several years older, and leaner, Kai recognized in his every movement the lethal force of a skilled warrior.

Kai knew the captain required further proof before he would admit a stranger into Arden's castle gates, and he secretly approved of such cautiousness. Kai removed his left riding glove and pulled up his sleeve to reveal the unmistakable sign of the Sauraii on the underside of his forearm, a snake coiled around a dagger. It hadn't faded in the twelve years since he'd received it. He tapped the center of the coiled snake with his right index finger, and the snake's body moved, wrapping itself around the dagger in a slow, sinuous motion. Though some had tried, no one could replicate the mark.

Kai knew that as a seasoned knight, Tarvok had mastered his expressions well, but he saw the lines around the older man's eyes relax. Behind Kai, one of the guards shifted his weight. Kai tensed, prepared to drop into a defensive stance, his hand automatically moving to the pommel of his sword. There were only three people in the room, but he had no way of knowing how many others waited outside.

A corner of Tarvok's mouth twitched in amusement. "Your orders, Captain Darkwood?"

Alert for signs of an ambush, Kai retrieved an intricately folded parchment bearing the king of Darbor's seal and handed it over.

After breaking the seal and reading the missive, Tarvok folded the document and tucked it away. "I'll assign a squire to you and have someone show you to your quarters. You've been offered accommodations in the castle."

"I'll stay in the officers' barracks," Kai said without hesitation.

Tarvok raised a brow. "You're the king's honored guest."

Kai chose his words carefully. "I don't know your customs, Captain, and I mean no insult to the king, but I came here to train knights, not fraternize with courtiers."

Tarvok eyed him with a calculated stare, but Kai thought he saw a flicker of approval. "I can't speak for the king, but I doubt he'll be insulted by your decision. Very well. Officers' quarters it is. I'm going to the training arena. Do you wish to come observe the knights train? Or are you too tired from your travels?"

Kai wasn't sure if there was a challenge in that question or not. With the long journey barely behind him, he wanted nothing better than a hot meal, a bath, and a bed.

Instead, he replied, "It would help me to determine where I should begin their instruction if I could see them in motion."

Tarvok nodded, and Kai had the impression he'd passed yet another test. Kai followed Captain Tarvok outside the guard tower. Two sentries stepped aside to let them pass. Outside, Kai caught the aroma of cooking food, underscored by the musty smells of men and animals. Voices made a low murmur, punctuated by the smith's hammer. A pair of knights laughed raucously as they strode across the yard. A two-wheeled wagon clattered toward the gate, drawn by a bent old man.

Braygo remained where Kai had left him—in the care of a boy who gripped the duocorn's reins as if he might fall without them.

Tarvok caught the direction of Kai's stare. "Don't worry about your duocorn. The stable lads will take care of him, and I'll have your gear brought to your quarters."

"He's wounded." Kai gestured to the long scratches on Braygo's flank made by the fearsome beast he'd battled only an hour ago.

Tarvok halted. "Trouble on the way here?"

Kai managed a casual shrug. "It's minor. I cleaned up the scratches and applied some salve I carry with me, but I'd like the head stable master to treat him."

He groaned inwardly as he recalled that disaster. He'd risked his king's relationship with a trusted ally by killing a rare and honored animal. His untimely appearance and wrong assumptions had brought disaster upon a girl who was, at the very least, a nobleman's daughter. And worse, he'd made her cry. Not the tears of a spoiled child who'd been denied her petty desires, but the tears of someone who'd lost everything. He'd never felt like such a cad. By the moons, today already had proven not one of his proudest days.

Captain Tarvok made a quick gesture to the boy who held the duocorn's reins. The lad nodded and led Braygo away. Kai kept pace with Tarvok through the castle grounds, amazed by the graceful architecture and expansive gardens. Everywhere he looked, he beheld fragile beauty.

Unfortunately, the castle appeared to be built to please the senses and not to withstand a siege. The outer walls were too narrow and the buildings of the nearby town stood too close to the castle walls. Other problems became painfully clear—too many to enumerate. Kai hoped the inevitable war would take place on a battlefield far from such delicate and impractical beauty.

At the training arena, Kai and Tarvok halted inside the entrance and watched knights spar in pairs.

"Do you want me to call them to attention?" Tarvok asked.

"No. I want to see how they move." Kai watched them, noting where their skills lacked and where their strengths lay.

Right away, he saw that their moves were too predictable and that the knights were grossly inexperienced. These men fought more like squires than knights, appearing to have received their knighthood only as an honorary title. Or perhaps the title came from their ability to fence, which was fairly good. But fencing was a pastime to display one's skill in precision; sword-fighting an enemy required a completely different technique.

Aware that Tarvok was waiting, Kai chose his words carefully. "You've done a fine job with them, Captain Tarvok. Their basic skills are solid."

Tarvok snorted. "Be honest. They wouldn't last a day in battle."

True, but Kai refrained from agreeing. "Their lack of experience is obvious, but not as bad as I'd feared for men whose country shuns extensive instruction in weaponry."

"We Ardeenes love philosophy and the arts, and have little tolerance for men who embrace violence and bloodshed."

Kai raised a brow at the mocking tone in Tarvok's voice and wondered if the captain had grown up scorned for his chosen profession as a warrior. "I understand Arden hasn't seen war in several generations."

"Over a hundred years."

"But you've been in battle."

Tarvok lifted one shoulder slightly. "I'm something of an anomaly. I fought in the Govian Wars before the king offered me a post."

"I did too."

Tarvok's gaze flicked to him, but Kai couldn't guess his thoughts.

He tucked his gloves in his belt and returned his gaze to the sparring knights. "We'll make sure they're battle-ready when the Hanorans arrive next spring, Captain Tarvok."

"That will take considerable effort."

Kai felt one side of his mouth turn up. "They aren't that bad."

"They are, but that's not what I mean. No one here really believes we face war."

Taken aback, Kai stared. "Truly?"

With a grimace, Tarvok folded his arms. "They think they'll find some diplomatic way to keep peace with the Hanorans."

Kai frowned in disbelief. "Impossible. I've fought the Hanorans. Their king is utterly bloodthirsty. No amount of token offers or pretty speeches will appease him."

"An Ardeene's faith in his own powers of speech is astounding," Tarvok said dryly.

"Then why did your king request me to come and train his army?"

"Precautionary measure, I suppose. Show of force."

Kai dragged a hand through his hair. Trying to train reluctant knights in preparation for a battle most of them believed they would never fight would be a difficult task. "King Farai warned me before I left Darbor that I might meet with some naivety about the possibility of war, but I had no idea my presence here would only be a display."

"We need you. We don't know it yet, but we do." Coming from a battle-hardened warrior, that admission had to have cost Tarvok.

"I'm here to serve."

The corners of Tarvok's mouth pulled upward, and he offered Kai his hand. "Welcome to Arden, Captain Darkwood."

Feeling as if he'd won a major victory, Kai grinned and clasped Tarvok's forearm below the elbow in the warrior's grip.

"There's a ceremony tonight at seven bells in the throne room to welcome you. Plenty of food and pretty ladies. I need to go check the gate sentries during the changeover. I'll see you here in the morning." Tarvok turned to leave.

A ceremony? Kai almost groaned out loud. "Captain."

Tarvok turned back and waited.

Kai gritted his teeth. He despised his uncertainty, but if Tarvok could admit needing help, so could he. "About this ceremony tonight, is there anything I need to know?"

Kai was all too aware that his role at Arden included acting as an ambassador of Darbor. Pity, since he'd always despised diplomats. But he'd fall on his own sword before he'd fail his king.

Tarvok shook his head. "It's only a formality. King Darvae will welcome you and give you your rank and title. They won't expect a speech or anything from you, merely a vow of loyalty. There will be a feast and probably a dance. Nothing to worry about."

A grand feast and a dance with royalty sounded almost as appealing as blood and torture. Kai let out an unhappy sigh. "Formal dress, I presume?"

"Of course." A devilish light entered Tarvok's eye. "Surely a Sauraii master has no fear of that."

"Will you be there?"

Tarvok made a sound that might have been a cough. "Royalty and honored guests only."

Disappointed that he'd be facing the formalities without an ally, Kai nodded. "I'll see you at dawn."

Tarvok broke out into a full grin, saluted, and after a smart, military turn, strode away.

Kai returned his gaze to the knights and watched them until he determined the best way to begin his instruction in the morning. Then he wandered up on the battlements.

The view caused him to pause. Unlike the rugged terrain and craggy mountains of his homeland of Darbor, Arden was green, with smooth, rolling hills. The sea shimmered silver in the distance on one side of the castle, and rounded mountains rose up into low clouds on the other. A fine mist blew off the water and formed tiny droplets on his face. The salty air was both invigorating and soothing.

Below the outer wall, Kai noticed a man with a slight build speaking to a hooded figure. Something in the furtive manner of their conversation caught Kai's interest. The slender man, wearing the clothes of a nobleman, passed something to the hooded figure, who jumped astride a duocorn and cantered toward the open gates. Kai watched the nobleman as he turned and swaggered out of view. Something about the exchange didn't feel right, and Kai decided it would be wise to keep a sharp eye on the nobleman.

Kai stilled. Keep an eye on a nobleman? Possibly a trusted member of the royal council? What a ridiculous notion! Perhaps the journey had fatigued him more than he thought. Even if he could have the king's ear at some point over the next few days, voicing doubts about a nobleman was not the best way to begin his role in Arden.

The sun scattered golden-red rays through the clouds, reminding Kai that he should begin preparing for the welcoming ceremony. He descended the battlements and approached a sentry.

The knight, apparently recognizing Kai, snapped to attention. "Sir!"

"The officers' barracks."

The knight pointed to a cluster of low buildings on the opposite side of the bailey. "That way, sir."

Kai nodded his thanks and headed toward the barracks. As he crossed the bailey, a servant girl approached and dropped a curtsy.

"Forgive my boldness, sir, but are you looking for someone?" Her eyes traveled over his face, and she blushed slightly as her hand moved to rest on her throat. She took another step closer to him, her eyes moving down his body.

Kai looked down at her in amusement. "The officers' barracks."

"Ohhhh," she breathed. "I love your accent. Where are you from?"

"Darbor."

Running footsteps neared. "Captain? Captain Darkwood?" A rosy-cheeked lad skidded to a breathless halt in front of him.

"Yes?" answered Kai, noting the girl's glare directed at the lad.

"I'm Romand, your squire during your stay here, if you approve."

Kai offered Romand his hand. When the boy hesitantly held out his, Kai gripped the squire's forearm below the elbow in a greeting between knighted warriors. "I'm honored, Romand."

The boy beamed as he returned the warrior's grip. "I'll show you to your quarters," he managed. Then he noticed the girl and faltered. "Oh, uh, am I interrupting?"

The serving girl moved away but turned and glanced back over her shoulder at Kai with a come-hither smile. Reminding himself that it would not reflect well on his king if he appeared late to his own welcoming ceremony, he resisted the urge to follow her.

Instead, he turned back to his squire. "You're not interrupting, Romand. Your arrival was timely."

"This way, sir," the boy said with an expression that bordered on worship.

"Thank you." He followed the boy, whose smile threatened to divide his face in half.

"I had your gear taken to your room already, and your duocorn's been seen to. Are you really a Sauraii master, sir?"

"I am."

Romand paused, chewing on his lower lip as if struggling with the propriety of a question he desired to ask. "Are you here because we're really facing war from the Hanorans, or are you just here to help the knights perfect their swordplay?"

Kai paused. "That depends on who you ask."

"I'm asking you, sir."

Kai suppressed a grin at the boy's cheekiness. "I'm here because my king ordered me to come and help an ally train his knights."

"To prepare for war?"

Kai admired the boy's determination. "Yes, Romand. To prepare for war."

Not only had Darborian spies reported that Hanore was amassing its armies and targeting the tiny kingdom of Arden, but Darborian mages had also foreseen an invasion of Arden. When, the mages could not say, but they knew it would be soon. King Farai's grandmother had been an Ardeene princess, and his daughter had married the eldest Ardeene prince, thus further cementing a long-standing alliance. Moreover, some feared once Arden fell, the Hanoran king would turn his greedy eye on all the rest of the kingdoms. Darbor had many reasons to care about the outcome.

If the Hanorans attacked now, Arden would fall in a day.

"Would you do anything your king asked?" Romand wondered.

"Of course. I've sworn an oath of loyalty," Kai replied without hesitation.

Romand looked up at him with round eyes. "What if he asked you do to something wrong?"

"He wouldn't. King Farai is one of the wisest men I know."

"But what if he did?"

Kai's practiced exterior almost cracked at the lad's guileless charm. "As a knight sworn to follow my king, I do not question his command. But as a man, I trust him implicitly. So, I will never face the choice between obeying my king and doing what I know is right."

"What was your final test for your Sauraii training?"

Nearly reeling from the abrupt change of topic, he glanced at Romand, then said with a straight face, "I had to bring back the heads of thirteen boys who ask too many impertinent questions."

Romand gulped.

Kai grinned. "I'm only ruffling you, lad."

Sheepishly, Romand met his eye. "Yes, sir. Sorry, sir. My father often tells me to hold my tongue."

"You can ask me anything you want. I may choose not to answer you, but I won't skin you for asking."

When Romand looked up, Kai knew he'd won the boy's undying loyalty. The squire paused outside a doorway. "Captain Tarvok said these are your quarters in the barracks, but I thought you were staying in the guest wing in the castle."

"I want to earn the knights' respect based on my knowledge and skill, not because of my reputation as a Sauraii. That will be better accomplished if I live among them instead of in the castle like some kind of lord."

Romand glanced up at him in puzzlement. "The knights are all sons of noblemen and lords. No commoner can be a knight; they can only be ordinary soldiers."

Kai didn't volunteer to the squire that the same held true in Darbor normally, that he had been knighted despite his common blood. "Do any of the knights live in the castle?"

"No, only the royal family. Oh. I see what you mean."

Kai ducked his head slightly to enter his quarters. The furniture consisted of a bed that actually looked large enough for a tall man to sleep in comfortably, and a trunk with his bag lying on top. Small, clean, uncluttered. Perfect.

A servant arrived with a basin and hot water. Romand helped Kai remove his chain mail, but when the squire prepared to help Kai bathe, he replied firmly, "Thank you, Romand. That will be all."

Clearly surprised, Romand hesitated and then moved to the door. "I'll wait out here until you need me."

Kai scrubbed away the dirt and grime, blackening the water. After shaving and changing into the full dress greens of Darbor, he dragged a comb through his wet, clean hair and pulled on his boots.

Outside the window, the sun sank closer to the mountains, and the two moons glowed pale against the purpled sky. A few stars winked dimly. Kai paused, his eyes moving up to the stars.

Perhaps the far-off world where the souls of the dead rested lay among one of those glittering lights. His hand moved to touch a strand of braided hair attached to a leather thong around his neck and brought it to his lips.

"Good night, my love," he murmured. Only a faint ache in the broken pieces of his heart came in reply.

Romand knocked hesitantly. "I'll take you to the throne room if you're ready, Captain Darkwood."

"Almost."

He carefully packed away his sword and the usual assortment of daggers he normally carried. It would not do to show up fully armed to offer his services to the king of Arden. He would only carry what he absolutely must. He picked up two of his smallest daggers. One he tucked in his boot, the other he strapped to his forearm underneath his sleeve. Though trained in the martial art of nordichia, where one fought with empty hands, Kai preferred to have a blade when he faced an enemy. Not that he expected to find an enemy within the castle, but one never knew.

Kai followed Romand to the main doors of the castle, feeling naked without his chain mail or heavily padded training shirt. He also missed the reassuring slap of his sword against his leg.

When Romand led him inside the castle proper, its splendor took Kai's breath away. The nobleman whose actions had seemed suspicious out by the bailey crossed the main hall, catching Kai's attention, and the Sauraii watched him narrowly.

"Romand, who is that?"

The boy followed the direction of Kai's stare. "That's Lord Alivan. He sits in council with the king."

Kai nodded his thanks but said nothing. Normally his instincts were reliable, but Arden was a strange land with strange customs. It would be best to wait and observe further before acting. As an ambassador of Darbor, he must not make a mistake of this magnitude regarding a nobleman of a country to which he was about to swear an oath of loyalty.

He certainly had been wrong about the young lady in the woods being in danger from the fearsome-looking animal.

Kai drew a steadying breath and braced himself. He must face getting through this ceremony without bungling it, surviving a meal with royalty without committing an unforgivable breach of etiquette, and then participating in a dance he couldn't hope to know.

He wished he could spend the evening in the training arena instead. Or perhaps rethink his decision not to follow the serving girl who smiled so invitingly in the bailey. Or go find the girl in the woods and beg her forgiveness. Learn her name. Touch her silken hair again.

She hated him. She thought him a bloodthirsty murderer.

Why that twisted in his gut like a knife, Kai couldn't guess. He shouldn't care. He'd left one entanglement behind in Darbor. His orders to go to Arden had been a relief, the perfect excuse to end the relationship, ensuring that he was safe from forming any dangerous emotional attachments. The last thing he needed was to risk another involvement.

He didn't care what the girl in the woods thought of him. He didn't care. But the tragedy in her eyes haunted him.

He kicked a loose stone and sent it skittering across the rock-paved courtyard. How could he have known it was a magical and honored animal? He'd heard a roar loud enough to shake the leaves off the trees, and seen a beast bigger than a duocorn, with more teeth than a pack of wyrwolves, standing over a lady who lay on the ground. Any sane man would have assumed she'd been about to be devoured. Any knight would have acted as he had.

To his everlasting annoyance, that knowledge did nothing to assuage his guilt.

Chapter Three

*R*eeling from the events of the afternoon, Jeniah trudged through the castle halls.

"There you are!" Mora called. "You're late. The ceremony will begin soon. Come, come, you must change."

The aged lady-in-waiting took Jeniah by the hand and trotted toward the stairway to the royal family wing. As Jeniah stumbled to keep up with Mora, her father and her eldest brother descended the stairway on the opposite side, both wearing full formal dress and crowns.

". . . to train the knights," her father said to Aven. "I haven't yet decided if I'll have him train the common soldiers as well."

Jeniah paused and bowed her head in deference to the king and the crown prince, even knowing they would pass her without glancing in her direction. She knew better than to ask what they discussed. No doubt they'd either be annoyed by her interruption, or simply pat her head and tell her to not concern herself with the matters of men.

To her surprise, the king nodded briefly to her. Aven gave her a wink. She gaped at their uncharacteristic acknowledgement. A slow warmth thawed the edges of the icy lump in her heart.

"Darkwood might have a recommendation," Aven said as they passed by.

"Quickly, now." Mora tugged her hand.

Servants holding torches paused from their duty of lighting the candles lining the castle corridors and stepped back to let Jeniah and Mora pass. Each servant suddenly had a face, a name, a story. Somber from her chayim's death, and overcome at her startling new awareness of people around her, Jeniah wanted to weep for her past blindness to the humanity all around her.

Inside Jeniah's bedchambers, candles flickered from every sconce on the polished walls. The large bed commanded the eye with its carvings of mythical scenes, its heavy velvet draperies, and its colorful, overstuffed pillows. The rich reds of the intricately embroidered fabrics filled the room with warmth.

Jeniah watched the play of the candlelight on the polished stone floor while Mora unfastened the buttons that ran down the back of her gown, chattering on about something Jeniah could hardly follow.

". . . and oh, so handsome. I wonder if he has an older brother? Too bad his father isn't still alive."

Jeniah managed a wan smile over her shoulder at her maid as she stepped out of the gown pooled on the floor. After helping her wash, Mora dressed her in a deep purple gown embroidered with gold thread, then fastened it down the back before fluffing and arranging the sleeves. Jeniah sat at the dressing table, her fingers carelessly tracing the carving on the burled wood while Mora went to work on her disorderly curls. After a moment, Jeniah realized Mora had fallen silent and was watching her with a worried crease in her forehead.

"You're very subdued this evening. Is anything wrong?"

Jeniah hesitated before replying. "I'm merely tired."

"Are you unwell?"

"No, Mora, truly, I'm fine. No need to worry." Out of a desire to change the subject, she asked, "You mentioned a ceremony tonight?"

"To welcome the new Darborian Sauraii."

Without any true interest, Jeniah asked, "The Darborian what?"

"Sauraii. It's a title for an elite weapons master. There aren't many who bear that title in all the lands, certainly none in Arden. Your father was so impressed with the Sauraii the last time he and the prince visited Darbor, that he arranged to borrow him from King Farai to train our knights."

"So a Sauraii is merely another kind of warrior."

"A highly skilled warrior," Mora amended. "You've never heard of them?"

"No, and I'm surprised you have."

Mora looked sheepish. "I knew very little of them until today."

"Why this sudden interest in warriors?"

"Since they came in the form of Kai Darkwood. Haven't you been listening to me? He's the most handsome man I've ever seen. His father was the legendary Daris Darkwood. Apparently Kai's skills have surpassed his father's, and he's reputed to have never lost a battle."

A Darborian warrior who had arrived today? That had to be the warrior in the woods claiming to be a knight. It explained much, not the least of which was the ease with which he slew her chayim.

Mora sighed dreamily. "There's enough good looks in him to spread around a whole regiment. Ah, to be twenty years younger . . ."

The maid droned on about the many virtues of the Darborian, but soon Jeniah stopped listening. She had no interest in hearing about a soldier, especially the one who'd murdered her bonded chayim, not to mention her future. But as she realized she would have to face the knight again, a slow dread curled in her stomach. Could she be civil to him? Since her father regarded the man so highly, she had better suppress her emotions.

If the visitor were a new minstrel or a group of players, Jeniah would understand the excitement. Men who spoke with such beauty and eloquence, who knew nothing of war or weapons, were fascinating and certain to be kind and peace-loving. But a warrior? Especially this one?

When she could get in a word, Jeniah said, "And to welcome him, we must have a big, formal ceremony tonight."

"Don't frown so, little one," Mora urged. "It's time you become interested in state matters. When you marry, there will be many more."

"That will be the end of my freedom."

Instead of scolding her, Mora looked at her with a gleam in her eye that Jeniah had never seen before. "Just wait. Being married can be wonderful. You can have more freedom than you might expect, particularly if you marry a man of intelligence or responsibility."

Jeniah eyed her dubiously, unable to break through her grief enough to truly care.

"The busier a husband's mind, the more a wife can effortlessly conceal. And who knows? Perhaps you'll wed someone handsome like the Sauraii from Darbor and then all the fun will begin," she said lustily.

"Mora!"

Unashamed, Mora continued, "Oh, little one, you really have no idea what amazing things can happen when you do come of age and get married. You'll see. Much of it is quite . . . wonderful."

Mora spoke that last word with such enthusiasm that Jeniah

frowned. She knew little of matters of love, but from what she'd heard, it was an arrangement that suited the man more than the woman. She shook her head, driving away images of a loveless marriage. Instead, she thought of the man from the forest, and his ferocity as he dealt death to her chayim. She shivered.

"Hold still, I'm almost finished." Mora placed the golden circlet upon Jeniah's head, pinned a wayward curl, and smoothed Jeniah's hair. "There. You look perfect. Now let's go to the throne room and enjoy the ceremony. I, for one, can hardly wait to feast my eyes upon the Darborian captain again."

Poised enough to please even the queen mother's sharp notice, Princess Jeniah glided into the throne room with her lady-in-waiting. She sank into a deep curtsy to the king and queen, and then to the crown prince, who sat on the dais beside them.

Despite her apprehensions and roiling emotions, the throne room enraptured Jeniah. She had not been there in ages and had almost forgotten its splendor. Soaring ceilings, polished marble, and rich tapestries combined in an opulence clearly designed to impress and intimidate.

Jeniah took her place to the right of the dais with the other lesser royalty and nobility. They stood murmuring among themselves, their voices soft. She glanced at her brother Aven, but he failed to acknowledge her.

Trumpets interrupted her thoughts and caused an excited hush. The massive doors at the far end of the throne room opened wide, drawing Jeniah's attention. She steeled herself, determined to keep her emotions under control.

"Presenting Sir Kai Darkwood, Sauraii, captain in the Darborian army, and royal high instructor of the knights and the home guard of Darbor!"

Jeniah's mouth went dry. Closing her eyes, she took a breath and composed herself at the unavoidable prospect of facing her chayim's slayer. Once she was confident that her face appeared serene, she opened her eyes and forced herself to look at the honored guest.

The Darborian's long, muscular legs carried him from the doors toward the raised dais that held the king, the queen, and the crown prince. All heads turned and followed the tall visitor who strode down the carpet.

The warrior from the woods, just as Jeniah had feared.

Her heart thumped so loudly that she half expected everyone around her to stare. She rubbed sweaty palms against her skirts and blurred so she would appear no more noticeable than one of the many courtiers in the throne room. It was an act of cowardice, but at the moment, facing the ruthlessly skilled warrior seemed too much to bear.

As he drew nearer, she drew in her breath sharply. Jeniah's memory failed to prepare her for the masculine beauty of his face. The man from the woods had bathed and shaved, revealing strong, square features under suntanned skin. The Sauraii master's head was uncovered and his dark hair shone in the flickering candlelight. Confident and authoritative, his bearing rivaled royalty and testified of his years as a leader. His green and gold tunic bore the Darborian king's emblem. Though he looked solemn for the formal ceremony, good humor touched his well-formed mouth.

Jeniah remembered his light touch as he'd brushed a tear from her cheek, stirring her awareness of him as a man. An involuntary shudder rippled through her body. She took her thoughts in hand. Ladies nearby whispered their approval and sighed, and Jeniah rolled her eyes. So he was handsome. He was also one of those dreaded warriors, a breed all those simpering ladies soundly condemned.

With the eyes of the assembly upon him, the Darborian

knight climbed the steps to the dais and went down on one knee. Bowing his head, he placed his fist first on his chest and then on his forehead in homage to the king and queen of Arden.

"Welcome, Sauraii Master Kai Darkwood," the king said with a gesture. "We are honored that you have come to aid us."

"It is my honor to serve you on behalf of my king, Your Majesty," the captain replied with an incline of his head.

As her father launched into a welcome speech, Jeniah shifted her weight inconspicuously. Ardeenes thrived on ceremony and tradition, a mindset that forced strictures upon all aspects of her life.

Then, as she watched her father, she realized more than ever how he deeply, passionately loved Arden. He feared for its safety and felt strongly that its customs and traditions should be honored. She knew he would do anything to protect Arden's people and preserve their way of life.

When the king's speech ended, he stood. "I award you, Sir Kai Darkwood, the rank of captain of the army, knight of the realm, and royal high weapons trainer of the knights and the Home Guard of Arden."

A nobleman acting as an aide moved to Captain Darkwood and murmured something in his ear.

On one knee, the captain nodded and raised his voice. "I, Kai Darkwood, pledge my hand, my sword, my loyalty to you, Your Highness, all my life, to my death, or until you release me."

The Ardeenes cheered as the Darborian captain arose and faced the audience. Jeniah watched the Sauraii look out over the assembly and smile all the way to his eyes. His conscience did not appear to be bothering him. He probably no longer possessed such an annoyance. How many times did a person have to kill before his or her conscience died?

Jeniah no longer truly blamed this foreign knight for his role in her chayim's death, but the plain truth remained that he was a seasoned warrior, a professional killer, a man of violence and death.

When the formalities came to a close, Jeniah watched as the captain graciously received congratulations and words of welcome until the crowd closed in around him. Jeniah turned her back toward him.

Later, when the throng moved from the throne room to the great dining hall, she stopped blurring and took her place at the far end of the royal table with nobles and courtiers. She caught sight of Captain Darkwood seated at the royal family's table to the right of the king. The captain and her normally reserved brother, Prince Aven, were in animated conversation. As Jeniah seated herself at her place, her eyes drifted to him again. This time, he appeared to be listening carefully to the queen as she spoke. He nodded, looked the queen directly in the eye, and smiled. Jeniah blinked.

Few men in Arden possessed such a heart-stopping smile. Pity it belonged to a warrior. How had Mora described his smile? *Lethal.* A very apt description in many ways.

As the music began, Jeniah found a place to sit at the far end of the room. Her heart was too heavy to receive any enjoyment out of dancing, even if she dared risk the Sauraii recognizing her.

Three noblemen stood nearby, their voices carrying to her. "Why are they so sure the Hanorans won't declare war until after spring?" one asked.

Jeniah froze, her heart in her throat. The Hanorans were about to declare war with Arden? Unthinkable!

"Because our spies have reported that they are massing their armies in Hanore, so we know for sure they're still there," replied another nobleman. "And the mountain passes are already impassable due to ice and snow. They'll have to wait until the spring thaw to cross over the mountains."

"You sound sure they're coming," said the third nobleman.

"They're coming," came the grim reply.

The third made an impatient gesture. "But we can't be sure they're coming after Arden. They have no quarrel with us. They're probably going after the Govians again."

The second speaker folded his arms. "The Darborian mages are sure the Hanorans are targeting Arden."

There was a snort. "Mages? When have we ever trusted magic? Consorting with the powers of evil cannot be reliable."

Jeniah's heart stalled. Was she consorting with the powers of evil whenever she blurred? A familiar, sinking fear whispered that she was. Yet, hadn't her chayim assured her the power she had was good, and that it would play a vital role of her destiny?

The noblemen spoke again. "Do you think the Sauraii will be able to prepare our armies if the Hanorans do declare war?"

There was a pause. "If he can't, I pray the Darborian king will send an army to come to our aid. Otherwise, we're all lost."

A bolt of dread shot through Jeniah. Could Arden truly be in danger? Surely not.

She stood. Weary right down to her soul, she headed for the nearest door. She wanted to sleep for a week—to escape the excruciating memories of finding and losing her chayim, escape the whispers of war, escape the noise and the crowds. Most of all, she wanted to escape the presence of the Darborian Sauraii.

She wormed her way through the clusters of people near the edge of the dance floor. An instant before she reached the door, she realized she'd unintentionally passed near Kai Darkwood of Darbor.

The blood drained out of her face. He idly glanced at her, and then looked again. She realized that she'd lost her concentration and was no longer blurring. The last thing she wanted was to be forced to speak with him. And now that he'd visually marked her, she could not blur.

For an instant, the captain's expression betrayed his surprise, then, looking determined, the Darborian began to move toward her. With a cry of dismay, she fled. She prayed she'd never again be forced to speak with this warrior who left death in his wake.

Chapter Four

Inside the castle training arena, Kai watched the knight beside him balance a sword in his hand. Kai nodded in satisfaction. "Much better. That other was too heavy for you. The ease with which you wield your sword is more important than the size of the blade."

The young knight flushed, glancing back at the sword he had discarded a moment ago. "It's a family sword, sir."

Kai grasped the young man's shoulder. "And one you will use with honor, Sir Gallen, when you are ready. But not today."

Sir Gallen nodded unhappily. "Yes, Captain."

How such an inexperienced youth had earned his knighthood—even in Arden—was beyond Kai's comprehension, but it was not his place to make that determination. His duty was to train these men in the hopes that they could defend their country from the Hanoran barbarians, and stay alive in the process, but this boy appeared far too young to court a maid, let alone face a battle.

Unfortunately, most Ardeenes believed that war was unlikely, and until they felt any urgency, they would not progress at the rate they must in order to be prepared. If the Hanorans declared war sooner than expected, the battle would be a slaughter.

Kai felt the weight of the trust two kings had placed in him. In the little time he had, he hoped he could teach these inexperienced men what they needed to know to survive a battle and defend their country. He drew a deep breath and let it out slowly. There was much work to be done.

Kai drew his sword and took a defensive stance. He nodded in approval when the lad mimicked him. "Now come again. Keep your blade up and don't let me get in close. The further away you can keep your enemy, the less dangerous he is to you."

The youth lost some of the terror he had worn the first time they sparred, but he still gripped his sword with white-knuckled fear.

"Now watch your footwork. Don't be an easy target," Kai advised.

The youth adjusted his technique.

"Better. Now come at me again."

Once the lad realized Kai wasn't going to use the first opportunity to thrash him, he began to relax and swing more naturally.

"Good," Kai encouraged. In direct opposition to most of his masters, Kai gave praise readily when deserved. "Remember to go back into the ready stance, Sir Gallen."

Their blades rang as they clashed, drowning out the sounds of the other knights as they sparred against each other, implementing the moves Kai had taught them that day.

"Let your strength come from your whole body, not just your arms," Kai reminded the young knight.

While Kai kept up a stream of instructions, the two slashed and parried. Sweat poured off their bodies underneath their mail, despite the cool fall breeze. Gradually, a look of determination overcame Gallen's features, and Kai pressed him harder, hoping the boy would rise to the challenge. He wasn't disappointed. After parrying a grueling series of blows Kai dealt him, the youth went on the offensive instead of simply trying to stay alive. Kai easily warded him off, pleased at his pupil's progress. A moment later, the young knight left himself clearly open and Kai drove his blade in under the young man's arm where armor left him vulnerable, but stopped short of actually piercing him.

Alarm leaped into the boy's eyes. "Peace," he cried in a strangled voice.

"You lost your concentration. You were doing well until then." With a slight whistling sound, Kai removed his sword from Gallen's torso and slid it back into its scabbard. Many masters had used the flat of their blade to punish an errant student, but Kai believed the lesson could be well learned without such measures.

"And never show fear," Kai said. "Keep your face expressionless. It helps in battle as well as in games of chance." He grinned at the youth.

The lad nodded, attempting a smile in return. "Yes, sir. I'll try to remember that."

"Go find your sparring partner and continue, Sir Gallen."

The boy nodded again, his face showing clearly a mixture of relief and disappointment that his private lesson with the Sauraii of Darbor had concluded.

Captain Tarvok appeared at Kai's side. "If you've finished humiliating my men, shall we go shout for our noonday meal?"

Kai wiped his sleeve across his forehead, looking up at the sun directly overhead. "Yes. A fine idea." He turned to the men. "Dismissed!"

As their squires took their gear, Kai clapped Romand on the shoulder. "Tomorrow, come early and I'll work with you alone before the other men arrive."

Romand's grin nearly split his face in half. "Yes, sir!" He trotted off.

Kai walked beside Tarvok to the dining hall in the barracks. Inside the warm, dimly lit dining hall, fragrant food smells mingled with the pungent odor of bodies. Serving maids scurried to bring the hungry men plates of steaming food. A dark-haired girl caught the corner of Kai's eye. His heart leaped into his throat until he realized that she was not the one who had haunted his dreams.

He shook his head. Of course not. The breathtaking nymph in the woods he had seen on his way to the castle of Arden would barely be mistaken for a mortal, much less a serving girl. He remembered the way the sunlight shimmered in her dark brown ringlets, the depth of her enormous gray eyes, the flawless ivory complexion, the full lips that promised the kiss of eternal joy . . . or madness. At first he thought she was one of the fairy folk said to populate the woodlands. Then she had looked upon him with scorn and spoken biting, angry words.

He thought he'd glimpsed her in the castle dining hall the night he arrived during the welcoming ceremony, but she'd disappeared in the crowd. Perhaps his obsession had contrived that vision.

He resisted the urge to look out the door toward the road. He had no time to go on foolish rides through the woodland roads in the hopes that the ethereal maiden would show herself to him again and give him a chance to apologize, or at least to explain, to smooth away the tragic look in her eyes when she informed him that he had taken an innocent life.

It didn't matter. He was here to train the knights of Arden, not pine after a vision he would unlikely see again, except in his dreams.

After eating, Kai returned to the training arena, where he planned to meet with Prince Aven. In his place stood a messenger.

"Captain Darkwood. Prince Aven sends his regrets but he is unable to meet with you this afternoon due to a conference with the ambassadors."

Kai nodded. "Very well." Perhaps he should find Romand and train him now instead of waiting until tomorrow. He'd spent so much time with the knights since he'd arrived, that he hadn't given his squire as much personal attention as he liked. Kai left the training arena and headed for the barracks, passing the stairs to the main castle doors.

Out of the corner of his eye, he saw a figure descending the stairs and halted. He stood frozen in place, his heart pounding so hard he suspected everyone in the castle could hear it.

A young lady whose beauty rivaled the fairies of the Black Forest in Darbor stood at the top of the castle steps. She shimmered in the sunlight, her face glowing in ethereal splendor. Pure and untouched, she clasped together her small, white hands, which clearly knew nothing of human drudgery.

She looked so different today that it took him a moment to recognize her as the girl from the forest. Had it only been nine days ago? He wondered how he could have lived and worked in the castle for nine days and never encounter her. Hardly daring to breathe, he gazed upon her.

The first time he'd seen her, she'd been tear-streaked and disheveled, but fearlessly facing a beast that would have challenged the courage of any knight in Darbor. Today, every dark hair was plaited and woven with threads of gold and pearl. She wore a white gown, meticulously embroidered with gold designs, and long, tightly fitted sleeves with outer sleeves cut wide enough at the underside to almost sweep the ground.

As he watched her regally descend the stairway, he realized her identity and almost smacked his own forehead. Tales of the unsurpassed beauty of Arden's princess circulated the countryside and had even reached Darbor. According to rumor, the sight of her struck awe in the heart of every man—nobleman or peasant—who laid eyes on her. Even Captain Tarvok had warned Kai that the princess possessed disconcerting beauty, but Kai had rested safe in his belief that either the tales were grossly exaggerated, or that he would be an exception. He was wrong on both counts.

Thunderstruck, Kai stood frozen. Their last meeting had been a disaster. She might be angry and refuse to speak to him. Or worse, a thoughtless word from him could send her straight to the king to relay the tale and demand that he be sent back to Darbor in dishonor. How important were these chayims to Ardeenes?

Kai knew he should leave but found it difficult to obey his better judgment. Overwhelmed by her beauty and desperate to atone for his rash act in the woods, he stood caught in an appalling state of indecision, gazing upon her and knowing he would never use the word "beautiful" lightly again.

Apparently sensing his stare, the princess lifted her head. Those bewitching gray eyes fixed upon him and one brow rose. She continued descending the stairs in queenly elegance.

Kai moved toward her. The whole situation was preposterous. Kai seldom found himself at a loss for words. Beautiful or not, she was still just a girl.

But as his eyes locked with hers, he realized that this was not an ordinary young lady. Beyond her astonishing beauty, something in her eyes challenged his resolve. The unexplainable feeling that his life was about to become intertwined with hers, and that it would be forever changed, struck him with such force that he had to call upon all his courage to refrain from bolting.

First recognition then displeasure overcame her features. "Captain Darkwood," she acknowledged with an edge to her voice.

Attempting to gather his scattered wits, he bowed. "Your Highness."

She came down the final step and approached. "I assure you, I'm in no danger. No innocent animals to kill here."

Kai forced himself to not wince, to keep his hands open and at his side with the mantra "Never show emotion to an opponent" running through his thoughts. Apologizing while maintaining dignity had never been easy.

"I hope you will forgive me for my actions in the forest. I've never heard of a chayim, and had no idea an animal that large and dangerous looking would be anything but . . . dangerous. I wouldn't have acted as I did if I had known. I deeply regret my misunderstanding of the situation. And my actions. And the distress I caused you." He fell silent when he realized he was babbling, and he cursed the fluttering in his stomach.

She remained silent, her gaze fixed impassively upon him. She was so tiny that her head barely reached the middle of his chest, and so finely wrought that she might have been a fairy. Two knights hovered nearby, yet distant enough that they would not overhear any conversation. Guards, apparently. With satisfaction, he recognized two of the more skilled knights, Breneg and Ciath. Mentally, he saluted Captain Tarvok. If Kai had handpicked guards for a member of the royal family, this pair would undoubtedly be among them.

The princess watched him coolly, her chin lifting. "I'm sure that after all your training as a warrior, your first impulse is to kill. Perhaps you simply cannot resist." Her incisive words cut through him as deep as her accusing stare.

Kai kept his tone deferential. "My first impulse is to defend those in danger. I do not lurk about waiting for an opportunity to kill."

Those disturbing eyes remained fixed upon him as if trying to determine his sincerity. At last, she said, "I believe your motives were pure, if not your methods."

It wasn't exactly forgiveness, but it was a start. At least the enmity in her eyes faded.

The tension in his shoulders eased. "Thank you, Your Highness," he replied with what he hoped was the correct amount of gallantry.

Her voice softened. "Being from Darbor, you couldn't have known."

The silence stretched as he struggled for words. By the moons, he was behaving like an inexperienced squire who had never spoken to a pretty girl. He collected his wits and forced them into submission. "I hope you will give me the opportunity to make amends."

She blinked. "Why?"

He faltered. Why indeed? She was not someone of personal significance to him. As the princess of his king's ally, it was unlikely that he, as a mere knight, would see much of her royal self during his stay in Arden. She, no doubt, spent most of her time in the castle, while he spent most of his time in training with the knights. Inexplicably, her opinion mattered, more than he cared to admit.

"The hurt and anger in your eyes has haunted me." His honesty surprised even himself.

Her eyes darted between his as if trying to divine his thoughts and then she lifted one shoulder slightly. "Do not be overly concerned, Captain. My feelings are of no consequence. And it's doubtless anyone would believe me should I relay the tale."

"I'm sure you underestimate your influence, Your Highness."

"Perhaps." Something flickered in her eyes and then she looked away, but in that brief moment, he understood.

The Darborian princess, Karina, had been married to Prince Aven of Arden, a man she had never met, for the sole purpose of reinforcing an alliance. As far as Kai knew, her wishes were never consulted, a common occurrence among royalty. Princesses were seldom valued beyond their ability to create or reconfirm alliances.

Princess Jeniah moistened her lips. "As a stranger here, you probably know nothing about chayims. Would you care to learn more about them, Captain?"

Kai paused. This might be his best opportunity to win her forgiveness. Why that seemed so important, he did not dare examine too closely. "Yes, I would."

"I'm going for a ride. Would your duties permit you to accompany me?"

"As it happens, I'm not needed elsewhere at the moment."

She paused. "As I'm riding unchaperoned, it would only be appropriate for you to accompany me to serve as part of my guard, if you are willing." She glanced toward the two knights who stood unobtrusively nearby.

Kai nodded at Breneg and Ciath. They snapped salutes.

"Princess Jeniah!" A middle-aged lady wearing clothing that rivaled royalty hurried up to the princess. "You forgot your cloak," she panted as she reached them.

A corner of the princess's mouth lifted. "Thank you, Mora." She turned around and allowed the woman to place the cloak over her shoulders and fasten the clasps down the front.

The lady smirked at Kai. She might have been pretty once, but the ravages of time and sorrow had taken a toll upon her features, yet she had a pleasant face, and her affection for the princess was obvious.

"Captain Darkwood, my lady-in-waiting, Lady Mora of the House of Kerrien."

Mora sank into a curtsy, her eyes making an unashamed appraisal of Kai, yet when she spoke, there was a note of warning in her tone. "I trust you will guard both her life and her virtue, Captain Darkwood?"

Kai inclined his head. "With my very life, my lady."

With a nod, Mora grinned at the princess as if they shared a private joke. The older woman gave Kai another bold, admiring stare before she turned and left.

Kai escorted the princess to the stables. As they arrived, the stable boy brought out the princess's small, white duocorn. With a look of adoration on his face, he glanced up at the princess, then blushed and dropped his eyes quickly. "Your Highness."

She accepted the reins with a gentle smile. "Thank you, Grenly."

As she mounted her duocorn, Kai re-saddled Braygo, a gift from King Farai of Darbor. The powerfully built duocorn had proven a friend in battle more times than Kai could remember.

They passed through the gates of the castle and wound their way through the streets of Arden City. The road branched off into three directions outside the city gates: one way led to the waterfront and the wharf; another was the Old Road, the main highway that spanned the length of Arden; the third wound along the seashore. Kai had never traveled this third road.

A few clouds drifted across a glorious blue sky in a breeze cold enough to be invigorating. The duocorns pranced side by side, nickering to each other. Gold, brown, and burnished red leaves drifted, coaxed by the gentle breeze, down to the ground. Many trees were already bare, their naked limbs leaning away from the shore and its constant breeze. Overhead, a flock of birds fled the coming of winter, calling to each other in excited cries. The air was alive with the scurry of small animals, the song of birds, and the rustle of leaves.

When they reached a break in the trees that allowed a clear view of the shoreline, the princess stopped, giving Kai a chance to take in the view. The bay's deep blue water clearly revealed the sandy bottom many fathoms below the surface.

Continuously moving, the water appeared alive, as if some great beast stirred far below the surface. The water lapped rhythmically and the topmost edges of the waves were peaked with white. Transfixed, Kai watched as a wave approached the shore. It grew in size and power until it crashed against the sands, collapsing, roiling and foamy, as it reached for the dry sand further up the beach before it slid back into the water to be replaced by another wave.

The sheer power and majesty touched a place deep inside him. "It's beautiful," he murmured.

"Take a deep breath, Captain. Isn't that the most wonderful smell? Whenever we travel inland, I miss that."

"I can understand why," he agreed in a hushed voice.

They enjoyed the view of the ocean for a few moments in silence before slowly going down the hill, where the trees blocked their view. At the bottom of the hill, Kai followed the princess off the road down a well-worn path leading to the beach.

Her eyes sparkled as she looked up at him. "I'll race you." Then, before Kai could reply, she urged her duocorn into a gallop.

He let out a yell of mock outrage at her early start, but almost immediately he caught up with her. As they raced along the shore, seabirds scattered at their approach. Kai reined in so that their impromptu race ended in a tie. His Braygo, bigger and stronger than her Egan, could have easily won, but Kai hated unfair advantages.

As he rode next to the princess, his eyes were again drawn to the seascape. Great jagged rocks jutted out of the sand like black, clawed fingers. The waves crashed thunderously upon them and then streamed in foaming white waterfalls down the craggy sides. He glanced back but the guards were out of view, probably sweeping the area for danger.

"It's low tide," the princess said in satisfaction. "My favorite time to come to the shore."

Rather than reveal his ignorance, Kai refrained from asking what "low tide" meant.

After they dismounted, the princess surprised him by sitting down and removing her slippers and stockings. She wiggled her toes. "I love to feel the sand on my bare feet. Soon it will be too cold to do this." She looked up at him with a smile. "Do you wish to know about chayims, Captain Darkwood?"

Momentarily speechless, Kai could only stare at her surreal beauty. He swallowed hard. "Yes, very much."

She motioned him to sit beside her. "They are very old and very rare," she began, her voice taking on the tone of a storyteller. The sea breeze played with her dark hair, loosening it from its careful plaits until she appeared much as she had that day in the woods.

"Because chayims shun humans and are able to blend in with their surroundings, they are difficult to see despite their size. According to legend, maidens tame them with their gentleness and purity, but what entices a chayim to accept one maiden and not another remains a mystery. It is always a rare honor, one that has not occurred in generations."

Kai pushed his fingers through his hair, dismayed at the news that he'd destroyed not only a creature, but an event of great importance.

The princess looked out over the water, her face wistful. "Acceptance by a chayim forms a lifelong bond. The chayim communicates directly into the maiden's mind, imparting some of its wisdom and knowledge to her. Chayims are also said to have magical powers of healing and protection over the maiden whom they accept."

"So you desired the magical properties of this chayim?"

"Partially." She turned to face him. "It's also a great honor and elevates the maiden's status. Peasant girls who are chayim-bonded become nobility."

"But you are already a princess."

She dropped her eyes. "A maiden who forges this bond is honored, revered, and given much freedom and often power. If I had come home chayim-bonded, I would have become more valuable to my father. The chayim's protection and healing extends to all in her household and even to her country."

Kai digested that. "You think it would protect your family from war?"

She blinked. Perhaps she was as oblivious to the true threat of war as the rest of the Ardeenes. "I suppose it would, but I desired to be chayim-bonded for more selfish reasons. I hoped that my father would let me stay home and choose my own husband later when I'm older. Or at least consider my opinion in the husband that he chooses for me."

Sadness touched her lovely face, leaving Kai with the absurd desire to help her. What he could do for her, he had no idea.

She looked him boldly in the eye as if desperate to explain herself. "But that truly wasn't my only reason for wanting to be accepted by a chayim, Captain. It's something else, something deeper. I've longed for this bond since my childhood, long before I understood my use to the king. I'm not sure I can explain it, but I always believed I was meant for such an honor, a dream I nurtured all these years. Perhaps my destiny."

Kai closed his eyes. If only he had traveled through the forest an hour sooner, or an hour later. If only . . . "I slew much more than a chayim that day."

She remained quiet a long moment. When she spoke, her voice softened. "You are a stranger here. Our culture must seem very foreign to you. It is not possible to know all of our legends, or the animals unique to Arden."

"Still, if I had known . . ."

"I know. You would have acted differently," she said gently.

"Did I say I'm sorry?"

An unexpected smile touched her face, humanizing the untouchable perfection. His stomach did an odd flip.

"Yes, Captain, you did."

By the moons, even though they sat several hand spans apart, her presence sent tremors of awareness through him. "If I can do something to atone for my actions—"

She held up a hand. "No, please don't. You acted with courage and gallantry. I forgive you. Speak of it no more."

Though reluctant to leave her presence, he realized that agreeing to ride with her may have been a bad decision. He might loose his wits and say something stupid, or worse, improper. What was wrong with him? She was not even of age yet. According to Tarvok, Ardeenes reached their age of adulthood at nineteen years, which meant he was at least seven years older than she. She was far too young for her opinion to be of consequence. Practically a child.

No, not a child. A breathtakingly beautiful young lady with eyes that threatened to dissolve his will. He took a steadying breath. Facing an army was less daunting than facing this woman-child.

"Thank you for your graciousness and your explanation."

She smiled and his heart slammed into his chest. Desperate to distract himself, he picked up a handful of sand, letting it sift through his fingers. "It's much finer than desert sand." He had spent far too much time battling Hanorans in the desert.

"Have you killed many men, Captain?"

Her sudden turn of thought caught him off guard.

She fixed an unblinking stare on him and added, "I know as a warrior you've probably killed hundreds."

"You disapprove of my profession."

"I'm not saying we don't need men like you. Without you, the northern wild men and their ogres would probably have destroyed all of civilization. I've heard that they are as bad as the barbaric Hanorans of the desert. But I question the motives of men who willingly spend their lives learning how to kill with more and more efficiency. Why else would a man spend all of his waking hours learning how to fight with every imaginable sort of weapon?"

Though her words revealed an attitude common among Ardeenes, Kai felt a knot form in his stomach. "There is a great deal of skill involved, and I enjoy the challenge of perfecting my technique. It's a form of art. But most men train for defense, to protect themselves or their families and homes. Surely you understand that, especially with the threat of war hanging over Arden."

"But warriors take pride in their ability to destroy."

"I understand what you are saying, but I'm not a Sauraii because I enjoy killing. Life is precious and I would gladly give mine protecting others. That's what I do every time I go to battle— protect the innocent. Now I teach others how to survive a war and protect the ones they love." He turned to face her fully. "Do you think that makes me someone who enjoys killing? Do I seem that cruel to you?" It was inexplicably important that she believe him.

Her eyes upon his face, she took a long time in answering. "No, you don't. I believe I've misjudged you." She turned and looked out over the water, her eyes upon the horizon.

Kai could not resist driving home his point. "Knights serve their king and country out of loyalty and a desire to protect them, Princess. I've yet to meet a bloodthirsty knight in Arden or Darbor."

Knights were usually arrogant and boasted shamelessly, Kai admitted to himself. He had sat in many groups while men relived their glorious battles. He was even guilty of that himself, and he well understood the kind of euphoria that comes after a well-fought battle. Most men, at least those in Darbor, enjoyed the prestige that came with being a knight, but few loved to kill. In fact, the knights here in Arden had never even taken a life . . . yet.

Clearly pensive, the princess nodded slowly. She turned her eyes upon him and he had the oddest feeling that she could see right into his very soul. "I understand. Please accept my apology, Captain."

"Apology accepted," he replied as unreasonable relief flooded through him.

She held out a hand. "Can we be friends?"

He looked at her in astonishment. "I would like that, Your Highness."

She smiled. It was fortunate he already sat, or his knees might have failed him. When her fragile hand closed in his, the same warmth he had felt when he touched her hand in the forest traveled up his arm and spread, stirring a place inside his heart he thought had died years ago. He swallowed and withdrew his hand.

They stood and walked side by side on the white sand. Then the princess veered off and clambered up onto the massive rocks with the agility of a duocorn. Birds flew overhead, some perching on a nearby rock, some bobbing in the water. Small, multi-legged creatures scuttled in and out of their homes in the rocks. Unseen animals bubbled and sputtered in the sand, while long-legged birds ran along the waves, occasionally burrowing their beaks in the sand. Waving, swimming, and crawling things populated the sandy seabed.

"Follow me, Captain. I'll show you my favorite place." She disappeared inside a deep cave.

Kai halted at the entrance. He hated closed-in places. Not about to confess a weakness, he drew his courage and scanned the area until he found one of the princess's guards, Breneg. After

Kai caught the guard's eye, he motioned that he and the princess were going inside the cave. Breneg looked unhappy but nodded, moving in closer.

Kai braced himself and went in after her. The sunlight streamed in through the mouth of the cave, but she moved beyond the light. When his eyes had adjusted to the gloom, he saw the princess with her skirts tucked out of the way, scrambling up the side of the cave. He glanced nervously back at the mouth of the cave and gritted his teeth. Carefully placing his hands and feet on the slippery rocks, he followed her up until he reached a ledge where she perched. Darkness closed in around them.

Kai eased himself onto the ledge beside her. It was wide enough to comfortably sit, and long enough for them both to stretch out if they chose. The ceiling hung only a few hand spans over their heads. Kai forcibly controlled his breathing, reminding himself there was plenty of air.

"This is the best hiding spot." The princess dangled her legs over the edge. "When it is high tide, the water comes up to here." She indicated with her foot a place a few hand spans below them.

Kai suppressed a shiver.

"I came here once to hide from Aven," she added, oblivious to Kai's discomfort. "He was furious with me, so I ran away and came here."

"Prince Aven? I find it difficult to imagine Aven getting that angry with anyone. He's always so composed."

"I suppose baby sisters have the unique ability to annoy even a holy man to the point of murder." Her smile was wry.

He laughed and concentrated on her face, which took some effort in the dim light until his eyes adjusted to the gloom.

The princess grew sober. "But by hiding here, I only made matters worse. When the tide came in, I was trapped. The water grows turbulent at high tide and it would have either dashed me against the rocks or caught me in an undertow and dragged me out to sea, so I had to stay here until low tide."

As vivid images of being trapped in a cave with dark water cutting off his only escape filled his imagination, Kai wondered how cowardly it would seem if he suggested they leave now.

Clearly unaware of his silent struggle, the princess continued her story. "By the time I could get out, half the Home Guard was looking for me. I've never seen Captain Tarvok so frantic. Or angry. Then I had to answer to my parents." Then she added brightly, "But you have to admit, this is a really good place to hide."

"Yes, wonderful," Kai agreed sarcastically. "If you don't mind suffocation, undertows, high tide, total darkness, or drowning, it's a charming place."

Her laugh washed over him. "I admit I tend to lose my common sense frequently, but I have some wonderful treasures here." She gestured to a nearby collection of shells and odd-looking dried plants. Her voice took on a hesitant tone. "This probably seems really childish to you, doesn't it, Captain?" She looked up at him with vulnerability.

"Everyone needs a place to go when they want to be alone." His eyes were drawn to her lips, but he gave himself a mental slap. She was the princess, not someone with whom he could indulge in a dalliance. He looked away. "Are there many caves like this?"

"The whole coastline is riddled with them. I've explored a lot of them, but as far as I can tell, this is the only one that doesn't completely fill up with water during high tide." She watched him curiously and he realized his expression must have revealed his alarm at the thought of being trapped inside a dark, water-filled cave. "Do you wish to go?"

Kai nodded, past caring if she knew of his fears, and immediately began to climb back down. To his relief, the princess did not question him and followed him down. Out in the sunlight, he took a deep, steadying breath.

Breneg stood near the entrance on full alert as if poised to come charging to her rescue should the princess have made any cry. Kai nodded and the knight nodded back, clearly relieved to have the princess in his sight. A part of Kai wanted to needle the guard for thinking Kai would be so dishonorable as to try to harm the princess, or stupid enough to risk execution. But the rest of him wanted to salute the man for his loyalty and caution. Breneg dropped back to make another sweep of the area.

They walked close enough to the water that the waves splashed them, but Kai's well-oiled boots repelled the water and the princess's skirts were tucked up almost to her knees to keep them dry. She didn't seem to mind that her feet and legs were both wet and sandy.

"Do you have any brothers or sisters that you annoyed?" the princess asked.

Kai averted his eyes from her graceful, slender limbs. "I probably annoyed them some, but I'm the oldest, so they annoyed me more. My half-brother got really good at talking his way out of trouble."

"Tell me about your family."

He glanced at her curiously. Usually women sought him for his fame or his looks or his status; very few actually expressed a desire to discover his real self. The princess had made her request in such a gentle, genuinely interested way that, despite his normal inclination to keep his personal life private, Kai wanted to comply.

"My father died of a fever when I was a child, but I remember many days out in the lists learning swordplay from him. My mother remarried an old family friend a few years later." It had seemed to Kai as though his mother betrayed his father's memory by remarrying, but he kept that portion of the story to himself. "The rest of my childhood was spent on his farm. My two half-brothers and I stirred up mischief and really tormented our sister." He smiled. "My mother arranged to have me foster with a Sauraii master. Out of respect for my father, the man took me even though I was too young. I'm sure the farm was more peaceful with my absence."

The princess smiled, her eyes soft. With growing dread, Kai realized that his feelings for this girl might easily grow into something more than respectful duty, more than desire for a beautiful young woman. He could not allow that to happen.

Fingering the braid tied to a thin leather thong around his neck, Kai remembered, and the empty place in his heart ached.

The princess's voice broke through his thoughts. "You are looking very serious, Captain."

He swiftly came back to the present and summoned a smile. "Forgive me. It grows late. We should return to the castle."

Oddly subdued, the princess nodded, her eyes probing his, and he realized that she knew he hid something. That alone was a disturbingly astute observation. Normally, others could not even discern when he applied self-defensive measures. She could. Alarm shot through Kai.

While she lowered her tucked skirts and donned her shoes, the princess's eyes continued to penetrate his mask of discipline. Kai positioned a carefully neutral expression on his face and kept his tone light as he chatted with calculated ease.

"Captain, is something wrong?" the princess asked quietly.

Fortifying the shields over his eyes, he put on a disarming smile. "Of course, not, Your Highness. I don't remember when I've enjoyed myself so much. Thank you for a wonderful afternoon—" The hackles on the back of his neck rose.

He scanned the terrain behind them, his hands moving

automatically to his weapons. Something was wrong. Danger lurked nearby. He realized that he hadn't seen her guards in several minutes. His muscles bunched, screaming for action.

"Get back inside the cave," he ordered tersely. "Here." He handed her one of his daggers hilt first. "Use this on anyone who comes near you."

She accepted the dagger, holding it with her thumb and forefinger as if it were some sort of filthy rodent. He resisted the urge to reposition her hand on the hilt. The weapon was purely precautionary; he would ensure that no one would get close enough for her to need it.

He waited until she was inside the cave before moving to the line of trees. The forest sounds around him noticeably absent, Kai reached out with all of his senses.

There. A furtive movement. Not a guard. Kai soundlessly withdrew a dagger and let it fly. A strangled groan sounded. Kai glanced back at the cave but no one came near the princess's hiding place.

He crept into the woods, searching for additional threats. All the forest sounds had hushed. Kai moved forward and discovered Breneg's lifeless body, pierced by darts. Controlling his anger, Kai slowed, moving more cautiously into the trees. The rustling of leaves led him to a dark young man with Hanoran features, writhing on the ground. The hilt of Kai's dagger protruded from his chest and his face twisted in pain.

Kai leaned over him. "Are you part of a strike team, or are you a spy?"

Hatred glittered in the boy's eyes and he clamped his mouth shut.

"How many more of you are there here?" Kai pressed.

As the Hanoran struggled for a last breath, he spit at Kai. Then he was dead.

Kai cursed. He hadn't meant to kill the Hanoran. A prisoner who could provide information was far more valuable than a corpse. He retrieved his dagger, cleaned it, and continued to search. There. Another.

Footsteps darted away and Kai made chase. Again, he let his dagger fly, this time aiming carefully for the legs. The man went down. He, too, was undoubtedly Hanoran. As Kai approached, the Hanoran placed something in his mouth. He was dead from his own poison before Kai got to him.

Swearing at a second missed opportunity, Kai resumed his search, but there were no signs of others nearby. Keeping one eye on the vicinity of the cave housing the princess, he swept the area thoroughly. He found the body of the second guard, Ciath. He clenched his fists, silently raging at the loss of two lives. Kai made another pass before he went back to the dark mouth of the cave.

"Princess? It's Darkwood."

"I'm here." She appeared out of the darkness and immediately handed him his dagger.

"We're returning to the castle now," he said grimly.

"What's wrong?" She looked up at him in innocent fear.

Normally, Kai's first impulse would be to shield a lady under his protection from the knowledge of a threat so nearby, and simply take her quickly to safety. He also did not wish to offend the king if his intent had been to keep his daughter uninformed. But after recent events, her ignorance would be a greater danger. At least now, the Ardeenes would be forced to take the Hanoran menace seriously.

"Two Hanoran scouts."

She blinked at him in disbelief. "Here?" She visibly struggled against the improbability of his words.

He lifted her into her saddle. Then, after grasping the reins of the guards' duocorns, he mounted and led out, urging them to a run. He'd send someone back for the knights' bodies later rather than retrieve them now and upset the princess.

She looked back. "Where are Breneg and Ciath?"

"Dead."

She emitted a cry of sorrow, and Kai regretted his bluntness. They cantered along the road, Kai alert for danger while the princess fell silent. He did not slow their pace until they were safely inside the inner castle walls.

All nearby guards snapped to attention as Kai dismounted. "Where is Captain Tarvok?" he demanded.

"The south guard tower," one of them answered, picking up on Kai's state of alarm. "Trouble, sir?"

"You and Eriq escort the princess inside and see that she's safely in the care of her lady-in-waiting. Gaebe, send a message to the king that I must see him immediately." While the men scrambled to obey his terse instructions, he turned to the princess. "Do not go anywhere without at least two guards with you at all times. I'll speak with Captain Tarvok about the assignments."

She was pale, her eyes wide with fear and shimmering with unshed tears. "You're sure they were dead?"

He blinked. He had not told her that he had killed the Hanoran scouts. Then he realized that she spoke of Breneg and Ciath. Touched at her distress over the lives of her guards, he nodded and reached out to her, but balled his hands into fists instead. "Breneg and Ciath were good men, Your Highness. They shall not be forgotten."

Tears leaked out of her eyes and ran unimpeded down her cheeks. She nodded and went inside the castle, flanked by two guards. Kai headed for the south guard tower. On the way, he passed Lord Alivan, who shot him a look of annoyance. Then, obviously noticing the grim expression Kai knew he must be wearing, the nobleman studied him more closely and halted.

"Troubled by something, Captain?" Alivan's tone was mocking.

"Only if you call lurking Hanorans and two dead knights trouble," Kai shot back. Normally, he would keep such news quiet until he had spoken to both Tarvok and the king, but some instinct in him urged him to speak, and observe the lord's reaction.

Alivan's expression changed and then was quickly masked, but not before Kai detected a touch of fear. Fear, not surprise. Interesting.

The nobleman made appropriate sounds of shock, and then mumbled something about a meeting. Stifling his desire to interrogate Alivan right then, Kai moved on in search of Tarvok to report the loss of two of his finest men and the presence of at least two Hanorans.

War was imminent.

~ Chapter Five

*J*eniah stood in the council chambers, hoping no one could hear the thudding of her heart or see her shaking hands. Since she had received the summons to appear before the Grand Council, a sinking dread had clutched at her until she could hardly breathe. Mora and two other handmaidens had fussed over her with such meticulous care that she might have been posing for a portrait.

The moment Jeniah had entered the chambers, all conversation had ended and she had found herself the focus of attention. The chairs at the council table were all occupied. All the usual advisors and leaders were present, including the king's brothers, who had arrived in the castle with their families only two days before.

Finally, King Darvae spoke. "Princess Jeniah of Arden." He inclined his head in a royal bow.

Jeniah swallowed at the unprecedented event of her father bowing to her. She remembered her manners and sank into a well-rehearsed curtsy, grateful that she didn't wobble or fall.

"In light of recent events, we, the council, have made a decision with regards to the Hanorans. We call upon your duty as a princess to come to the aid of your country."

He paused, and her sense of dread deepened. She'd known all of her life she had been raised for a political alliance, but facing the day her father would pronounce her fate seemed surreal.

"It has been determined that, in the interest of goodwill and to form an alliance with Hanore, you will marry the prince of Hanore."

Aghast, Jeniah stared. Marry the prince of Hanore! The words tolled like a death bell.

"You shall depart as soon as your Ascension Ceremony is complete, to your husband and your new home. We are confident that our offering will not be refused as you are a maiden and your beauty is rare . . ."

Jeniah hardly heard the rest of the king's words as a buzzing noise in her brain dulled all sound. A shudder rippled through her. She stood wide-eyed, rooted to the floor in disbelief.

"Marry a barbarian?" The words fell out of her mouth before she could stop them.

The king's eyes narrowed. "It is not your place to question my ruling, or the decision of the council."

Jeniah flinched.

"For this you have been born and bred."

"Of course, Your Majesty," she whispered.

"You alone can preserve peace, Jeniah. All our hopes rest upon you." He gave her a sad smile, and for a moment, she saw how agonizing his decision had been.

Disarmed by his regret, her eyes traveled slowly over those seated at the council table. Prince Aven, too, wore a look of sympathy.

Captain Darkwood's expression appeared perfectly neutral at first glance, but then a crack showed through his façade, and Jeniah saw his anger and dismay. Somehow, his show of emotion cut through her shock and touched her heart.

Captain Tarvok of the Home Guard kept his eyes averted. The faces of the princes and other leaders and advisors were grim and determined. This had not been an easy decision.

Her heart hammered. Lightheaded, she bowed and murmured what she hoped was an appropriate response about duty to country and king. Then, as hastily as etiquette allowed, she retreated. In the corridor, Jeniah rested a hand against the wall to try to steady herself.

Marry the prince of Hanore.

She couldn't move, couldn't breathe, couldn't think.

A nearby guard held out a hand toward her. She pulled herself together enough to begin walking, but her legs moved unsteadily and a terrible weight pressed on her chest. The hallway closed in around her like a tomb.

Voices echoed and faded as the council adjourned and vacated the council hall. Jeniah forced herself to keep moving. She would not break into a run, or break down.

A warm presence next to her edged through the heaviness. Kai Darkwood fell in step with her, his blue eyes searching her face with an expression she could not decipher.

"Your Highness, I . . ." He swallowed. "I wish I could say something to bring you comfort. Ladies have a role in life that I do not envy."

Feeling vulnerable, she looked up at him. "Thank you, Captain." Her words sounded hollow even to her own ears. With effort, she managed to keep her tears at bay.

His eyes darted over her face, and then he turned to leave as if he could not bear to be in her presence any longer. "Good day, Your Highness."

The heaviness returned the moment the captain left, but Jeniah forced herself to keep moving. Marry the prince of Hanore. The enemy. The enemy who threatened their way of life, their very existence. The thought left her with crushing dread.

This could not really be happening. Her family would not do

this to her. There had to be another option! This could not be the only way to avoid war. Had the council simply viewed her as the most obvious solution? A commodity?

Remembering her father's display of grief quickly dispelled that thought. Whatever else he was, he was still her father and he loved her. Though he had acted in the best interest of Arden—not just the country, but its people—she knew that he would have viewed this decision as a last resort, only when all other options had been exhausted.

Still, to marry a Hanoran!

She could run. The urge to ride far away lured her with a song of freedom so strong that she actually considered it. But that would be treason, and besides, she had nowhere to go. She could only blur for a short time, and that would not protect her indefinitely. If father were right, she alone held the key to peace, and she would not risk the safety of all of Arden. She was trapped by duty and responsibility. It was her purpose, her destiny.

In the privacy of her room, Jeniah sank down across the bed. After weeping until exhaustion hushed her tears, she sat by a window. She rested her head on the leaded windowpane and closed her eyes, chilled down to her soul.

Many people married for love. Why were the privileged royalty condemned to marry for position or power with little hope of true joy? She had known all of her life that her marriage would be arranged by her father for political gain, but that event had always rested in the distant future. Now she faced the immediate prospect of marriage, not only to a stranger, but to the enemy.

She would leave Arden and live in a desert among barbarians who practiced pagan rituals and human sacrifices. They were savage, ruthless. Their king practiced black magic.

With a gasp, Jeniah realized she would be sharing a bed with this kind of man. If the Hanoran prince was sadistic with his subjects, he would probably be the same with his wife. Horror squeezed her stomach until she became ill. She emptied her stomach in a washbasin before weakly slumping onto the window seat. She rested her forehead on the window. The first snowfall of the year had arrived the day before, dusting the countryside with pristine whiteness. But in the courtyard below, the snow had been cleared away from the paths to lie in dirty piles in the corners. Jeniah's eyes drifted beyond the castle walls to the sea. The calmness of the water mocked her turbulent emotions as she watched a flock of birds fly overhead. How many more days would she see this view?

Her Ascension Ceremony would take place in only a week, and preparations had already commenced. It marked the end of her life as she knew it. Then she would be taken away, so far away. To marry a monster.

Jeniah moved to the bed and collapsed on it face down. Her tears returned and she had sunk into violent sobbing when the bed sank beside her. When no one spoke, she turned her head expecting Mora, but instead found the queen.

Jeniah closed her eyes, expecting her mother to scold her for behaving improperly. Instead, a gentle hand rested on her back.

"I know you are frightened, Jeniah," her mother soothed as she rubbed her daughter's back. Jeniah's sobs faded into shudders while the gentle hand continued moving up and down her back. "Your father is heartbroken over this, but he truly felt he had no choice. And he had to answer to the council."

"I've heard such terrible things about Hanorans," Jeniah moaned.

"I know. But often those stories come from those who do not truly know. I was so frightened when I learned I was to come to Arden, I nearly ran away."

"What stopped you?"

A faint smile touched the queen's mouth. "Loyalty to my father and to my country." Her eyes softened. "When I arrived, I discovered, pleasantly, that I had been misinformed about both Arden and the king. I knew when I met your father that he was a man of honor and I had nothing to fear. We did grow to love each other, and now I can't imagine life without him."

Jeniah sighed. It seemed impossible that she could find honor in a Hanoran, especially one bent on conquering Arden.

"It's possible King Rheged might not be as ruthless as we believe, and even if he is, perhaps his son is nothing like him." The queen leaned down on one elbow to look her in the eye. "I know I've been hard on you. I've demanded much and given you little time to yourself. I wanted to you be prepared for anything, any challenge. You can do this. You are stronger than you know."

Jeniah stared at her in surprise. She had never heard such praise from her mother. "I will never be like you," she began timidly.

"No, you will be *you*. And as you face challenges, you will discover who you are. I sense in you an ancient magic. You will be able to do great things." Her hand continued its circular movement on Jeniah's back.

"Magic? How?"

"Daughter, out of respect for the Ardeenes, I never told you this before, but there is a Tiraian matriarchal magic that flows in your blood. It only surfaces every two or three generations. My grandmother had great power. I suspect you have a trace of it too. Trust your heart."

Jeniah sat up. "Then you don't believe all magic is bad?"

"I believe it is a tool that can be used according to the will of the user."

Jeniah stared up at the ceiling, recalling that her chayim had said much the same thing during their brief bond. The thorn of pain returned at the thought of his death.

"Things often look the worst before they improve. You are strong. Meet your adversities with your head high, and you may find strength and joy you never imagined."

Her mother's words brought her more comfort than she might have guessed. Hearing that the queen believed she had potential helped quell the panic, and Jeniah thought she just might survive her fate.

When the queen left, Mora crawled into bed with her and held her, calling her "little one," and cried with her. And when Jeniah realized Mora would no longer be with her when she left Arden, her tears began anew.

⁂

Kai lowered his sword. His arms shook with fatigue from the workout he had demanded of himself. Practice had ended hours before and the men had all left. The sky had darkened, and snow had begun falling again, but Kai had been determined to keep training until he cleared his head. Instead, his thoughts spiraled back to the council, to the moment when the king ordered Princess Jeniah to marry the Hanoran prince. A savage.

The thought made Kai ill. He had been present as the elders discussed possible solutions to prevent the looming war and knew they had spent days discussing options. This union seemed the only plausible answer, but he hated it. Even now, he desperately searched for an alternative. It wasn't his place to oppose the king; he wasn't even Ardeene. But he could not stand the thought of a Hanoran beast married to the young, pure princess. Any son of King Rheged would surely be a cruel husband.

With a sound of disgust, Kai sheathed his sword. No matter what he did, the terror and hopelessness in the princess's eyes haunted him.

Kai handed his gear to his exhausted squire. "We're done for the day, Romand. Go find something hot to eat and get some rest."

"Thank you, sir." Romand managed a tired smile.

Kai hardly felt the cold despite forgetting to don his cloak as he stalked from the arena toward the barracks. In the inner courtyard, a soft presence washed over him and he looked up to see that the object of his thoughts had taken form directly in front of him. The snow fluttered down gently, dusting her hood.

"Princess Jeniah," he said in greeting.

"Captain." Her voice was barely a whisper as she passed him on the path. Her face was pale, and purple shadows under her eyes told of many sleepless nights. He felt as if someone had kicked him in the stomach.

"Princess," he called softly after her.

She stopped and turned toward him. "Yes, Captain?"

He swallowed. "I . . . " He wanted desperately to speak with her, but words of comfort were beyond him.

She waited patiently, her eyes upon him.

"Are you well?" he finally managed. It was feeble, but he could think of nothing else.

The faintest curve touched her lips. "I am. Thank you for your concern, Captain."

Brave words. Not true, but brave. The princess's eyes remained upon him as he searched for appropriate consolation. Her guards moved back out of earshot while keeping her carefully in view.

She came to his rescue. "I've prepared all of my life for a marriage of my father's choosing, Captain. Do not trouble yourself for my sake." She spoke with quiet resignation, her eyes dull.

"I shall make a formal request to accompany your escort to Hanore." He had not consciously decided to make such a request, and he did not even know if his presence would offer her comfort, but the words had come from his mouth almost at their own accord.

"Then I'm sure to have a safe journey. Thank you, Captain." Her chin lifted a degree, a ghost of a smile flitting across her lovely features.

Kai turned at the sound of nearing footsteps and saw the princess's lady-in-waiting.

"There you are! The dressmaker needs you to come for the final fitting."

The princess looked at her. "Very well, Mora, I'll be there momentarily." Her eyes flicked back to Kai. She nodded to him, a smile of appreciation touching her mouth before she turned.

Kai's footsteps took him outside near the outer bailey. Earlier that day, the knights had trained there in earnest. Kai understood the importance of the Ascension Ceremony to the culture of Arden. The grand, coming-of-age event began with a three-day tournament. The knights trained with a good deal of boasting about their prowess in each event and who would be the overall winner. The knight with the most victories would be named the Princess's Champion, a coveted honor. Traditionally, the champion would be her escort over the next year, unless she married first. In this case, that champion would command the guard during her journey to Hanore. For reasons he did not care to examine, Kai determined to be included with that guard.

The messenger with the offer of an alliance between Hanore and Arden had departed a few days before, so it would be at least a moon cycle before Arden received a reply. Hanore could refuse, of course, but it seemed unlikely, unless King Rheged was simply bloodthirsty—a distinct possibility.

Kai allowed himself the luxury of hoping that the offer would be refused, but instantly shame struck him. If the two countries went to war, thousands would die. But the princess would be spared from a marriage prospect that horrified her. She deserved to be married to a man who knew her. A man who would cherish her. A man like him.

Kai grimaced and raked a hand through his hair, banishing this futile line of thought. His battered heart would never be whole enough to allow anything more than a casual relationship. Moreover, she was royalty and he was a commoner, which made a union between them impossible.

A lone rider galloped through the gates as they began to close. The rider stopped inside as if looking for someone. A guard questioned him but let him pass. There was something familiar about this rider. Immediately, a shadow detached itself from the wall and moved toward the rider.

As Kai crept upon them, he recognized Lord Alivan, whose actions had seemed suspicious the day Kai had arrived in Arden. The rider and Lord Alivan left together, turning down a narrow side street. Kai followed them stealthily, knowing he appeared no more noticeable than a shadow.

". . . and are waiting for your arrival before they send in the first wave," the rider said.

"Already? They were supposed to wait until after I leave on my diplomatic mission," Alivan replied with alarm in his voice.

"Tonight."

"This wasn't part of the plan." Alivan sighed. "Very well, I will depart immediately." He handed the rider an object that had the distinctive jingle of coins.

All of Kai's instincts screamed that Lord Alivan was engaged in treason. Walking toward the two men, Kai called out boldly, "Something wrong, my lord?"

Even in the dim light, Lord Alivan blanched visibly, and the rider beside him put his hand on his sword.

"Nothing that concerns you, Darborian," Lord Alivan snarled.

"Then you won't mind telling me."

Alivan and the rider drew their swords and moved toward him.

Kai grinned darkly. "I'm impressed with your devotion to perfecting your swordplay, Alivan, but this isn't really the best time to spar."

"I'm going to kill you, you overconfident braggart."

Kai raised his eyebrows in amusement. "Oh? Did you suddenly develop skill with a blade?"

Alivan lunged at him while his co-conspirator circled around. Their swords rang as they struck. Kai threw Alivan off easily while whirling to ward off the blow the rider tried to deal from behind. He maneuvered himself to a more advantageous position and then pressed them mercilessly. Under Kai's blade, the rider fell, bleeding and writhing. Alivan stumbled and went down but before he could rise, Kai placed his sword at the hollow of the nobleman's neck.

"Tell me what you are doing, Alivan, while I still have the patience to spare you."

"I've nothing to say to you, Darborian." Alivan lay on his back, glowering up at Kai.

Kai pressed his sword tip against the nobleman's throat until he gasped. In a soft, deadly voice, Kai said, "Tell me, or I will be forced to hurt you before I drag you before the king."

Alivan's face paled further. "You can kill me but you'll not get a word out of me."

Kai applied more pressure to Alivan's throat until a thin line of blood trickled down his neck, knowing if he was wrong about this, he risked execution and war between Darbor and Arden. He kept his voice cold. "I won't kill you, Alivan, I will only carve you up. Slowly."

"You wouldn't dare!"

"I fear the safety of Arden is at stake. It is my duty to protect it, even from a traitor."

When Alivan still did not reply, Kai moved his sword to the base of Alivan's left ear. The nobleman held his breath.

Kai deepened the chill in his voice. "They taught us many things when I trained to become a Sauraii. One is to never show mercy to an enemy."

Alivan's face paled even further, but he remained silent. Kai bent over him and with a swift stroke, brought the hilt of his sword down over the lord's head in a controlled strike, knocking him unconscious.

Kai sighed. He had hoped that the nobleman wouldn't call his bluff. He sheathed his sword and threw Alivan over his shoulder. The rider had stopped moaning and lay unconscious on the street.

"Ho, there!" called a voice.

Kai halted.

A guard ran up to him. "Captain Darkwood?"

Kai gestured toward the rider on the street. "Bring him for interrogation. And dispatch a messenger to the king. I must see him immediately."

The guard's eyes flicked to Alivan's limp form draped unceremoniously over Kai's shoulder, but he carried out the orders.

Kai carried the unconscious lord toward the king's private study. The eyes of the sentries were upon him as he trod through castle corridors, but after Kai shot a fearsome scowl at anyone foolish enough to attempt to speak to him, the guards all fell back.

After being admitted inside the king's room, Kai lay Alivan down on a rug and straightened. He stepped back and bowed, falling into formality.

"I haven't hurt him, Your Majesty," Kai said hastily to the king. "He's only unconscious."

Standing unflinching before the king, Kai then recounted everything he knew of Alivan's dubious behavior, beginning with the day he had arrived and ending with the nobleman drawing his sword on him.

Prince Aven stood nearby, looking thunderous as he glared at Alivan's unconscious figure on the rug. Kai glanced at Tarvok, who looked grim. Even now, Tarvok's men were massing at the outer defenses, and Kai knew the captain of the guard longed to be with them.

The king paced the floor, each movement jerky, and Kai could not be certain if the monarch's fury was directed at him or at Alivan.

"You know Darkwood speaks the truth, Father." Aven's words, quietly spoken, were filled with righteous indignation. "All along, Alivan has thwarted our efforts to train the knights. He argued against bringing the Sauraii here, he argued against fortifying the walls. In short, every effort we have attempted in preparation for war has been stymied by him."

The king ran his hands over his face. "I know."

The desolate resignation in his voice twisted like a knife in Kai's stomach. Silently, he watched the noble king of Arden come to terms with a painful betrayal.

Kai swallowed against a dry throat. "Sire, he said the first wave was coming tonight. We face imminent invasion."

Looking as if he'd aged twenty years in moments, the king nodded. "Sound the alarm. Evacuate the women and children. Arm everyone else. Dismissed."

They bowed and left the room, calling for their squires and sending out messengers. Kai felt sick down to his soul. There were few adequately trained knights in the castle, and even if they had all been Sauraiis, so few against a full army of savages made defeat alarmingly probable.

Kai clenched his fists. They should be meeting in a battlefield, not defending themselves at their very door. He had barely finished donning the padded shirt that protected his skin from the metal edges of his armor, when the horns sounded.

"We're under attack!" Voices picked up the warning.

Adrenaline flowed through Kai's body, energizing it and sharpening his senses. He ran through mental exercises to clear his mind as his squire helped him don his chain mail and strap on his weapons.

Ragged breathing caught Kai's attention, and he turned to see Romand's expression of sheer terror.

"Pick up your sword, Romand, and stay close. We fight for our country. There is no greater honor than that."

King Farai of Darbor had once declared Kai invincible. Tonight would test that claim in a way no battle ever had. For the sake of the Ardeenes, Kai prayed that the Darborian king was right.

Chapter Six

*J*eniah awoke in terror. Every nerve in her body screamed danger.

"Mora!" She leaped from her bed, picked up the lit candle, and rushed to her wardrobe. After flinging the doors open, she began searching through her clothes. She found a plain riding gown and cloak, and as she shed her nightgown she called again, "Mora!"

The sleepy-eyed lady-in-waiting came into her room. "What is it?"

"We're in danger."

Mora blinked and rubbed her eyes. "Little one, I'm sure it was only a dream."

"No. No, it's real." Jeniah couldn't explain how she knew, but blind terror had dragged her from sleep and urged her to flee. She stepped into her clothes and fumbled at the ties with shaking hands.

The wail of a horn broke the stillness of the night. Jeniah froze. Mora blinked. "What—?"

A shout came from outside the castle. "We're under attack! Enemy approaching! Evacuate the city!"

More voices picked up the alert and grew stronger as the message passed from mouth to mouth.

Someone pounded on her door. "Princess!"

White-faced, Mora hurried to open the door while Jeniah pulled on her stockings and shoes.

A guard stood in the threshold. "Dress quickly, my lady. We must get you and the princess out of the city."

"What is it?"

"The Hanorans are upon us. They're at the outer gates."

Jeniah felt the blood leave her face. "They are here? Now?"

"I thought Jeniah's marriage would prevent all that," Mora said.

The guard shook his head. "Lies, all of them. Quickly! There is no time."

Jeniah grabbed two cloaks and handed one to Mora. The guard made an impatient gesture and then urged them down the hallway. As they descended the grand staircase, another knight stopped beside them. "We're surrounded. Take them to the queen's solarium." Without waiting for acknowledgement, he ran on, his armor clinking loudly.

Distant cries sounded. Then an earsplitting noise shook the castle, and the screams grew closer. Jeniah hurried to a window at the end of the corridor and parted the hangings to look outside. Fire illuminated a city in chaos. The sound of clanging metal and the distant cheer of men rang out. Much closer came the clashing of swords and then a strangled cry. The smell of blood assaulted her nostrils.

A sound like thunder rent the air and another shudder rippled through the castle. The guard let out a shout and grabbed Jeniah by the elbow, thrusting her behind him.

The wall exploded, the impact throwing them to the floor. Debris and shattered glass showered over them. Dazed, Jeniah pushed herself up and coughed as a cloud of dirt arose. Freezing wind blew in from a yawning hole where the outer wall and window had stood only a moment ago. As the dust settled, Jeniah saw the guard lying next to her underneath several large, ragged blocks of stone.

"Sir Knight?" Jeniah touched his grimy, bloodied face and felt for a pulse in his neck. Finding none, she let out a sound of distress.

Mora put her hand over her mouth. Nearby, the floor had collapsed, leaving a chasm where the corridor had once been. They were cut off from their path to the queen's tower. Jeniah peered over the edge. An enormous boulder lay on the next floor below them, surrounded by chunks of stone that had once made up the floor.

"How can this be happening?" gasped Mora. "What should we do?"

Jeniah had never seen Mora so frightened. She took her hand. "We've got to get to my mother's tower. This way."

As the sounds of battle raged outside and smoke burned their eyes, Jeniah led Mora to the back stairwell. Another explosion shook the walls around them as they stumbled down the stairs. At the bottom, they paused. The main hall had become a battlefield. Many of the armed men were Ardeene knights, but others wore strange armor. These were not her people; they were dark and long-haired. Hanorans.

Somehow, they would have to cross the main hall to get to the stairway leading up to the queen's solarium in the central tower.

A nearby Hanoran wielding a curved sword sliced through the Ardeene knight he faced. Mute with horror, Jeniah watched helplessly while the knight crumpled. The Hanoran turned, seeking a new opponent.

Jeniah swallowed, trying to gather her courage and her wits. She and Mora would never make it to the other side of the great hall to the central staircase without being detected. She could blur, of course, but that would not help Mora.

Mora turned to her. "I know you can hide yourself, little one. You must do so now. Go to your mother in her solar. Be safe."

"We'll find a way through together."

"Go on your own. I'll try to get through alone."

Terrified that she would never see Mora again, Jeniah clutched at her. "No. Stay with me."

Mora crushed Jeniah against her bosom. "I love you, child. As if you were my own."

Then, roughly, she pushed Jeniah away and darted into the great hall. Keeping to the shadows, she zigzagged her way through the battling men. Jeniah blurred and followed, careful to touch no one and reveal herself. They might make it.

Mora almost reached the stairs before an enemy soldier marked her. With a lunge, he grabbed her and threw her to the ground. He raised his sword, about to deliver a killing blow.

"No!" Jeniah shrieked.

She charged at the soldier and threw herself upon his back in an attempt to knock him to the floor. In surprise, the Hanoran staggered, but did not fall.

"No, foolish girl!" Mora screamed. "Run!"

"I'm not leaving you!"

She rolled off the soldier's back and darted out of the way, realizing belatedly that she'd forgotten to remain blurred. The second the Hanoran lost eye contact, she blurred. He turned, swinging his sword, and then blinked. In confusion, he scanned the room. Mora climbed to her feet and started for the stairs again, but the swarthy soldier grabbed her around the waist and threw her down again.

Jeniah picked up a sword from a downed knight. It was much heavier than she expected. She knew nothing about battle, but she knew which end of a weapon to use. Standing behind him, she plunged the sword into the Hanoran's back. Her blade met with more resistance than she expected, and there was a sickening sound of cracking bone and tearing flesh. The Hanoran stumbled, dropped to his knees, and fell face down.

Aghast, Jeniah dropped the sword and looked down at the blood spattered on her gown. She'd killed a man!

Mora seized her hand and pulled her toward the stairway. Fighting nausea and the bile in her throat, Jeniah staggered. Then she realized she had lost her focus and was no longer blurred, but she couldn't find the strength to do it again. They climbed the stairs and stumbled over a body lying in their path. With dismay, Jeniah recognized him as an Ardeene knight. She stepped carefully over him as if she feared hurting him further, her stomach twisting at the sight. Again, they encountered a lifeless knight. At the top of the stairs were several more motionless forms, both Hanoran and Ardeene. The door to the queen's solarium lay in splinters on the floor. Another knight lay face down in a pool of scarlet on the threshold.

Fearing the worst, Jeniah looked inside. Only a glance around the room confirmed that none of the royal family remained there. The queen's room had been ransacked. Her indigo brocade furniture lay on end, its fabric hanging in slashed ribbons. Pillows were strewn haphazardly about. A candelabrum lay on the floor, the candles' flames drowning in their own wax. The fire in the fireplace had died down, its light casting a pale glow over the destruction.

"They must have been moved to a safer location," she said to a stunned Mora, while a darker fear whispered in her mind.

The lady-in-waiting wrung her hands and turned anguished eyes upon Jeniah. "Where do we go? How am I to protect you now?"

"We must get out of the city," Jeniah said, trying to think clearly.

She stepped into the room to give her eyes something other than the dead men to focus upon while she fought to gather her thoughts. The view inside was only mildly less disturbing.

Mora hugged herself. "Surely someone will realize you're missing and come back for you."

"Ah! Two more birds have flown into the cage," a guttural voice said from behind them.

Three Hanoran soldiers stood on the stairs, weapons drawn, clothing smeared in gore. With hatred and something far more sinister glittering in their eyes, they advanced upon Mora and Jeniah.

Mora pulled Jeniah behind her. "Stay back, fiends."

The nearest soldier laughed at her empty bravery. Tortuously slow, the invaders continued to move forward, backing Mora and Jeniah further into the room.

"That must be the missing princess," said one of the soldiers, glowering at Jeniah.

"Yes," agreed another. "I think we've found her. And I think we shall enjoy her first." They all laughed in cruel glee.

"It would be a shame to not enjoy the spoils of war before we turn her over to the commander," rejoined the first.

The nearest soldier made a quick lunge for Mora, his sword slicing through her midsection. Jeniah screamed as Mora crumpled. Shocked and enraged, Jeniah stared. Mora couldn't be dead. None of this was real. None of this was happening.

"Come, little girl. Which one of us do you want first?" taunted a soldier.

Cold fear skittered down Jeniah's spine. She picked up a fallen candlestick and held it with both hands in front of her. He smirked. He made a jab at her and laughed as she clumsily tried to ward him off. His sword came up and effortlessly knocked her weapon out of her hand. It made a loud clunk as it hit the floor.

The soldier licked his lips. Jeniah shrank back against the wall near the black fireplace, her heart throbbing in her ears.

"I outrank you both, so I claim her first," he called over his shoulder to his comrades, without taking his eyes off her.

His eyes smoldered as he set down his sword. Grinning hideously, the soldier lunged at her and threw her roughly to the floor. She screamed as he fell upon her and nearly crushed her with the weight of his body. The savage's hands tore her gown from the neckline to the waist. His breath was hot and foul upon her face. She screamed again. Kicking and scratching failed to move him.

Jeniah's flailing hand came into contact with a fire poker. She pulled, but it hung by a hook and she could not pull it loose. Her free hand clawed his face and pummeled his chest. Twisting her body, she kicked anything her legs could reach.

Sharp claws of panic raked her heart, and then primal fear swept over her, bringing untapped strength. She tore the fire poker free, then smashed it down upon the head of the Hanoran soldier. The brute straightened and cried out. Jeniah swung her weapon across her body and struck him again, this time on the side of his head, knocking him off her. As he fell sideways onto the floor, she struggled to her knees.

Her attacker dabbed at the blood trickling from the side of his face and looked down at his hand smeared with his own blood. With a murderous cry, he threw himself at her. She braced herself and plunged the pointed end of the fire poker deep into his chest. He gurgled and fell back, then lay still, eyes open in surprise.

Sickened, Jeniah climbed shakily to her feet. The other soldiers paused, staring first at their fallen comrade and then at her. She turned toward them, still brandishing the bloodied fire poker.

A shadowed figure burst into the room, and the Hanorans whirled to face the new arrival. With a battle cry, the shadow lunged at them, moving as lithely as a dancer. A sword flashed and both Hanorans fell lifeless. The shadowy form turned, his armor and sword dripping with blood. Dark panic welled up inside Jeniah, nearly strangling her. The man rushed toward her.

Grimly wielding her fire poker, Jeniah faced her new enemy.

Chapter Seven

I feared I was too late," Kai gasped breathlessly, his chest heaving.

The glow of fire from outside the windows illuminated Princess Jeniah's terror-filled face. She showed only a glimmer of recognition. Kai's gaze moved down her torn gown to the blood that smeared her exposed skin and splattered her clothes. Her hand gripped a bloodied fire poker. A Hanoran soldier lay dead at her feet.

She stared at Kai hollowly, and his breath left him as if a giant fist squeezed his lungs. She'd suffered the worst sort of violence from those monsters. He tried to steady his voice and held out a hand toward her. "Come with me, Princess. I'm getting you out of here."

When she made no move, he approached as he would an injured animal. Averting his eyes from her near nakedness, Kai removed his cloak and placed it around her. She did not resist. After fastening the cloak, he pried the poker from her hand and tossed it onto the floor.

The princess shivered, her breath ragged, her eyes wide and unblinking. He took her hand and gently propelled her to the door. At the top of the stairs he paused, his senses straining for possible ambush in such a closed space. Satisfied that the stairway was empty, he led her out. Stepping over bodies, they wound their way down the steps. In an attempt to spare the princess, he maneuvered himself so that his body blocked the sight of so many corpses strewn about. He could not begin to estimate the death toll.

He had failed them all. Sick with bitterness, he forced himself to keep moving, driven by a single thought: the princess must be protected.

Footsteps approached, echoing on the walls of the circular stairway. Bobbing torchlight illuminated the stairway, closing in on their position. Kai drew the princess into the shadows and stepped in front of her, listening for the telltale clink of Hanoran armor. He waited until they were close before he leaped out at the Hanorans. Before the enemy even realized their danger, two lay lifeless on the floor. The motion sent a wave of pain through his wounded side and shoulder. The remaining four Hanorans attacked but he parried and countered, and they soon fell.

Kai sucked in his breath, laboring against the pain, and then straightened.

He looked back at the princess. "Are you all right?"

She nodded mutely. He took her hand again and led her down the stairway. They descended the steps to the main floor, where a few brave Ardeenes still fought the Hanorans. Kai's instincts urged him to help them, but the Ardeenes had already lost the battle. He could do nothing for them. He must get the princess to safety.

In the inner bailey, he stole through the noise and confusion. Tongues of fire spread, hungrily licking anything in their path. The castle itself was built out of stone but everything else blazed. Glass windows shattered as fires roared inside buildings. Kai tightened his grip on the princess's hand and picked his way across the courtyard to the gate. The head of the king was stuck to the end of a pike like a gruesome banner. Carefully shielding the princess from the ghastly sight, he propelled her through the burning gateway and the relative, if temporary, safety of the shadowy walls surrounding the castle.

When Kai whistled, Braygo appeared, his head and chest blood-spattered and his horns thick with gore. Kai scooped the princess into his arms and mounted, biting his lip in pain and stifling a groan. He settled her across the saddle in front of him and urged the duocorn to a run. Around them, Arden City had erupted into complete bedlam. Bodies lay in the streets, many of them women and children.

The princess let out a low cry of horror.

Kai couldn't blame her. He'd known the Hanoran barbarians knew no bounds to cruelty and dishonor, but tonight exceeded everything he'd ever seen. No soldier from Darbor would have committed these atrocities.

Holding his precious charge, he fled through the streets of Arden City, dodging the chaos and fire and bloodshed. Every jolt sent searing pain through his body, but he refused to slow. All that mattered was getting the princess to safety.

Hanorans barred the main gate, but a hole in the outer wall to his right appeared large enough to ride through. He urged Braygo toward it, trusting the duocorn's surefootedness among the rubble. A shout rang out, and by the time they passed through the breach, mounted men were in pursuit.

Kai turned Braygo off the Old Road to cut through the forest. It had snowed a few days before, but the snow had refrozen and crusted over. Hopefully, Braygo's tracks would not be discernible. Black, naked tree limbs reached out like clutching arms, but enough moonlight filtered through the branches for the fleet-footed duocorn to bear his passengers safely through.

Clouds drifted wraith-like across the two moons, making their light shine intermittently.

Kai knew wyrwolves populated the forest, but at the moment, he'd rather face them than the Hanorans. The sounds of the pursuing men reached his ears, frighteningly close, and arrows whistled by as Braygo darted through the forest. The duocorn dashed along the bank of a frozen river that shined silver in the moonlight, while the sounds of their pursuers gradually faded. A lone wyrwolf howled in the distance.

Kai could feel Braygo begin to tire, each step coming more slowly. As the princess brushed against his wounded side, he stifled a gasp and had to fight to breathe against the pain. When he could move, he shifted her more comfortably in front of him.

She craned her neck to look behind them. "How close are the soldiers?"

He had expected her to be either hysterical, or mute and passive with shock, but her voice sounded strong.

"They've fallen further back." The Hanorans were out of sight, but they couldn't be far behind.

"Your duocorn is getting tired. How much longer can he outrun them?"

"Long enough." He hoped.

"He needs rest."

"He can rest once we reach the docks." With any luck, Tarvok had rescued other members of the royal family and was on his way to the rendezvous point. The princess ran her hands along Braygo's neck, no doubt feeling sweat and the strain of their pace. The duocorn coughed and his hoof beats broke rhythm, yet he kept running.

"Do you think we can we make it that far, Captain?"

Truthfully, Braygo could not keep up this speed much longer. He had already been in the middle of a battle, and this full run had sapped him quickly. Kai drew a breath, sending fresh pain shooting through his body. "We don't have much choice."

Jeniah straightened, peered out at the darkness, and pointed to a large, rocky outcropping. "That's Praying Mother." Then she motioned to a spot slightly behind them. "The cave I took you to is over there. We could hide inside and let your duocorn rest."

When another wyrwolf howled, much closer this time, Kai felt his options narrow. He turned Braygo toward the coastline. In the pale moonlight, Kai grew disoriented, but the princess guided him without hesitation to the cave.

His courage faltered at the sight of the darkened cave opening. "Is it high tide?"

"It's coming in," came her reply.

Water already churned at the mouth of the cave. Kai's muscles clenched at the familiar, suffocating fear lurking at the edge of his mind. "And you're positive water never fills it?"

"There's no sign that it ever has."

Swallowing his apprehension, Kai urged Braygo inside the darkness. The water swirled around the duocorn's knees but the surefooted animal remained steady. Inside the cave, they slid off Braygo's back and fought the current as they waded through the icy water to the wall.

"How long will we be trapped here by the water?"

"Only a couple of hours."

Kai nodded. He could do this. He felt his way along the rocks and began to climb. His wounded shoulder and side sent waves of agony knifing through his body each time he used his left arm to pull himself upward. Warm blood ran down his side.

Following the princess, who climbed in the darkness above him, he forced himself to keep moving. Since wild duocorns originally came from steep, rocky mountainsides, Kai knew that his fleet-footed Braygo scaled the rocks easily behind them. The churning waves muffled the noises they made as they climbed.

At the top, Kai pulled himself up and hauled his body onto the ledge, feeling around for a place to sit while Braygo scrambled up beside him. Fortunately, the long, narrow ledge afforded enough room for all of them. Kai sat back, breathing heavily, his eyes aching in the blackness as he listened to the water rising toward them.

"You're sure water could never reach us up here?" He hoped his voice sounded steadier than his nerves.

The princess's voice came from close beside him. "There would be water marks, or shells or something, but I've never found any."

Kai would rather go back outside and face the overwhelming numbers of the enemy than remain in the cave. Moreover, hiding felt cowardly, but he had to consider the safety of the princess. With the soldiers in such close pursuit, a tired Braygo would never be able to carry them to the rendezvous point designated by Captain Tarvok. Taking her into such danger would be foolhardy.

The initial wave of panic that always came when Kai entered a small space seeped through him. His breath caught and refused to move down to his lungs. Sweat poured down his back, and he pressed his shaking hands against his eye sockets. He found the presence of mind to run through his Sauraii mind-clearing exercises. Gradually, the dark terror faded into something manageable.

"Captain?" Fear laced the princess's voice.

"Yes?" He sounded strangled even to himself.

"Why did the Hanorans attack us after our gesture of peace?" She sounded like a lost child.

Kai sighed. "Making peace with the Hanorans was an unreasonable hope. They don't want allies or trade agreements.

They want power. And blood." He heard the hatred in his voice as it echoed faintly, competing with the rushing water.

She paused. "What happened tonight? And how did it all happen so fast? I heard the alarm and then they were already there."

"The Hanorans surrounded the outer wall. They used catapults and battering rams to break through on all sides."

"Where is the rest of my family?"

"Captain Tarvok is bringing them to a meeting place. We'll put you on a ship to Tirai until it's safe to bring you back." The queen's homeland and a trusted ally for generations seemed the best possible place for the royal family to find sanctuary. They would be safe there until Arden could be regained. If it could be regained.

The princess breathed a sound of relief, as if she had feared the worst. "After you see me to the ship, will you go back and help them win the battle?"

Kai removed his helmet and ran his fingers through his matted hair. He let out his breath in a long, ragged, weary exhale. "The battle is lost, Princess."

"My father would not concede so quickly. He must be regrouping his men."

She did not understand the magnitude of the loss, poor girl.

"Captain?"

Kai hesitated, wanting to spare her from the awful truth.

"Captain, please tell me." A touch of desperation colored her voice. She had seen the destruction and would know soon anyway. Sparing her would be impossible.

"The king fell in battle. He's dead." He spoke more bluntly than he should have, but he knew of no way to soften the blow.

The princess let out a low moan. Then, more timidly, her voice broken with tears, she asked, "Aven couldn't rally the knights?"

"Prince Aven also perished. The Ardeene army was completely annihilated. There is no one left to rally."

The slaughter that took place on the battlefield, which only hours before had been a peaceful city, would probably haunt Kai all his days. Perhaps it would have been better if he had died with them. No. Then the princess would be in their hands. Kai knew he had to live to see her protected.

"Aven," she whispered, her sorrow growing more pronounced. "Poor Karina. She loved him so."

Kai wasn't certain if Aven's wife Karina had lived either. With luck, Tarvok had gotten her and others out of the castle to safety.

"And my mother?"

"Captain Tarvok and his men are bringing all survivors to a meeting place."

The princess sagged against Kai, crying and shivering. He shifted until his back rested against hers, in an attempt to keep them both warm. Time dragged by at a maddeningly slow pace while Kai battled pain and a pervading sense of defeat, and listened to the water in the cave rise steadily. His thoughts returned to the battle. He cursed himself. He should have done more, fought harder, trained the Ardeene knights better. He had survived countless battles without losing one. King Farai had once predicted that Kai Darkwood could never be defeated. That had ended tonight. Tonight he had failed.

He knew it was arrogant and foolish to believe that he alone could have prevented the decimation of the Ardeene army. After all, they naively believed there was no true threat and that they had plenty of time to prepare. And Lord Alivan's duplicity only fed those beliefs.

If only Kai had known how little time they had before he had left Darbor. An army of Darborian knights could have swept away the Hanoran invaders.

The princess continued weeping silently against Kai's back. He could think of no words that might console her. Wanting to offer her comfort, he reached toward her but halted. He couldn't take the princess into his arms.

The image of her torn and bloodied gown, and the look of horror in her eyes, burst into his mind. His jaw clenched in anger. The thought of the barbarian's filthy hands on her blinded him with rage. He wanted to kill every Hanoran in the land for the brutal crimes they had committed tonight. With effort, Kai pushed his hatred aside. He had to think clearly now. At least the princess was alive. And he would give his life protecting her. As long as he had breath, she would never be hurt again.

The shivering princess scooted closer and rested her head on his shoulder, apparently unbothered by the links of his chain mail. He put his arms around her and felt whispers of guilt for touching her. Yet she already had his cloak; he could give her nothing else to keep warm.

The heat of Braygo's body behind Kai blended with the warmth of the princess against his chest. Occasionally, Kai felt water droplets splash on his face as the water churned a mere hand span below their ledge. Stale air, filled with the scent of fish and salt, made breathing increasingly more difficult. The panic threatened again, but Kai fought it back. He needed to stay calm for the princess's sake.

Her silent weeping finally subsided and she leaned heavily against him, her breathing deep and steady. Kai wished he could sleep but didn't dare.

When the cadence of the water changed, he straightened. The water was receding. He peered downward until he could make out the faint outline of the mouth of the cave. When the water was finally low enough to allow them to escape, he gently woke the princess.

"Your Highness, the water's down enough. Let's go."

She made no reply but sat up.

Kai crawled to the edge and began to lower himself down. A sudden, blinding pain in his wounded side made his breath come in gasps. He braced himself and kept moving, but finally his strength failed and he lost his grip. He only fell a few hand spans before he hit the water. Steeling himself, he struggled to stand in the chest-high icy water and fought to keep on his feet in the surprisingly strong current. Then, as the ocean's salt water soaked through his clothes to his open wounds, searing agony ripped through him. Kai clenched his jaw and smothered a groan.

"Captain?" The princess clung to the rock wall, keeping all but her feet out of the water.

He sucked in his breath, unable to reply, and leaned against Braygo, who remained steady against the tide. The cold quickly numbed his pain enough to allow movement. He turned and helped the princess mount.

She took his hand, her face drawn with concern. "Are you well?"

He gave her a quick nod and fought the waves as he led Braygo forward. At the mouth of the cave, Kai placed a hand on her arm and mouthed, "Wait here."

He drew his weapons and moved cautiously outside, searching for danger. The moons were still up, the grayness low on the horizon, hinting of sunrise yet to come. Kai waded through the water to the beach. After he reconnoitered and found no sign of danger, he circled back around.

As the numbness wore off, the salt began to burn the open sores again, so he pulled back the torn edges of his shirt under his damaged chain mail and poured some fresh water from his water skin down his wounded side. Once he remounted, the princess huddled against him, shaking.

They rode in silence, listening for sounds of soldiers. They backtracked several times, Kai using every tracking skill he possessed to conceal their trail, but his knowledge was rudimentary at best and he feared it would be inadequate.

Nocturnal forest creatures who braved the winter squeaked as they scurried away. Great trees stood like sentries, stretching toward the cold sky. The moons set and predawn light crept over the land.

Smoke from Arden City rose in billowing, black clouds in the distance. Kai cantered Braygo on the empty main road leading to the waterfront. Dark silhouettes of silent ships nodded in the fog as they waited at port, and warehouses stood vacant. No sign of life appeared anywhere. Everything lay in a breathless hush. Kai battled waves of pain and fatigue as the sun rose.

He guided Braygo to a small, winding street facing the bay, then slowed to approach a small tavern. All was as Captain Tarvok had described. Kai listened carefully, all senses straining. When he was sure all was still, he whistled softly. An answering whistle sounded. Kai responded with a variation of the whistle—higher, longer.

From the tavern came a cloaked and hooded figure. The hood was lowered, revealing Captain Tarvok's bandaged face. "Darkwood, hurry, get the princess inside."

After they dismounted, another knight appeared and took Braygo to the stable in the back. When they were all inside, Tarvok closed and bolted the door to a room that held only a few chairs and a broken table. A darkened stone fireplace sat in the corner of the room.

"The Hanorans have already been here, so I don't think they'll be back right away." With obvious disappointment, the captain of the guard glanced at the princess, who sunk into a chair by the fireplace. "No one else?" He kept his voice barely above a whisper.

Kai shook his head.

Tarvok's mouth tightened. "They've taken control of the port. Getting her to a ship for Tirai is out of the question. You'll have to take her to Darbor."

"Travel to Darbor will be risky," Kai said quietly. "They will be looking for her when they realize she's missing. Aren't there any other harbors we can use?"

"This is the only safe harbor for a hundred miles in either direction. There are too many cliffs and off-shore reefs anywhere else."

"You didn't get anyone out?"

Looking defeated, Tarvok shook his head. "I was too late. They executed the entire family and most of the nobility. Even Lord Alivan. I guess they no longer found him useful."

"He was stupid to think they'd actually fulfill their bargain with a traitor." Kai ran his fingers though his hair, letting his breath out slowly. "I should have come to you or the king as soon as I suspected Alivan's treachery."

"We cannot waste time laying blame. You must take her away now while you can."

Kai glanced back at the princess. She sat curled up, staring at the wall. He considered the length and difficulty of the journey they faced. He had traveled on the highways during good weather without anyone else's needs to consider, and it had still taken him nearly two weeks to make the trip from Darbor to Arden. A flight during winter, dodging the enemy all the way, would make the journey much longer. And without any comforts, such a trek might prove too much for someone of the princess's delicate breeding. But there were few options.

Kai crouched down next to the princess and touched her

shoulder. "Princess, we need to leave now before we lose our chance."

The princess raised her head.

"You can't stay in Arden," Tarvok added. "The whole country is teeming with Hanorans. Captain Darkwood will take you to Darbor."

"Darbor?"

Kai nodded. "King Farai will protect you. You will be safe there."

"What about the others?"

Tarvok spoke. "You are the last survivor of your family."

The princess rose unsteadily to her feet and stared at him in clear disbelief. She looked from Tarvok's solemn face to Kai's and back again. Putting her hands on either side of her face, she closed her eyes and whispered, "No."

"The rest of the living royalty were rounded up and executed publicly. Even the children," Tarvok declared soberly.

She looked up at Kai, her eyes tearing again. "Everyone?"

"I'm sorry." Kai could barely stand to look her in the eye.

"No, that can't be." Moaning, she slid down the wall and curled up in a quivering heap on the floor.

There was nothing either Kai or Tarvok could offer as consolation. This delicate creature who had lived her life among the plush riches and comforts of the palace, adored and pampered, was now forced to live as a fugitive, without even the necessities of life.

Once again, fury at Lord Alivan's deception, and the underhanded victory of their enemies, rushed through Kai. The most beautiful city in all the kingdoms was in ruins. Countless innocent people and good, brave men had died, and for what? Kai resisted the urge to smash his fist through a wall.

"You're hurt," Tarvok observed, eyeing Kai.

Kai glanced down at the dark stains on his padded shirt, barely visible underneath his chain mail.

"It's only a graze."

"I'll send for a healer."

Kai looked through the shutters of the window at the lightening sky. "There isn't much time. I'll be all right." He helped the princess stand. "Princess, we must go while we can still get away. If the Hanorans have a good tracker, they will find you here. We have to move on."

She sniffled and looked up at him with childlike vulnerability.

Kai put a hand on her arm. "I will protect you and get you safely to Darbor."

"Do you really think we have a chance?"

"I will use my last breath if I must, but I will bring you to Darbor unharmed," he said with fervor. He exchanged glances with a grim Tarvok. "I'll send you word when we reach Darbor."

"I will keep the effort going." Tarvok found a blanket and placed it around the princess's shoulders over the cloak Kai had given her. "You are the last living member of Arden's royalty. Our one hope. You are our rightful queen now."

"Queen," she whispered in disbelief.

Looking at this young, frightened, ragged creature, Kai understood her trepidation.

"Captain Darkwood will take you to safety until Arden can be regained. I will find anyone who can wield a sword and continue the fight. It's not over, I promise you." He bowed his head. "Your Majesty."

The princess nodded and managed to reply with grace, "Thank you, Captain Tarvok. Your loyalty and bravery will be remembered."

Tarvok removed his own cloak and handed it to Kai, and

they clasped arms in a warrior's handshake. Before emerging cautiously from the tavern, Kai checked in all directions. Braygo, who had been watered, fed, and rubbed down, was led back to his master.

Kai tossed a coin to the stable lad. "My thanks."

The tavern shrank behind Kai and Jeniah as Braygo bore them toward Darbor. They rode in silence, listening for the sounds of enemy troops. All was mercifully still. Fatigue crept upon Kai, but somehow he kept himself upright and conscious.

The distant thunder of many hooves sent Kai into full alert. He reined Braygo to a halt and listened breathlessly to make sure, then urged the duocorn to a run until they reached a thicket, where Kai quickly dismounted and helped Jeniah to the ground. They hid in the densest part of the trees, hoping their tracks were not noticeable on the icy ground.

A regiment of Hanoran soldiers came dangerously close, but the riders galloped past without pausing.

Only when he let his breath out did Kai realize he had been holding it. He exchanged glances with the princess before they remounted. They rode hard while the sun crept slowly across the sky.

As the shadows deepened, Kai began looking for a place to camp. Before long, he found a cave.

"Great," he muttered, "another cave."

Leaving Jeniah on the duocorn, he briefly explored the cave and found that it was fairly shallow, yet deep enough to provide shelter, with a ceiling that rose many feet above his head. A common carnivore, fat from a summer and fall of gorging, hibernated inside. Kai remounted and doubled back several times before returning, hoping no skilled Hanoran tracker had found their trail. He listened with straining ears for sounds of pursuit. All remained quiet.

Kai slew the sleeping beast, then checked for further signs of danger. When he found none, he dragged the carcass outside. Sharp waves of pain knifed through his body but iron control kept him upright and moving. Though the cave was dry and relatively warm, Kai could see his breath.

After helping the princess dismount, he retrieved a blanket from his saddle and spread it out on a soft bed of dried leaves that had belonged to the former resident of the cave. The princess stood, staring blankly, and offered no resistance when he led her to the makeshift bed. She sank down on it wearily.

Kai brought his duocorn into the cave. "You were a brave warrior last night, Braygo."

The animal nickered and nuzzled Kai's neck as he untacked him and unloaded the saddlebags. Kai withdrew a firestick, snapped it open, and set it on the ground near the princess. Its radiant heat filled the small cave with warmth.

Though he had trouble keeping his eyes focused, he could not allow himself to rest until he made sure they would not be discovered. He went outside and buried the carnivore he had killed, lest it should attract other beasts. Favoring his injured left side, Kai cut a few branches from an evergreen tree and arranged them in front of the cave so it appeared as if a thick bush grew there. Then he stood back to survey his work. The entrance to the cave was difficult to see, even looking straight at it. He circled the area, pausing frequently and listening, but the forest was quiet. After erasing their tracks and laying out a powder that helped throw off the wyrwolves from their scent, he went inside.

Braygo lay down on the cave's floor next to the princess, his slender legs tucked underneath him. In the semi-darkness, Kai knelt down beside him and gave him a thorough rubdown, thanking the moons for Braygo's invaluable presence during the battle and subsequent flight. Then, suddenly lightheaded, Kai leaned an arm against the cave wall.

"Princess, I need your help removing my armor."

She moved like a sleepwalker but followed his instructions until they managed to remove the armor. After they were finished, she curled up in the blankets. Kai leaned against Braygo to try to absorb some of the warmth from the duocorn's body. With the princess's eyes upon him, he managed what he hoped looked like a reassuring smile.

"We'll be safe here tonight, Princess. Get some rest. Braygo will alert us if anyone comes near."

She nodded somberly and within minutes, sank into slumber. Kai listened for sounds of the enemy, but all was silent. He finally allowed sleep to overtake him. In his dreams, Hanoran soldiers swept the country, looking for the princess. The dream became a nightmare.

Chapter Eight

*J*eniah woke slowly, aware at first only of a cold room and an uncomfortable bed. She opened her eyes. The dim light cast dark shadows in every corner. Instead of draperies around her bed and a large fireplace, she saw dirt walls with roots snaking along the sides. Stones littered the floor.

This was not her room. She was inside a cave.

On the ground lay a smooth, round stick, broken in half. Both halves glowed as if made of hot coal. Jeniah studied the stick curiously. It was not a common stick from nature; it had been crafted. She hadn't known such a thing existed, but then she had never slept outside of her bedroom with its well-tended fireplace.

A huge silver duocorn lifted his head and looked at her with soft eyes. He lay protectively close to a motionless form on the ground wrapped in a cloak. In the gloom, she recognized the shapeless form as Captain Kai Darkwood of Darbor.

Memory returned, and with it, a living nightmare that renewed Jeniah's terror. Events unfolded of the night her life as a princess ended. Her family was dead. Her home lay in ruins. She hid in a cave. Hunted. Exiled.

Braygo watched her as he lay next to his master. Without the faithful mount, they surely would have been captured and she would be dead now. Like her family.

Jeniah thought of her home, her father and mother, her brother, her cousins, Mora who had served her for so many years, the shy stable boy, her faithful guards, Breneg and Ciath—all were gone. She was alone. Yet she'd cried so much, she had no more tears left to shed.

A soft moan drew the princess's attention and she took command of herself. The dying ember-like stick on the cave floor softly illuminated the captain's face. Sleep lent the fearsome Sauraii master a boyish appearance. One of the ladies in waiting in Arden had described the Darborian as "dangerously handsome," but at the moment, he looked as harmless as a child.

As she watched him, her fears abated. He had risked all and beat terrible odds to keep her safe. Only a knight of his caliber could have protected her as he had. And now Jeniah must put her life, and the fate of her people, into the hands of a trained killer.

But he wasn't a killer, not really. He was trained to defend. Still, could she truly trust a man who'd killed hundreds?

Her stomach gnawed at her with a hunger she had never before known. Her feet were freezing and she longed for a hot bath and a change of clothes. Miserably, she shifted upon her rough bed of grasses.

The captain stirred and opened his eyes, but when he tried to speak, he lapsed into coughing, wincing with each cough. Jeniah crawled closer to him. He was deathly pale, and when she touched his face, her fears were confirmed. He burned with fever. Alarmed, she began digging through his saddlebags until she found a water skin. She slid one hand underneath the captain's head and supported it as she placed the water skin to his lips. He drank in gulps and then coughed again.

A line of dried blood caked one side of his face. She pushed back the hair on his forehead to find a deep cut barely outside the hairline.

"I don't know much about healing, Captain, but I can clean your wounds."

His mouth moved but no sound came out.

She needed something to use as a cloth. Her gown would do; it already hung in shreds, so a few more missing pieces would make no difference. As she reached down, she realized she wore two cloaks—hers and a much larger one that obviously belonged to a man. Touched, she glanced at the Sauraii.

She tore a few strips from her gown, then poured water on a folded piece of cloth and gently bathed the cut on his face. When she unfastened his cloak, she found a bloodstain high on his shoulder. Carefully, she peeled away his heavy padded shirt to examine the wound. He appeared to have been shot with an arrow or dart, but judging from the wound on his back above his shoulder blade, it had passed all the way through.

Jeniah cleaned the wound, trying to avoid hurting him. The wound bled at her touch but the captain did not complain; only his labored breathing betrayed his pain. Further down on his left side, she found a large tear in his padded tunic with a dark red stain. Jeniah widened the tear to find a much larger wound, still bleeding and surrounded by an enormous purple bruise. When she bathed it with the wet cloth, the knight flinched and let out a soft gasp.

"You need a doctor, Captain."

He spoke with visible effort. "Can't risk it."

"I don't know what to do for you." Feeling helpless, she bit her lip. "Do you have any salve in your bags? Anything I can give you for the pain or the fever?"

"No. Just need rest," he mumbled as he drifted off to sleep.

She repositioned his cloak until it fully covered him. Her eyes strayed to something tied to a leather thong around his neck. Careful to not disturb him, she picked it up. It was a narrow braid of golden brown hair. She glanced up at the sleeping warrior's face as if answers lay there. Jeniah did not know the customs of Darbor, but in Arden, such a token only came from a lady whose regard was highly valued. Someone from his past? Or someone to whom he was returning in Darbor? A curious sadness settled over her at the thought of him loving another. But that was foolish. Of course he had a life and a family in Darbor. His stay in Arden had only been a temporary arrangement, and now he would return home to his loved ones. Jeniah pushed back the agonizing remembrance that she had no one waiting for her at home.

Her stomach complained again. With the captain injured, the task of locating something to eat fell to her. Inside the saddlebags she found a large tunic, which reminded her of the state of her clothing. She removed both cloaks and put on the tunic over what was left of her gown. After replacing the cloaks, she went back to the saddlebags. She found some dried meat, tough and leathery, but she ate a few strips, wrinkling her nose in distaste. There had to be something better. Perhaps something wild grew nearby. Parting the tree limbs that served as their door, she peeked out.

It had snowed the night before while they slept, covering everything in a thick, pristine whiteness. The early morning sun reflected blindingly off the snow. Shading her eyes, Jeniah scanned the area. Only a few hand spans away from the mouth of the cave grew a bush laden with seedpods.

"Ah!"

She listened cautiously for several minutes until she was certain that the forest was silent. She looked down at her feet and frowned. Too bad she had donned her slippers instead of having the foresight to put on her riding boots. Slippers would not protect her feet from the snow, but at the moment, her hunger overpowered her need for warmth.

She ran quickly into the freezing air outside the cave, grabbed as many seedpods as she could carry, and ran back. Her feet felt frozen, but she smiled triumphantly and kicked off her wet slippers.

Inside each pod were several large seeds. During winter festival, it was traditional to roast them over a fire as a special treat, although half the fun was the anticipation as they sizzled and popped. Jeniah wasn't sure how filling they would be or how they would taste raw, but perhaps they would satisfy until she could get something more substantial.

She crushed the outer pods with a stone and picked out the seeds. After she ate them, she washed them down with water.

Her eyes were drawn to the slumbering captain. The light was better now, revealing how pale his face had grown. The cut on his forehead looked worse than before.

She touched his shoulder, gently waking him. "Here, Captain, have some more water."

She placed the water skin to his mouth, again holding up his head so he could drink. Clearly, it was a battle for him to stay awake, and his blue eyes were ringed in shadow.

"Thank you," he mumbled.

His strong, calloused hand dwarfed hers as he gripped her hand with surprising strength. A surge of tenderness for him washed through her and she touched his face with her free hand in a way that she hoped would be soothing to him. The captain closed his eyes and turned his head toward her touch. His breathing deepened as he went back to sleep. As she continued caressing his face, the barest hint of a smile touched his mouth as he slept. She never would have touched him, or even studied him so closely if he were awake, but now she took advantage of his state of unawareness. Jeniah let her hand travel down his face, exploring the planes and angles. A few stubbles of a beard had begun to grow on his chin and jaw, giving his chiseled, masculine beauty a rugged appearance. He looked much the way he had appeared at their first meeting. The cut on the side of his forehead heartlessly marred his face in a vain attempt to flaw his handsome features.

She stroked his hair as Mora had done to her when she had been sick or hurt, while the other hand remained locked in his.

His fever climbed until the heat from his skin almost burned her hand. Finally, she withdrew her hand from his and gave him the last of the water. Her slippers were still wet, but she put them on and went back outside. Finding a clean pile, she pushed as much snow as she could through the narrow mouth of the water skin. Her hands and feet throbbed from the cold before she had filled the water skin and returned to the cave. She stepped out of her slippers, stripped off her stockings, and rubbed her feet vigorously until they warmed.

Outside, the sun sank and the forest hushed. The mournful wail of a wyrwolf sounded in the distance, and Jeniah realized how helpless she and the captain were. Would the wyrwolves find them? The captain's enormous sword lay in its scabbard next to him, but she doubted that she could even lift the weapon, much less actually use it to defend the two of them.

When there were no further sounds, her fear dimmed and fatigue crept upon her. The strange stick ceased to glow, and the cave darkened, growing steadily colder until her breath came in white puffs. She hated to disturb the captain, but they needed warmth.

"Captain?" She touched his shoulder. "I don't know how to make a fire."

He could barely open his eyes. "Firesticks. In the pack. Snap it open."

In the captain's belongings, she found another stick like the one lying cool and gray on the floor and snapped it open. Immediately, the center sparked and began to glow like a hot coal. She set it down on the floor to avoid getting burned. A surprising amount of heat emanated from the firestick, which now glowed red. Her head whipped up at the sound of the captain's voice.

"Ariana," he called weakly. "Where are you?"

Puzzling over the name, Jeniah bathed his face with a wet cloth. Dangerously hot, he mumbled, thrashed, and tried to tear off his cloak.

"It's all right," she soothed, running her hands lightly over his hot face.

He quieted at her contact, but a moment later he tossed restlessly again. He moaned, pushing at the blanket. "Forgive me, Your Majesty."

"Shh. All is well, Captain."

He pushed at the cloak. Deciding to try and cool him, Jeniah unfastened his tunic and shirt with fumbling fingers. He calmed at her touch. The muscles of his lean body were hard and deeply defined, and a soft patch of light brown hair grew on the center of his chest. She had never seen a man in this state of undress before, and she blushed at her own boldness. She bathed his burning skin but the cloth warmed quickly and she had to constantly rewet it to keep it cool.

In the course of her ministrations, she found a small dagger at each wrist inside his sleeves, a brace of throwing knives in his belt, one long dagger fastened lower against his hip, and a knife in each boot. Jeniah smiled. Even without his sword, the Sauraii was a walking armory.

After bathing his skin repeatedly, she removed the blanket from her pallet and placed it over him. She dozed, leaning against the cave wall, rousing each time the captain cried out in delirium. Much of what he uttered was unintelligible.

"I failed you," he mumbled and then cursed himself.

When she pressed the water against his lips, he drank, but he showed no sign of recognition. Desperately helpless, she bathed his face and chest and tucked the blanket carefully around him.

"We lost so many . . . so many men . . . no time to mourn . . . must prepare . . ."

"You're safe, Captain." She combed her fingers through his hair and caressed his cheek.

The cry of a wyrwolf sounded terrifyingly close, and Jeniah jerked awake, pulse pounding in her ears. Braygo snorted, his eyes wild, his ears thrust forward. In the dim glow of the firestick, she made out the faint outline of something large outside the mouth of the cave beyond the tree branches. She needed a weapon.

The captain's sword lay in its scabbard near the saddle and bags, but Jeniah feared she'd cut off her own foot before she figured out how to use it to defend herself and her sleeping patient. Her success in killing two Hanorans gave her no hope that she would succeed against a pack of wyrwolves. And if naturalists were correct, the animals used their noses as much as their eyes, so blurring would afford her no protection. It certainly wouldn't help the captain.

Without much hope of her success, her trembling fingers closed over the sword and she withdrew it. The blade was lighter than she'd guessed, but it still felt enormous. She gripped it with both hands and stood over the captain, her gaze glued to the cave entrance, praying she would not have to attempt to use the weapon.

Several more calls sounded, each progressively closer. Shadowy forms at the mouth of the cave grew larger. Scratching sounds came from the entrance. The wyrwolves were clawing their way in through the branches protecting the cave.

Braygo got up and began prancing nervously. Blood pounded in Jeniah's ears, and her muscles screamed from the tension.

The branches fell away, revealing a gaping hole. Out of the darkness, two shaggy bodies leaped inside the cave. Snarling, they crouched to spring. Fear nearly strangled Jeniah, but she held the sword in front of her. The ugly, human-like faces grinned at her, tongues lolling out one side of the mouths.

As one wrywolf leaped at her, and Jeniah brought up the sword, but it only sliced through air as the beast leaped back. The two carnivores tried to circle, but Jeniah backed up, keeping the blade between her and them. Braygo lowered his head and brought his long horns down like a weapon. He pawed at the ground.

A terrifying roar broke the night's stillness, and the wyrwolves turned away from Jeniah toward the new sound outside the cave. Outside the cave, the pale moonlight illuminated several shaggy wyrwolves, forming a loose circle around a large animal. A low warning growl came from the animal. It sounded like the same growl her chayim had made when he was threatened by the captain. That day seemed ages ago.

Outside, the wyrwolves snarled and paced, and the two in the cave suddenly sprang out to join them. With a roar, the large, shadowy shape launched toward them. The wyrwolves charged. They met in a clash of teeth and claws, the sounds of rending flesh and howls of pain filling the air as the combatants tore into each other. With trembling hands, Jeniah gripped the sword and watched wide-eyed as the battle raged outside. After several heart-thumping moments, the wyrwolves slunk away and left their dead bleeding in the snow. All was silent.

The creature that had attacked them returned to the cave entrance and waited noiselessly outside. Something about that form felt familiar. Jeniah picked up the firestick with a wet cloth and held it out toward the shape. The golden, furry muzzle of a chayim stared back at her, its eyes glimmering in the light. Standing on all fours, he appeared enormous, but smaller than her first chayim. He dipped his head down toward her and blew into her face.

"Oh," Jeniah said in a soft voice. "It's you."

Pushing aside the branches, Jeniah stepped outside the cave, her hand held out. The chayim leaned toward her hand and she reached out to touch him. A low purr came from the chayim as she petted him. His mane was shorter than her first chayim's, but just as soft.

Twice in her lifetime, she had been chosen by a chayim. No other maiden in all the lands had received such an honor.

"Thank you, my friend," she whispered.

He gave her a gentle nudge in return as she stroked his shaggy mane. Her skin tingled and she felt light as his mind enveloped hers in gentle warmth. No, not his mind—*her* mind. The chayim was female, the mate of the other who had chosen her.

She bore no malice for her mate's death, for his spirit now resided within her in a more intimate manner than he ever had in life. Visions of the land changes, the years, the understanding of the symbiotic relationship between all the creatures alive came over Jeniah. She saw herself as a being of great worth, a necessary part in the order of the universe, with a role that could affect others, either for good or ill. Her chayim showed her the burden of her own destiny. All of Arden depended upon her to save them from slavery and death.

Her chayim showed Jeniah that her ability to blur was only the smallest part of an ancient and powerful magic, a magic that would change the course of humanity, not only in Arden, but in many nations. Crushed under the weight of the responsibility, Jeniah's limbs gave way and she collapsed. The connection remained. The chayim told Jeniah her name. *Maaragan.*

Jeniah understood the sacredness of knowing a chayim's name, and the power and responsibility attached to that knowledge.

Maaragan's mind withdrew slowly, leaving Jeniah feeling both humbled and ennobled.

The air cooled tears on Jeniah's cheeks, and she threw her arms around Maaragan's neck. Her chayim growled softly, leaning into her embrace. Then Maaragan turned, padded silently away, and disappeared. After a lingering look, Jeniah returned to the captain inside the cave to bathe his face and hush his anguished calls.

Calmer now and lying next to his master again, Braygo nuzzled the captain. Jeniah smiled at the beast's loyalty and concern.

She sat lost in thought, grappling with her own self-worth, overwhelmed and frightened at the knowledge bestowed upon her by her bonded chayim. She faltered as it occurred to her that she alone had claim on the crown. She would be the rightful queen, and she must free her people. A daunting prospect. Her mother believed her capable of it and so did her chayim. But how could she, a girl of not yet nineteen, save all of Arden and influence many nations?

The captain let out a strangled cry. Visibly tormented by his delirium, he thrashed. Jeniah gave him water and unwrapped his bandages, only to discover that his wounds looked even worse. The terrible gashes gaped open, festering. His fever soared.

Jeniah knew she had to do something or he would die.

She had never tried to care for another person. The thought of this man's life in her hands was terrifying.

Once, Jeniah had watched the stable master clean a wound on Egan's leg by holding a hot cloth against it to draw out the sickness until it bled clean, and then sewed it closed.

She held her hand out over the top of the broken middle of the still-burning firestick to test the heat. It might be enough to heat water. She had seen a small pan in one of the packs earlier. After digging it out, she went outside to fill it with clean snow.

Maaragan was nowhere in sight, but a moment later, she

quietly appeared and bumped her muzzle against Jeniah's shoulder. Jeniah rubbed her face and mane before returning to the cave. Maaragan sat in front of the cave, guarding it.

To Jeniah's relief, the firestick heated the water to a slow simmer. Jeniah rolled the captain over onto his side and began the painstaking process of trying to release the infection from his injuries. He cried out in sleep.

"I'm sorry, Captain."

She traced her free hand over the bare skin of his chest while the other held the hot, wet cloth against his wound, and soon he quit fighting her. As she held the cloth against his wounds, the sickness soaked into it until finally the wounds bled clean. Once the worst of the injuries on the captain's side were cleaned, she turned her attention to the wound piercing his shoulder. Then she looked to the gash on his forehead. It was healing better than the others, but she cleaned it carefully, hoping it wouldn't scar too badly.

With nothing in the packs that she could use to sew the dangerous cuts in his side, she could only re-bandage them. If only all her studies had included the healing arts.

Then her mind caught hold of an idea. She must find something to clamp the skin together until the wounds could heal. Her eyes fell on the shrub that the chayim had come through. It was a reshle shrub, heavily laden with the same seedpods she had been eating.

After picking several reshle pods, Jeniah pried apart the edge of the pod enough to fit a fold of fabric between the two sides, but it snapped open and broke. She let out her breath in disappointment. Trying again, she carefully pried open the edges, not so far that it would break, but enough to place it over the hem of her tunic. This time it remained intact, and when she let it go, it snapped closed, effectively gripping the material like tiny jaws.

She glanced back at the captain. It would be painful but it might work. She gently lifted the two sides of the gaping wound on his side and pulled them together. Wishing she had two more hands, she slid her fingernail between the seedpod halves and opened it enough to slip it over his skin, which she pinched between her fingers. When she released it, the seedpod snapped shut, holding the two ragged edges of skin closed.

She flinched, anticipating his reaction. He moaned and turned his head, but did not awaken. Braygo stared accusingly at her as if he suspected her of trying to hurt his master. She patted the duocorn's neck and murmured assurances before returning her attention back to the injured man.

It was difficult work, and Jeniah broke more pods than she used, but in the end, about a dozen seedpods held the wound closed like giant stitches. She smiled ruefully. Hopefully, when he awoke to see her unconventional form of medicine, he wouldn't think she'd tried to kill him.

But what if he never woke up?

Chapter Nine

*K*ai woke to pale fingers of light reaching into the cave. The branches he'd cut and used to block the entrance were trampled and cast to the side. Princess Jeniah, wearing his spare tunic with the ragged pieces of her gown showing below the hem, sat with her back against the rock wall, her hand resting on his chest with a cloth in her limp fingers, her head tilted to one side in sleep. The warmth of her hand felt soothing.

Kai ached all over and his mouth felt like a desert. When he reached toward the water skin, pain lanced his body. He fell back, and the movement sent another jolt of pain through him. An involuntary moan escaped his mouth.

The princess's eyes opened blearily and she blinked a few times before focusing on his face. She touched his cheek. "How do you feel?"

"Thirsty," he managed to croak.

The princess retrieved the water skin and cradled his head while he drank. Her tired eyes revealed her concern. As she carefully laid his head down, she held her cool, soothing fingers against his cheek.

"How long have I been asleep?"

"I lost track. Three or four days, I think."

"That long? We can't remain here. We have to get you to

Darbor where it's safe." He tried to rise, but fire shot through his side, cutting off his breath.

Wearing a curious smile, the princess put her hand on his chest and gave him a gentle push until he rested his head. "Don't worry, Captain, we are safe here. And I really don't think you are well enough to go anywhere yet."

Kai let out a sigh of exasperation. "They're looking for you. We have to keep moving."

"Your fever has come down some. I should clean your wounds again." She pulled back a blanket tucked around him.

Kai stared at his side. "What is that?"

"Uh . . . seedpods." She sounded embarrassed. "I didn't know what else to do. I didn't have anything to use to sew your wounds closed, so I had to improvise."

Kai felt one corner of his mouth lift. "Inventive. It might work."

He stiffened as she began cleaning his injuries, but she carefully avoided touching the seedpods holding his skin together.

"I'm sorry, Captain. I'm trying not to hurt you."

"I know. It's all right." He braced himself and clenched his teeth so he wouldn't flinch each time she touched him. Instead, he focused on watching her. Even in her rumpled state, her beauty was bewitching.

"I'm glad you're finally awake. It will be easier to feed you now. You weren't terribly cooperative before."

When she had finished tending his wounds, she spooned some very bland, warm liquid into his mouth and laughed softly at his expression. "I'm sorry about the fare, Captain. Not only is this my first attempt at cooking, but the only thing I had to use to make a broth was the dried meat I found in your pack in the saddlebag."

Drowsiness returned and he could only eat a few sips of the broth. As sleep crept in, he was aware of her gentle hands on his face.

During the night, a noise brought Kai bolting out of his blanket, hands on weapons, fully alert. The motion sent a blinding shot of agony through him and a cold sweat beaded on his skin. He fought to avoid screaming in pain.

The princess cried out in her sleep and began calling for someone named Mora. Wasn't that her lady-in-waiting? Then her voice took on a desperate edge. "No. No!"

Kai let out a steadying breath as he realized there were no tangible threats. The princess's voice had awakened him. He leaned over and touched her arm. "Princess."

She jerked away from his hand as if it were a hot coal, then shot up to a sitting position, her eyes wild and unfocused.

"Don't be afraid, Your Highness. You're safe."

Her breath came in ragged gasps as she stared at him unseeing. Slowly, the terror in her eyes faded. After blinking several times, the princess put her hands over her face.

Instinctively, Kai reached for her, but then he withdrew his hand. It would not be appropriate for him to touch the princess. He had taken that liberty in the cave filled with water, but she had been too distraught to notice or care.

He remembered the enemy soldiers in the queen's room, and the shattered look in Jeniah's eyes. He knew that if she relived that moment in her nightmares, she would not be receptive to comfort from him—or any man. While helplessness and anger swelled within him, he lay back down to stare out at the darkness beyond the cave, trying to clear his mind. He listened to the noises of the night and wished the muse of the poets, who spoke with beauty and eloquence, would inspire him tonight. They would know the right words to say to her. Nothing came to Kai's mind. All he could think of was how badly he wanted to kill the Hanorans who had hurt her.

Gradually, the princess's weeping subsided. She lay back down, pulling the blanket around her. Kai turned his head to look at her, but her eyes were averted.

"Are you all right?" he whispered. He knew it was a foolish question, but saying nothing seemed insensitive.

Without looking at him, she nodded and then turned over with her back toward him. A moment later, she said, "I'm glad you're here, Captain."

That sweet statement startled him. Somehow, it meant more to him than he would have ever admitted out loud, or even thought possible.

⚜

Another few days' rest quieted Captain Darkwood's fever, and his color returned to normal. Jeniah fed him dried meat from his packs, along with reshle seedpods, which he ate with more enthusiasm than she did. When he fell asleep again, she stayed nearby, worrying that he might relapse, but he slept peacefully.

Hunger drove the Darborian to get up from his sickbed earlier than he should have. Against Jeniah's words of caution and still clearly favoring his injured left side, he left the cave, declaring that he would retrieve the beast he had buried in the snow, if some wild animal hadn't found it.

When he returned to the cave only seconds later, he exclaimed, "There are tracks everywhere and blood on the snow."

"I know."

"What happened?"

"Wyrwolves came, but a friend protected us."

"A friend?"

She smiled, still in awe over it. "I was chosen by another chayim, which, I think, has never happened before in Arden's history. When the wyrwolves came, she defended us."

Clearly stunned, the captain slid down the wall to a seated position. "I left you defenseless and another had to take my place."

"You were hurt; you had no choice. And we weren't defenseless."

His eyes met hers. In that moment, his walls lowered and she saw self-recrimination.

"You haven't let me down, Captain Darkwood."

He grimaced and dragged a hand through his hair, wincing as his fingers brushed the cut above his temple.

Jeniah touched his arm. "She bears you no ill will for killing her mate."

"Her mate?" he repeated with apprehension.

"He acted impulsively, and had he waited, he would have understood you. But with so many armed men infiltrating the land, he saw your sword and believed you one of them. She understands all this. And she understands who you are."

He fixed an unreadable expression upon her as he considered her words. A moment passed before he nodded and climbed slowly to his feet and disappeared outside. He returned with a large slab of meat, already cleaned and skinned, and several dried branches, which he used to build a spit.

"With the Hanorans so near, we don't dare use a fire, but we need to eat something more substantial. Cooking the meat over the firestick will take longer, but it can be done."

The smell of the cooking meat made Jeniah's mouth water. She sat next to the firesticks and willed the meat to cook faster.

The Darborian searched for something in his clothing. "I'm missing a dagger," he said.

"Oh, I forgot. Here." She handed it over and couldn't resist teasing, "I'm surprised you missed it, with all the weapons you carry."

"I never know when I might need one." He eyed her. "What else happened while I was asleep—besides the chayim and the wyrwolves?"

She checked things off with her finger. "I discovered raw reshle seeds lose their appeal after two meals, I figured out how to boil water, and I decided that your dried meat is not palatable even stewed."

He chuckled. "I see you got to have all the fun without me." His eyes moved to her feet. "Are those slippers the latest fashion in Arden?"

Jeniah looked down at her feet. She had wrapped strips of cloth around her palace slippers in a feeble attempt to keep warm and protected during her ventures outside the cave. The thin, embroidered slippers had been adequate for the smooth floors of the palace, but offered little protection from the snow or the rough terrain of the wild.

She wriggled her toes. "All fashionable ladies of the court favor these."

"Some women have no sense of practicality when it comes to clothing and shoes," the Darborian quipped as he pushed himself to a stand.

"What are you doing? You need to rest."

Kai grinned and waved her off. "Don't be concerned."

Soon he returned, carrying the saddlebags. With great care, he settled himself back down and packed all of the contents of both his leather saddlebags into one. He cut up the empty bag and oiled the pieces to help repel water.

"It's a good thing you have tiny feet."

He reached for her feet. Curious, Jeniah did not resist when he placed them on his leg. With her ankles resting on his thigh, he wrapped the leather pieces around her feet and ankles over her thin castle slippers and stockings, and wound a thin leather strap around the whole, making a crude boot.

"These are lovely," she declared.

"Ah, yes. My workmanship is fit for royalty. They are a nice compliment to your gown." He grinned. "My tunic has never looked so good. You fill it out better than I do."

As she looked down at herself, a shadow settled over her spirits. The captain looked questioningly at her, but she could not meet his searching eyes.

"What is it?" he asked.

She made a slight face and shrugged. She did not want to speak of the Hanoran soldiers in her mother's solarium, or the personal violence that had left her gown in rags.

"Tell me," he urged gently.

When she looked up at him, he nodded, encouraging her to speak. He might understand. After all, he'd killed many. But she wasn't sure if taking lives troubled him. Perhaps he'd think her silly, or overly tenderhearted.

She couldn't bring herself to speak of it yet. Instead, she voiced another thought that had occurred to her that morning. "Today would have been the celebration of my ascent into maidenhood, called the age of ascension."

"The knights spoke of it often. Many of them trained specifically for that tournament. There was a great deal of boasting about who would become your champion."

"Was there?" Jeniah asked in surprise. "None of them ever paid the slightest attention to me. I suppose winning the tournament and being named the princess's champion would bring a certain distinction."

"No, it was more than that. They all wanted to be *your* champion."

She wrinkled her nose. "I think you exaggerate."

When she fell silent, he prompted, "Tell me about the ceremony."

Images of the tournament, the fair, the entertainers who performed, the ceremony itself, the great feast, and dancing filled her thoughts. But now, in light of everything else she had lost, it all seemed insignificant. All her life, she knew that as a princess, her value was much less important than her brother's, but at least she belonged to a family then. Where did she belong now?

"Princess?"

His look of compassion almost proved her undoing. "It no longer matters, except to remind me how much I've lost." Her voice caught, but she managed an apologetic smile. "Forgive me, Captain, I do not mean to complain."

"No doubt anyone would feel as you do."

"We're fortunate that the Hanorans did not wait until closer to my ceremony to strike or there would have been hundreds more people in the city. Normally, people come from miles around for the fair and tournament."

The captain nodded slowly. "That would have been worse." He finished turning the meat and inspected it. Holding the skewer toward her, he announced, "My lady, dinner is served."

The meat was unseasoned and quite tough, but they feasted on it ravenously. After days of nothing but dried meat and raw seeds, Jeniah couldn't remember when anything had tasted so delicious. She and the captain grinned at each other over their dinner, and she licked her fingers in a manner that would have shocked the court.

"Your Highness, there is a city not far from here on the border of Arden and Lariath. We can purchase some provisions and more suitable clothing."

She brightened. "How soon?"

"We should be there in a few days. Hanoran spies are probably there, so we must assume that everyone is our enemy, but it is a large city of commerce with merchants who come from all over, so I believe we will blend in—" he paused "—if you behave as a commoner."

Jeniah nodded, seeing the wisdom in his words. If anyone recognized them, they would be captured. How odd it felt to be a refugee in her own country. But it was not hers any longer. She was a fugitive.

She drew a breath. "I will do my best, Captain."

"That means I must not use your title once we reach the city."

"I understand."

He paused as if trying to put his thoughts into words. "I fear that we may attract notice regardless of our precautions. I don't dare leave you behind alone while I go in for supplies, but I'm reluctant to risk taking you there."

Jeniah knew then that she needed to trust him with her secret. In a land where magic of any form was viewed as evil, her old fears rose. But her chayims—both of them—had assured her that her magic was not a power to mistrust. And her mother had told her the same. She could, of course, simply blur as he watched her, which would allow him to still see her in her true appearance and only fool the eyes of others, but some intuition whispered that he needed to know she possessed this ability.

"Captain Darkwood, there is something that I feel you should know about me."

He looked at her with raised brows.

"I've never told anyone this before, but I think my lady-in-waiting suspected somehow." She moistened her lips. "I have a way of disguising myself to appear as something other than I am. I call it blurring, for lack of a better word. It is a way of blending in, or becoming unnoticeable. I must concentrate, and it takes a great deal of energy so I can't maintain the illusion for long, but I can appear no more remarkable than anyone or anything else."

"You're a shape-shifter?"

"No, I can't actually change form. I only create the illusion of becoming something else. Look outside, and then look back at me."

The instant his eyes left her face, she blurred. When he looked back, alarm widened his eyes. "Princess?"

"I'm still here," she reassured him.

He reached out to her blindly. When his hand came in contact with her arm, first puzzlement and then wonder came over his features. "You still feel like a person, but my eyes tell me there's nothing there but an outcropping of rock."

She stopped blurring.

He jerked his hand back. "That's incredible." There was no condemnation in either his tone or his expression, only fascination. "Truly, this is a great magic. To my knowledge, other than the high priestess and a few mages, only a few lucky Darborians actually possess magic."

Surprise and relief flooded her. She did not know why his approval mattered, but somehow it did. Perhaps if a warrior who placed his faith in his weapons saw no reason to mistrust magic, she shouldn't either.

"How long can you maintain it?"

"Only a few hours at a time."

"Have you been able to do this all your life?"

"I'm not sure. I discovered it quite by accident in my early adolescence and have used it many times over the years."

"Do it again," he urged, his eyes filled with admiration.

"If you are looking directly at me when I first begin to blur, you can still see me."

"Really?" he appeared intrigued.

"See?" She blurred again while he looked at her.

He blinked. "There's a slight . . . I'm not sure what to call it, but the outside edges of your hair and clothes look a bit fuzzy." He grinned. "Blurry. But you're right, I can see you."

"That's how I escaped my guards that day in the forest when I found my chayim—the day we met." She smiled sadly. "Poor Breneg and Ciath. I know it frustrated them that they often could not find me. How badly I treated them."

The captain took her hand, his thumb lightly rubbing across the back of her hand. The casual contact made her skin tingle. Then, as if catching himself, he released her hand and leaned back heavily, his eyes closing.

Concerned that he had overtaxed his strength, Jeniah touched his face, looking for signs of fever. He was still cool but his face was drawn and tired and the cut above his temple stood out against his pale skin.

"I'm all right, Princess. I just need rest."

⋯⋯

The following morning, Kai insisted that they leave the safety of the cave and start their journey to Darbor. He didn't dare remain in the heart of enemy territory and risk the princess's safety. Before they left, he tore off his rank and insignia and disguised everything that might reveal their identity.

Disguising Braygo would prove more difficult. Anyone could see he had been bred as a kingly mount. Kai muddied him a bit, under the animal's reproachful stare, and hoped it would be enough. Perhaps he would appear as a mercenary enjoying a steed he'd taken during looting.

Once he swept the area for danger, he helped the princess

mount Braygo and swung up behind her. A well-rested Braygo danced against the reins eagerly. Soon they were off, moving as quickly as Kai dared.

The sun was at its apex when he heard the sounds of mounted soldiers. With a silent curse, he left the road for the thick brush and dismounted. The princess slid off Braygo's back and looked up at Kai with frightened eyes. He drew her down into a crouch beside him. Breathless, they waited. Hanoran soldiers burst into view, riding hard and fast. They wore white cloaks and rode white, hairless mounts. Kai knew from past battles that they were not the regular army, but part of a special force, highly trained and deadly.

The princess's breath came out in unsteady gasps and her face was pale with terror. Kai put a hand over the princess's in an attempt to lend her courage. The soldiers moved past them without stopping, but Kai waited several more minutes to ensure they were out of danger before cautiously remounting.

That evening Kai cut down several branches to fashion a lean-to so they could sleep sheltered from the winter. By the warmth and light of the firestick, the princess dressed his wounds again. He steeled himself, but her touch was so light that the pain was tolerable.

"When did you realize you wanted to become a Sauraii?" the princess asked in an obvious attempt to divert his attention.

"I've always known. My father was a Sauraii who served the king of Darbor all of his life. He taught me to move and think like a warrior."

"Tell me about your father."

"He was the son of a blacksmith. A traveling Sauraii met him and saw greatness in him. My father became a legend even before his death."

"What happened to him?"

"He died of a fever when I was only a youth, but he was a truly great man—strong, honorable, committed."

"And you wanted to be exactly like him?"

"It never occurred to me to even consider learning a trade. I always knew I'd be a Sauraii."

"Tell me about it."

He paused, again wrestling with the odd desire to actually reveal himself to another. Yet the princess looked at him with such genuine kindness that he found himself opening his mouth.

"When my mother remarried, we moved to my stepfather's farm and I lived there with them until I left to study under a Sauraii master. After three years, the master said there was nothing more he could teach me." Kai grinned self-consciously. "He said I had exceeded him, but I know he was still much greater. I was probably too much of a troublemaker and he'd grown weary of my antics. He sent me to Domari."

"Domari?"

"The school where Sauraii apprentices are trained."

"What was that like?" One hand rested against the bare skin of his back. Soft and warm, it sent shivers of pleasure through his body.

Hungry for more but resisting the lure to lean against her touch, Kai swallowed and remained still. "Grueling. We trained for sixteen hours a day in weaponry, hand-to-hand combat, and survival skills."

"And I thought my studies had been rigorous," the princess commented with admiration in her voice. "How long where you there?"

"Two years."

"That's a long time for such intensive training."

"It's actually faster than normal. Most finish in three or four, if ever."

"How old were you when you were received the title of Sauraii?"

"Fourteen. I went straight from there to offer myself to the king. I've been in his service ever since."

"Fourteen? No one in Arden is knighted that young. You are a remarkable man, Kai Darkwood. I'm fortunate to have you with me. I've never met anyone as driven or as duty-bound as you."

She moved to sit next to him and looked him in the eye. When their gaze locked and held, tenderness for this lovely young woman welled inside him. Her gray eyes mirrored trust and something soft that he wasn't sure he wanted to see. He clenched his fists and looked away, wishing his heart was whole, yet grateful it was not. He couldn't risk an attachment, not with her, not with anyone.

After he pulled on his shirt, he checked the perimeter of their camp and drove off a snake, then stood looking up at the stars.

"Good night, my love." He brought the braided hair around his neck to his lips. Unaccountably, his gaze returned to the princess. Then he snatched his eyes away and refocused on the stars, feeling as if he had been caught with another woman.

Chapter Ten

Pressed by a sense of urgency, they traveled late into the night, Braygo as tireless as Captain Darkwood. Sitting across the duocorn's strong shoulders, Jeniah let her head fall back against the captain's chest behind her, then woke with a start when Braygo halted. The captain peered intently into the forest. Jeniah tried to focus on what he saw but nothing looked unusual.

Eyes straining in the darkness, she finally saw a booted foot protruding from behind a tree. Soft snoring reached her ears.

Putting a finger to his lips, Kai slipped off Braygo and stole stealthily to the large tree. He flattened himself against the trunk and peered around it. Then he crept noiselessly back to Jeniah, his body thrumming with tension. She knew by his grim face that he'd found a contingent of sleeping Hanoran soldiers. Jeniah's chest seized until she couldn't breathe. Then Kai rested his hand on her arm, and she was comforted enough to draw a breath.

The Sauraii urged his duocorn forward and they rode for several minutes in silence before Jeniah looked back, but there was no sign that the soldiers had been alerted. They rode on until well after the middle of the night before they stopped to camp, and the captain was up again before sunrise. He looked flushed and pained but would not rest. They only stopped briefly to eat and see to personal needs before the Darborian urged her on.

By that afternoon, the captain's normally straight posture began to slump against her back as they rode. Jeniah glanced back at him. His ragged breathing and flushed face betrayed his pain. She reached back and touched his cheek. Hot. He was relapsing.

He managed a brave but weak smile. "I'm all right."

"We should camp, Captain."

"I can go on a while longer," he insisted.

If she had been any less concerned about him, she might have smiled. He certainly seemed to have a strong aversion for showing any weakness. That trait may be common in warriors, but Captain Darkwood epitomized it. Perhaps he was being brave for her sake, but she suspected that his overdeveloped sense of both inner and outer strength was a deeply ingrained part of his personality.

"I'm rather tired, and I'm getting cold and hungry," Jeniah said. "Couldn't we stop now?"

The captain wearily eyed the darkening sky. It was still early, but he nodded. Whether he agreed out of courtesy for her comfort, or because he was grateful for an excuse to stop, she could not discern. Regardless, the Sauraii guided Braygo up to the side of a knoll. Two large, leaning boulders underneath a towering evergreen tree created a sheltered area. Captain Darkwood reined, helped Jeniah down, and then swung his leg over to dismount, his lips tightening in pain.

She helped him remove Braygo's saddlebags and tack. The captain leaned over to rest his hands on his knees, bracing himself. The color drained from his face and he swayed.

Jeniah grabbed his arm and tugged on him. "You need to rest."

He stubbornly resisted. "Not yet."

"Rest." She pulled hard on his hand. "I insist."

His knees gave way and he slumped to the ground. Jeniah draped a blanket around his shoulders. He lay back and fell asleep almost instantly.

While he slept, Jeniah finished setting up camp. Realizing their shelter would not protect them from wyrwolves, she took the captain's sword and kept it close. As complete darkness blanketed the sky, she heard the rusting of leaves and a twig snap.

Jeniah froze, her heart giving a lurch. Her breath came in small clouds. The steps neared. She listened, all senses straining. They did not sound like the footsteps of the silent, deadly predators she had feared. The light touch on her mind quieted her fears. A shrub parted and there stood her chayim, Maaragan.

"Good evening, my friend," she murmured in relief, holding a hand out to the beast.

Maaragan's breath warmed Jeniah's neck as the chayim nuzzled her. Jeniah plunged her hands into the golden fur, feeling a deep sense of well-being at the animal's presence. The chayim approached the captain's sleeping form and touched him with her nose, then sat over him as if she stood watch.

"Thank you, my friend," she said. "I'm glad you're here. I will rest well now that I know you are still watching over us."

The beast made no comment, only turned her maned head and let out a gust of breath.

Braygo appeared, sniffed in the direction of the chayim, and then disappeared again to forage.

The captain shivered. Chills. That could not be good. She lifted the blanket and pulled back the torn edges of his shirt to survey his wounds. His shoulder looked better, but his whole side was badly bruised and swollen. Scarlet mottled his skin. The seedpods had fallen off, their tiny jaws leaving ragged marks on his skin. Yesterday, when Jeniah had cleaned the large wound on his side, it had appeared to be healing well. Today, it oozed foul-looking liquids.

What if she had done this to him? With a weight pressing on her chest, she cleaned the cut until it bled clean. The captain moaned even in sleep. If only she had training in medicine! As she touched his face and smoothed back his hair, a profound sense of helplessness swallowed her.

"Please get better," she whispered.

She felt a presence behind her and turned to find Maaragan leaning down toward the captain. Her chayim sniffed the sleeping form briefly and then licked the wound. The captain cried out but Maaragan continued to lick the wound. Torn between wanting to stop Maaragan from hurting him and trusting her chayim's instincts, Jeniah sat still and watched. The great beast stopped, nosed the Sauraii, and breathed into his face. The tension drained out of his body.

Jeniah's heart dropped. Had he died?

With a cry of alarm, she touched him. His breathing was deep and even and his fever had broken. Relieved, she let out a shaking breath and covered him with the blanket. It appeared that chayims did indeed have healing powers as the legends had suggested.

Jeniah looked back at the form silhouetted against the night sky. The golden beast dipped her head down and looked her in the eye.

"Thank you my friend. I owe you my life," Jeniah said quietly.

A low purr came in reply before Maaragan turned to continue her vigilant watch.

Jeniah lay down beside the captain, who slept without delirium. With the shadowy outline of her chayim nearby, Jeniah drowsed.

The howling of wyrwolves woke her. She shot up, heart racing. Maaragan uttered a low growl in warning and padded out into the darkness. There were no further sounds from the predators. Beside Jeniah, the captain still slept. Shivering in the sharp cold, she curled up against his back, careful not to touch his wounded side, and let the heat from his body warm her.

The sky was gray when Jeniah awoke. The captain lay curled up against her, his lashes close to his cheek, one arm wrapped around her waist, his lean, hard body pressed against her. He was a large and powerful man; she was small and helpless in comparison. She shifted and his arm tightened, pinning her.

A dark fear grew inside her. She stiffened as panic seized her with sudden intensity. With a gasp, she struggled against his unyielding, muscular arm holding her so tight.

"Let go," she cried out in desperation.

The captain awoke with a start, immediately releasing her. She bolted up, gripped by an unexplained terror.

Fully alert, he drew his weapons. He paused, listening. Then he eyed her in puzzlement. "Did you hear something?"

A shudder ripped through her body.

"What is it?"

She flinched and backed away.

He blinked. "Princess?"

"I . . . " She could not speak steadily. She drew another breath and tried again. "I thought you were trying to . . . use me."

He opened and closed his mouth. "Use you? You mean force myself upon you?"

She cringed.

He stared at her with undisguised hurt. "Haven't I earned your trust?"

Shame drove away her unreasonable panic. "Of course you have. I . . ." She glanced toward the blankets that had served as their bed and swallowed hard.

"Princess, if I were a monster who would force himself upon a lady, don't you think I would have done that before now?"

"You couldn't. You were hurt."

"I've been strong enough for *that* for days," he countered, his voice tinged in anger. "I thought you knew me."

"I do. But I . . ." She swallowed, unable to articulate her fears.

She remembered too vividly the soldier in the castle—the weight of his body, his hands on her, tearing her gown. She had been trapped, helpless, and for a few terrifying moments, she thought she would suffer the most frightening and personal violence.

Beyond hurt, he looked stricken. "Princess Jeniah." His voice caressed her name, drawing her gaze. "You have nothing to fear from me."

She hugged herself. "I don't fear you, Captain, but . . . when you . . ." she looked back at the rumpled blankets.

He paled. "Did I *touch* you?"

Jeniah swallowed. "Not, well, not like that, but you did . . . uh . . . have your arm around me."

He closed his eyes. "Forgive me. I never would have consciously taken such liberties."

She drew a shaking breath and looked at him, really looked at him. This man bore no resemblance to the Hanoran who had tried to hurt her. There was no hatred, no lust for violence. Kai Darkwood was a man of valor and honor.

He let his breath out slowly, as if struggling to find the right words. "The soldiers violated you, didn't they?"

There was such compassion and tenderness in his eyes that her words came tripping out of their own will. "One of them started to, but he didn't . . . finish." She choked, remembering the sickening sounds of the poker piercing his body, the horror on his face, the blood on her hands.

"You killed him first."

A sob broke through and the images of that night overwhelmed her. "I was so frightened. He tried to . . ." Tears streamed down her face and she sank to her knees.

The captain kneeled in front of her and waited silently while she wept. Twice, his hand reached for her, but both times, he drew it back without touching her. The shadows faded and the dawn brightened before she brought her tears under control. She gave him a weak smile.

"Not much of a queen, am I?" she said ruefully, drying her tears.

His eyes were dark. "You did the right thing killing that man. You were only defending yourself. And it took great strength." He waited until she had regained her composure. "What he tried to do to you was an act of violence. It has nothing to do with matters of love. No one should ever endure that kind of brutality." His jaw set and hardened, the muscles in his neck visibly tightening. "While I protect you, no harm will come to you. Not from anyone. Especially not from me."

The fervor in his declaration dispelled the last of her fears. "I know, Captain. You are an honorable man. I never really doubted you. I do trust you."

The captain watched her for a moment as if to assure himself that she believed her own words. One corner of his mouth lifted. He arose, helped her up, and stood straight and tall, with a healthy color and without any sign of pain.

"I'm glad you're feeling better," she said, touching his face to assure herself that his fever was truly gone.

"Thanks to you," he murmured.

"Thanks to the chayim. She was here again last night and licked your wounds, and you immediately began to improve. They truly do have magical healing powers, it seems."

"Then I owe her much."

They ate and packed. In reply to her questions, the captain assured her repeatedly that he was well enough to travel.

Finally, he chuckled softly. "I'm quite well. Stop worrying. Your chayim has worked her magic."

Jeniah conceded and stopped pestering him. As they traveled that day, a new awareness of him as a man grew, and she acutely felt his arms around her as they rode together on Braygo. Arms of strength, of gentleness. He had ceased to be just her protector and had become something much more.

"Captain?" the princess's voice floated to Kai on the cold morning air.

"Yes," he responded absently as he saddled Braygo quickly and gave the last strap a good tug. They had eaten more of his soldier's rations of dried meat and prepared to depart. Today he would watch for game; fresh meat would be a welcome change. The hesitation from behind him stilled his hands.

"What made you come for me that night?"

Kai's thoughts returned to the streets of Arden City, which had become a battlefield. A war of emotions left him empty inside.

He turned to the princess. "Your father asked me to protect you and get you to safety."

"My father," she whispered in amazement.

"He fell in battle. I got to him at the last moment, and in his dying breath, he commanded me to save you and the queen."

"He thought of me at the moment of his death."

Kai turned away, clenching his fists. "I came to help your people. I failed them. I failed my king and your king." Then with renewed purpose he added, "But I will not fail you, Your Highness. I swear I will get you safely to Darbor."

He didn't tell her he would have come for her even if he hadn't vowed to find and protect her. He spoke little after that, lost in his own thoughts, and the princess seemed equally preoccupied.

Snow fell again as they traveled, blanketing the world in silence. The princess rode Braygo with her head down to shield her face from the cold, but Kai peered into the silent snowfall, ever watchful for Hanorans.

The princess had surprised him on many levels. Remarkably strong and uncomplaining, she had tended him when he, for the first time since his childhood, had fallen helpless. She cared for him, unflinchingly, not because she needed him to protect her, but because she was a young woman of compassion and warmth.

He glanced down at the top of her head. "I don't think I ever thanked you for caring for me when I was hurt. You saved my life."

She looked back. The sweetest smile he had ever seen came over her lovely face, causing his heart to pound. "I've never been needed like that before." She lowered her eyes. "You saved my life. I owed you."

"You never need to feel indebted to me," he replied. His arms longed to tighten around her, but he kept them still.

That night, they slept in the hollow of an enormous tree. Kai awoke twice to walk the camp in a guarding pattern but all was still. Just after dawn, he awoke with all senses screaming danger. From outside came the sound of crunching snow. A twig snapped. Braygo, who was out grazing, would never have made that much noise. Two Hanoran soldiers, looking down at Braygo's hoof prints, came into view. In moments, they would find them.

Kai reached for his daggers, soundlessly drawing them from their sheaths. As the Hanorans followed the tracks, he waited. When they were within range, he took careful aim and let his daggers fly. Both men dropped without uttering a sound. Kai let out a breath in relief that he hadn't been forced to fight them; he didn't know if his newly healed side would bear up under a fight.

The princess awoke in alarm. Kai went to retrieve his daggers and cleaned them on the clothing of one of the fallen soldiers.

"We must go quickly. There will be more nearby." He grabbed their things and stuffed them into the pack. Then he froze. Hoof beats. The jingle of tack. Mounted men approached and they were sure to find the men Kai had killed. There was not enough time to escape.

"I'll have to fight." He didn't know if he could do it wounded, but he was determined to not fail her. "Stay back."

The princess shrank against the inside wall of the hollow tree. When he looked back, all he saw was the empty middle of an old, hollow tree. Good. She had blurred.

Kai whistled for Braygo and the duocorn came bounding out of the trees to him. With a running leap, he mounted Braygo bareback.

Eight Hanorans broke through the brush. They stopped, looking first at their fallen comrades and then at Kai. He turned Braygo and charged directly at them. He took down the Hanoran archer with his dagger. Then, after drawing his sword, he struck out at the two closest soldiers, who crumpled.

Braygo continued to plow into the path of the enemy, goring the soldiers and their beasts with his horns. Enraged, the Hanorans surrounded Kai as he parried their attack and countered. Hanorans fell with every stroke. Within minutes, he was left alone with a complement of Hanoran soldiers lying lifeless in the snow. It was not until the danger had passed that he felt the dull ache from his wounds. He dismounted, retrieved his dagger, and cleaned his weapons. The princess went to him with a look of alarm.

Kai shook his head as she approached. "I'm not hurt." He cleaned the blood from Braygo's muzzle and horns. After tacking up the duocorn, they mounted and cantered through the forest to the highway.

"We're almost to the border city between Lariath and Darbor."

"Do you think they are still neutral? Or might there be repercussions?" The princess gasped as if something had occurred to her. "What if the Hanorans conquered them, too?"

"Lariath has nothing to offer a man like Rheged. Except for their one trade city, the country isn't much more than a few scattered farms. They're totally neutral, and much too close to Darbor." Men such as the king of Hanore were difficult to predict, but Kai offered a reassuring smile. "We'll get some provisions and stay in an inn tonight."

The princess let out sigh of delight. "A real bed! It sounds too wonderful. I'm so tired of waking up with sticks in my hair and rocks in my ribs."

Kai chuckled appreciatively. "You've been remarkably good-natured about your travails."

She dropped her head. "Sorry. I didn't mean to complain."

"You haven't complained at all. You surprise me."

She looked back at him with one eyebrow up. "Oh? You mean for a girl, or for royalty?"

He chose his words with care, knowing how particular women were about words and their hidden meanings. "Both. But you've proven me wrong."

She stared straight ahead. "I've been taught to bear up under difficulties. My mother had no tolerance for complaining. She said that we must always be calm and gracious, regardless of our circumstances." Her voice dropped almost to a whisper. "I disappointed her often."

Kai leaned in. "She always spoke highly of you and with great pride. She would be pleased with your conduct."

The princess fell silent but her posture straightened. Before the shadows were long, they arrived at the outer edge of the city.

"Now would be a good time to blur," Kai suggested.

She nodded and Kai recognized the faint, softening edges around her body.

"What are you projecting as an image?" he asked.

"A plain, unnoticeable peasant girl."

"Perfect."

It sounded unbelievable that someone of her beauty could appear plain. But if she could masquerade as a rock or a tree, a peasant girl should be easy.

⊶⊱⊹⊰⊷

They rode through the city gates with the rest of the peasants and merchants who passed in and out in droves. Jeniah felt the captain's tension as he remained watchful. With the Sauraii guiding Braygo, they fell in with traffic. The city was a bustling, busy maze of narrow, winding streets where dirty piles of snow lay in corners. They followed the main thoroughfare, lost among all the activity. People hurried by on foot, astride duocorns, and inside carriages without a second glance at the forlorn pair. Shops and booths lined the street, the vendors haggling with shoppers over prices. Animals and livestock cried out and stamped, their musty smells lingering in the air. Ragged children ran among the noise and chaos, looking for excitement and perhaps an unguarded purse.

Jeniah's eyes darted around as she rode in front of the captain, taking in all the sights of the city.

She had been to bazaars, but they did not prepare her for the marvels unfolded before her here.

The captain stopped at a shop and purchased two new cloaks of an inconspicuous dark brown cloth, like those of peasants but made of the warmest material available. Anxious to be as anonymous as possible, they both put the plain cloaks on over their clothes. At a dressmaker's shop, they looked at fabric for a dress to replace Jeniah's ragged gown.

"Do you have anything already made that we may purchase?" Captain Darkwood asked the dressmaker.

"No, not unless you want to buy some of my own," she replied with a wry smile.

"That would be acceptable," the captain said.

She paused and looked at him oddly. "Do you jest, sir?"

"No. I'm willing to purchase anything you already have."

"Very well." She disappeared.

Across the street at a bakery, a young girl came running out the door wearing a look of terror, with the cook, red-faced and furious, storming out after her.

"You stupid, clumsy wench. I'll wring your neck!" the cook shouted.

The scullery maid turned a corner and crouched down next to a heap of refuse. Jeniah wished she could protect the girl. She had never really tried such a thing, but wondered if she could project a blur over the quaking scullery maid. She concentrated on shielding the girl, making her blend in with the bricks of the building. A soft shimmer touched her outline. Jeniah watched, delighted, as the cook ran right past the girl. The maid let out a sigh of relief.

"Mag?" came another voice, softer, concerned. An older woman came out of the bakery.

Jeniah stopped projecting the blur as the maid stepped out of the shadows toward the woman.

"Come, you can take these deliveries. Don't worry about Cook. He'll have forgotten all by the time you return. I'll clean up the mess in the kitchen."

The maid nodded and obediently followed the older woman back inside the bakery. A moment later, the girl returned, balancing two baskets, and disappeared down the street.

The knowledge that Jeniah had protected the girl from an undeserved beating gave her a quiet joy. She could not save her people yet, but she had saved someone.

She turned away and found the captain's blue eyes upon her. A tiny smile tugged at his mouth.

"Did you do that?"

Feeling both shy and proud, she nodded.

"I thought so." Approval shone in his eyes.

A moment later, the dressmaker reappeared with a blouse, a skirt, and a bodice that laced up the back. "I don't have anything really fine, but these belong to my daughter. She's not as tiny as you are, milady, but if you lace it up tight, it should do."

Although the clothing was coarse, dull, and thinning in areas, Jeniah accepted it gratefully. The captain bought a change of clothes from a traveling merchant who was similar in height, although a bit portly. The merchant was only too happy to sell an old set of clothing for enough money to have some fine new ones made.

At the cobbler's shop, they purchased a pair of fur-lined boots for Jeniah. The captain had to negotiate for a pair that had been made for another customer and finally paid double the price in order to persuade the cobbler to part with them. The boots were a bit too big but when two pairs of warm stockings were added, they fit well enough.

"I don't think I even remembered what it was like to be truly warm," Jeniah said dreamily as she wore the boots out of the shop.

They passed a number of shops and taverns, then turned down a side street toward a quieter neighborhood on the outskirts of the city. A small inn stood sheltered by evergreen trees.

After leaving Braygo with a stable hand and promising a tip for his superior care, the captain took her inside to a dining area crowded with several tables and a bar on the far side of the room. A middle-aged man with thinning hair and a round belly served mugs of foaming liquid to customers from behind the bar.

He looked up at their approach. "Welcome," the man said in a pleasant voice.

"Good evening," replied the captain cheerfully. "We need a room, two baths, and two meals."

Alarm jarred Jeniah at the thought of sleeping in the same room with him. Now that they were in civilization, she had assumed that they would each have their own room. She glanced at the captain but his face remained ambiguous. After taking a steadying breath, she reminded herself that he had proved an honorable man repeatedly and that he would not suddenly transform into a monster the moment they were alone in a bedroom. Then, realizing that her nervousness made her lose her concentration, she strengthened her blurring illusion.

The innkeeper nodded. "I've a nice room available." The innkeeper named his price and Captain Darkwood paid him out of his shrinking money pouch.

Jeniah wished she had some coins to contribute and made a mental note to repay him if she ever had money of her own. Not just repay him but reward him.

A middle-aged woman appeared beside the innkeeper.

"My wife will show you the way." The innkeeper turned to his customers who called noisily for another round of grog.

The innkeeper's wife gave them a friendly smile and pushed back a wayward strand of graying hair. "This way."

She led them down a narrow corridor to a door. Inside, they found a clean room with a large, comfortable-looking bed. Against a wall sat a bureau with a washbasin and a screen to change behind. Although bare compared to the luxurious chambers in the castle, to Jeniah it was a haven.

"Your baths will arrive shortly, milord. We begin serving dinner at six bells. Come early. We are busy most nights, and dinner is only served as long as it lasts. My name is Mirre. If you require anything else, let me know."

"Thank you, Mirre," the captain said with a disarming smile.

Mirre blushed and faltered. Then she smiled back, no doubt overwhelmed at receiving attention from such a handsome man. The door clicked behind her.

Alone with the captain, Jeniah's irrational fears returned and she tentatively looked up at him. "One room?"

"I can't protect you if I can't see you. And we cannot discount the possibility that the Hanorans may have traced you here. Two people arriving together asking for two rooms might be enough to lead them to us even if you aren't recognized."

Jeniah nodded and sat down on the bed. The only bed in the room.

Very softly, he said, "You can still trust me, you know." His expression begged for her confidence.

How could she not believe him? "I know."

A humble knock on the door announced the arrival of the tub and buckets of hot water. The captain stepped out of the room while Jeniah bathed. She had almost forgotten how wonderful a hot bath felt, but she was surprised at her own helplessness in bathing and washing her hair. Mora had always done it for her. Jeniah spared no few tears over the loss of her friend and faithful lady-in-waiting. Then, reminding herself that the captain waited outside the door, she pulled herself together.

Despite her awkwardness, she scrubbed her skin heartily and felt glorious. Dressing proved challenging as her fingers struggled clumsily with the clothing. The simple blouse with long sleeves and a brown woolen skirt, much like those she had seen peasant girls wear, looked beautiful compared to the ragged gown and borrowed tunic of the captain's she had worn the last few weeks. The laces in the bodice, however, were impossible, and finally Jeniah made up her mind to do without and threw it down.

She had to work at her hair for some time to comb out the tangles, a task she had never had to do. Her hair had nearly dried by the time she coaxed out the last snarls. Mora had done it with such ease, and had often admired Jeniah's hair as she arranged it.

Mora. How Jeniah missed her beloved and faithful companion. Pulling in her emotions, she took a breath and looked down at herself. She looked better than she had in days. Indignation welled up inside of her as she realized she could now easily pass for a peasant girl without even blurring.

Her life as a princess had ended. She lived in exile.

Then she squared her shoulders and lifted her head, refusing to brood over it. She glanced at the door, behind which she knew Captain Darkwood waited in the corridor. With Kai Darkwood at her side, she could bear anything.

She refused to consider what she might do if he were gone.

Chapter Eleven

*K*ai knocked at the door to their room. "May I come in?"
"Yes," came an answer from behind the door.

The princess's smile met him like sunlight after a storm. A few damp ringlets clung to her lovely face, which shone from the bath, and she smelled like sweet herbs and flowers.

He let his eyes move down her slender, curvaceous body. The princess turned with a flourish as if parading a lovely gown, innocently assuming he was looking at her attire.

He redirected his thoughts to her clothing. "Something is missing."

She wore a blouse tucked into a skirt, but there was no bodice. The thin fabric of her blouse did little to conceal her figure beneath it. Kai spotted the bodice lying on the floor.

As she followed his line of sight, the princess frowned in embarrassment. "I couldn't manage that alone."

He successfully suppressed a smile. "These can be tricky things. Would you care for some assistance?"

A look of horror came over her and she crossed her arms over her chest. "You mean . . .? No, no that would not be—"A blush crept into her face and her teeth caught her lower lip.

Kai picked up the bodice. "I don't have much experience with these. Not much different than lacing boots, I would assume."

Her blush deepened and her eyes dropped.

"Here. Allow me," he persisted.

She looked as though she might bolt. "Very well," she said in a hushed voice.

He could almost feel the heat of her blush. She bit her lip and waited, shame-faced, while Kai placed the bodice around her and laced it up, trying not to allow his hands to linger too long and make her uncomfortable, or to indulge his imagination. He finished lacing her and rested his hand at the curve of her waist.

She glanced back over her shoulder and their eyes met. She held her breath, her eyes darting to each of his. Tension rippled between them. The princess grew very still, and he knew that she was aware of him, not only as her protector, but as a man. His hand lingered at her waist and then slowly slid up her back and along her shoulder. He touched the exposed skin above the neckline of her shirt. The softness of her skin surprised him, and a surge of need shot through him. His chest tightened and he could barely draw a breath. He ached to touch her, to taste her. It was almost more than he could bear. By the moons, where was his self-control? After his declaration only moments ago, he could not fail her now.

Breaking eye contact, Kai leaned down and picked up the boots. "May I help you with these, too?"

Clearly shaken by the current that had passed between them, she turned away, and he waited while she composed herself. She nodded. "Only if you will show me how to do it. I won't have you dressing me like a handmaiden."

He raised an eyebrow and replied wolfishly, "I found it interesting, actually."

"Captain!" She looked scandalized, but a smile touched her mouth.

He chuckled lightly and was gratified to see that she finally relaxed. After he laced her boots, the princess stood up.

"Compared to the lovely slippers you made for me, I don't know if I can bear to wear these ugly old boots," she teased as she turned to allow him to look her over again. "What do you think? Am I common-looking enough?"

"You are far from common-looking. But yes, I believe the clothing will do."

She grew somber. "Captain, am I . . . beautiful at all?"

Kai was taken aback at the question. Didn't she know? He hesitated. Speaking honestly might not be prudent, but her expression begged for reassurance.

His mouth opened and words came pouring out. "Never in all my life have I seen anyone who could compare to your beauty."

She studied him as if to determine his sincerity. "Thank you. I'm not sure why, but I really needed to hear that." Her eyes focused on something far away.

The princess looked so vulnerable, standing there hugging herself, that Kai longed to take her into his arms. That urge seemed to be hitting him more frequently, and it was becoming increasingly more difficult to resist. He told himself that after all she'd been through, and his earlier vows, his wish to hold her only stemmed out of an innocuous desire to comfort her. But knights weren't supposed to lie.

When more hot water was brought, Kai laid a hand on her arm. "Remain inside the room. I'll bathe behind the screen."

The princess waited quietly, resting on the bed. He could almost feel her discomfort. Kai stripped down and submerged himself. The hot water soothed his sore muscles. He scrubbed his skin and examined his wounds. They were scarred and red, but healing well. He glanced toward the princess on the other side of the flimsy barrier, achingly aware of her nearness. So tempting.

He drew a steadying breath and scrubbed his hair as he thought back over their conversation only hours before. She had doubted his motives for getting only one room. The thought came like a blow to the gut. Hadn't he proved himself to her? But then, because of her ordeal with the Hanoran soldiers, any woman would feel as she did. And if she had any idea how much he wanted to take her into his arms, she would have good reason to doubt his intentions.

"While we are here, don't you think you should get your shoulder and your side looked at by a doctor or a healer?" she called.

"No. I'm mending."

"Your wounds looked serious."

"I know, but a healer would recognize them as battle wounds and might draw conclusions. The Hanorans are everywhere. I can't risk it." He finished bathing and began drying.

"I'm worried about you, Kai."

He froze, and the towel slipped from his hands. That was the first time she had spoken his name. Before, she had always called him "Captain." He began dressing and tried to keep his voice casual. "Don't worry. Your chayim worked her magic."

After he dressed, he slipped over his head the leather thong that held the braid. He eyed it, feeling a sting of guilt that he hadn't thought of her as often as usual, and brought the token to his lips.

The dinner bell rang and the pair of refugees ate their food hungrily. Of all the sumptuous feasts served in the castle, the princess later said, none could compare to this, the first real meal they had eaten since their flight from Arden. Kai ate in silence but his ears remained alert. He hoped no one paid close attention to the princess or noticed her mannerisms, which were obviously that of the well-bred. Though she ate quickly, her posture was too erect, her hand position on the utensils too formal, her bites too tiny and proper. Every motion screamed high-born. He could only trust that her blurring would be an adequate protection from any suspicious eyes present.

Most of the conversation coming from the tables around them centered on livestock or the weather. Some discussed their business in the marketplace. Then the conversation took a more meaningful turn.

"I heard that the castle of Arden fell in only one night and that all the royalty were publicly executed. Even the children."

Beside him, the princess swallowed hard and put her last bite of bread back down on her plate, her body rigid.

"Except the princess," interjected another. "They didn't find her in the initial raid. The Hanorans are carrying out a widespread search for her."

"Troops are combing the countryside, and all the main roads out of Arden are blockaded," replied another. "It's made traders unhappy."

"Traveling has become a terrible nuisance," agreed another.

"I pity the princess," said the innkeeper, joining in the conversation. "I hope for her sake the wild beasts get her before the Hanorans do."

The princess made a choking sound.

"She'll meet a more humane end," agreed the innkeeper's wife, Mirre, as she paused to refill their tankards. "Did you hear how brutally they executed the royalty?"

There were murmurs of assent. The princess went pale and shook visibly. Her blurring faded until her own features blended with her illusion.

The innkeeper's wife passed by and then stopped. "Are you unwell, milady?" Her eyes narrowed as she carefully studied the princess.

Alarm shot through Kai. He stood. "She's tired from our journey. Perhaps she should rest now." He put his arm around her and helped her up. They left the room with a few curious stares following them.

Inside the room, Jeniah began to weep. At first, she tried to hold back, but finally she gave in to the flood of tears that overwhelmed her. She looked so forlorn that Kai could not resist the need to comfort her. When he put his arms around her, she did not push him away but instead leaned against him, sobbing quietly as he held her.

Outside the shuttered window, the cloak of night spread over the land. Spent and exhausted, the princess rested against his chest. Tenderness swelled up inside him and he tightened his arms around her, reveling in the feel of her against him.

She sniffed. "I'm sorry. I seem to do nothing but cry."

"You've been through a great deal."

She leaned against him more deeply, her tremors dying down.

Kai stroked her hair and kissed the top of her dark head. "Get some rest."

She did not resist as Kai laid her back on the bed. At least she had eaten a decent meal and finally had a proper bed. She sank into sleep almost instantly, and he prayed her dreams would be sweet.

Kai stood over her, admiring her. Her radiant beauty made him ache. Banishing such thoughts, he shook himself and removed her boots before pulling a blanket over her. As he rolled up in his blanket on the floor by the door, Kai attempted to forget the lovely, desirable young woman in the bed only a few hand spans away.

Thank the moons for his Sauraii training, or he might never sleep. He ran through mental exercises until he cleared his mind enough to rest.

Kai awoke to a soft knock at the door. Immediately alert, he leaped to his feet, a dagger in each hand. Pale, silver moonlight shone in between the shutters of the window. He heard the princess's soft breathing, but no other sound.

"Who's there?" he called softly.

"Forgive me for disturbing you, sir. It's Mirre," came a reply barely above a whisper. "May I speak with you, please?"

The princess stirred but did not awaken. Kai sheathed one of the daggers and quietly opened the door. The innkeeper's wife stood alone in the passageway. After stepping outside, he eased the door closed. She glanced first at his dagger, and then up at him. He re-sheathed it.

"I apologize for awakening you, sir," she said in a low voice. "I know you are both weary. My husband thought it would be better if I spoke with you. We didn't want to frighten either of you." She looked furtively about, then began in a softer whisper. "We believe it would be better for you both if you left now. The Hanoran soldiers have tracked the princess to the city."

A tremor started deep in Kai's stomach as his mind sifted through different avenues of escape.

"They are making a house-by-house search for the princess," continued Mirre. "You don't need to say anything—my husband and I know who you are . . . or rather, who she is. We are assuming you are her protector." She quickly added, "You have nothing to fear from us, Sir Knight. We are loyal to Arden's royalty. I used to work in the castle before I married. Your lady bears a strong resemblance to the queen."

Kai dragged his fingers through his hair. As he'd feared, they'd been recognized. He wondered who else had seen them. If someone had recognized the princess, they would have taken note of his face as well.

Mirre continued, "I wonder that I didn't recognize her when

you first arrived. No matter. We want to help. We have gathered provisions and extra blankets for you, and a tent. It won't protect you from the cold but it will keep you dry."

"How far away are the Hanorans?" Kai asked tersely.

"Still in the center of town."

Kai laid a hand on her arm. "I cannot adequately express my gratitude to you, my good woman."

"It is not necessary, sir. Keep her safe. I pray Arden can be restored someday. Hurry, there's no time to delay. My husband awaits you at the stable. Speed and safety go with you." She hurried away.

Kai awakened Jeniah. Disoriented and irritated, she mumbled. "What is it?"

"The Hanorans have tracked us here, and the innkeepers know who you are. Others might know as well."

Suddenly more alert, the princess snatched her cloak and pulled on her boots, her shaking fingers fumbling to lace them. "I drew attention at dinner. I'm sorry."

"You said you can only blur for a few hours?"

"Yes, but I think I can blur us both like I did the scullery maid. I'll try."

Outside, the air was so cold that it hurt to breathe. By the stable, the innkeeper advised Kai on the best route to take to get out of the city, and then wished them well. Kai gripped his hand in gratitude. The innkeeper bowed to the princess and hurried inside, hopefully to help his wife erase all signs of their presence.

As she and Kai mounted Braygo, the princess whispered, "You might feel a bit strange when I blur us."

An odd, prickling sensation raised the hairs on his skin.

"I think it's working," she added in a whisper.

He nodded and gently placed a finger over her lips to caution her to be silent. They rode through the dark, deserted streets, all of Kai's senses straining for any sign of danger. He caught the distant sounds of shouting. Outside of town, they left the road for the forest. Huge, twisted trees met overhead and the forest thickened and darkened.

Kai urged Braygo forward, grimly determined to protect Jeniah from danger, regardless of the cost.

Jeniah's fears made the dark forest terrifying. Light from the twin moons cast sinister-looking shadows that, to her growing imagination, became great, vicious beasts lurking, crouching, awaiting a chance to make a kill. The grotesque trees sagged and bent under years of heavy snow, their bark peeling back raggedly where wild duocorns had fed upon them. Jeniah's breath came out in ragged puffs in the freezing air.

She resisted the desire to cling to the captain as Braygo wound his way among the writhing, clawing masses of trunk and limb. A large bird of prey flew across their path, chasing a small rodent that scurried, squeaking, among the naked trees. Night insects called, and somewhere in the distance a wyrwolf howled.

The moons shone on the surface of a stream. The captain led Braygo to the bank, dismounted, and then paused for a moment. With his head turned up toward Jeniah, he covered her shaking hands with his. Moonlight shadowed his face, but his gesture touched her heart. It meant a great deal that he'd take a moment to reassure her when he might have been preoccupied with their danger. He took the reins and led the duocorn with Jeniah still astride, carefully testing the ice with each step before allowing Braygo to follow. They walked down the middle of the frozen river for several leagues before heading for the riverbank.

As they reached the other side, Kai remounted behind her and gave her an encouraging smile. "Everything will be all right."

She managed a smile in return, admiring this fearless, gentle knight who had sworn to protect her.

They continued cautiously until the blackness faded to predawn gray. Jeniah's head began to nod, but Kai, riding with his head erect and his shoulders square, never appeared to tire. Even with his recent injuries, he seemed fully fresh and alert, eyes and ears aware of everything. She let her head fall against him and wondered if she imagined that he tightened his arms around her.

Suddenly, Kai stiffened, then quickly guided Braygo off the path only moments before a contingent of Hanorans rounded the corner. They spread out and began a search pattern.

"I can blur us," Jeniah whispered.

Kai nodded. They remained motionless as she projected over them an image of shadowy plant life. Kai's heart thudded against her back and he sat tensed as he poised to fight if her ruse failed. The white-cloaked soldiers rode past slowly, carefully. One came within a few hand spans of them but looked right over them. Eventually, the leader of the regiment called them together and they moved on. Kai waited for several minutes before urging Braygo forward. Fearful that some of the soldiers lay in wait, Jeniah continued to shield them until her strength gave out and she had to stop.

They rode breathlessly all the next day, watching for any sign of discovery. When none came, they relaxed. At nightfall, Kai set up and lashed together the poles of the tent. Jeniah pulled out the blankets the innkeeper had provided.

"We'll reach Darbor in a few days," Kai said. "It's more rugged than Arden, with steep mountains rather than gently rolling hills, and the trees are different, but it is beautiful. I think you'll like it there. The king is known for his fairness and bravery. He will welcome you with open arms, Princess, and he will fight to help free Arden and make you queen."

No doubt if she had been born a few years earlier, she would have married one of King Farai's sons and Darbor would already be her home. She removed the bags from the saddle.

"I never thought I would be queen of Arden. Aven was to inherit the throne. I assumed someday I would marry a Govian or Tiraian prince and spend the rest of my life having children and attending public functions, not making decisions that will affect a whole country. I'm not prepared to be queen."

"I'm sure you will rise to it. People often have inner strength that goes undiscovered until a challenge reveals it." Kai began draping the tarp over the wooden frame.

He spoke much the same as her mother had when she'd comforted Jeniah after her father announced that she was to marry the Hanoran prince. She stood silently digesting Kai's words while he tugged at the tent. A corner had gotten caught on the end of a pole and he was having trouble pulling it clear.

"Here, let me help." She reached up to free the uncooperative piece of cloth.

Working in comfortable silence, they finished setting up the shelter and then spread a large blanket over the ground cloth that made up the floor of the tent. Neither one could stand up inside, and the tent's base was not much bigger than a large bed, but it would keep them dry and protect them from the wind.

Kai walked the perimeter of the camp, moving so silently that Jeniah would never have known he was there if she couldn't see him among the trees. He paused, looking up at the stars. He stood stiffly, his shoulders rigid, his fists clenched. He drew in a labored breath, his normal reserve falling away and stark despair shining through.

Jeniah's heart lurched. She'd never seen such grief, such hopelessness, such unspeakable pain. He bowed his head, clutching something at the base of his throat. She remembered the braided hair he kept there and wondered at its origin and its meaning to him. Someone he'd loved. Someone he'd lost.

He straightened and returned, his expression hard, controlled. Jeniah looked away and pretended she hadn't been watching him.

"Your chayim appears to be standing watch."

She nodded. "She'll protect us while we sleep."

When everything had been brought inside the tent and Braygo was freed to roam wild, Jeniah crawled inside and sat hugging her knees. Kai climbed in after her and fastened the tent flap closed. Jeniah stared at him, searching for the pain she'd witnessed only moments ago, but it had vanished.

"I used the last firestick yesterday and was unable to find any in the city. And it's much colder tonight than it has been so far." He smoothed the blankets and scooted closer to her. "If we sleep back to back we will stay warmer."

As he neared, she caught his familiar scent, felt the warmth of his body. His nearness sent a wave of caution through her—not exactly fear, but something close to it. She was increasingly aware of him on a physical level, and she suspected that he saw her no longer as just a princess and his charge, but as a woman. She knew he'd never hurt her. Still, she couldn't stop the tension in her body or the nervousness coiling in her stomach.

He spread the blankets over them both and lay down with his back toward her. Nothing untoward appeared to be on his mind.

Jeniah hesitated before lying down on her side with her back toward his. He scooted closer to her until their backs touched. Her back warmed where it touched his. She wanted to turn over and nestle against him, to put her arms around him. She shivered, not in cold, but in a new and foreign feeling she couldn't quite identify. She wanted to learn and heal the source of his pain the way her chayim had healed his physical wounds. She wanted to put her arms around him and soothe him, comfort him, touch him. She wanted to explore these very womanly feelings sweeping over her.

She chided herself. Kai Darkwood was an experienced man who no doubt only saw her as a naive child. He probably had a lady waiting for him in Darbor, someone he missed and loved.

She curled up into a ball and tried to not picture him with another woman in his arms.

⁂

Kai lay very still while the princess trembled against his back. It might have been from the cold, or from her fear of lying so close to him, but whatever the cause, her tremors gradually lessened and she settled in more comfortably. As her body relaxed, she fit perfectly against him.

In the predawn stillness, Kai awoke. During the night the princess, wrapped tightly in her own blanket, had snuggled up against him for warmth, her head resting against his shoulder. He knew she would never have done that consciously, but his heart whispered that she belonged there.

He admired her sleeping face. One curl lay over her eyes. Carefully, so as not to wake her, he picked up the wayward curl and laid it back with the rest of the dark ringlets spread out behind her head. Her long, thick lashes rested against her cheeks. Her skin was as fair as an angel's and her lips, full and pink, parted slightly.

He touched her cheek very lightly, reveling in the texture of her skin. She smiled in sleep and turned her head toward his hand. There was something else about her beyond her rare beauty that cracked the walls he had carefully built around his shattered heart. She reached him in a way that he had thought was past reaching. His protectiveness toward her extended far beyond his oath to her father. He felt tenderness, gentleness, and something more. No. He drew back. She was his charge and nothing more.

Ignoring the irritating voice in his head that called him a liar, Kai arose. The princess stirred and woke. Still lying in the blankets, with her hair mussed and her eyes heavy-lidded with sleep, she looked breathtakingly beautiful. When she looked up at him with sleepy affection, his lungs seized and he had to leave the tent.

After they ate bread and cheese provided by the innkeeper, Kai took down the tent while the princess saddled Braygo. A smile came unbidden as he watched her do things that, as princess of Arden, she had always had a servant to do for her. Without voicing complaint, the princess simply adapted to her new way of life, remarkably resilient to her circumstances.

She caught him smiling at her and raised her eyebrow inquiringly, but he refocused on his task without speaking. With some trepidation, Kai acknowledged that his esteem of Jeniah, princess of Arden, was increasing rapidly. But if he allowed such feelings to continue, he would be lost. Besides, she would be queen of Arden, and there was no place for a low-born knight in her life. Indulging his affections would lead nowhere he wished to go, so he rebuilt the shields around his heart, taking every defensive measure he could. He would not lose control, for if he did, the dark and broken place inside him would utterly consume him.

⌐ Chapter Twelve

now fell heavily. Jeniah wore a blanket over two cloaks and kept her head covered as she rode Braygo. Even so, her hands shook and her feet kept going numb.

Her thoughts strayed to the night the Hanorans attacked and destroyed her home. She remembered the soldier who'd assaulted her and the way she'd defended herself. If she hadn't killed him, he would have hurt her in ways she could not begin to imagine. That knowledge failed to ease the tightness in her chest every time she remembered it. Because she'd killed a living, breathing human being, she felt as if a part of her had been broken off and lost. Still, it had been necessary.

She lifted her head. "Kai, would you teach me to use a weapon?"

Walking beside the duocorn, he looked at her in surprise. "Do you really want me to?"

"I realize what you've known all along—that knowing how to fight doesn't make one a murderer. I had to defend myself in Arden against the Hanoran soldiers, but it was luck that saved me, not knowledge or skill. If I ever find myself in that situation again, I don't want to be helpless."

"That's wise," he replied thoughtfully. Although his blue eyes were shielded, Jeniah sensed a sudden tension in him.

Her words came out in a rush as she tried to explain herself. "I know it isn't customary for a lady to use weapons, but in Govia, the women are as much warriors as the men and—"

"You don't have to explain. I think it's a good idea, and I would be honored to teach you." He paused. "Normally I would take a new student to the armory and have him choose a weapon that fits. Very young squires use wooden weapons their first few times. Perhaps we can improvise."

That evening, after they had set up camp, Kai hunted for the right stick and then carved it while Jeniah groomed Braygo. Brushing the animal had a soothing effect on her. The duocorn nuzzled her before wandering away in search of food.

She felt a familiar presence at the edge of the firelight, a lure so compelling that she could not have resisted if she had wanted to. "I'll return in a moment," she said to Kai.

He glanced up. "Stay close."

Her chayim waited patiently while Jeniah wound her way through obstacles in the darkness toward her. The moment Jeniah's hand made contact with Maaragan, the soothing warmth of the wise one's mind enveloped her. Jeniah's heartbeat slowed and she nestled against the chayim. Reassurance and approval flowed from the great beast into the princess, not only for Jeniah's actions, but for the woman she was becoming. The vision changed, and Jeniah became Maaragan, looking down at the human snuggled into her mane. Though this female was small, she had great power, great potential. She possessed duty, courage, and valor uncommon in humans. Magic was uniquely manifested in her to defeat the evil lurking over her people, over all of Arden. She alone could defeat the darkness looming over the land. When the vision withdrew, Jeniah sank weakly against Maaragan. A sense of well-being permeated her soul, yet she felt overwhelmed by her task.

"Can I really do this?" Jeniah murmured.

Maaragan growled softly and nuzzled her.

Jeniah drew a breath. When she felt steady, she pushed herself to a stand. Maaragan turned and melted into the darkness.

By the time Jeniah returned to camp, Kai had whittled the stick down to a rough sword shape. "I'm not much of a woodworker, but try this." He paused and gave her a searching look. "Are you all right?"

She met his eyes and nodded. "My chayim expects much of me."

He waited.

"She thinks I'm my people's only hope."

"Of course. You're the rightful heir."

She didn't try to explain, since she wasn't entirely sure she understood either. Instead, she took the wooden sword from Kai and held it out in front of her. He corrected her grip and taught her the ready stance and a few beginning moves. It surprised Jeniah how difficult it was to follow him. He made everything look effortless and she moved clumsily, but he was encouraging and patient. Her arms quickly tired. When the night grew too dark, Kai called for a stop.

"You did very well for the first time."

"Not really."

"I've had squires who didn't do as well their first time."

She knew he was only encouraging her, yet she took pleasure in his praise. They ate, crawled into the tent, and without thinking about it, Jeniah scooted back until she felt the warmth of his body. His nearness was reassuring and she felt safe.

Snow fell at an angle as wind murmured in the evergreen trees. They traveled along a river with a steep bank. Large chunks of ice floated silently downstream, and a layer of solid ice lined the river's edges.

To save Braygo's strength, Kai walked, leading the duocorn. He glanced back at the princess astride the animal. She stared absently at the river, looking as though she might collapse. She was thin and pale. Even though she insisted on training with him each evening as they stopped to camp, she had trouble concentrating and fatigued quickly. He didn't know how much longer she would last. She was so tiny and fragile that he could hardly believe she'd had the resiliency to survive this long.

He wished he could put her back in silks and jewels, dine with her on the finest foods. He missed her smile, her laughter, the playful gleam in her eyes when she teased him. He wanted to make her feel safe and warm, burrow his face into her fragrant hair, gaze forever into those endless eyes . . .

His boot slipped on the ice. He snapped his attention to his footing but his feet were growing numb and he could barely feel the ground.

The princess slid off Braygo and began walking to get warm, her head lowered against the wind as they followed the almost-frozen river running sluggishly beside them. Kai peered ahead and thought he saw a small building just ahead. He squinted into the onslaught of snow. There was indeed a tiny structure on their side of a bridge spanning the river. A bridge house, perhaps.

"Shelter."

Princess Jeniah raised her head.

Kai quickened his steps as he led Braygo forward toward the small building. Suddenly, a sharp gust of wind hit him with such force that it threw him off balance. His foot slipped and he fell to his knees. He grabbed the reins to keep his balance, but Braygo stumbled and fell against the princess. With a cry, Jeniah clutched Braygo's mane but teetered at the edge of the river. Wild fear leaped into her eyes. Kai reached for her, but, as one, they slid down the steep banks, then landed hard on the ice at the water's edge.

Kai's ribs flared in pain, and he lay in stunned silence. Then, a sickening crunch echoed in his ears as all around them the ice cracked. It gave way under Braygo's weight first and the duocorn fell in. The rift widened, crumbling underneath the princess, who lay nearest the duocorn. She screamed, clawing at the ice. Kai lurched to his knees and made a desperate grab for her.

His fingers barely brushed against hers but he couldn't get a grip. She screamed again as she slid into the churning water, drifting away from him. His heart leaped into his throat and almost strangled him. *No!* He couldn't lose her—not now, not like this.

The ice collapsed beneath Kai and he plunged into a world of silence. His limbs flailed desperately as he fought against the current that pulled him further down from the light. Weakly, he battled his way upward, and finally his head broke through the water's surface. Gasping, he groped for something solid to hold on to but his hands only slid off jagged ice. The current pulled at him, but his strength failed and he slid back into the icy water. Over his head was only solid ice.

He was trapped. His pulse hammered and a roaring noise built until it deafened him. Blind panic overtook him. He barely registered a dark shape nearby. Numbly, his fingers intertwined with long, flowing hair. A force pulled him upward toward the light. He broke through the surface, gasping as his head came above the water. Coughing, he struggled to open his eyes as he was pulled out of the water. Numb and shaking, he scrambled on the ice, something dragging him along, until he finally felt solid ground.

Kai opened his eyes. He lay on the steep riverbank, his hands twisted around the golden mane of a wet creature that clambered up onto the bank, clawing footholds into the ice, pulling Kai until they were both safely off the river's edge. Kai blinked up at the large golden muzzle of a chayim. The princess's chayim.

The golden shape released him and leaped back into the river. Kai looked around wildly. He was alone.

"Jeniah!" he screamed, but his voice sounded choked.

Silence was his only reply. He'd lost her.

"No. No, no, no!"

The chayim's head burst through the river's surface downriver with a struggling, dark-headed form that clutched beast's mane.

"Jeniah!"

She called to him, breathlessly. She was alive.

The chayim hauled her coughing form to Kai. He crawled to her, slipping on the ice, and pulled her into a crushing hug. "By the moons, I thought I'd lost you . . ."

She wrapped her arms around him, shivering violently. The snow fell harder now and the wind blew in fierce gusts. From above Kai's head, standing firmly on the riverbank, the chayim shook the water off her hide, sending droplets of water in all directions. She snorted before she turned and vanished into the forest. That was three times the magical beast had saved Kai's life, all after he killed her mate.

Braygo nudged his master and nickered. How the duocorn had gotten out of the river, Kai couldn't guess. Astonished that all three of them had survived, he twisted his hand through the hanging reins and looped his other arm around Jeniah.

"Braygo, pull us up," Kai commanded.

They slipped and scrambled but with Braygo steadily pulling them, they managed to climb up the bank and onto level ground.

"There," Kai said as he pointed to the bridge house he had spotted earlier.

Jeniah mumbled something unintelligible.

With one arm around Braygo's neck and the other around Jeniah, Kai stumbled toward the bridge house. The door was locked, but he kicked it open, sending shock waves through his numbing legs. Jeniah was barely conscious when he pulled her inside. With Braygo safely in with them, Kai pushed the door closed, but he had broken the bolt when he kicked it open, so the wind kept slamming the door open.

They were in a room furnished only with a pallet, a table, a chair, and a cupboard. A thick layer of dust lay over everything, and the air was stale. A fireplace stood in one corner, however, and the walls were solid enough to keep out the wind and blowing snow. The previous occupant had left a generous supply of firewood stacked neatly beside the fireplace. Kai pulled the chair in front of the door to keep it closed.

With numb, shaking hands, he clumsily built a fire and turned to rouse Jeniah. "We need to get out of these clothes."

The fire roared to life, but Kai felt no warmth. Jeniah faded in and out of consciousness while he tried to peel her stiff, frozen clothes off her. Though she whimpered and pushed at him, he spoke to her reassuringly as he patiently worked to get her undressed. Her skin was a sickly blue. He pulled a blanket out of a saddlebag that had miraculously stayed dry and wrapped her in it, then laid her next to the fire.

His stiff fingers fumbled to strip off his own clothes. He wrapped up in the only other dry blanket, and with Jeniah snugly against him in spoon position, he huddled close to the fire. Braygo curled up behind Kai with his hooves delicately folded under him. Kai leaned back against the duocorn, but hardly felt any warmth from Braygo's body. Jeniah mumbled incoherently, her skin still frightfully cold. He had to do something to warm her.

He laid her against Braygo and climbed stiffly to his feet. After melting snow over the fire, he tested it first to make sure it wasn't too hot. The heat slipped comfortingly down his throat. He held Jeniah's head and pressed the cup to her lips. "Jeniah, drink."

She roused enough to obey but murmured something unintelligible. When he pressed the cup against her lips, she drank again. The fire crackled and the hut gradually warmed. Kai worried that the smoke would draw unwelcome attention, but the immediate danger was freezing to death.

He built up the fire until it roared in the hearth. With the warm water in his belly and a fire at his feet, the numbness left, but pain came on its heels. Eventually, his limbs quit hurting and he grew warm and comfortable.

Jeniah still shivered and her hands and feet were icy. Kai urged to her drink more warm water and began rubbing her limbs gently.

She woke disoriented. "What happened?"

"We fell in the river, but we're safe now."

She nodded and snuggled up to him before falling asleep again. He wrapped his arms around her and held her close. At the edge of his consciousness, he remembered only one other woman who had felt so right in his arms.

Kai woke tired and cold. The shutters of the small window let in a faint glimmer of gray sky, as well as a fair amount of wind. Without disentangling himself from Jeniah, he reached for the woodpile and tossed a few more logs onto the dying fire. He looked down at the beauty asleep in his arms, curled contentedly against him. He indulged himself as he let his eyes travel slowly over her slender body. The blanket had slipped down enough to show the graceful curve of one shoulder. He became acutely aware of the nearness of her body.

He touched that inviting shoulder and slid his hand along her creamy skin. She sighed and opened her eyes. Warmth and tenderness shone in her face. He traced the soft curve of her shoulder, down her arm, and back up to the ivory column of her neck. He craved her like a man in the desert craves water. Seeking the warmth and sweetness of her mouth, he leaned in. Her lips parted in invitation.

Out of nowhere, his conscience woke up and gave him a swift kick. She wasn't his.

With a groan, he leaped to his feet, holding his blanket firmly around himself. He picked up their clothes that he had laid out in front of the fire and shook them out with more vigor than necessary. Without looking at her, he tossed hers at her.

"Our clothes are dry. We need to move on. I'll step outside so you can dress."

Outside, the snow had stopped falling but the wind still whistled. With chattering teeth, Kai dressed hurriedly.

What kind of a man was he? Even when he was at his worst as a youth and had earned the rakish reputation that still followed him, he had never pressed his advantage upon a young woman as pure as she. And worse, she was the future queen of Arden. He had sworn to protect her. Where was his honor?

Besides, if he broke down now, he might lose control of his heart, and that he could not abide. He wanted to run out into the forest and yell in frustration. Instead, he gulped the cold air until his head cleared, and firmly shut down his yearnings.

Jeniah watched Kai as they broke camp and prepared for travel, but he refused to meet her eyes.

"At least the wind has stopped," she ventured after uncomfortable silence.

"The snow has, too."

They said nothing else for some time as they traveled. Finally, the forest ended and they crossed through a valley with nothing but bleak, stark whiteness. They rode Braygo, who struggled through snow so deep it nearly reached his belly.

Self-doubt tugged at Jeniah. Was Kai so protective of her virtue, or did he resist because he truly did not want her?

He had seemed to want her, at least for a moment. She should be grateful he was so honorable.

By dusk, Jeniah had grown so hungry and disheartened that she wondered if they would survive the journey. Snow fell heavily again, and her only relief from the cold and hunger was Kai's reassuring presence.

As he set up the tent, Jeniah helped him automatically, lashing the poles together like a seasoned outdoorsman. Her hands had become chapped and calloused, her nails ragged, but she had ceased to care about her appearance.

Grumpy and weary, Jeniah glared at the snowfall. "How long did it take you to get to Arden from Darbor?"

"About three weeks, but I came by the main highways with a caravan. And the weather was good. Going across country like this, dodging soldiers, and in harsh weather, takes much longer."

Jeniah heaved a sigh. "How close do you think we are now?"

Kai paused and gazed at her in sympathy. "About three days."

Three days. Jeniah nodded. She could survive another three days.

Normally when royalty traveled, an army of servants accompanied them and they brought a mountain of baggage containing every possible comfort. This trip had been nothing like that. Jeniah stole a glance at Kai. It had been a unique journey in many ways. Suddenly, it didn't seem so bad.

After Kai made his usual perimeter check and ensured that the chayim was standing guard, he returned to Jeniah inside the tent. As he pulled the blankets over them both, he glanced at her. "I know this has been hard on you, but you've borne it remarkably well."

"I hope I haven't been a burden."

"Not at all."

Her eyes traced the lines of his chiseled, handsome face. His hair was a little longer and the stubble on his normally smooth-shaven face had grown into a short beard. The scar that ran up his forehead into his hairline had faded to a thin, pink line. It did not detract from his raw handsomeness.

"I haven't checked your wounds in days."

He shrugged. "They've healed over."

"Let me take a look."

Humor curved Kai's mouth as he removed his tunic and shirt and allowed her to inspect him. Goose bumps appeared on his skin. Large, ragged scars and faint, yellowed bruises were all that remained of his near fatal wounds. Jeniah traced the scars, thinking how close she had come to losing him.

"There's still a lot of bruising," she murmured in sympathy.

"It's of no consequence."

When he picked up his shirt, she noticed a wide, white scar on his forearm. "Another battle scar?" she asked as she gestured toward it.

"No. I got that sparring with a friend. I lost my focus. If we hadn't been using blunted blades, he might have taken my arm off." He looked at her with a wry smile. "I never lost my focus again." He pulled his shirt over his head.

"I'm sure you didn't," she replied soberly. "With as many battles as you have fought, I'm surprised you aren't covered with scars."

He pulled on his tunic over his shirt, keeping his eyes averted from her inquiring gaze. "I never took a blow in battle before," he confessed quietly.

Jeniah stared at him in astonishment. "Never?"

He shook his head soberly. "The king once claimed I was untouchable, that no battle I fought would ever be lost." He made a sound of disgust. "I guess I proved him wrong."

She laid a hand on his back. "I'm sorry that the only time you were ever hurt was defending my country. It wasn't even your fight."

"The undefeatable, untouchable Kai Darkwood." His tone was bitter. "A failure in Arden." He lowered his head and raked his hands through his hair.

"No!" Horrified that he saw himself so, and that she had caused him to reopen that inner wound, she threw her arms around him, not even sure if he would accept her comfort. "No, not a failure. The entire country was not in your hands alone. No one expected you to do more than you did. You were wounded and yet you still had the determination to find me and take me away from harm. Without you, I would have been executed with my family. Because of you, there's still hope for Arden."

To her surprise, Kai didn't resist her. He leaned against her, his head resting on her shoulder. She tightened her arms as he shuddered, the muscles of his back quivering underneath her hands. Jeniah held him as he struggled in a rare display of emotion that nearly broke her heart.

And then she knew that this man was far more than her protector. She'd do anything, risk anything, sacrifice anything. For him.

Chapter Thirteen

As they emerged from the mountain pass that marked the southwestern border of Darbor, sunset spread its glow across the sky, turning the clouds amber and red. Confident that the Hanorans would not dare to cross the border into Darbor, Kai cantered along the main highway. As darkness grew, turning the blue sky indigo, Kai scouted for a place to camp.

"We'll be there before nightfall tomorrow," Kai assured the princess as they dismounted.

Hope lit her face. "I look forward to staying in one place for a while. And sleeping in a bed. All night, not just a few hours."

Kai glanced at her.

"I know you get up several times every night to walk the camp. You must be exhausted, never sleeping all the way through the night."

He shrugged. "It's an old campaign trick. But I admit I'd like to get a decent night's rest." Even with the chayim standing watch, he'd awoken regularly to circle the camp and ensure for himself they were safe. He had always prided himself on being quite capable of sleeping on his sword through a rainstorm, but he, too, grew weary of the lack of comforts.

They had just finished eating a fowl Kai had killed when the dreaded call of a wyrwolf reached their ears. Wide-eyed, Jeniah turned to him, her hand moving to rest upon his arm. They waited, listening. The howl echoed again, raising the hackles on Kai's neck. Noiselessly, he handed his longest dagger to Jeniah. They waited, back to back, poised for battle. She stood so near him that her back almost touched his. All his senses alert, he waited.

He whirled around as the wyrwolves charged from behind, their huge, shaggy bodies lunging from the darkness. He let his daggers fly, each one finding its mark. Still, their pale, eerily human-like faces came at them, snapping their dreadful jaws. His daggers had no effect. Kai drew his sword.

Jeniah pressed against his back, her frightened breathing drowned out by the wyrwolves' snarling. Kai thrust and sliced, but the furry bodies always managed to stay barely outside of the reach of his sword. The soft moonlight illuminated their eyes, making them glow yellow in the darkness. Snapping and growling, they bared their wicked, curved fangs. They circled and charged as a pack, trying to get to Kai's back, but he kept his blade moving.

Jeniah's cry warned him when one of the jaws caught the hem of her cloak. She stabbed at the beast with her dagger but the creature jumped out of her reach and fell back with its brothers. Kai's sword found its mark in the advancing wyrwolf. He plunged the sword in deep. Yelping, it staggered, went down, and lay lifeless. Jeniah moved with him as he continued to spin, their blades flashing in the pale moonlight.

As one, the bloodthirsty monsters charged. Kai's blade plowed into their bodies, wounding some, killing others as their howls rose to deafening levels. He fell into a rhythm of striking and turning, all senses alert to any wyrwolf that might be ahead of his blade's pass. He found a state of calm where he could read their strategy and anticipate their moves. Constantly pivoting, and fully aware of the princess, he battled on. For each wolf that fell, another took its place. His newly healing shoulder and side felt the exertion but Kai kept up his battle. Gradually, the enemy's numbers decreased.

The beasts no longer came in as close, instead leaping and then falling back as if they hit an invisible barrier. Kai's blade continued to slash and cut unimpeded, but the wyrwolves could not get near him. He wondered if Jeniah was somehow responsible.

The last wyrwolf died. Silence fell, almost as tangible as the noise of the battle. Kai waited, breathing hard, for further sounds of attack, but none came. He lowered his arm, calmed his heart, and pulled Jeniah close. Wrapping his arms around her, he let her softness soothe him.

"You did it," she murmured.

As his breathing slowed and his muscles unclenched, he lifted a corner of his mouth. "We did it. Thanks for watching my back." Then another thought struck him. "I wonder why your chayim didn't come."

Jeniah's brow furrowed in concentration. "I can't feel her any longer. I think she's bound to Arden."

"But we left Arden weeks ago."

"I think it has to do more with natural barriers rather than political lines. I sensed a kind of parting from her a few days ago when we passed through that last valley."

Kai nodded, disappointed at the loss of their silent guardian.

<hr />

Jeniah's gaze fixed on the castle crowning a rocky hill, surrounded by several tiers of walls in a pentagon around the castle. A high tower sat at each corner. The castle itself was a large, sprawling structure made of gray stone, rough-hewn and without any adornment. The walls were at least four times the thickness of Arden's walls. The fortress lacked the grace and beauty of Arden's architecture, but was functional and clearly impenetrable.

"Once we reach the city, we will go directly to confer with the king. It will be his decision as to what Darbor can offer you in the way of sanctuary."

Jeniah had been so focused on reaching Darbor that she hadn't thought of what would happen once she arrived. She was completely at the mercy of the king. Darbor and Arden were staunch allies. The Darborian king's mother had been the former princess of Arden, and his daughter Karina had married Jeniah's brother Aven. The king of Darbor and her father had been friends since boyhood, often hunting together. Still, there was no guarantee that King Farai would grant her sanctuary. Would he view her as a burden, an unnecessary risk? Darbor was a large and powerful country with nothing to fear from the Hanorans, but Jeniah doubted any leader would want to create animosity with the Hanoran's war-loving leader.

"What do you think his reaction will be?" she asked Kai with some trepidation.

"I cannot speak for the king."

"Will he be angry that I've come?"

He turned to look back at her. "No, of course not. He will welcome you." Then he added with pride, "Do not be concerned, Princess. The king of Darbor has no reason to fear Hanore."

As they neared the castle, Kai slowed Braygo. "There's a secret entrance that leads into tunnels below the city and up into the castle. I had planned on getting you in through the city that way. But if you think you can shield us long enough, we'll ride in through the castle gates."

"I can do it," she replied confidently.

"You should probably blur us both until I can confer with the king. My arrival might be enough to tip off a spy watching for you."

Jeniah nodded, surprised at her own confidence. "No one will even notice us."

They rode up to the city wall and through the open gates. Several alert sentinels stood guard but barely glanced at the peasants and their pack animal who passed by. Jeniah smiled. This was getting too easy.

The gates opened to a large tunnel. The tunnel, about thirty hand spans long, led to another set of gates.

"Are all the walls this thick?" she asked.

"They are. All the way around the city."

"Arden needs walls this strong. I wonder how long it would take to build some like this."

"I couldn't say."

The next set of gates stood open. They too were guarded, and again, the sentries paid them no attention.

Kai grinned. "That was my closest friend and he barely glanced at me."

Jeniah turned to look at Kai, thinking how little she truly knew about this man. He had a life here that she knew nothing about. She wondered if she would even see him now that his mission to bring her to Darbor was accomplished. The idea of living in a strange land without a friend left her unsettled, and the thought of not seeing Kai every day opened up a hollow ache in her heart.

They passed through the city streets. Everything had been laid out as if on a grid, engineered with straight lines. It was efficient and symmetrical but austere, without any thought for beauty. It was, however, clean and orderly.

Kai reined at the gates surrounding the castle proper. "The gates remain locked at all times, and one must either be expected or have clearance to enter. I'll have to reveal myself if we go in this way. But there's another way in."

He rode around the side of the castle wall, away from the main gate. He stopped in front of an expanse of stone wall.

Jeniah eyed the solid wall dubiously. "A hidden entrance?"

Kai nodded. After they dismounted, Kai looked up at a sentry patrolling the top of the wall.

"He can't see us," Jeniah assured him. "We're completely invisible." It was odd to her how confidently she knew this.

Kai traced strange markings carved into the face of the cliff, carefully going over each graceful line and curve.

"What are those?" she asked when he finished.

"They are called runes—primitive writings."

He spoke strange words. Cracks appeared around the stones where there had been solid mortar a moment ago. Jeniah stared mutely as the cracks widened and formed the outline of a door. He placed each hand on the wall and pressed. A slight scraping noise answered, and the stone door swung inward, revealing an empty room. Kai stepped through the door and paused, listening, before lighting a torch in a sconce. Once they were inside, he pushed the stone door closed and pressed a rune carved in the door. Again, he spoke words of another language that caused the cracks to disappear.

"How did you do that?" she asked in wonder.

"It's an ancient magic, placed here generations ago to protect the royal family."

"Magic?"

"It's completely benign, with no price to pay and no inherent abilities as a magic-user required," he reassured her quickly. "All one must do is touch the runes and repeat the proper words. Your ability to blur is a form of magic, is it not?"

Jeniah knew Darborians were superstitious, but she had always believed the magic they accepted was only myth. She had heard of ancient dark magicians who tore the land asunder and caused the Great Wars, and that the Hanoran king practiced a portion of their dark art. She'd also heard that the Darborians accepted mages. Kai seemed to accept it as commonplace.

"Yes," she confessed reluctantly. "I believe blurring is magic. That's why I never told anyone about it. I feared its source was dark, although my chayim and my mother said otherwise."

"From my youth, I've been taught that magic is neither dark nor light, but rather a tool to be used. A magic-user is either light or dark, not the magic itself."

Jeniah stared at the nearly verbatim repetition of her mother's words. Her heart whispered that Kai spoke the truth. She smiled, feeling lighter as she let go of the last vestiges of fear and doubt she had carried for years. "I can't tell you how liberating that is."

After tying up Braygo, Kai untacked him, rubbed him down, and covered him with a blanket. "Let's hope no one finds him before we get back."

"I don't think I can blur him if he's out of my sight."

"It's all right. This room doesn't look well-used."

He led her to a door opposite their entrance and turned back to her. "Blur. We may meet someone along the way."

She projected the image of plain servants over them. Beyond the inner door lay a wide corridor lit with smokeless lamps. Kai led her through the corridor, passing a few servants along the way, and around a corner to a door.

"The king's chambers," he explained. "We're deep inside his private quarters, which is why there are no guards here. They are all outside the main doors." He knocked boldly.

Jeniah withdrew her magic from around Kai so his king would know him.

"Enter!" came a command from inside the door.

Inside sat a man about the same age as Jeniah's father, but there the similarities ended. A trifle shorter, he resembled a barrel with a jovial face. His clothing was much less formal than her father's, and his only adornment was a medallion around his neck.

Bowing his head, Kai placed his fist first on his chest and then on his forehead.

"Kai, my boy!" With more dexterity than his form suggested, King Farai leaped from his chair to catch Kai by the forearm in a warrior's grip and then pulled him into an embrace. After slapping Kai on the back several times, the king pulled back, laughing and wiping his eyes. "At last, you've come! I had almost begun to fear the worst." Then with a curious look toward Jeniah, he asked, "You brought someone along?"

Kai's eyes darted about the room.

"You may speak freely, here, Kai. This room is completely secure."

Kai nodded. "Your Majesty, may I present Princess Jeniah of Arden."

She stopped blurring, pushed back her hood, and sank into a courtly curtsy.

The king's eyes widened but he recovered quickly. "Your Highness." He stepped forward, kissed her hand, and looked her directly in the eye. "You look so much like your mother. Please accept my deepest condolences for your loss. Your father was a great man and a dear friend."

"Thank you, Your Majesty." She inclined her head.

"I grieve for the loss of my daughter as well," he added quietly.

"It was a privilege to know her, Your Majesty."

The king turned back to Kai. "I had heard the rumors about the princess but I didn't put much stock in them. I figured they were either started by the Ardeenes to give them hope of being freed from the Hanorans someday, or by the Hanorans to give them an excuse to terrorize both Arden and Lariath searching for her. Now that I know that you were with her, I can see how it could be possible for her to escape."

He ran a hand through his thinning gray hair, making it stand on end. The Darborian King looked more like a grizzled war veteran than a regal ruler. "The kingdoms are outraged at the Hanorans' actions. I didn't imagine even Rheged would be capable of such barbarism."

As the king's eyes fell upon Jeniah, his face softened. "I'm glad you're both here. First, you must eat and rest. My impulse is to keep you locked away for your protection, Princess, but I do not wish you to feel that you are a prisoner. I will assign two of my own personal bodyguards to you. They will remain with you at all times until this is settled. I would like to believe that there are no spies within Darbor, but I would be foolish to count on that. You will need an alias, as well." King Farai smiled, taking her hand into his. "My dear Princess, I hope that you will consider this your home until Arden is freed."

She looked up into his kind eyes. "Thank you, Your Majesty. I'm very grateful."

Kai spoke. "Your Majesty, do you think she should stay with someone outside the castle? It might be less conspicuous."

The king stared at her, his thumb stroking his chin. "I'm reluctant to introduce any sort of intrigue. Those often have a way of playing out for the worst. And I prefer her to be kept here in the castle proper. Keeping your anonymity will be impossible, Princess." He studied her face while sadness touched his expressive mouth. "At times such as these, I very much miss my queen."

The king continued to study Jeniah as he thought. "Hmm. You have obviously Tiraian features. Anyone who travels would see that instantly, so we might as well say right from the start that you are Tiraian to avoid speculation that you might be the missing Ardeene princess." He clicked his tongue if he were debating the details of the plan in his mind.

"Your Majesty." Jeniah moistened her lips. "I'm able to appear as other than I am." She paused. Telling Kai had been much easier than telling this virtual stranger. "I call it blurring. It's a form of matriarchal magic. I can't do it for more than a few hours, but I can make myself appear as a serving maid, or a lady in waiting, or even a tree or a piece of furniture."

The king's face lit up in obvious pleasure. "Truly? Ah, that's how you arrived so quietly. That is a unique ability. Lady Zayla is a shape-shifter, but she must remain in similar size and cannot blend in that effectively. The high priestess is an empath and a prophetess with a great deal of magic. I must arrange a meeting. Otherwise, she will pester me. Perhaps she can help you discover other abilities you don't yet recognize. It could be of great value to your people."

"I would like that, Your Majesty."

"Meanwhile, since you cannot remain in disguise indefinitely, we must still find you a new identity." He tapped his chin. "You were visiting your distant cousin, the queen of Arden, when Hanore attacked. We will introduce you as Lady . . ."

"Illané?" Jeniah supplied. It was the name of a favorite heroine in a Tiraian story she had read repeatedly since her early childhood.

"Very well, Lady Illané." The king inclined his head. "And the reason you came all this way with Kai is because . . ."

Jeniah could almost hear the gears spinning inside his head.

His gaze moved from her to Kai. His eyes danced. "Because you and he fell in love while you were both visiting Arden and have decided to marry." He snorted and turned to look at

Kai. "Although, with your reputation, some people might have difficulty believing that." He chuckled while Kai managed to look properly offended.

"Sire, my reputation has been grossly exaggerated."

"Yes, I'm sure," the king replied dryly. "Do you agree to my plan?"

Instantly enjoying the intrigue, as well as the idea of pretending to be promised to the handsome man for whom she was already developing strong feelings, Jeniah looked back at Kai.

"As you wish, Your Majesty," Kai replied as if the king had given an order to call a meeting with the advisors, his face perfectly impassive. "Although I fear she will draw unwelcome attention, even with a new identity."

"We can use that to our advantage. Anyone seeking her will expect us to keep her secret, hidden, not out in the open. In fact, we'll start a rumor of our own. It wasn't the princess who escaped, but the prince, and he's here, somewhere in Darbor, hidden safely away where you have put him."

Kai paused and then nodded.

King Farai turned to her. "Princess, do you agree?"

Jeniah looked up at him in wonder. The king actually sought her permission, rather than simply advising her of his decision. Perhaps it was only a courtesy, but to have her opinion considered by a king was an unprecedented honor. "I've no objections, Your Majesty. But is it appropriate for us to carry on a ruse of this kind?" It had occurred to her that she might be required to play the part in every way.

"As long as you do not mind being seen frequently with Sir Kai, dining, dancing, and so forth. Any further display of affection in public is purely optional." His eyes twinkled.

"It might avert speculation," Kai offered, his body rigid with tension, his expression stony.

Only the touch of quiet resignation in his voice gave any indication of emotion. Jeniah frowned. Something bothered him or he wouldn't be shielded so tightly.

"Very well, Your Highness. I will behave as though I'm about to marry Kai," Jeniah said, wondering at the fluttering of her heart. It wasn't as if it were true, but she decided to enjoy her role. However, she would feel better about it if Kai wasn't so guarded. What were his misgivings?

They left the same way they entered the castle, even riding all the way back out to the outer city gates while Jeniah blurred them. Riding in front of Kai, she felt the familiar warmth of his body. And she felt his tension.

"You're opposed to us posing as betrothed?" she ventured.

"No. I agreed to it."

"You are not happy about it."

"I've no reason to object."

Clearly, he was not willing to discuss his feelings, but Jeniah's instincts screamed that something troubled him deeply. Her safety? No, Kai's carefully guarded distress stemmed from a more personal nature. She wondered if the enigmatic Kai would ever trust her with his thoughts, however deeply hidden.

⊙ӝᴈ⫷ⵜ ⫸ᴈ⫷ⵜᴈⵜᴈ⊙

A league outside the castle, they rode Braygo down the main highway until they reached a bend in the road that blocked the castle from view. In the deepening dusk, shadows lengthened and the sky was awash with color.

"It's time to reveal ourselves to the guards." Kai's voice belied his misgivings.

Jeniah removed the illusion and they retraced their steps, cantering directly up to the main gate. Guards at the outer city gate recognized Kai immediately, and many called out friendly greetings. In response, Kai gave them a very military salute, but he grinned as he called them by name. Inside the wall, they continued through the city to the castle proper and entered those gates as well, passing another set of sentinels.

Kai helped Jeniah dismount, and a servant came to lead Braygo to the stables. Kai put his hand under Jeniah's elbow as he guided her toward the main castle doors.

In moments, they were surrounded by soldiers gripping Kai's arm and pummeling him on the back, enthusiastically welcoming him home in their charming, lilting Darborian accents. Kai slid his arm around Jeniah and pulled her into the protective shelter of his arm as he greeted them.

A golden-haired knight with a wide, boyish smile rushed up to them. "You made it!" he said with a whoop. "I knew you would. You always manage to beat the odds."

Kai's face lit up. "Garhren."

The knight pulled him in for a brief hug and a hearty slap on the back. "It's good to see you in one piece, Kai." He shook his head, his voice sobering.

Kai exchanged a meaningful look with him and then turned to Jeniah. "My lady, may I present Garhren Ravenwing, knight in the Home Guard, and all-around troublemaker. Garhren, this is Lady Illané of Tirai."

Garhren's eyes fixed boldly upon Jeniah's face and traveled downward to make a thorough appraisal. He bowed deeply. "My lady, I'm your humble servant." He turned to Kai with a raise of his eyebrows and flashed a wolfish grin.

Kai rolled his eyes and clapped his friend's shoulder. "Garhren, I need to speak with the king, but I'll come find you later."

"Good. I just got off duty. I'll buy you a grog."

Word of Kai Darkwood's safe return spread quickly, bringing

throngs of people out to meet him in a sort of impromptu parade. The king came out to meet him at the front steps of the castle. Kai kneeled, bowed his head, and placed his fist first on his chest and then on his forehead, a gesture of respect only offered to the rightful king. Beside him, Jeniah sank into a curtsy. King Farai greeted Kai as enthusiastically as he had in his private chambers, giving no indication that they had already spoken.

Kai grandly presented Jeniah. "May I present Lady Illané of Tirai, a cousin of the late queen of Arden. Lady Illané has agreed to wed me, and I seek your blessing on our betrothal."

The king beamed. "Welcome to Darbor, Lady Illané." He cheerfully gave them his blessing and then called for servants to lead the weary travelers away.

At the threshold to the bedchamber assigned to Jeniah, Kai looked in and made a visual sweep of the room. A young girl with large, brown eyes waited inside. Kai nodded to her and made a swift gesture to the trailing guards, who immediately took position in the corridor on either side of the door.

Kai squeezed the princess's hand. "I'll leave you to rest."

She nodded and felt oddly lost when he left.

"Welcome, my lady," the lady-in-waiting greeted her warmly. "My name is Lavena, and I'm honored to serve you."

"Thank you, Lavena."

"I understand you have traveled a great distance. You must be very fatigued."

Jeniah nodded. "To be sure."

"I'll have dinner brought to you on a tray in your room. I'm sure you want to bathe first."

"That would be wonderful!" Jeniah instantly liked Lavena's gentle, nurturing manner.

Lavena opened the door to a closet, from which she retrieved various articles of clothing and small jars and put them into a bag.

"If you'll follow me, my lady, I'll show you to the bathhouse."

Bathing in Darbor was a unique experience. The castle, Lavena informed her, had been built over a natural hot spring that provided an unlimited supply of fresh warm water. People went into a special bathhouse, which was divided inside into several different rooms. In some rooms, many people bathed together socially with much talk and laughter. Others, like Jeniah, bathed in privacy with only an attendant on hand to assist. Jeniah lay back against the side of the large tub, reveling in the comforting feel of swirling water as it eased the soreness out of her muscles and made her truly warm for the first time in ages.

"I never fully appreciated how lovely it is to be clean," Jeniah murmured as she stretched languidly.

Drowsy from the bath, Jeniah stood while Lavena dried her and dressed her in silken undergarments, a night dress, and a luxurious robe. The slippers were too big, but she curled her toes to keep them on as she followed Lavena through the castle corridors. Back in her room, Jeniah yawned so often that she could barely eat the hot meal placed in front of her. Lavena tucked her in bed, and Jeniah drifted off to sleep, warm and contented. Yet the absence of Kai's arms around her left her strangely alone and incomplete.

Chapter Fourteen

*E*xhausted from their long and difficult journey, Jeniah slept late into the next day. Lavena must have been hovering nearby, waiting for signs of life, because the moment Jeniah sat up in bed, the handmaiden came in.

"Are you feeling better, my lady?" she asked cheerfully.

Jeniah stretched luxuriously. "I feel like a new person."

Lavena threw open the window coverings. The glass windowpanes were thicker and much more difficult to see through than the windows in Arden, but the sun shone in, flooding the room with light. Another maid came in with a tray of food.

Lavena held a robe for Jeniah to don before she seated her at the table. "You slept past the morning and midday meals. You must be very hungry."

"Indeed, I am." The food looked unlike anything Jeniah had ever seen, but she ate hungrily, enjoying a hot, filling meal.

"There's to be a feast and a ball in honor of your arrival and Sir Kai's safe return," said Lavena.

"I look forward to it." Jeniah curled up in the large armchair and sipped hot, spiced wine from a carved wooden cup.

"Sir Kai looked in on you twice," Lavena informed her with a smile. "He was concerned about you, but I assured him you merely slept. Arden is a goodly distance away, and if you fled during the invasion, you must have come without any comforts."

Jeniah nodded, but with the sweet wine slipping comfortingly down her throat and loosening her limbs, the horrors of that night, and the hardships she had faced since, seemed a mere dream. Only Kai and her growing feelings for him seemed real.

After Jeniah had finished eating, Lavena offered to take her to the bathhouse again, and Jeniah enthusiastically agreed. After the bath, Lavena dressed her in silken undergarments and then went to work on Jeniah's hands and feet. The maid trimmed, shaped, and buffed Jeniah's nails and rubbed rich cream into her rough and cracked skin. Then she lowered a gown over her head, fretting over the fit of the borrowed gown and assuring Jeniah that she would alter others for her immediately until the royal dressmaker could come and measure her for her own wardrobe.

As Lavena fastened the buttons down the back, Jeniah admired the deep blue-green gown with a much lower neckline than Ardeene fashions would have ever permitted. It showed off her neck and shoulders, making them look graceful.

Lavena plaited Jeniah's hair in several thin braids and wound them around the back of her head. The style and weight of her hair made Jeniah feel grown up.

Lavena pulled some tiny strands from the pile of braids to curl in tendrils beside Jeniah's face and around her neck, skimming her shoulders. Jeniah stared into the mirror, barely recognizing her own reflection. Not only was she thinner, but she looked older, with a new air of wisdom and maturity in her face. The sheltered, innocent girl no longer existed. Wearing the elegant gown and hairstyle, Jeniah saw that she did, indeed, bear a startling resemblance to her mother. It was a bit unsettling.

"Are you not pleased, my lady?"

Jeniah laid her hand on the maid's arm and smiled. "Thank you, Lavena. I'm well pleased."

Lavena lowered her eyes. "It is not necessary to thank me, my lady. It is my pleasure to serve you."

"I hope I shall never take your assistance for granted. I haven't felt this grand in ages."

"You are beautiful, my lady," Lavena replied sincerely as she made a few final adjustments. "Even dressed as you were for the journey, you were lovely. Seeing you like this seems proper. There. Now you look perfect."

Having to dress and groom herself in a new land with unfamiliar styles and customs would have been difficult without knowledgeable help, and being waited upon seemed a great luxury. Impulsively, Jeniah hugged Lavena. The maid's arms went around her and she returned the embrace with an embarrassed smile.

When Lavena escorted Jeniah to the grand hall, Kai was already there. All the light in the room seemed to emanate from him. Jeniah's breath left her lungs and her pulse quickened. Was it possible that she had forgotten how handsome he was? Clean-shaven and wearing the clothes of a nobleman, he stood half a head taller than the men surrounding him. His dark hair shone in the lamplight. His black leggings emphasized his long, muscular legs, and his scarlet doublet over a white linen shirt made him look positively kingly.

Kai glanced around the room as if looking for someone, and Jeniah knew the moment he spotted her. With eyes that seemed to devour her, his gaze fixed upon her face, then moved slowly downward and back up again, approval and admiration shining clear. A smile touched his mouth and then broadened.

Jeniah's face warmed in pleasure under his unabashed stare. He moved deftly through the throng, avoiding the giggling ladies who vied for his attention, took her hand, and raised it to his lips. Her hand tingled from his touch.

"I don't think I can come up with a word to do you justice. 'Beautiful' seems pitifully inadequate."

Glowing from his compliment, Jeniah truly felt beautiful at that moment. Kai led her to the king's table.

King Farai stood. "My lady." He planted a fatherly kiss on her cheek. "My sons are unable to be here tonight. Tray is in Govia, and Janden is home with his wife, who recently bore him a son. My third grandson." His chest puffed.

Jeniah's lips twitched in amusement. Grandparents boasted so proudly of their grandchildren, one would think having them was the greatest feat a person could accomplish. "Congratulations, Your Majesty."

"Please." The king indicated the chair to his right.

Jeniah had never sat in a place of honor before and felt so overwhelmed that she found it difficult to speak. Kai sat directly across from her at the king's left.

"I hope you were made comfortable?" the king asked solicitously.

His easy manner helped her relax. "Yes, Your Majesty, thank you."

Kai's eyes never left Jeniah's face. "Did you enjoy the bathhouse?"

"Yes. A most unique and wonderful experience."

Dinner was served with less ceremony than was customary at Arden. Kai guided Jeniah gently and unobtrusively through the correct etiquette until she fell into a sort of rhythm. None of the food was recognizable, but the unusual flavor combinations were surprisingly delicious. Jeniah soon felt at ease in the presence of the king. He was a warm, cheerful man with a dry sense of humor, who displayed a true personal interest in Jeniah that she was certain had little to do with her future status as queen.

Before dinner had ended, Jeniah, Kai, and the king chatted comfortably together as if they were all dear friends. The king's fatherly affection for Kai was obvious, which endeared the king to Jeniah even more.

As the diners finished their meal, musicians began playing a dance tune. Jeniah watched the dancers file out to the floor as tables were cleared and moved against the walls. What surprised her was the position the dancers took with their partners. The man put a hand on the lady's waist while she rested her hand on his shoulder, their free hands clasped off to the side about shoulder height. In Arden, dancers only touched one hand and danced in small groups. The Darborian dance position seemed very intimate. After watching the dance sequence repeat, Jeniah understood the steps to the dance they performed and believed she could remember them if the occasion arose.

"Perhaps your betrothed would care to dance, Sir Kai?"

Jeniah turned to see the king nudge Kai and smile at him slyly.

"Uh, yes, sire." Kai cleared his throat, offered his arm to Jeniah, and in an exaggerated formal voice asked, "Lady Illané, would you care to dance?"

Jeniah gave him a smile designed to take his breath away and was not disappointed. "I would love to dance." Wickedly, she turned her head and scanned the crowd of dancers. "Can you recommend anyone?" she asked with almost believable innocence.

The king chuckled.

Kai pressed hand over his heart. "You wound me, my lady."

She laughed and then in a demure voice replied, "Sir Kai, I would be delighted to dance with you. Thank you for your kind offer."

He winked at her. "That's better." Then, to the king, "I think the lady has an incisive sense of humor."

The king grinned. "My boy, a woman with spirit is more diverting than a woman who is meek and obedient. Although" —he rubbed his chin— "spirited women are more trouble."

"I agree."

Jeniah glared at them both, then said sweetly to Kai, "Are we going to dance or not?"

Again Kai offered his arm and bowed low. "My lady, I await thee."

Jeniah's smile was genuine as she rose and accepted his arm. On the dance floor, sudden shyness overcame her as Kai placed his hand on her waist and took her hand.

"My mother would have thought this scandalous," Jeniah murmured with a self-conscious smile.

"Ardeenes take morality to a new level."

"You don't approve of our morality?" she baited as she smiled up at him.

"I'm sure it has its benefits," Kai replied evasively.

Not wanting to spoil the evening or the lovely feeling of having his arm around her, she changed the subject. "You surprise me, sir. I didn't realize Sauraiis were instructed in the art of dance as well as weaponry."

"Years in court forced me to develop other skills."

"You do it very well."

"King Farai's late queen took a special interest in me when I first arrived and made sure I was taught such courtly manners, despite my resistance." Kai's stony expression softened. "I suppose she felt sorry for me and my backwards ways."

"Nonsense. You have a strong, confident bearing, and you dance with more grace than many noblemen."

His teeth flashed. "You didn't know me at fourteen."

Feeling light and very alive, Jeniah followed Kai's skillful lead. They released each other, took several steps to the side, and circled, touching with one hand. She loved the feel of his large, strong hand in hers as they faced each other, stepped back into the closed dance position, and began repeating the figure.

She looked up into his handsome, weather-beaten face. His rugged strength was real and unpretentious, his muscular arms and broad chest solid. Jeniah tingled in response to his nearness, his masculinity.

As she gazed at him, she realized that her feelings for him had surpassed friendly affection. At that instant, she freely and willingly gave him her heart, even sensing that he still shielded his against her. In time she would discover the cause of all those barriers and his need to protect his emotions. When she did, and when she found a way around the barriers, she would discover the Kai inside, the Kai she saw only in glimpses now. It would be difficult, but it would be worth it.

⚜

Kai was keenly aware of the stares of admiration that followed Jeniah everywhere she went. She was magnificent. He began to think that letting her roam the castle so openly, without blurring, had been a mistake. In fact, he dreaded the end of the dance when he would have to relinquish her hand.

"My lady, I know that this is not your Ascension Ceremony and dance, but I hope it can be something of a substitute," he said.

She wrinkled her nose in mock annoyance. "Well, I suppose if I can't be the center of attention, at least I'm dancing with the center of attention."

"I may be the one they are honoring, but you are drawing all of the eyes."

All too soon, the music ended, and a nobleman approached wearing clothing so exquisite and fine that a woman would envy the rich velvets and gilded lace.

Kai grimaced. "I do not wish to share you with anyone else, my lady, but Darborian dance etiquette demands I relinquish your hand to any who approaches you. And Lord Kavin is coming."

"And if I refuse?"

Kai sighed. "He'd be offended. He's a powerful lord. Offending him may not be the best idea."

When he reached them, the dandy put on a charming smile and bowed. "Sir Kai, I beg you to introduce me to your delightful lady."

Kai resisted the urge to growl at the pompous man. "My lady, may I present Lord Kavin. My lord, this is Lady Illané, my betrothed." He stressed the last two words as a warning to the man.

Jeniah sank into a graceful curtsy as Lord Kavin bowed with a flourish, giving no indication that he heard Kai's warning. "My lady, I beg you to honor me with a dance."

"The honor is mine, Lord Kavin." She accepted his outstretched hand.

With jealousy eating a hole in his stomach, Kai inclined his head and retreated. He took a seat near the dance floor, unable to keep his eyes off Jeniah. He clenched his jaw at the reminder that she belonged in this world of glitter and finery, this world that always made him feel like an awkward oaf. He didn't belong here, especially not with a future queen. He accepted a goblet from a passing tray and drank deeply.

Again he became aware of many other stares fixed upon the princess. He scanned the crowd and found the king's bodyguards, fully alert and keeping a close watch, already wearing the look of worship every man in Arden had worn. The princess created such a sensation that he wondered if the king's discarded idea of locking her away under guard would have been better. Kai sighed. It was too late now. Besides that, she would have been miserable in isolation.

As he tossed back the contents of his goblet, the corner of his eye caught a familiar figure. Steeling himself, Kai arranged his face in a neutral expression as he set down the goblet and turned to face Zayla.

"Welcome home, Kai," she murmured in a sultry voice as she reached him.

He looked down into the face of the beautiful, blond woman, who wore a red gown that flaunted her ample bosom and showed off her graceful neck and shoulders. He had almost forgotten her beauty.

"Zayla," he murmured in greeting.

Fire lurked in her eyes. "That's all you have to say to me? I thought you had been killed in Arden. Then I hear you're alive and back safely and you didn't bother to even come see me yourself!"

"You look beautiful as always." He gave her his most disarming smile.

Some of the anger left her eyes as she sank down in a chair beside him. She studied him and then said quietly, "I've missed you."

Kai kept his face impassive. "Zayla—"

"I know. When you left for Arden, you made it clear you were leaving me, too, and that when you came back, you would not be coming back to me. But you have to admit we were happy together. We can be again." There was a provocative lilt to her voice.

Kai thought back over their time together. Zayla had more substance than most of his former lovers, but she had started getting too close, and letting himself fall in love was not an option.

"I hear there was someone in Arden, too," she stated softly. Her casual tone failed to fully mask her jealousy.

Kai's eyes automatically flew to Jeniah, radiant as she danced and laughed with her current partner.

Zayla followed his gaze. "She's lovely. Rumor has it that you are going to wed her, but I knew it couldn't be true."

Kai had to draw upon his training to make his lie sound convincing in both voice and face, training that served him in more battles than just those fought with a weapon. "It's true."

Zayla stared at him in clear disbelief, then swallowed and said slowly, "I see. Well, she must be an extraordinary girl."

"She is," he replied truthfully. "I've never met anyone like her." He finally met Zayla's gaze, and at the hurt he saw there, he felt a sting of regret. "I'm sorry."

"No, don't. You made no promises, and I have no regrets. I knew from the beginning that our time together would be temporary and that I was a fool to hope otherwise." She stood. "Congratulations."

Kai watched Zayla leave, hating himself for lying to her. It had been difficult to part with her, yet even if he'd stayed in Darbor, he would have stopped seeing her. Their relationship had reached a crossroads, and leaving her was the only way out, the only way to protect his heart from a terrifying vulnerability.

Then he thought of Jeniah, and the beautiful and passionate Zayla faded in comparison. He searched the couples and found her dancing with a new partner. As though called to her side, he wound through the dancers to Jeniah and whisked her away before the final note of the dance music ended.

"Forgive me, sir," he said with barely a glance at the startled nobleman. "I have this next dance."

Jeniah's face was flushed from the vigorous dance and her eyes sparkled. "Of course, Sir Kai. I haven't forgotten."

Not certain what he would have done if she hadn't played along, he possessively wound her hand through his arm.

"Why Sir Kai, I hadn't thought you capable of jealousy," she teased.

But her comment hit too close and he stiffened. "Merely playing the part," he ground out under his breath.

The light in her eyes faded and she looked away. "Of course."

Kai mentally kicked himself, then laid his hand over Jeniah's where it rested on his arm. After a searching gaze that made him feel as if he'd entered a melee without his armor, she turned her hand over and squeezed his. He turned in relief as his friend Garhren approached.

Garhren flashed a lopsided, boyish grin. "I came to see if your betrothed has changed her mind about you now that she sees you in better lighting."

"I've been deliberately keeping to the shadows for fear of that very thing, my friend," Kai replied mournfully.

Garhren's gaze swept over Jeniah. "My lady, I had heard Tiraians were beautiful, but you have surpassed all of my imaginations." He bowed low and kissed her hand. With a sidelong glance at Kai, he added. "Although, I question your judgment regarding men." He ducked, laughing, as Kai took a playful swing at him. "Good to be back?"

"It is," Kai replied wholeheartedly. "Not much appears to have changed while I was gone."

Garhren looked offended. "There have been different women."

Kai chuckled. "I wasn't discussing your romantic pursuits, Gar."

Garhren shrugged. "What else is there? Yours have obviously changed. And improved." He grinned rakishly at Jeniah. "Forgive us. We've been through much together, not all of it honorable."

"Really? Please explain." Jeniah cast a sly smile at Kai.

Kai groaned. "Believe me when I say you do not want to know."

"Dance with me, my lady," Garhren said, "and I shall regale you with tales designed to change your mind."

Jeniah smiled. "You may tell me anything you like, Sir Garhren, but you shall not change my mind. I'm immovable. However, my next dance is promised to my betrothed."

Kai resisted the urge to puff out his chest. Instead, he waved her off. "Go ahead. I'll wait." He suppressed another ugly flair of jealousy as his best friend led Jeniah away. He did, however, claim the next dance, and the one after that. He remained by her side all evening, greeting the knights and nobility who came to speak with them. He introduced her to more people than she would probably remember. By the time the celebration came to a close, he became so comfortable playing the part of a betrothed man that he almost began to believe it. As the lights burned low and the music played softly, her nearness stirred an ache in him, and he wondered how he could ever let her out of his arms.

Then the king rose and bade them all a good night, marking the end of the festivities. Kai escorted Jeniah to her room, with her guards following at a respectful distance.

"Kai," she said with a glance back at the trailing guards. She lowered her voice. "When you are with me, they are unnecessary."

"I take no chances with your safety, my lady. Neither does the king."

"You are better protection than a whole regiment of men. No one else could have brought me here unharmed the way you did."

"I gave you my word that I would not fail you."

"I know. That's what I mean. As long as you are here, nothing could happen to me."

Kai stopped walking and gazed deeply into her eyes. The affection he saw there was intoxicating. He took a step closer, his heart pounding wildly. Every nerve in his body came alive.

He leaned toward her, craving her touch, his lips demanding a taste of hers. She trembled as her lips parted. She lifted her chin and leaned toward him. He brushed his thumb over her lower lip, fascinated with its fullness, then trailed his fingers along her smooth cheek as he bent over her.

Their lips met. Hers were amazingly warm, soft, pliant. He inhaled her breath spiced with sweet wine and breathed in her fragrance of perfumed soap and oils, combined with a scent that belonged uniquely to her. Her hand curled against his chest and she moved closer. He pulled her in, pressing her soft curves against him. Her kiss was unpracticed, but so willing. She received him and gave more in return. Kai's very soul stirred. The darkness within shuddered and drew back, making room for light that hadn't touched his heart since . . .

What was he doing?

He pulled away and let out a shaky breath. Jeniah slowly opened her eyes.

He took a step back. "Forgive me," he whispered.

She blinked in bewilderment. "Kai—"

"Please, don't say anything, Your Highness. My behavior was inappropriate."

"'Your Highness' again, is it?" she said quietly. "I thought we had gone beyond that."

Making no response, Kai carefully kept emotion out of his expression as he continued walking with her down the corridor.

At the door to her chambers, he bowed and turned to go, but she caught his arm.

"Kai."

He maintained his invisible armor. "Good night, Lady Illané. Sleep well."

Kai bolted down the hallway, trying to escape the fire in his blood. He wanted to fight, to work off this frustration that threatened to drive him mad. He didn't know how much longer he could restrain himself, but kissing her had only made it worse.

No. He *must* resist her. Completely.

As desire burned in his veins, his heart thudded wildly and he thought he would go mad. Instinctively, he went to the training room. This he could understand. He lit the lamps. Because of the hour, he didn't find Garhren or some other poor soul to vent his energy on. He tore off his doublet and shirt, then lifted the enormous two-handed broad sword in the armory. He ran though every training exercise he had ever learned and began to slay invisible enemies.

Kissing Jeniah had sent him flying into the realm of beauty and love. Then reality set in. Having held her like that, tasted her, he knew he was totally and completely hers. Somehow, she had touched the broken pieces of his heart and made them feel again.

He could not slay these demons. He had no defense against the tireless enemy that threatened to destroy him.

When his bruised ribs throbbed and he could no longer raise his arms, he dropped his sword. The sound of metal on stone echoed in the empty room. His anger and madness faded, leaving only quiet sorrow.

Chapter Fifteen

In Darbor Castle, the morning meal was an informal affair. People simply came and went at will and helped themselves out of trenchers that servants brought out periodically. Every few minutes, a new trencher appeared filled with fresh, hot food for the newest batch of diners to feast upon.

All around them, green plants and glorious flowers of every description grew in pots and planters, a stark contrast to the white, frozen landscape outside the glass wall. Jeniah could almost forget that they were indoors instead of in a garden in the middle of spring. She bid Lavena good morning, then spied Kai at a table alone near the wall of windows. He stood at her approach.

"Good morning, my love," Kai sang out with false cheer as he kissed her hand.

Jeniah knew the stoic man she loved would avoid discussing the previous night and the obstacles between them. For now, she would allow him that.

"Good morning, Kai. How did you sleep?"

"Well, thank you. You?"

"Wonderfully." She watched him shrewdly, and even though he kept his eyes averted, it was obvious that he had gotten very little sleep, if any. Sleep had eluded her most of the night as well. It was during the quiet, early-morning hours that Jeniah had begun to understand. She knew now that Kai's feelings for her did run deeper than a duty to protect her. Yet his honor would forever stand in the way of a marriage between them. It was almost unheard of for royalty—especially an heir to the throne—to marry a commoner. Kai would never cross those boundaries. And although his heritage did not matter to Jeniah, tradition was an unyielding master, and Kai followed an exceptionally strict code of honor.

There was also a second wall of resistance inside Kai, one she had first glimpsed back in Arden. It caused the momentary flashes of pain to enter his eyes when his guard was down. Clearly, something had hurt him deeply, and he was determined to not repeat it. Which obstacle would prove the most difficult to overcome, Jeniah could not guess, but as she watched him, her love for him grew. She vowed to make whatever sacrifices she must to be with him.

"This is amazing," she commented. "I've never seen anything like it. A room with glass walls? It's wondrous."

Kai grinned. "I thought you would enjoy it. I believe you will find that there are many new diversions here. I hope to be able to introduce you to a few of the better ones."

"I look forward to that, sir," she replied genuinely.

"I hope you will forgive me, my lady, but I will be somewhat absent today as I'm required in council. However, ladies often gather here, and I know they would welcome you."

The king had told the princess she would be filled in on everything regarding decisions to help free Arden. In order to protect her identity, this would occur in a private meeting. Not even the elders or chief advisors had been advised of her presence.

"Can we meet later and continue my defense lessons?" She missed working on her newly acquired skills almost as much as she missed spending time alone with Kai. Perhaps the lessons would bring back the Kai she knew during the journey, before he became so closed up.

Kai's eyebrows pulled together. "It might raise suspicions. Do you think it is wise to do things that may draw attention?"

Jeniah's shoulders slumped. If her mother was an indication, no Tiraian lady would consider learning the ways of a warrior. Going against tradition might be a flaw in Jeniah's masquerade, which could cause someone to question her identity and discover the truth.

"No, I suppose not," she answered quietly. Then she brightened. "But I could blur and look like a squire with an easily forgettable face."

Kai considered. "I'll see what I can do." Then he stood up and called to two young women, "Ladies."

One of the girls looked as though she would faint at the honor of being addressed by the strikingly handsome Sir Kai, but the other hurried over to him, pulling her friend along. They both wore lavishly embroidered gowns cut low in front.

When Kai put his hand at the small of Jeniah's back, the simple contact sent swirling warmth through her. "This is Lady Illané of Tirai, my betrothed. Would you please introduce her to the other ladies?"

"Of course, Sir Kai," gushed the bravest of the pair. She turned to Jeniah. "Welcome, Lady Illané. I'm pleased to meet you. I'm Nali and this is Carrine."

Carrine never managed to drag her eyes off Kai, who seemed completely unaware of his effect on her.

"We are going to a poetry reading," Nali continued. "Won't you join us?"

Jeniah put on her most gracious smile, although she would have been more enthusiastic if they had invited her to go riding.

"I would be delighted, thank you."

Kai bowed to them. "I hope you enjoy yourselves." He took Jeniah's hand and kissed it. "My lady."

Carrine watched him go. "Sir Kai is so handsome."

"You are most fortunate, Lady Illané," added Nali.

Jeniah couldn't help answering a bit wickedly, "Yes, he's not as dull as others I know. I suppose he's better than some."

They both stared. "If I searched the world far and wide I would never find anyone as perfect as he," declared Carrine.

Jeniah only smiled, but she silently agreed.

After Nali introduced Jeniah to the other ladies, they all went to a separate sitting room ,where chairs and benches had been set up facing the fireplace. Jeniah's lady-in-waiting, Lavena, arrived with several others. When the appointed hour arrived, the poetry reading began.

As the minstrel began reciting the poem, Jeniah closed her eyes and listened to the words. The poem was about a forbidden love, a couple who defied the odds and sacrificed everything to be together, only to have their love discovered and exploited. Eventually, they conquered all, and they spent the rest of their lives together. The poem was beautifully read, and when it ended, there was not a dry eye in the room. As the attendees sprang to their feet to express their appreciation, the minstrel bowed.

Jeniah noticed a lovely, tall woman with hair the color of spun gold and a figure that made Jeniah feel childlike. Drawn to the woman, Jeniah made her way toward her, but as she neared, she was met with an icy stare. Undaunted, Jeniah approached.

Lavena appeared at Jeniah's side. Indicating the blond women, she said, "Lady Illané of Tirai, may I present Lady Zayla."

Zayla inclined her head in greeting, eyeing Jeniah coolly.

Jeniah smiled, hoping to thaw the ice. "Lady Zayla."

"Lady Illané. You must feel most strange here in Darbor."

Jeniah got the double meaning but chose to ignore it. "It is different here in Darbor, but lovely."

Zayla nodded, her eyes raking over Jeniah. With a contemptuous smile, she turned to speak with another lady, clearly dismissing Jeniah.

Puzzled and hurt, Jeniah glanced inquiringly at the lady-in-waiting who shrugged and offered an apologetic grimace.

Later, as the ladies sewed together, Jeniah made a point to seat herself near Lady Zayla. "My lady, you have the most beautiful hair I've ever seen," she said sincerely.

"Thank you," Lady Zayla replied stiffly, her needle nearly flying. Without looking up she said, "I understand you and Kai are to wed."

"Yes, we are." She believed with all her heart that someday that would be true.

"I'm surprised to hear that."

"Oh?"

"He prefers women, not little girls."

Feeling color rise to her face, Jeniah swallowed and answered deliberately, "I may not be as mature as you are, Zayla, but I am of age."

Zayla's gaze slid over Jeniah dismissively. "He's probably six or seven years older than you. Well, no matter, as long as he's happy." Her voice was heavy with forced civility. She stood. "Excuse me, ladies."

Lavena turned to Jeniah after Zayla's exit. "You mustn't blame her, my lady. She and Sir Kai were romantically involved for over a year before he left for Arden. There was much speculation that he had chosen her."

"He shields his heart too carefully," interjected an older woman.

Jeniah searched Lavena's face. "Was he truly a philanderer?"

The older woman answered, "It seemed that way when he first arrived in the castle. He certainly made a sensation—young and handsome and terribly gifted, a Sauraii and then a knight all before he was even of age. Almost every young lady in Darbor openly pursued him. Not many young men his age would resist all the offers of companionship he received, not that anyone expected him to refuse. He still gets them, I'm sure, but he has grown up. He's had to. He takes matters of love seriously now. Perhaps too seriously. You must be a very exceptional young lady to have won the heart and hand of Sir Kai."

Jeniah knew there was more, but the woman seemed disinclined to divulge it. "I'm fortunate to have him," she responded fervently. "Truly, I would be lost without him."

Kai arrived then and motioned to her. As the ladies giggled and chattered about young love, Jeniah arose, excused herself, and went to him.

Kai kissed her cheek and whispered, "The high priestess has asked to see you."

Jeniah could not help the smile or the warmth that traveled through her at his touch. Knowing he only kissed her cheek for the benefit of those watching did not diminish her pleasure. They linked arms and leisurely walked as if they had nothing better to do than enjoy one another's company.

He took her to an obscure corner of the castle and up a winding stair inside a high tower. The walls of the tower had been carved and painted with vines and flowers, the workmanship exceeding anything Jeniah had ever seen. The ceiling bore mysterious carved runes. She and Kai climbed the stairs winding around the tower until they reached the top, where an archway bent over a curved door. The runes along the arch had been painted silver, making them appear to glow. The arched door shimmered and vanished, leaving an open entrance.

The moment she crossed the threshold, Jeniah knew she had stepped into the presence of a powerful being. A woman of indeterminate age stood in the center of the room, wearing multi-colored robes and adorned with several different lengths of decorative chains, like jewelry without any gems. Her long, dark hair hung loose like a cloak over her clothing.

"Thenisis, the high priestess," Kai introduced in a hushed voice.

Thenisis smiled and outstretched her hand. "Jeniah, future queen of Arden, you are most welcome here. Sir Kai, please remain, as this affects you as well."

The high priestess released Jeniah's hand. Then, with both hands, she made sweeping motions over the door, which shimmered and then appeared as a solid door again. Thenisis began removing her jewelry.

"The metals block my powers. They protect me from the barrage of emotions that often overwhelm me when I'm not wearing them. But now that I've sealed the door, I can tap into the life forces without drowning in others' emotions."

Jeniah wondered if her natural reluctance to wear jewelry sprang from this dampening effect on her own magic.

After seeing them comfortably seated, Thenisis took Jeniah by the hand again and looked deeply into her eyes. At first touch, Jeniah felt infused with light. Then she recognized the presence of the priestess inside her mind, hearing her thoughts, feeling her emotions. It seemed invasive and Jeniah stiffened. While similar to the way her chayim communicated, the priestess's mental contact seemed rougher than her chayim's whisper touch. Suddenly desperate for Kai's reassurance, she reached for him. His large hand enclosed hers. Emboldened by his touch, Jeniah resisted the urge to pull away from Thenisis.

The priestess waited until Jeniah's natural protective

inclinations hushed before probing deeper. This time, the mental contact no longer felt invasive as the priestess probed Jeniah's mind, seeking her secret, latent powers.

"You are chayim-bonded," the priestess murmured in wonder. Jeniah could hear her thoughts in her mind and knew that Thenisis articulated them for Kai's benefit.

Thenisis continued speaking. "There is much your chayim can teach you. Let her guide you as you ascend your throne." Jeniah saw brief images of her future coronation, a room filled with Ardeenes, herself crowned and sitting upon the throne.

"Is this what shall come to pass, or only a possibility?" Jeniah asked out loud for Kai's sake.

"It is your destiny. It shall come to pass if you do not fail."

Kai stirred. A dark emotion she could not quite identify rippled off him before he guarded it.

"And my magic?" Jeniah asked.

"You call it blurring, but it is a form of shape-shifting known as fading. Your fears blocked your power until you embraced your magic. One day soon, you will use your power to manipulate form, rather than create mere illusion. When you face your greatest enemy, you must reveal her illusions and the falsehood of her power. Your chayim must be with you when you face her, for she will strengthen you so that you can defeat your enemies. Alone, you will surely fail. Together, you may succeed."

The prophetess paused, probing deeper, and Jeniah felt her despair. "Terrible travails await you, worse than you have yet faced. Great evil combines against you. Remember who you are. Remember that you serve your people. Only when you are willing to sacrifice all, can you hope to succeed. But you must face your worst fears alone."

Stunned, Jeniah felt all the warmth leave her body. She'd already faced the destruction of her home, the loss of her family, and the difficult journey with its cold, fear, and hunger. What could possibly be worse?

Until that moment, the hardships she had suffered had been bearable because Kai had been with her. Yet, soon she must go on alone, without Kai. She nearly collapsed with dread.

Chapter Sixteen

Inside the king's council room, Kai clenched his hands, wishing he could enclose them around the neck of the pompous lord addressing the council. Seething in frustration, he tugged at the collar of his shirt.

Finally, unable to contain his aggravation, Kai leaped to his feet. "You fool. That's exactly what they're counting on."

At Kai's uncharacteristically impassioned outburst, the council members stared.

"Sir Kai, I understand how you feel, but—"

"Lord Kavin, with all due respect, you could not possibly understand how I feel. You were not there. They ravaged and murdered every woman they found. They killed children. It wasn't a war, it was a massacre! There was no declaration of war, no established battlefield. There was no time to assemble the knights or the army. The Hanorans simply swooped down on Arden City in the middle of the night and slaughtered hundreds of innocent people."

"Sir Kai, I've heard the reports," began the diplomat. He was so self-righteous and smug that Kai had to resist the urge to plant a fist into his face. "But diplomacy must be observed, and we must carefully weigh the consequences of our actions before we act. We cannot afford to be hasty."

"If you were there, you would not be so certain, you pompous—"

"Sir Kai, sit down," the king commanded. "We must resist arguing among ourselves. We must be united."

Kai dragged in a breath. "Yes, sire, of course. My apologies." He sent a withering glare at Lord Kavin.

Unruffled, Lord Kavin continued. "Your Majesty, I am not in any way condoning the Hanorans' actions. I'm simply trying to protect Darbor from suffering the casualties of war. We must always have options to consider."

"Thank you, Lord Kavin," said the king. "I agree that we must keep an open mind to all possibilities. But now that we know the Ardeene prince still lives and is safely hidden away in a secure location, we can justify taking action to free Arden and restore the rightful heir to the throne."

A chief advisor spoke. "Hanore would be foolish to consider threatening Darbor. Our army is much stronger and better trained than theirs."

The king nodded. "King Rheged faces imminent civil war with his own son. And with his people so divided, Rheged cannot afford to wage another war. The Hanoran prince promises a return to their old values and has attracted loyalists." The king's words hung as the council members considered. "I believe a short recess is in order."

There was a murmur of ascent as the council members rose from their seats and spoke among themselves. Kai jumped to his feet and began to pace.

"Kai, walk with me," King Farai said.

Kai fell into step with the king as they left the council chambers. Their footsteps echoed hollowly in the hallway.

"You look terrible," the monarch commented.

Kai gave him a rueful smile. His squire had carefully pressed

Kai's clothes and shone his boots, so he knew the king did not refer to his dress or grooming.

"Spend all night in the weapons room again last night?"

Kai glanced at the king. Little happened in the castle that escaped the king's knowledge, even Kai's personal life, apparently. He nodded glumly.

The king watched him shrewdly. "It's about your 'betrothed.'"

"Yes, sire."

"She obviously returns your feelings." The king studied his face. "What will you do?"

Tight-lipped, Kai said, "Restore her to her throne."

⊶⊰⊱⊷

Jeniah paused at the threshold of the king's private study, her hands clasped, hoping she showed more composure than she felt. King Farai added to a stack of papers that threatened to topple off the desk, then he stood and indicated a chair. "Come in, come in."

After closing the door, Jeniah sat across from him by the fire and waited expectantly.

"We've received word from our allies, Tirai and Lariath, who have pledged their assistance. Even Govia has agreed to help. He fears Hanore won't stop at Arden and will conquer every kingdom in the land. He has a valid point, although I don't believe they will try to expand so soon with their armies divided between Hanore and Arden. However, our allies stand ready. They stand by you."

"Has your ambassador of goodwill gone to pay his respects to the new king of Arden?" Jeniah could not keep the ire out of her voice at the idea of acting as if Darbor had accepted the new sovereign of Arden, King Rheged.

"My spies tell me the ambassador was well received, and that Captain Tarvok is keeping the rebellion going enough to ward off any suspicion of a major attack from outside."

Jeniah breathed a sigh of relief that the loyal captain of the guard was still alive and well. "What's our next step?"

"We wait for the allies to get into position."

She wished her studies had included battle tactics, or that she at least had been included in matters of state. In Arden, she had always been excluded from "affairs of men." After years of forced ignorance, it felt strange to be included in these discussions. If King Farai had been any less approachable, Jeniah might never have found the courage to open her mouth. He'd made it clear that as queen and the only living member of the monarchy, she was now instrumental in restoring Arden's freedom from Rheged's brutal military rule.

"Could we come up with some type of diversion to help Captain Tarvok's forces?"

Mild surprise crossed the king's face. "Actually, yes. We discussed that in council today. Rheged will probably be expecting retaliation from Tirai. If the Tiraians staged a sea strike, it would provide a diversion for our counterattack. Give the king a reason to watch the sea rather than the land."

Jeniah nodded thoughtfully. "You mentioned that King Rheged is facing civil war."

"According to our spies, his son has opposed him with continued boldness this past year. He's gaining supporters, promising them a return to their old values and to banish the dark magic wielded by his father. Some of the Hanorans have rallied to him. Others are either seduced by the king's dark magic, or are too terrified to resist it."

"Then the rumors about the king are true."

"They are. The prince is cautious about whom he approaches

for the insurrection, so it may be some time before he's able to present any sort of threat to Rheged."

Jeniah stood and began to pace. "Would making an ally out of this son be foolhardy?"

King Farai stared. "Join forces with the Hanorans?"

"Not with Rheged. With his son—Aragaëth, isn't it?"

"Correct."

"If we could help Aragaëth overthrow his father, he might become an ally. It was Rheged who led the invasion against Arden. And it's Rheged who wields dark magic, the same magic his son professes to hate, correct?"

King Farai looked thoughtful. "With so few numbers, he's doomed to fail if he attempts his rebellion any time soon, but he will surely be a good distraction to his father." He paused. "We must proceed with extreme caution. I will send word to our spies and see what they can tell us further."

"How quickly can we coordinate this?" she asked.

"It will take at least another three weeks."

"That long?"

"There is much to do yet, and it takes time for messengers to travel."

Jeniah let out her breath in frustration. "Everything takes too long."

Reports of the destruction and pillaging Rheged caused in Arden continued to arrive. And worse, every morning, King Rheged sacrificed an Ardeene child to his pagan god.

Jeniah's people needed her. She would not fail them. If only she could strike back at the Hanorans now instead of just waiting!

After her meeting with the king, Jeniah sat in the empty atrium staring at a book while her thoughts skittered in impotent circles. She felt torn between rushing to help her people and staying here with Kai. If all their plans succeeded, she would go back to Arden and become queen, a stark reminder that she and Kai were of incompatible social classes. Accepting her duty could mean losing Kai completely. She wished royalty could make the customs, rather than be slaves of them.

Snow glittered outside the glass windows, an odd contrast to the lush foliage inside the warm room. Jeniah looked up at approaching footsteps. Garhren Ravenwing loped up to her, his golden hair tousled, his lopsided grin wide and inviting.

"Lieutenant."

"Lady Illané. I won't bow, if you won't salute."

She laughed softly. "Very well, Garhren." She lowered her book and motioned for him to sit next to her.

With a gleam in his eyes, he plopped down easily beside her and made himself comfortable. "As Kai's friend, I have a duty to find out what your intentions are toward him."

She raised an eyebrow.

"Oh, that's very good. I've never seen a woman do that with her eyebrow."

She smiled. "My intentions?"

"Yes, you know, what are your plans with him?"

She moistened her lips. "Propriety in Darbor is certainly different than it is in Arden." Alarm shot through her as she realized what she'd said. "Or Tirai," she added, hoping he wouldn't catch her blunder. "If we were in my homeland, you would not be so brazen as to ask such a personal question, and if you were, I would tell you it is of no concern of yours."

"I'm glad we're in Darbor, then, for a number of reasons." Garhren's chin lifted slightly in challenge.

Jeniah returned his gaze with equal directness. "Very well, I confess. I plan to marry him, give him a dozen children, and spend the rest of my life making him blissfully happy."

"Very well, I suppose you do have good intentions." With a

wicked glint in his eye, the knight leaned in with lowered voice and said, "In that case, I should warn you that Kai isn't as perfect as he may seem."

Her lips twitched in amusement. "Oh?"

Garhren nodded in mock sadness. "Yes. I'm afraid it is true. On the outside, he's so perfect you almost want to hate him, except he's too likeable." Then he said with great relish, "But I could tell you stories about him that would make you blush." He furrowed his brow. "Although, if I did, then I would be revealing too much of myself. Most of the time, I'm usually the one who gets us into trouble. You see, deep inside, he wants to be wicked. That's why he likes me. I help bring out the scoundrel buried deep within him." He kept a straight face for a moment before breaking into his irresistible grin.

"He's not nearly the scoundrel you are, I suspect."

"No, I'm much worse. His strong sense of honor keeps getting in the way of him being truly bad. It gets rather bothersome, at times."

"And the rumors that he had a new lover every week?" She kept her voice light, as if she cared little for the answer. She held her breath, fearing the truth.

"That was when he was younger." Her face must have revealed more than she intended, for he hastened to add, "See, in Darbor, manly men are expected to—"

"Please." She held up her hand. "I don't want to know. I suspect you're just as bad as he was."

"Well . . . maybe not quite as much. I haven't left quite as long a trail of broken hearts as he has, but I've made a valiant effort." He looked over at her appreciatively. "I'll reform my wicked ways and settle down when I met the right woman. Someone like you. In fact, if I liked Kai any less, I might try to steal you away from him."

Jeniah had never been flirted with this brazenly before. She liked it. She leaned in closer and in a provocative voice said, "If I liked Kai any less . . ." —she paused for dramatic effect and focused on his mouth as if tempted to kiss him— "I still wouldn't go anywhere near you."

"Ah!" He threw a hand over his heart and fell against the pillows of the couch. "You, my lady, don't need a sword to rip out a man's heart."

Seeing a potential opportunity to unravel part of the mystery around Kai, Jeniah chose her next words carefully. "How long have you known Kai?"

"Hmm, I guess about twelve years. The first time I saw him was when he was taking the King's Test to become a member of the Home Guard. He was only fourteen at the time, the youngest man to ever attempt it, although it is nothing compared to what he had to do to earn Sauraii a few moon cycles earlier. I wasn't even in the king's service then, but I loved to watch the tournaments and the King's Test."

The knight's voice took on a tone of awe. "I've never seen anyone move the way he does. He's amazing. The way he fights . . . it's like the weapons sort of grow out of his body like another arm. I immediately started following him around and begging him to teach me. A friendship grew out of that. He was too serious and overly good, but I did my best to corrupt him." Garhren grinned at the memories.

Jeniah smiled with him, engrossed in his tale.

Then he sobered. "I'm not nearly the warrior Kai is, though. If he hadn't spent so much time working with me, I wouldn't be serving on the Home Guard."

"What else can you tell me about him?"

Garhren looked at her through narrowed eyes, all trace of humor fleeing. "He hasn't told you, has he?"

Jeniah's heart quickened. Garhren knew Kai's secret hurt. She knew she trod on dangerous ground, but couldn't resist the urge to press him to tell her something that might help her understand Kai.

"I know his feelings for me are genuine, but he holds back as if he's afraid to love with all of his heart. He has suffered terrible pain, and it haunts him."

Garhren watched her without speaking for a long moment. Then, slowly, he said, "It's for him to tell. Kai is a very private person. He only reveals what he must. What I know of him, I've witnessed for myself, not because he told me. You, however, he probably trusts enough to confide in, but it will be when he's ready, and no sooner. Prying will only close him up more."

Garhren was right. She needed to win Kai's complete trust; only then would he reveal himself. Not knowing the enemy that stood between her and Kai's heart left her frustrated, but only gentleness and love would melt that mysterious barrier.

Jeniah let out a long and troubled exhale. "Then I suppose I have no choice but to wait—"

"Oh, no! Not you two together." Kai strode up to them with an enormous grin. "Let me guess. Gar is either trying to steal you away from me or he's telling you all about all the terrible things we've done together."

Garhren snapped back into the guise of the irrepressible cad. "Too late. She already told me how she feels about me."

"That bad, huh?" came Kai's sardonic reply. "I'm surprised you're still smiling."

As Garhren chuckled, Kai sat down on the other side of Jeniah and kissed her hand. "Don't even pretend interest in what he has to say, or he'll talk until next spring."

"A perfect conversation all by himself?" Jeniah said with a teasing smile at Garhren.

"Right. And if you ever want to spread the word quickly, all you have to do is tell Garhren, and in an hour the whole castle will know." He shot Garhren a sideways grin. "He hasn't perfected the skill of being silent and mysterious."

Garhren rolled his eyes. "You do that well enough for both of us." He stood. "Kai, I can't imagine why, but it seems that she's determined to be faithful to you. I guess I'll go see what trouble I can stir up elsewhere. There must be a woman in the castle who hasn't yet had the pleasure of my company." He gave them a loose salute and swaggered away.

Kai looked more relaxed than he had in days. "Did he scare you away from me by telling you all about my tainted reputation?"

"No. I already knew all about your tainted reputation," Jeniah assured him. Then she added with a tender smile, "Nothing would ever scare me away from you, Kai."

"Glad to hear it." His blue gaze caressed her face as he kissed her hand again and then pressed it against his cheek. Slowly, he turned her hand over and kissed her palm, then her wrist, sending her senses swirling. Oh, how she loved this man!

Conscious of the nearby guards, she lowered her voice. "Is this all part of the ruse too?"

Instantly, his smile faded. "I agreed to play the part of your betrothed, and I will continue to do so as long as necessary."

"That's not what I mean and you know it."

Without actually walking away, Kai retreated. His body stiffened, his jaw hardened, and the lines of his mouth narrowed, the familiar, carefully mastered shield coming up between them once more.

Silently, Jeniah scolded herself. She should have known that pushing him would only make him pull away even more. She'd have to be patient and give him time, just as she had vowed to do a few minutes earlier.

"I will always be here when you need me, my lady." His strangely detached voice whittled away at her hope. "It's a rare sunny day. Shall we go for a walk?"

Jeniah summoned a smile despite her falling spirits. "I'd love to." She donned a cloak and took Kai's offered arm.

In the gardens, he cast a sideways glance at her. "Are you happy here in Darbor?" His breath came out in great clouds.

"Of course. I'm warm and comfortable. I hope I never take those things for granted."

Their footsteps crunched softly in the snow. The gardens were still, as if the whole world slept.

"I confess that all this waiting to coordinate efforts is driving me mad." With lowered voice she added, "I feel terribly alone— never able to confide in anyone, always on my guard, careful to never reveal my identity. And I miss you. You're completely untouchable now."

Kai did not reply, but under her hand, his arm muscles tensed. His mask of neutrality did not shift except possibly to thicken. How might she reach through the barriers? Garhren had warned her not to push, but she could not meekly wait for him to come to her. He might not ever find his way back through all of the walls he continued to build.

Laughter and voices floated to them on the cold air as a group of knights and courtiers strolled by. Jeniah spotted Garhren, who had clearly chosen his next conquest and was skillfully winning her favor, if her giggling were any indication.

Jeniah shook her head as she watched him flirting so brazenly. "Do you think a man like Garhren will ever marry?"

"A man like Garhren?"

"He's chasing after someone new all of the time, and from what I hear, he has compromised many of them."

"Morality is different here than it is in Arden, you know."

Her face warmed, unwilling to speculate as to the number of conquests Kai must have made among the ladies. "I wonder if he'll ever have a reason to marry if ladies continue to grant him privileges that only a husband should have."

"People marry in Darbor, Jeniah," Kai replied quietly, his hand moving to touch the braid that hung from his neck.

She followed the movement of his hand, aching to know his secrets. After reminding herself not to push him, she asked, "Is Garhren really that much of a gossip?"

"Why do you ask?" he asked, clearly caught off guard.

"He seems so different than you that at first I found it hard to believe that someone so jovial and shallow could be your best friend. Now I believe there is more to him than is apparent at first glance."

"He plays his role with relish, but he's a friend I can rely upon. There's no one I would rather have next to me in battle."

"Is he really unable to keep a secret as you have suggested?"

Kai's guarded expression softened. "If you expressly forbid him from revealing something, he will keep silent. I think it causes him bodily pain, but he's capable of doing it."

"Is there a story behind that?"

"Not really, but as a knight, he's privy to certain information he has sworn not to divulge, and he takes his duty very seriously. Although," Kai said with a smile, "once, I decided to test his fortitude. I purposely told him something particularly scandalous and then made him promise not to tell. The next day I asked one of the prettiest ladies in the castle to try to wring it out of him. She used every feminine charm she possessed—and she possessed a great deal—but he never breathed a word."

Jeniah smiled up at him. "I'm glad you have him for a friend. Everyone needs someone that loyal."

Kai nodded slowly. Jeniah's gaze drifted over the landscape

and she admired the snow glittering in the sun. Impulsively, she bent down, scooped up a handful of snow, and threw it at him. It was dry and powdery and did not stick together well, but she effectively showered him in the sparkling white stuff.

He retaliated. Soon, snow was flying until they fell down into it, gasping and laughing in the freezing air.

He raised up on one elbow. "Ever gone sledding?"

"What?"

"You sit on a piece of wood and slide down the hill."

She laughed. "Sounds dangerous. I want to try it."

Kai rummaged around a storeroom and produced an odd-looking wooden slat that curved upward on one side. Jeniah trudged up a hill outside the castle wall behind Kai while he pulled the sled to the top of the hill. Her guards remained nearby, looking as though they could not decide whether to be alarmed or amused.

Kai motioned to the sled. "Go ahead and sit."

Ungracefully, she climbed in and tucked her skirts around feet. Kai pushed the sled until they had built up some momentum, and then jumped onto the sled behind her. They gathered speed as they slid downhill, and the wind stung Jeniah's eyes. Kai leaned to steer the sled around obstacles in their path. At the bottom of the hill, they slowed to a gentle stop.

Jeniah leaned back against Kai and laughed heartily. "That was wonderful! Let's do it again."

They tromped up the hill and slid down repeatedly until they were thoroughly wet and cold. For Jeniah, days of pent-up frustration melted away like spring thaw.

Without any warning, Kai went on alert. He fell into a defensive stance in front of her as weapons seemed to instantly appear in each hand. He stood unmoving and peered into the snow-covered trees lining their sledding hill. He made a sharp gesture to the guards, who immediately ran in that direction. Her heart thumping, Jeniah rested her hand on Kai's broad back, drawing courage from his nearness. Kai would protect her as he always had. Snow slid off a tree branch and landed in the slow with a soft plop, but she heard no other sound.

They waited in breathless silence.

Was it possible the Hanorans had tracked her all the way to Darbor?

Moments later, the guards returned. "We saw no sign of intruders, sir."

Kai nodded but did not look relieved. He stared in that direction for a long moment. "Perhaps we should return to the castle."

"I'm wet and cold anyway," Jeniah said, partly because it was true, and partly out of respect for his caution.

Kai cast one final glance in the direction of the trees. As they passed the guard gate, he ordered a perimeter check, and he refused to leave Jeniah's side for the remainder of the day.

Jeniah delighted in his constant presence, but couldn't shake the feeling that somehow the Hanorans had found her.

Chapter Seventeen

In spite of his flighty exterior, Garhren Ravenwing was a man of determination. When he cornered Kai and grimly barked, "We need to talk," Kai knew he was in trouble.

Unwilling to allow Garhren to believe this was going to be an easy victory, Kai shot the man a look of annoyance as he racked his weapon. After making certain no one else lingered nearby, he faced this next battle with a fearsome scowl. "What is it, Garhren?"

Garhren folded his arms, clearly unimpressed. "You are about to marry the most charming and beautiful lady I've ever seen. Yet you are stalking around, scowling, muttering, and training at all hours."

Kai rubbed his tired, aching eyes. "I'm not in the mood, lieutenant," he hedged, knowing full well that Gar would never give up even if Kai stooped to pulling rank on him.

"Get in the mood quickly, because a girl like that only comes around once in a hundred years. And I'm going to knock your head off if you break her heart. Then I'm going to steal her away."

Furious, Kai rounded on him. "Don't you touch her!"

Garhren's slow grin told Kai he had been baited. He swore

under his breath and stalked out of the room with his friend trotting beside him.

Sometimes he wished he could actually confide in Garhren. There were few secrets between them, and this was one he did not want to bear alone.

Garhren began to muse. "She's Tiraian, and if I remember my social customs correctly, she's making you wait until marriage, but I know that can't be the only reason for all of this."

"You would know the mating customs of every country in the world," Kai growled.

"Thank the moons Darborian women aren't that prudish! But that's not it, is it?"

Kai stopped walking and turned to face him, heaving a sigh. "No, that's not it." He struggled against the raging tide of emotion. "I . . . shouldn't feel this way for her."

"What? Are you insane? You shouldn't love the girl you're going to marry?"

Kai started walking to escape his friend's scrutiny, fearing if there were a crack in his armor, Garhren would find it.

Garhren gripped his shoulder. "Is this about Ariana?"

Kai felt the wind go out of him. His fingers found the braid he wore around his neck, and he gripped it like a lifeline.

Ariana.

He leaned against the wall and squeezed his eyes shut. The sound of her name pierced him like a barb, reopening all his wounds.

"Kai, you're not betraying her. And you're not forgetting her. You're living again."

Ariana.

"If you need more time, Lady Illané will understand, but you need to tell her why. She deserves to know," Garhren said softly. "She's hurt by your distance."

Kai stood unmoving, his eyes still squeezed tight. He barely felt Garhren's hand on his shoulder.

Garhren's voice sounded close to his ear. "She's been avenged, Kai. She's at peace. Don't you think you should have a bit of peace too? That she'd want you to move on?"

Ariana.

There was another squeeze on his shoulder before Garhren's footsteps moved away. Kai stood alone with his memories and the pain they invoked—Ariana's rounded belly under his hand, the baby kicking from within, the scent of her hair as he held her close and kissed her, the sweetness of her voice when she told him she loved him and would miss him. Then she had lifted the braided hair from his chest, a token she had bestowed a year before, and pressed it to her lips. "To remember me," she had said.

Kai began walking again, following the familiar paths of the castle corridors. Would loving Jeniah mean losing Ariana completely? He slammed a fist into the stone wall. His feelings for Jeniah didn't matter, because she would be queen. Utterly untouchable.

The only two women he ever loved were out of reach. One would soon be on a throne. The other lay in a cold grave.

⁂

Since that day in the snow when he was certain they were being watched, Kai had forbidden Jeniah to leave the inner castle, yet he knew her confinement must be driving her mad. In the hopes of distracting her from her restrictions, he sought her out as much as his duties allowed, but each encounter chipped away at his resolve to shield himself from emotional attachments. Still, he couldn't abandon her.

When he arrived to escort her to the noon meal one day, he found her frowning in a corner just as a theatrical production ended.

"What is it?"

She waved her hand impatiently, her lower lip trembling. "It was a tragedy."

He smiled at her tender heart. "It's only a story."

"I know, but I don't like sad stories. And I hate it worse that she took her own life. I can't imagine being so completely without hope that I would actually kill myself."

Suddenly and unreasonably annoyed, Kai withdrew his hand, making an impatient gesture. "That's because you are young."

With uncharacteristic anger, she turned on him with blazing eyes. "Kai Darkwood, how dare you take such a patronizing tone with me! Even after—" she broke off and glanced at the others, but no one else was close enough to hear. Still, she lowered her voice, but it was laced with anger. "Even after I lost my family and my home, I never considered suicide, and don't tell me it was because I was too naive to think of it. Do you actually think that I know nothing of loss, just because I'm young?" Her face was flushed and her chest heaved.

He stared, startled at her intensity. She had endured worse than anyone he knew. Through it all, she had shown great courage and strength when others might have given up and lost their will to live, or at least melted into self-pity. The princess had done neither. Instead, she had risen above it, enduring a difficult journey without complaint, and had graciously adapted to the customs of a strange land. Jeniah had ceased being a pampered, sheltered princess long ago, and it was wrong of him to continue to treat her as such.

Kai took a breath. "Forgive me."

Her anger faded, replaced by fervency. "All I'm saying is that there is always hope."

"Not every story has a happy ending."

Jeniah's lips pressed into a line. After giving him a long look, she stood and moved away.

Kai let his breath out in frustration. "Women," he muttered even as he went after her, walking swiftly to catch up.

As he reached her, he grasped her elbow to stop her. Then he slid his hand down her arm to her hand. "I'm sorry." Jeniah's face was solemn rather than angry, and she let him raise her hand to his lips. He tugged at her gently. "Walk with me?"

"If we can go outside."

He stiffened, remembering the prickling sensation that someone had been watching them. Finally, he nodded. "The gardens."

After stopping for their cloaks, they went out to the walled gardens directly behind the castle, her guards distant enough to allow them a private conversation. Gray clouds hung oppressively low, and an occasional snowflake swirled in a faint breeze.

"Kai, have I done something unforgivable?"

Feeling a sharp pain in his chest, he enclosed her hand with both of his. "No, of course not. I'm sorry for my thoughtlessness. I seem to be quite irritable lately, and I apologize for turning my temper on you."

"Am I the cause?"

He stopped walking and turned to her. He skimmed her soft cheek with his fingers. "No."

Her eyes searched his. "If being in my presence causes you discomfort, then—"

"Being *out* of your presence causes me discomfort." He cupped her face with a hand.

"Sometimes I wish we had never come here. I would rather still be cold and hunted than warm and comfortable, if losing your affection is the price." She blushed. "At least, you seemed to have feelings for me while we traveled together. Perhaps I misunderstood?"

"No, Jeniah."

"I loved having your arms around me when we rode Braygo and when we slept." She blushed deeper, looking sweet and charming. "But most of all, I miss how easy it was to talk to you. Here, you are on guard, always proper, always . . . distant. You are either angry or completely unapproachable." She closed her eyes but tears squeezed out between her eyelashes.

Her tears almost broke Kai's heart. He had wanted to protect her from sorrow, but instead he was causing it. He wiped the moisture from her face with the pads of his thumbs, pulled her into his arms, and rested his cheek on the top of her head. Wordlessly, he held her, wishing he would never have to let her go.

"I do have feelings for you," he confessed softly. "But only royalty marries royalty. It would be foolish to pursue a hopeless relationship. I never had the audacity to try to court one of King Farai's daughters."

Her voice was muffled by his cloak as she spoke. "If I take the throne, I lose you. If I reject the throne, I fail my people. Where does that leave us?"

"Alone."

She pushed away, and all the warmth seemed to leave him. "No. We don't have to be alone."

"I can't do this. I can't—" Kai curled his hand around the braid hanging from his neck, seeking strength.

She placed a gentle hand over his. "It hurts to see you suffering like this. There's more to it than bloodline. You once asked me to trust you. I do. Can't you trust me in return? What is this secret hurt that tortures you?"

If those words had come out of any other woman's mouth, he might have accused her of being manipulating, but he knew

Jeniah enough to know she would never stoop to such pettiness. And as he met her eyes, he saw only concern, tenderness, love.

Love. By the moons, she loved him.

Kai raked his fingers through his hair. He owed her an explanation. He hadn't spoken of his pain to anyone; he could barely stand to remember it. But Jeniah deserved to know.

He held out a hand to her. Though they appeared fragile, her fingers felt strong as they curled around his. When he started walking with nowhere in particular to go, Jeniah fell in step with him, and he shortened his stride so she could comfortably keep up.

After drawing a fortifying breath, Kai began, "I had a wife."

He heard Jeniah's intake of breath.

Fixing on a distant point on the horizon, Kai automatically followed the path winding through the sleeping gardens. "Four years ago, I received orders to take a company of knights out on maneuvers. I wanted to move my wife, Ariana, from the village to the castle for her safety, but she was with child and her time of delivery was near. The midwife feared traveling might bring the baby too soon."

Steeped in memories, Kai could almost feel Ariana's warm mouth as she had kissed him at the door. He had returned her kiss and then pressed his lips to her rounded abdomen. Then he had gone, fully expecting to see her again soon.

He tried to order his thoughts, steady his voice. "We finished maneuvers and began the trip back to the castle. News reached us that our village had been attacked by the Gandon robbers. They were a bunch of cutthroats who struck without warning and then fled back into the mountains. Years had gone by without any difficulty from them. Some even speculated that they had died out. They were wrong." At the memories, Kai's anger returned fresh. "I sent the rest of the knights back to the castle with my first lieutenant. I raced back to the village. Garhren came with me."

Kai's throat closed over as he relived his fear for his wife that long night during the journey home. When he had crested the hill and looked down into the valley, only smoking rubble met his eyes. Kai had searched through debris, smoke stinging his eyes, hot cinders burning his hands. After screaming his wife's name until he grew hoarse, he finally found her lifeless body curled around her abdomen, as if trying to protect her unborn child.

Much later, Garhren had pulled him from the stupor into which he had sunk, and pried his hands off Ariana's cold body.

A strangled groan now escaped Kai's mouth. He pressed the heels of his hands into his eyes, pushing that memory back, and struggled to breathe. Jeniah stood so close he could feel the warmth of her body. He did not dare look at her; it might prove his undoing.

"The robbers had killed many and burned the village. They also abducted a number of young women. After Gar and I," he swallowed, "buried my wife, we went after the Gandon robbers. We caught up with them outside the catacombs in the mountains and followed them inside to their secret lair. We left none alive, an act of brutality unworthy of Darborian knights." He reached the end of the path and turned back, keeping his eyes fixed on the ground.

"We reunited the prisoners with their families in the village. Then we went back to the castle. I couldn't think of anything else to do, and Gar refused to leave me."

Kai glanced up at the familiar castle turrets, a symbol of his reason for rising every morning these past four years. Immediately, he had thrown himself into his work and, in time, into the arms of amorous women willing to accept an uncomplicated and uncommitted relationship. His heart, he kept carefully protected, until now.

He finally looked at Jeniah. Her eyes shining with unshed tears, she tentatively reached for him. "Oh, Kai, I'm so sorry."

He ignored his first impulse to turn away. Instead, he pulled her into his arms and let her comfort him.

Holding her until he could breathe again, he wondered how he would ever let her go.

Chapter Eighteen

Still reeling from Kai's revelation, Jeniah touched his face, wanting to soothe him as she had when he was feverish and delirious.

Kai cupped her cheek and raised her chin. Her breath hitched and a longing ache arose in her as he slowly leaned toward her until their lips met in an infinitely gentle kiss. He brushed his lips across hers once before settling in. Warmth enveloped her. His lips moved tenderly and longingly, his kiss telling her what his words could not.

Jeniah knew then that he loved her. He loved her! She nearly staggered at the thought. Despite their bloodlines, even despite his anguish over losing his wife and the love he still obviously carried for her, he loved her.

Enfolded in his arms and embraced by his clean, earthy, masculine scent, she sank against him. She tightened her arms around him and poured all of her love into the kiss. As his lips continued to press against hers, she responded completely, giving all of herself to him. His kiss grew hungry, demanding. Melting in the heat of Kai's ardor, Jeniah sank against his strong body. His heart hammered against her chest, matching the frantic rhythm of hers.

When at last their lips parted, he kissed her eyes, her temples, her cheeks, then left a trail of warmth on her skin as his lips moved down her throat. As he held her tightly against him, he trembled with restrained desire. His lips found hers again. When Jeniah was nearly consumed by heat, he dragged himself away from her lips. They held each other in a crushing embrace, their breath ragged.

Kai swallowed hard and held her close. Then, pulling back from her, his eyes drank her in as if memorizing every detail of her face, her mouth. His smile was tender and sad.

Caressing her face, he whispered, "I've dishonored you by starting something we can never finish. Please forgive me."

Without giving her time to respond, he strode a few steps away. After making a swift gesture to the guards, he broke into a run. The garden lay as quiet as a tomb. Crushed that he'd left her, Jeniah stood rooted to the ground. Never before had she experienced such exquisite joy and pleasure. And never before had she felt so alone.

Then another emotion wormed its way in. For the first time, she began to hate Kai's dedication to his duty. How could he just walk away after such a profoundly intimate moment? Her hands curled into fists as anger simmered in her stomach. He was a coward, a cad.

If he thought he could toy with her the way he toyed with other women, he knew nothing about her. She'd find him and she'd make him see reason.

⚜

Kai ran all the way to the stables. After saddling Braygo, he rode far into the hills, trying to ease the intensity of his frustration, but he couldn't go far enough away to escape. Yet he did not run from her—he ran from himself. What a fool he was.

A cold sun flitted weakly through the clouds. Kai found himself at a village churchyard. After dismounting, he wandered like a sleepwalker through the headstones. He fell to his knees and ran his hand lightly over the stone grave marker.

Ariana Darkwood. Forever in my heart.

"I can't do this anymore, Ari. I want you, but you're gone. And I don't dare open myself up to anyone else. I can't be vulnerable again. It hurts too much. I miss you. I'm sorry I didn't protect you. I'm sorry I failed you."

He rested his head against the cold stone, aching for what might have been. He didn't know how long he sat there, but he was stiff and cold by the time his instincts brought him back from the haze into which he'd fallen. Raising his head, he scanned the terrain, his hands automatically reaching for his weapons.

A lone woman wearing a brown woolen cloak and carrying a basket walked into the churchyard. She hesitated at the gate as if waiting permission to enter.

Kai dragged his sleeve across his eyes and smiled. "Mother."

She returned the smile. "I saw you at the crossing. I hope I'm not intruding."

"Never." He held a hand out to her.

She came toward him with an unhurried stride. "You haven't visited in ages." There was no reproach in her tone, only a gentle reminder.

"I have been remiss. I'd planned to come to the farm later today."

As she knelt beside him, he eyed her carefully. The lines around her warm blue eyes had deepened, and there were a few more gray hairs mingled in with the dark, but her cheeks were rosy and her face glowed in happiness.

Kai pulled her into an embrace and kissed her cheek. "You look well."

She brushed the hair back from his face. "You look troubled." She nodded down at the headstone. "Still hurts, doesn't it?"

"I haven't visited here in a long time, either."

"It's best if you don't."

He stared. "You don't visit Father's grave anymore?"

"Not as often as I did at first. Returning frequently makes it hard to go on."

"I don't want to go on. It's seems unfaithful."

His mother shook her head, her mouth pulling into a sad frown. "Oh, Kai. It's possible to love a living person and a deceased one at the same time. It's just like a parent loving more than one child. Your love for one doesn't diminish your love for the other."

"Is that how you were able to remarry so quickly?" He hoped there was no sign of accusation in his voice.

She nodded, pushing back his hair again the way she'd done when he was a child. "Finding someone else helped fill in the hole left behind when you father died. Your stepfather was never meant as a replacement. He's someone new to love in addition to your father."

Kai nodded and a guilt he hadn't realize he carried began to fade. He could love Ari and Jeniah at the same time.

Then he scowled. If only he'd made room in his heart for a woman he could actually have. He shrank from the thought of suffering another profound loss when he and Jeniah would part ways, as they inevitably would.

"Have you found someone new?" Kai's mother asked, interrupting his thoughts.

He shook his head. "Only a fantasy. Did you walk all the way here?"

She smiled. "I like walking."

He stood and helped her up. "I'll take you home if you'll feed me some of your pie."

"Hazenberries are out of season, but I have some nutbread."

"Sounds wonderful." He lifted his mother to the saddle, noting that she'd grown comfortably plump, and swung up behind her. As they rode back to the farm, he thought about the last woman who'd been in the saddle with him, and wished she were here to introduce to his mother.

What did it matter? Jeniah would be queen of Arden. And he would go on serving his king.

※ ※ ※

Jeniah's stomach rumbled, bringing her out of her book. She lifted her head, realizing that the windows had darkened and she had missed dinner. Nearby, her guards stood at alert, never wavering in their duty. Too bad she couldn't train them to keep her aware of the time.

Placing her bookmark and tucking the book under her arm, Jeniah unfolded her legs and slid off the window seat where she'd been ensconced all afternoon. Hopefully, there would be something left to eat. Wondering if Kai were worried about her, she quickened her steps and burst inside her room to change.

Darkness met her; not even a fire burned in the grate, and she bumped into a table. Faintly illuminated by the lamplight in the corridor, a vase rocked precariously on the table.

From nearby came a muffled sound.

Something was wrong. Dark fear rose in her chest.

A shadow came out of the darkness, and Jeniah blurred instinctively. It was foolish, for in the darkness no illusion would be effective. Arms seized her. She struggled against them and took a breath to scream, but a cloth clamped over her mouth, smothering her sounds. Jeniah bucked and kicked against the vise-like arms that kept her pinned.

A strange odor assailed her. She grew weak and dizzy, her limbs falling heavily. All went black.

ᴄ⟶ *Chapter Nineteen*

After passing a pleasant afternoon with his family, Kai rode toward the castle, lighter of heart than he had been in ages. At the crossroads, he paused. Then, bracing himself as if for battle, he turned Braygo back to the churchyard. Ariana was gone, at peace among those departed souls in the stars. He needed to let her go.

Slowing, he approached Ariana's grave. As the sun set behind the mountains, he fell to his knees.

"I've met someone, Ari." He faltered. "I didn't want to, but I've developed feelings for her. She's out of reach." He let out a sound of disgust and ran his fingers through his hair. "She's the rightful queen of Arden."

He watched the sunset reach outward, spreading a glorious fusion of color across the sky and turning the underside of the clouds into gold. "It's time I let you go and let you move on. Let myself move on. I don't want to be alone all my life." He bowed his head. "I love you, Ari. I will always love you. Be at peace." He removed the braid from around his neck, kissed it, and then buried it next to the headstone.

He waited, expecting a sense of loss, but sweet peace slipped over him.

He took a deep breath, then mounted Braygo and returned to

Darbor Castle. He still couldn't see a future with Jeniah, and he hated to imagine one without her, but at least he could face the future with a whole heart.

He arrived at the castle well after dark, feeling a pain of regret that he hadn't arrived in time to dine with Jeniah. He passed the main hall only to find it empty. Whatever the evening's entertainment had been, it had ended. Making a mental note to make it up to the princess, he headed toward his room. Perhaps he could take her riding. She'd probably enjoy visiting the frozen falls in the canyon.

He paused at a junction in the corridor, looking toward Jeniah's chambers. He knew she would be abed, but the desire to see her again was so strong that he could barely withstand his need to go to her.

He had to resist. If he went to her now, he would make her his own and never let her go, defying both his duty and hers.

Inside his room he removed his cloak, outer tunic, and leather jerkin. He'd just reached over his head to pull off his shirt when a knock sounded at the door.

"Enter," he called, expecting his squire.

The door opened, but the footsteps and rustling skirts did not belong to a lad. He glanced up, then stared. "Zayla."

She wore a brocade dressing robe and soft-soled slippers. Her shimmering golden hair fell in tumbled curls over her shoulders, and her eyes glimmered with a sultry light.

A smile curved her lips. "Don't let me interrupt."

Kai tugged his shirt back into place. "You shouldn't be here."

"Ah, yes, everyone is talking about how very virtuous you've suddenly become. Worried someone will see us together and tell your little girl you aren't capable of fidelity?"

He ignored the barb about the princess. "I was faithful to you while we were together, Zayla."

Her mocking smile faded into one of tenderness. "I know you were. And we were together a long time. Long enough that I'd hoped maybe, just maybe, one day you would let go of that very tight hold you have on your heart and love me a little."

As Kai struggled to come up with a reply, she draped her lithe body over a chair and let out a sigh. "Actually, I came here to tell you I leave in the morning for Arden."

He nodded. "I knew you were on the advance team."

She grinned. "I do love to play spy. And if we can tweak Rheged's nose by putting the Ardeene prince back on the throne, all the better."

Kai didn't correct her. She would learn in her final briefing before the advance team departed that they were fighting for a princess, not a prince. "Your aid will be valuable."

Zayla traced her lower lip with her fingers, a provocative ploy. He watched as if hypnotized, then, desperate to break the spell she was weaving, stood and threw another log on the fire. "I wish you luck."

Her eyes followed his movement with undisguised hunger. He turned away from her and focused on the fire, battling the temptation to take her into his arms. Perhaps he could forget Jeniah and rekindle the passion and security he'd found with Zayla. Now that he'd decided to move on with his life, he might find it within himself to allow himself to love Zayla the way he couldn't before. Ariana would always remain tucked away in a special corner of his heart, but now there was room for another.

Zayla moved to him and touched his shoulder, then slid her hand along his collarbone to the parted shirt. As her fingers touched the bare skin at the base of his neck, he drew in his breath. She moved closer, brushing her body against his. He swallowed hard, tamping down his reaction.

"I've seen you wrestling with your inner demons, Kai. Let me heal you. Let me love you. There's been no one since you." She slid her arms around him and lifted her head for a kiss.

Though sorely tempted, he hesitated. Her nearness brought back sweet memories and tender moments. Zayla had taught him to laugh again and he'd been fond of her, but he hadn't been able to step toward the terrifying precipice of love. Now that he'd finally said farewell to Ariana, he could take that step and welcome the wholeness of loving and being loved in return.

But not with Zayla.

He pulled away, grasping her hands and pressing them together inside his. "I'm sorry, Zayla. I cannot give you what you want. My heart belongs to another."

Tears shimmered in her eyes. "You've finally let go of Ariana. But not for me." She stepped away.

"I'm sorry, Zayla. I did care for you."

She let out a derisive sound. "Not enough."

He watched her cross the room, her head high, her mouth pressed into a flat line. At the door, she turned. "May the god of the moons keep you safe." She slipped through the door and closed it firmly behind her.

Kai let his breath out slowly. He'd just rejected a woman who loved him, who was attainable and whom he might have loved someday. And he'd done it for a woman he could never have. Fate was indeed very cruel.

As he sat down to remove his boots, a feminine scream echoed in the corridor.

His first thought, his first fear, was for Jeniah. He raced down the corridor, rounded the corner, and skidded to a halt. His heart leaped into his throat. Jeniah's guards lay broken and lifeless, their weapons still sheathed as if the guards had been ambushed without warning. Zayla stood over them with a look of abject horror.

Kai stepped over the bodies and ran into Jeniah's room.

Her bed had not been slept in, and on the floor lay a rag that smelled of a sleep-inducing drug. She was gone.

Through the halls of the castle echoed Kai's scream of rage and revenge.

Chapter Twenty

eniah awoke to painful jarring. She lay motionless, trying to get her bearings. A crude, wooden door stood near her feet, and sunlight filtered in between the slats of wood that made up the walls of the small enclosure. With the jolting and rattling and the sound of hoof beats, she realized she was inside an enclosed cart. Aching, she stretched, testing her muscles. Cords tightly bound her hands and feet. Raising her head made her nearly faint with nausea. She recalled the foul-smelling cloth someone had clamped over her mouth before she lost consciousness, and she realized she'd been drugged.

Her guards in Darbor had always insisted on checking any room before she entered, but she had been in such a hurry to change for dinner that she had burst into her room without thinking. Vaguely, she wondered how an enemy could have gotten into such a heavily guarded fortress, and how her abductors got her out without anyone noticing.

The wagon creaked to a stop. Voices came from without and someone fumbled with the lock on the door. Blinding sunlight streamed in as the door opened, silhouetting a dark shape in the doorway. Hands grabbed her by the hair, forcing her head up.

"Yes, this is the one we're looking for, Commander. I'm sure of it." An unmistakably Hanoran accent brought back Jeniah's nausea tenfold.

"At last!" replied a Hanoran from outside the wagon. "Bring her out."

Rough hands dragged Jeniah out and dropped her on the ground. Squinting in the sunlight, she looked up at her captors. Their brown skins and black hair left no room for doubt that they were Hanorans. They wore white leather cloaks like the troop of Hanorans she and Kai had seen during their flight from Arden.

"The king will be pleased." The Hanoran who spoke wore an ornate braid on his uniform and a gold clasp on his white cloak—adornments that, since they were absent on the uniforms of the other soldiers, appeared to distinguish him as an officer. The officer dropped a bag of coins into the hands of the driver, a nervous-looking merchant. The merchant grabbed the bag, tucked it into the folds of his coat, and made a hasty retreat in his wagon.

Jeniah turned her attention back to the soldiers. Three stood nearby while several more waited in the trees, their eyes alert. A few soldiers held the reins of strange animals that resembled duocorns but were stockier and hornless. The Hanoran officer kneeled beside her, lifted her chin, and looked steadily at her. His eyes were like shiny coal.

She snapped her head back out of his hand. "Don't touch me," she hissed. At that moment she would have given her life for a weapon. Or a fire poker.

"Oooh, Commander. A woman with spirit," said a nearby soldier. There were a few appreciative laughs.

The commander silenced them with a look and asked Jeniah, "Can you stand?"

She glared at him. The Hanoran commander was young,

perhaps a year or so older than she. He had the same brown skin and black hair as the others, yet something in his bearing seemed different.

The commander scooped her up and began to carry her. Repulsed by his intimate handling of her, Jeniah thrashed so violently that he nearly dropped her before he had taken more than a few steps. The Hanoran steadied himself and placed her on the back of one of the hornless creatures. The beast was covered with smooth scales like the skin of a snake.

As he set her down, Jeniah kicked the Hanoran commander with her bound feet, hitting him squarely in the stomach. His breath let out with a *whoosh* and he fell to one knee. Delighted howls came from the onlooking soldiers.

"This one's going to be fun. Shall we tame her first?"

The commander rounded on the soldier. "No one is to touch her, Kryspyyn," he snarled. "I made that clear before we left."

Her hands still bound in front of her, Jeniah grabbed the reins of the scaly beast and kicked him into a run.

With startled yelps of surprise, the men scrambled to their mounts. It was foolish to attempt to escape, she knew, but she could not meekly follow her fate. She would die—or kill—before she would suffer a violent attack. She risked a quick look over her shoulder. If she could only get out of sight for a second, she could blur, but the commander's gaze fixed unblinkingly upon her from only a few hand spans behind.

He leaped off his mount and hurled his body onto her, the momentum throwing her off the beast. They landed painfully on the frozen ground.

Jeniah struggled as the commander tried to get a grip on her. He rolled on top of her and grabbed her bound-but-pummeling wrists in his hand, forcing them up over her head. She writhed and thrashed, but his body effectively pinned her. He lay full on top of her. She was trapped. Absolute panic seized her. A terror-filled scream tore out of her as she anticipated the sound of tearing clothing and the feel of his hands groping her body.

"Calm yourself, Princess, I'm not going to hurt you." Something in his voice made her stop fighting him. "I give you my word, no harm will come to you as long as you're in my charge."

She stared. He sounded like Kai.

No, this was no honor-bound knight. This was a savage from the desert, one who had destroyed her family and home.

Her breath came in harsh gasps. "What is that, the word of a Hanoran?"

"In my country, my word means a great deal," he replied crisply.

"In my country, Hanorans are murderers without conscience!"

The commander set his jaw and stood, hauling her to her feet. She nearly sobbed in relief when she realized that he did not intend to harm her in the intimate way the soldier in Arden had attempted. At least not yet. For now, the Hanoran threw her over his shoulder and carried her to the waiting mount. Hoof beats neared and the rest of his men surrounded them.

Jeniah struggled again but his arms clamped down over her, and with his shoulder pressing against her stomach, breathing became difficult.

"Your behavior will directly affect your treatment, Princess. Remember that."

In reply, she kicked and thrashed, growing short of breath and then lightheaded.

The commander hefted her onto the back of the scaly beast. Freed from the man's shoulder, she sucked in her breath. Scowling, the Hanoran wrapped another rope around her legs, binding them to the saddle. Then he tied her hands to the top of the saddle before he stepped away and appraised her, tight-lipped.

"You're only making this harder on yourself," he warned.

She glared at him. "What, you'll kill me quickly if I cooperate, but torture me first and kill me slowly if I resist?"

"You know nothing of torture," he growled.

She turned her head away and looked straight ahead. The leader mounted his own beast and took the reins of her mount in his hand. His soldiers closed in.

Jeniah kept her head high, fighting the fear coiling in her stomach. Her wrists and ankles throbbed where the ropes bit into her skin, but eventually the pain diminished as she started losing feeling in her limbs. The wind gusted, biting through her gown. Without a cloak, she shivered.

"Where are you taking me?" she demanded in an imperious tone of voice.

The commander gave her a curious glance, as if amused by her haughtiness. "To King Rheged."

She swallowed a cry of dismay. Instead, she raised her chin. "And then?"

"He will decide your fate."

Jeniah pressed her lips together and kept her head high as a bleak future loomed before her.

The team of twenty-five armed men traveled quickly and openly, staying on the main roads. People they encountered moved off the road with fearful expressions, not even looking at the prisoner. Occasionally, the Hanorans' guttural voices drifted to Jeniah, but the men rarely spoke as they rode. At sunset, the Hanorans stopped and set up camp near a stream.

The commander appeared beside her. "If you vow not to kick me again, I will untie you and let you off."

Jeniah wanted nothing better than to kick the man, this time in the face. However, her limbs were so numb she doubted she could. She nodded curtly in agreement.

After eyeing her silently, the Hanoran commander untied her from the beast and lowered her to a blanket on the ground. Kneeling beside her, he untied the knots in her bindings. The cords had bit into her flesh, leaving purple bruises and a bloodied ring around each wrist.

He reached into a pouch at his waist. "Here, this will help." He drew out a tiny clay jar, dipped his fingers inside, and withdrew them covered with ointment.

She shrank from him.

"Don't be afraid, Princess." His voice softened despite his harsh accent. His hand froze and his gaze locked with hers.

She had never seen such dark eyes, so black that his pupil could not be discerned. No hate or lust for violence glimmered in his stare.

He made no move. "With your permission, of course, Your Highness." One corner of his mouth lifted.

Did he mock her? Under her careful appraisal, the commander's amusement faded and he waited, hand still extended. An unexpected softness entered those dark eyes, and Jeniah knew then he had no malicious intentions. Stunned to find kindness in the eyes of her enemy, she nodded.

He gently applied the salve to her wrists and massaged it in. The rubbing helped restore the flow of blood but also renewed the throbbing.

"I'm sorry the ropes were so tight," he said softly, his fingers still coaxing the feeling back into her hands.

Her eyes narrowed. "Strange words for a Hanoran."

A trace of sadness entered his expression. "You must not judge a whole people based upon the actions of a few."

Rage boiled up inside Jeniah, and her words came out in

fragments. "You are a leader in the Hanoran army. You invaded my country and slaughtered my family, destroyed my home, enslaved my people. You tried to kill me. Hunted me. You forced me into a life of exile. Exactly what am I not supposed to judge?" Her chest heaving, she battled tears of fury.

His black eyes held hers, his expression fading to perfect neutrality. Perhaps all trained warriors possessed Kai's ability to become difficult to read when they so desired.

He broke eye contact and applied the salve to her ankles, which did much to relieve the pain in her flesh, but her heart felt as raw and open as if she had suffered her losses only moments before.

Though his hands remained gentle, the commander spoke curtly. "You may rest here. If you are going to be difficult, I'll restrain you. The choice is yours."

The feeling had returned to Jeniah's limbs, but she was still so weak that escape seemed impossible at the moment. After a brief deliberation, she finally promised, "I will behave."

One of his men approached. "Commander Lalen, the perimeter is secure and the watch has been assigned."

"Guard her, Dayel. I'll relieve you shortly."

"Yes, Commander."

The young leader went to join his men. Dayel eyed her, a suspicious scowl furrowing his brow as he stood a few hand spans behind her, his hands resting on his weapons. Jeniah wrapped her skirts around her legs and feet and hugged her knees in an attempt to stay warm. She wore only thin silk stockings and slippers fit for sheltered palace life, not the outdoors. Why was it that each time she found herself traveling, she never seemed to be properly attired?

Soon, a fire burned bright in the center of camp, bringing life to Jeniah's chilled limbs. A fragrant pot of stew simmering over the flames awakened her appetite.

"It's ready," announced the soldier who tended the food.

The men stood back as Commander Lalen spooned stew into two bowls. As soon as he had taken what he wanted, the other soldiers began serving themselves and eating noisily as they sat near the fire. Jeniah thought they sounded like a bunch of animals, the way they slurped and guzzled.

She turned away in disgust, hugging her knees tighter. The commander returned to Jeniah, squatted down in front of her, and held out a bowl of stew to her.

Her mouth watered and her stomach growled, but she hesitated, reluctant to accept food from the enemy. It crossed her mind to simply throw it in the Hanoran's face, but that would only incite him. At best, it would succeed in getting her tied up again. She glanced at the guard called Dayel behind her. His stare remained steady.

Still weak from the effects of the poison, Jeniah knew that going hungry much longer would only make her weaker. If she ever hoped to make an escape when the opportunity arrived, she needed her strength. As long as they were willing to feed her, it would be wise to eat. Still, she hesitated.

The commander waited without expression or comment. His bowl held the same food as hers and she'd watched him dish it up. It seemed unlikely he could have slipped poison into her food with her watching.

She accepted the offered bowl. "Thank you," she murmured automatically, and then bit her lip. Surely such manners would be wasted on a savage.

Commander Lalen raised a brow, and one corner of his mouth twitched. He sat on the blanket next to her. Jeniah tasted the stew and found it bland but hot.

The commander glanced at the guard. "Go eat, Dayel."

"Yes, sir." Dayel went to join the others.

Spurred by gnawing hunger, Jeniah ate quickly, spooning up every drop and wishing for more.

As the Hanoran leader ate, he watched her out of the corner of his eye. "I'm impressed you made it all the way from Arden to Darbor. It's a great distance, and we searched thoroughly. How did you do it?"

Jeniah hesitated. "My champion guided me." She almost informed him that Kai was both a Sauraii Master and a Darborian knight, which made him almost invincible, but revealing anything would be foolish.

"He must be very clever."

She knew it was unwise to provoke the commander, but the images of death and destruction in her head made her recklessly angry. She shot him a daring look. "He killed many Hanoran soldiers protecting me."

"A great warrior as well." The commander seemed to take no offense as he hungrily ate his stew.

She blinked. Did he truly take death so lightly as not to care that her champion had killed many of his countrymen?

"Have you ever been to Hanore?" When she shook her head, he continued, "It's very different from Arden. A desert."

"Is that where you're taking me?"

"No. We go to Arden." He finished his food and stood. "Dayel."

Her former guard returned. "Yes, Commander."

"You and Carnea have first watch over the prisoner."

Dayel nodded.

The commander looked down at Jeniah as though he would say more. Instead, he strode away. As the company bedded down for the night, their voices gradually died away. Three guards circled the perimeter of the camp. Dayel's and Carnea's gazes never left Jeniah. She would have to watch carefully to find the moment when she could blur. In a company of twenty-five men, escape seemed unlikely, but many of them would sleep, so it was not hopeless. Under a starless night, the land outside of the circle of firelight fell completely black, the darkest night she had ever seen.

The commander approached her. Under one arm he carried a large, thick fur; in his other hand were a rope and several strips of cloth. Jeniah shrank away from him at the thought of being tied up again, with the ropes biting into her already-raw skin.

He seized her by the elbow, his voice hard, "If you resist me, I'll tie them tight. But if you hold still, I'll make them loose enough not to hurt you."

She held very still. The Hanoran leader wrapped her wrists in the strips of cloth as a sort of bandage, then tied the ropes securely over the top of the cloth with her hands in front. Then he draped the sleeping fur around her shoulders.

Surprised at his show of compassion, she met his black eyes. "Thank you, Commander."

His eyes narrowed as he studied her. She unflinchingly returned the stare. He wore his hair longer than the noblemen of Arden or Darbor, with a heavy fringe of bangs and tapered sides that framed his face and hung below his jaw. Suddenly, a frown creased his brow. He grunted something unintelligible and stalked away.

She couldn't imagine what had annoyed him. With a mental shrug, she rolled up inside the fur, grateful for its warmth. She glanced often at her guards, but they never relaxed or looked away. Throughout the evening, Jeniah's eyes strayed to the young commander. He was no different than the others—not the tallest, nor the leanest, nor the darkest. Nothing outside of his decorated uniform made him stand apart. Yet he was different. In a gruff sort of way, he'd treated her with courtesy and compassion. These were not traits associated with the Hanoran barbarians. Yet, she harbored no hope that his kindness would extend to protecting her from his king.

As the night darkened, Jeniah pondered the hopelessness of her situation. Her fate seemed certain. She was to be delivered into the hands of the king of the savages who had ruthlessly slaughtered her entire family. What humiliation, what pain, would she suffer before the Hanoran king had her executed?

Jeniah curled up. She would die alone, and her people would remain enslaved. She'd failed them.

She sank into utter despair.

Chapter Twenty-One

*J*eniah woke to the sound of terse whispers nearby. She silently scolded herself. She shouldn't sleep; she should watch for an opportunity to escape.

"No, Kryspyyn, you heard the commander. She's not to be harmed."

She opened her eyes to see Dayel standing nose to nose with another soldier.

The other man glanced her way with an open leer on his face. "I'm not gonna harm her, just enjoy her a bit. She'll stay in one piece. More or less."

"Kryspyyn!" The commander's voice rang out over the camp. Boots thumped heavily on the frozen ground. The commander strode to Kryspyyn with fire blazing in his eyes. "I told you to keep away from her. The king wants her brought back untouched, do you hear me?"

"Why untouched?" Kryspyyn demanded.

"How should I know?" The commander said angrily. "Maybe he wants her for himself before he kills her. It doesn't matter. Your job is to obey orders."

"But we've been on the trail for moons with no companionship. She's young, probably nice and—"

A resounding crack rang out, causing Jeniah to flinch. She

stared openly as Kryspyyn staggered back and fell under the force of the commander's blow.

"Question my orders again and I'll tear out your heart and choke you with it!" In a towering rage, the Hanoran leader stood over the man on the ground.

"Yes, sir," Kryspyyn gasped, but his eyes glowed in defiance.

"I'll take next watch over the prisoner," the commander said more quietly to Dayel and Carnea. "Go get some rest." Then he called, "Bael, you're with me."

Her guards went to bed down as another soldier got up. Those who'd been awakened by the noise settled in again, and soon the snoring resumed while the perimeter guards continued to circle.

Terrified, Jeniah lay wide awake, her pulse throbbing. Someone approached quietly and Jeniah snapped her head up.

The commander crouched next to her, his black eyes unreadable. "Sleep, Princess," he whispered. "I won't let you be harmed."

She blinked, surprised to find that she believed him. "Thank you."

He gave her a brief nod, then stood and walked away. Strangely comforted, Jeniah relaxed. Despite her desire to remain awake to watch for an opportunity to escape, fatigue dragged her down to the irresistible lure of sleep.

The Hanorans were up when Jeniah awoke. They ate hastily, and one of the younger soldiers, a mere boy, brought her a bowl and a cup. He never looked her in the eye. Hungry, yet cautious, Jeniah hesitated. Would they stoop to poisoning her? She glanced at the commander, who talked softly with Dayel.

No, the commander wouldn't allow that. He wouldn't poison his prisoner after saving her from assault. She ate the bland, steamed grain and drank the bitter liquid.

After breakfast, they broke camp. As they rode side by side, Jeniah often noticed the commander's eyes moving to her.

He watched without any hint of threat. He was decisive and authoritative, his men respected him, and he treated her with kindness. He certainly did not seem barbaric. In fact, with the notable exception of the one called Kryspyyn, these men were disciplined and efficient. Hardly barbaric qualities. They were different than the average Hanoran savage. Perhaps that was due to the influence of their fair and honorable commander.

What was she thinking? He was the enemy! What part of her home had he set on fire? Which member of her family had he killed? How many of her countrymen died by his hand? Horrified, she eased her mount away from him.

Without the protection of her sleeping fur, she shivered and her teeth chattered. The sun never broke through the cloud cover. The Hanorans did not stop for a midday meal but pushed along at a steady pace, traveling through terrain she had seen only a few moon cycles before when she and Kai had fled Arden. The land slept under a blanket of snow, but the Hanorans openly traveled the roads and burned fires without fear.

A fierce wind and heavy snowfall forced them to stop before sunset. By then, Jeniah had developed a cough. She curled up with her head down and wrapped her arms around her legs. Her feet were numb with cold. The commander brought a sleeping fur and placed it around her shoulders, while his men built a bonfire and cut down branches to build rough shelters like the lean-to Kai had made before they acquired a tent. The commander untied Jeniah's ropes, handed her a blanket, and led her to the lean-to most sheltered from the wind and snow. Then he built a smaller fire at the edge of the shelter.

"Thank you, Commander."

With a faintly curious expression, he glanced at her before he went back to his men. Two guards kept her in sight. After lapsing into a coughing fit, she opened up her fur in front to let in the warmth of the fire and stretched her feet out toward the heat. She glanced at her guards, whose eyes remained fixed on her. They would have to look away at some point. When they did, she would blur and escape. How she would survive on her own in the winter, she did not know, but she would rather freeze to death than suffer the fate the Hanoran king had in store for her.

After seeing to his duties and his men, the commander sat down next to Jeniah under the lean-to and held out a wooden cup with something steaming inside. She eyed him dubiously.

His teeth flashed white as he smiled, and a strangely incongruous dimple appeared in one cheek. She stared in astonishment. He was actually quite handsome when he smiled. She recoiled at the thought.

"You're very cautious. Here." He took a drink. "See? I've no reason to harm you. You're far too valuable to me alive." He held out the cup to her.

"Wouldn't it be a terrible inconvenience if I died before you brought me to your wretched king?" she snarled.

He grinned again. "Quite."

She glared furiously at him, which only seemed to amuse him further, and snatched the drink out of his hands. She sipped it. It was almost hot enough to burn her mouth, but it tasted of sweet herbs and slipped so comfortingly down her throat that she drank it all. Warmth spread through her body and soothed her throat.

"Thank you."

His mouth pulled to one side, showing that dimple. "How do your wrists feel? Still sore?"

She looked down at them and nodded. He unwound the strips of cloth he had used as bandages and treated the skin with ointment before rewrapping her wrists. When dinner was ready, he brought it to her and sat next to her as they ate. Jeniah never looked at him, but she found his presence less intimidating.

"We'll cross into Arden in a few days," the commander said.

Jeniah nodded, oddly anxious to go back to Arden. She was the Hanorans' prisoner, and she knew their purpose in returning her to Arden was to execute her, but relief swept over her at the thought of returning home. The fire crackled and sputtered, sending out a glowing ember to one side.

"You surprise me, Commander. You're nothing like I expected."

His black eyes fixed upon her. "You mean for a Hanoran?"

"Yes. For a Hanoran."

She wondered if it were only in the heat of battle that Hanoran warriors turned vicious enough to have invaded Arden and massacred her family. At the moment, she had trouble picturing this young man doing any of those things.

"Perhaps I'm different."

"You treat me with kindness."

"I truly mean you no harm."

She leaned in and lowered her voice to a desperate whisper. "Then please let me go."

He stiffened. "You know I cannot."

"You are taking me to my death."

"I must take you back. There is no alternative."

Anger flared. "Were you part of the invasion?"

His black eyes bored into hers. "Do you really want to know?"

She hugged herself and squeezed her eyes shut but could not block the images swarming through her thoughts: gaping holes in the walls; the broken, lifeless bodies; Mora dying right before her eyes; fire, death, fear . . .

A sob escaped her mouth and she pressed her hand over it.

The commander's voice grew cold. "I'm a ruthless monster, Princess Jeniah. The sooner you accept that, the better off you'll be. I'm only keeping you comfortable so you won't get sick and slow us down. Or die before my king can execute you publicly."

She bit her lip and swallowed her tears. The commander remained unmoving, his face giving no clue to his thoughts. He silently tied her hands in front of her and nodded to the guards who watched her. The commander moved to speak with Dayel, who Jeniah had discovered was his first officer. Neither man glanced her way. She recalled the warning Commander Lalen had made when Kryspyyn defied him. None of the soldiers under his command seemed to have any doubt that he would carry out his threat. Perhaps he truly was capable of the violence she had witnessed in Arden. Of course he was! He was Hanoran.

Jeniah rolled up and burrowed inside the fur. She felt the commander's eyes upon her, but when she risked another look, he stood thoughtfully staring up at the moons.

The next morning when she opened her eyes, Jeniah saw the commander lying next to her, wrapped in his own bed roll. Asleep, without the weight of his responsibilities hanging over him, he looked serene. And young. He must be a very skilled warrior to have achieved a position of leadership at such a young age. His features were strong and square. Any woman in Arden would have considered him attractive—provided he wasn't pointing a sword at her and threatening her family.

He opened his eyes. He said nothing, merely fixed his unreadable gaze upon her.

Jeniah buried her face in her sleeping fur and smothered a round of coughing, wincing at a pain in her chest with each cough.

They ate and broke camp. Clearly, Commander Lalen took very seriously his duty to return the princess to his king. There were never fewer than two pairs of eyes upon her, making escape impossible. As they traveled, he kept her tied up unless she was eating. She never even had a moment of privacy to attend to personal matters, which made her increasingly irritable. The commander continued to bring her the tea of sweet herbs for her cough, and it brought temporary relief. Sometimes, however, a searing pain tore through her lungs as she coughed.

The soldiers talked softly and laughed among themselves, perfectly relaxed in this barren, inhospitable winter environment. Jeniah despised the soldiers. She hated the way some of them looked at her with triumph in their eyes, the nonchalance with which they were bringing her to certain horror and death. When their language became objectionable, something the one called Kryspyyn often instigated, Commander Lalen would silence them and ride closer to her, almost protectively. His presence was actually reassuring.

When he probably thought no one else was looking, Kryspyyn would leer at Jeniah as if he enjoyed watching her cringe, but he made no move toward her. Once, the commander caught him staring at her and glared with such warning that Kryspyyn slunk away, his hand moving to his heart.

After Kryspyyn left, the commander put a reassuring hand on Jeniah's arm. She realized then that his actions had nothing to do with orders from the king, but rather from a sense of honor. Who would have thought any Hanoran possessed honor?

One night, as the men set up camp, Jeniah's moment to escape arrived. For the first time during the journey, no one appeared to be watching her. She blurred, projecting an image of herself sleeping and bound. She had never tried to project a muffling sound before, but she tried, not knowing if she would succeed. With her hands and feet bound, she struggled to a seated position. The first thing she needed was a blade to cut her ropes.

How she wished for a knife! She eyed the guard's dagger but knew she would never manage to get it. If only she could project something real, something solid, instead of only illusion. She stilled. Hadn't Thenisis told her she could create reality when it mattered most? Jeniah couldn't recall the high priestess's exact words but knew she had to try. She concentrated on a knife, the feel of the handle in her palm, the sharpness of the short blade.

She started. She did feel a smooth handle in her hand. She craned her neck to look behind her and saw a small, curved dagger in her palm. Elation and wonder rippled through her. She sawed the ropes with the dagger. The awkward angle of holding a knife with her fingertips while trying to cut ropes around her wrists made it difficult, time-consuming work. Finally, the rope made a tiny snap. Jeniah froze. The nearest Hanoran guard glanced at the ground just below her, apparently seeing her lying asleep on the ground. He looked away, stifling a yawn.

She kept working the ropes until they fell away. With her hands free, she worked on the bindings at her ankles. When the ropes fell free, she sprang to her feet. The Hanoran guard looked up at her, but his gaze passed over her. She turned and darted into the forest.

She never knew what gave her away. Perhaps her projected illusion faded once she ran out of sight, or her feet crunched in the snow, or they saw her very visible footprints, but only seconds passed before someone shouted and several men began running, following her tracks.

Cursing, the commander came after her. Jeniah stopped running and flattened herself against a tree, trying to silence her breathing. He followed her tracks right up to where she stood. She held her breath and froze. His eyes followed the line of the tree trunk, his eyes passing over her as he searched. He looked up into the branches, but they were clearly too high to be climbed.

He moved so quickly that she did not have time to react. One minute she was standing a hand span in front of him. The next, she lay on her back in the snow with his body pinning her.

He swore viciously. "You're a sorceress!"

"No."

"Explain yourself!" His eyes blazed with such hatred that she thought he would kill her that moment.

She braced herself for the fatal blow.

He swore again. Still trapping her with his body, he reached inside his tunic and withdrew a heavy silver chain from around his own neck, then draped it over her head. Though only warm from his body, it almost burned her skin.

The high priestess in Darbor said she used metal to lessen her power in order to shield her mind from the noisy thoughts of others. Jeniah wondered how the Hanoran commander would know metals had a dampening effect on magic. Then she remembered that the Hanoran king was reputed to be a dark sorcerer. A man Commander Lalen served.

Still staring at her with open hatred, he said, "You are deceptively innocent-looking for a magic wielder."

Jeniah caught her breath. Did he believe only an evil person could use magic? If so, did he see evil in his king?

The commander shifted his weight, grabbed one of her arms, and roughly turned her face-down in the snow. He sat on her and tied her hands so tightly behind her back that the ropes bit into her flesh. She let out a cry that brought on a coughing fit. He bound her feet, gagged her, and pulled her roughly to a stand, disgust and loathing so strong in his gaze that she shrank from him.

"If you even *think* any magical words, I will knock you unconscious."

He scooped her up like a sack of grain and carried her back to camp, where he dumped her on a blanket. She did not dare move. Lying in between three guards, Jeniah watched the commander stalk the perimeter of the camp, snapping at any soldier foolish enough to speak to him. He repeatedly looked up at the moons and muttered.

Jeniah knew that as a man of honor, the Hanoran leader would continue to shield her from men like Kryspyyn, but he would never again look at her with kindness. She had lost him as an ally. That knowledge brought an unexpected loss, and an insufferable gloom permeated her spirit.

In a few days, these men would turn her over to their hateful king. She had no doubt he would sentence her to torture and death.

Chapter Twenty-Two

Nine days after Jeniah's capture, Kai carefully surveyed the landscape. The last mountain pass before the northeastern border of Arden lay directly ahead. The pass snaked, long and narrow, between sheer cliffs that rose so high that the sky could barely be seen above—the perfect place for an ambush. He was amazed that they had made it this far without being challenged.

Kai reined. "Hold. We wait for the scout."

Behind him, the company of knights halted and waited silently.

The Hanorans transporting the princess had made no effort to conceal their trail. Did they lie in wait? Or were they truly so confident in their success that they did not bother to ensure they could not be followed?

Flanking him, Garhren shifted in his saddle, looking as uneasy as Kai felt.

A large, tawny feline loped toward them. As it approached, it slowed, its body shimmering and melting into a woman. Zayla stood, brushed her hands off on her leather breeches, and flipped her golden braid over her shoulder. "They did pass through here and moved on without stopping. They made camp further on in the forest only yesterday. No signs of doubling back."

Confident in Zayla's scouting abilities, Kai gave the signal to continue on. King Farai of Darbor had agreed that it might not be too late to save Jeniah. King Rheged would no doubt wish to publicly execute the princess with much ceremony, in revenge for the embarrassment she caused them by evading them for so long. The sorcerer-king would probably use her as a victim in one of his brutal blood sacrifices. Kai's heart nearly stopped every time he thought of it.

He remembered only too well how the Hanorans had tried to ravage her in Arden. Unable to bear the thought of her helpless in the face of such monstrous violence, he kept reminding himself that they had found no evidence Jeniah had been injured. Yet.

The sun hung directly overhead when they reached the traces of another Hanoran campsite. They found footprints too small for a man—the princess, most likely. Yesterday, she was alive.

They pushed on, riding hard. Kai didn't want to stop to sleep, but the duocorns were exhausted before nightfall. As the team set up camp, he paced restlessly.

Garhren approached, chewing on his lower lip and eyeing Kai warily. "Permission to speak, Captain."

Kai gave him a curt nod, turned, and walked beyond the circle of camp with Garhren in step with him.

When they were out of earshot, Kai braced himself. "What's on your mind?"

"You are."

Kai nodded grimly. After Jeniah was kidnapped, Kai had told Garhren about the Jeniah's true identity, the escape, and her alias. Garhren had listened without judgment, as Kai knew he would.

Garhren waited until they could not be overheard. "She's well, Kai. I just know it."

"She has to be."

"We'll get there in time to save her."

"They're still a day ahead of us!" Kai fumed. "She may not have that long." He raked his fingers through his hair as he tried to rein in his helplessness and frustration.

"What are you going to do, go on foot? The duocorns are spent. We can't push them any faster."

"How are we ever—" Kai nearly choked, fighting with his emotions.

Garhren looked away. When Kai began walking again, Garhren matched his stride. "It's not your fault."

"Of course it is! I swore to keep her safe." Kai's voice cracked, but he swallowed hard and continued quietly. "I failed. I failed to help her people, and now I've failed her."

Garhren was silent for several moments. When he finally spoke, his voice was hushed. "You cannot control everything that happens to the people you love. And you cannot blame yourself if harm comes to them."

Kai squeezed his eyes shut.

"It's impossible to be there every second of every day. The king's best men were guarding her. Everyone thought she was safe." Garhren's grip on his shoulder was firm. "We'll find her before she comes to harm."

They made a wide circle around camp, neither of them speaking, while the team set up camp and tended to the duocorns. "You're not wearing Ariana's braid," Garhren observed.

Kai's mouth dried. "I buried it next to her grave." He glanced at Garhren, half expecting to see recrimination. If anything, Garhren looked relieved.

Kai took the first watch while the men bedded down. Sleep had eluded him for ages. He felt as if he would never sleep again. Jeniah haunted his dreams; harsh reality taunted his wakefulness. He found no rest. Guilt bored a hole through his insides, and pain filled in the hole.

Chapter Twenty-Three

*I*n the land of Arden, Jeniah let her gaze sweep over the forest to the meadow beyond. As the road turned and they neared the shore, Jeniah could hear the roar of the sea and smell the salty air. When at last they neared the shoreline and the trees thinned enough for her to see the ocean, Jeniah watched, spellbound, as the waves dashed joyously onto the rocks and danced along the sandy beach. She drank in the lovely view, longing to embrace the beckoning, pristine water. Every rock, every shell seemed like an old friend welcoming her back. A lump rose to her throat. She was home. All of the ugliness and the horror her kingdom had suffered seemed far away as she embraced the splendor of nature. At least the Hanorans had not spoiled the landscape. The snow had melted and the air warmed. Spring would not be far behind.

The moment they crossed the border into Arden, Jeniah repeatedly called to Maaragan in her mind, but her chayim failed to come to her.

When they stopped that night, Commander Lalen approached Jeniah with a steaming bowl of soup. He eyed her grimly.

"I will remove your gag and feed you, if you will swear by all you hold dear that you will not utter any dark words of magic."

She nodded. Her mouth raw and dry from the gag, she

looked up at his face. All touch of the softness he had shown her previously had vanished.

"I don't know any words of dark magic, Commander Lalen."

His eyes searched hers. "How did you disappear?"

She hesitated. Being honest with him could destroy any hope of escape, yet she had little to lose. The commander already thought she was a dark sorceress. Perhaps telling him the truth might soften his anger, his mistrust. Something about him, despite his fierceness, convinced her she could trust him. She might yet find an ally in Commander Lalen.

She moistened her cracked lips. When she took a breath, it aggravated her cough and set off a hot pain deep in her chest. A moment later, she explained, "I call it blurring. It's an illusion I project. It allows me to blend in to my surroundings and not be noticed."

"You're a form-changer?"

"No, I only become unnoticeable to the eye. I don't actually change."

"What else can you do?" he demanded.

"I can project an illusion momentarily. Nothing else."

He stared hard, his eyes unyielding. "I do not know if I can believe you."

She coughed again, and he looked down at the bowl in his hand as if he had forgotten it. She ate as quickly as he could spoon the soup into her mouth. The soldiers had not fed her all that day. They avoided her as if they thought she carried some sort of dreadful, contagious disease. She knew their aversion had nothing to do with her cough, but rather her magic.

"Commander, the ropes are pointless. Keeping me tied will not take away my ability to blur."

He snorted. "And I don't suppose you'll tell me how I can prevent you from using your magic."

"I'm no threat to you, Commander. Your metal chains have blocked my powers. Even so, whatever magic I possess is not dark. I've never studied the dark arts. I know no dark words. I cannot harm anyone." She looked up into his black eyes, silently pleading with him.

He sat back, considering her words.

She moistened her lips. "Please. My arms are throbbing and I can't feel my hands."

Suspicion leaped into his eyes, but he relented and untied her bindings. She rubbed her wrists, frightened at the bluish tint in her fingers. A ragged sore formed a ring around her wrists. The commander waited with his hands on his weapons, his body taut as if ready to spring at the first sign of flight or deceit. When the feeling returned to Jeniah's hands, it brought pain, but her skin quickly assumed a healthier color. He retied her hands in front of her but kept the ropes loose enough that they would not cut off the circulation again. He even pulled the fur more securely around her.

She looked up at him in gratitude. "Thank you."

He frowned darkly at her and stomped away muttering. She caught the words "soft" and "weakling."

The weight of the chains around her neck bore down on her, always hot, and she wondered if they were responsible for her chayim failing to come to her. Disappointment tasted bitter in Jeniah's mouth. She had been so sure the moment she returned to Arden and began mentally calling to her, that her chayim would help her escape, vanquishing Jeniah's captors the way she'd driven off the wyrwolves as Kai lay wounded.

Kai. Where was he now? Surely he knew she had been captured. He would be searching for her by now, probably with his best knights. But he might be too late. Jeniah curled into a ball and tried not to let despair consume her.

They rode hard over the next few days, pushing their mounts to greater speed, and riding much later after dark, as if they had a pressing deadline to meet. Late one afternoon, as Jeniah and her captors came around a bend in the main highway, the castle of Arden became visible. Even from this distance, the scars from the war were clearly visible. A sudden lurch choked Jeniah as she beheld how much had changed.

Arden now belonged to the hateful King Rheged. Jeniah's heart pounded and perspiration ran down her sides. She had to escape. It didn't matter that there was nowhere to go and that she would probably die alone. She had to get away.

Riding next to her, the commander watched her through narrowing eyes as if he sensed her rising fear. In a flash of desperate courage, she grabbed the sword from the commander's scabbard where it hung from his saddle and made a thrust toward his chest. With her hands tied, she couldn't get a firm grip on the pommel and she swung embarrassingly slow. He parried the attack with his dagger and thrust the sword back easily. Its weight threw her off balance, and she was forced to let it drop before it dragged her off her mount. Before the sword hit the ground, she turned her scaly mount around and kicked it into a run. Savagely, she kicked the animal harder in a vain attempt to outrun the close pursuers. The poor beast ran with all its might, but it was used for carrying packs, not for speed.

"No, don't shoot her!" shouted the commander from behind.

Jeniah risked a glance back. An archer stood in his saddle with an arrow nocked and aimed at her.

"We need her alive and unharmed!" Commander Lalen shouted again.

The sound of pursuit followed. The soldiers' younger, quicker mounts easily outran hers. When a rope was thrown around the neck of her mount, it obediently slowed. Jeniah slid off the scaly beast with the intention to run, but instead fell on her face. Her feet were still tied. She cursed her stupidity and struggled to stand. Heavy footsteps sounded directly behind her. Commander Lalen grabbed her around the waist and held onto her as she thrashed.

"Stop fighting me," he growled.

He used a foot to sweep her legs out from under her. As she fell, he straddled her with his knees. Tight-lipped, he untied her ropes, threw her onto her stomach, and bound her hands behind her back. She cried out as the ropes reopened the wounds on her wrists.

"I knew you would attempt to escape again," he said through clenched teeth.

She shouldn't care, yet shame trickled through her that she'd repaid his kindness by attempting to stab him.

He picked her up and dumped her on her mount, whose sides still heaved from the exertion of running. Silently, the commander tied her to the saddle.

He glanced up at her, his anger clearly mingled with a touch of admiration. "I would have done the same thing."

Jeniah fixed her gaze on the horizon in an effort to prove she didn't care about his opinion of her. Kai would have been disappointed in her weak attempt at using a sword. She kept her tears of frustration at bay by sheer willpower.

By mid-afternoon, they arrived at the outer gates. Jeniah choked down a sob as she looked up at the castle that had once been home. As they entered the gates to the city, she rocked back in shock at the profound destruction.

Most of the shops that lined the main thoroughfare were in ruins. Few homes or buildings still stood. Little more than charred timber remained of the thriving capital city of Arden. Except for the outer walls and gates, which had been patched crudely, no effort to rebuild had been made. Jeniah stared, horrified at the devastation.

As they traveled through the city, a few Ardeenes watched with frightened eyes from crumbling doorways, but most of the city appeared deserted. Only patrolling Hanoran soldiers walked out in the open.

An utter depression of soul, a sinking, sickening dread, crept over Jeniah, threatening to rob her of her sanity. The Hanorans had won. Soon she would face their king, who would humiliate, torture, and kill her.

"I'm finished," she whispered.

She had failed to save her people.

The young commander looked stony as they rode to the main castle stairs. The majority of the company broke away, leaving only a few of his men. After he dismounted, Commander Lalen cut Jeniah's ropes. She nearly fell as he placed her on her numb feet, but his hand shot out to catch and steady her until she could stand. Clutching at him to get her balance, she looked up into his dark eyes, sending a silent plea, searching for any sign of softening.

He held her for a moment, his gaze locked with hers, until he brusquely pushed her away. Surrounded by Hanorans, she mounted the stairs, each step bringing her closer to her doom.

With great effort, she gathered her ragged courage. She would not be truly beaten. Whatever they did to her, she would never give them the satisfaction of breaking her. With her mother's image firmly in her mind's eye, she lifted her head proudly, squared her shoulders, and went forward to meet her fate with all the grace and dignity of a queen. She maintained this façade as they led her through the castle to the king of Hanore.

King Rheged glowered down at Jeniah from her father's throne. Arden's banner had been replaced with the Hanoran king's. Such a thing seemed a desecration. King Rheged's face was so twisted with malignant evil that just looking at it turned her blood cold.

King Rheged gazed down at her as if she were an annoying insect. "So, the elusive princess finally arrives. Excellent. You will be publicly executed. That will end any hope the peasants have that their so-called rightful heir will ever return."

His glittering eyes bore down into hers, and Jeniah had to fight to maintain her composure. He would not break her. She raised her chin.

"What, no pleas for mercy? No crying?" Rheged mocked. He leaned forward.

Jeniah stared straight at him without a quiver, letting her distain show clearly.

His mouth twisted into a gruesome smirk. "You are a proud one, aren't you? How delicious. Perhaps, rather than a customary execution, I should allow you to take part in the Ceremony of Souls in place of the victim I had planned to consume. Your arrival could not have been better timed."

The king rubbed his chin thoughtfully. "Yes. You shall take part in the ceremony." He leaned forward gleefully. "Tonight, when both moons are aligned at their apex, I will make a petition to the god of the demons. Then I will cut out your heart and eat it even as it continues to beat."

Terror and disgust clutched at Jeniah and she had to concentrate to keep her face expressionless.

Smiling, Rheged obviously took great relish in telling her gruesome future. "One by one, I will cut out and consume your organs, then drink your blood. Finally, I will devour your soul."

This description went far beyond Jeniah's imagination. She drew upon all her strength to not show the unspeakable horror and revulsion that seized her.

"You will be conscious and feeling through the whole thing, of course. Pain provides the most power. The ceremony itself lasts nearly until dawn. A long and painful death for you. Exquisitely pleasurable to me and the Lamia. The Ceremony of Souls only happens twice a year. I look forward to it with great anticipation." Taking delight in the thought, he rubbed his hands together. "Nothing to say? No last requests?"

Jeniah remained silent.

His face reddened and a vain popped out in his forehead. "Say something!" he thundered.

Everyone in the room jumped, except Commander Lalen, she noticed, who stood beside her, ramrod straight.

Jeniah didn't twitch. She remained tall, head erect, eyes level and unflinching. This horrible, barbaric monster had no power over her spirit. She stood before them ragged, dirty, her hair hanging in a tangled mass. But she remained in perfect, dignified splendor, completely unruffled and with all the majesty of the rightful queen of Arden.

"Well, well," King Rheged finally said, admiration shining in his perverse face. "You are rare." He regarded her in silence for what seemed a long time. "It is not often that I meet one of such courage. I will enjoy consuming your spirit. You will give me great power." The king's gaze turned to the commander. "Well done, Aragaëth. You surprise me. I didn't think you would be man enough to find her and bring her to me."

Aragaëth?

The commander's jaw tightened and the cords of his neck muscles stood out as he glared back at his king.

King Rheged met his gaze with the barest flicker of approval. "Perhaps you will be a worthy son after all."

Son? Commander Lalen was Aragaëth, the king's son? Suddenly unable to breathe, Jeniah looked at him in disbelief.

This young man who had won her respect was the son of the most diabolical creature who had ever lived. She could barely conceal her shock and horror.

Prince Aragaëth glanced at her without a flicker of emotion before returning his eyes to the king. His father. Revulsion turned her stomach.

"Take her to the tower," commanded the king.

A new set of guards came forward and seized her arms. Outside the throne room, Jeniah fell into a coughing spell, white-hot pain shooting through her lungs. She glanced back at Aragaëth, who left with his men, never looking her direction. Jeniah's new guards prodded her up several winding flights of stairs into a part of the castle where she had never dared venture. She maintained her composure as they took her to the tower, shoved her inside a cell, and chained her to the wall. The air reeked of human waste and decaying bones. Insects and rodents were even more plentiful than prisoners. At least the oppressive gloom reduced visibility enough to spare her from the grisly sights. To her knowledge, the prison towers in Arden had not been used in generations, yet Rheged appeared to have made use of them immediately.

The door to her cell closed with a creak and a reverberating bang.

Chapter Twenty-Four

The tiny window in the prison tower above provided Jeniah some indication of the passing day. No matter how much she willed it otherwise, the cruel sun moved mercilessly across the sky and sank. Soon she would meet her death. She was running out of time.

No food or water had been brought, and her throat was raw with thirst. Her wrists and hands bled freely. Torn flesh hung below her shackles where she had worked all afternoon in an attempt to free herself. She'd tried magic, but the metal chains encircling her neck blocked her power and made her head feel as if it were about to explode. Using her blood as a lubricant, she twisted savagely. With a frenzied jerk, she wrenched her left hand free of the shackle. She began working to free her right.

Pushing through her lightheadedness, Jeniah forced herself to keep working. *Twist, pull, twist, pull, breathe, ignore the blood. Twist, pull, twist, pull, fight the nausea.* The pain was so bad she nearly succumbed countless times, but she drew courage from her success in freeing her left hand. She could do this. She must.

Sobbing in pain and desperation, Jeniah mercilessly twisted until she yanked her right hand free of the shackle. Blood splattered her gown and dripped from the empty shackles hanging from the wall. Freed from the chains, she bent over, trying to control her breathing as fiery pain lanced her arms. Her hands were a hardly discernible mass of torn flesh. In places, the bone was visible. If her wrists had been any larger, she would never have succeeded. Certainly a grown man never would have.

She looked back out the high window. A faint hint of gray remained. There was still hope.

First, she had to escape this cell. The narrow, barred window sat in the outside wall about ten hand spans over her head—too high to climb to and too small to get through. She pulled on the handle of the door. Bolted, of course. There had to be some way to escape.

A rodent ran over her foot. She stifled a shriek as she jerked her foot away. Quickly, she snatched the squeaking creature by its tail and held it up. Its body contorted as it dangled from her fingers.

"You have done that too many times today, my friend," she muttered with disgust. "Either you, or one of your brothers."

From the other side of the door, she heard a voice. A key slipped into the keyhole and made audible click. The door swung open, its hinges squealing sharply. As a shadow appeared in the door, Jeniah flung the rodent at the intruder. A young man's yelp of surprise replied. She lunged at the faceless shadow. Her victim wore the clothing of a guard but no armor or helmet.

She threw her elbow upward into his face. He cried out in pain, but before he could react, she spun him around. Using her body weight and all of her strength, Jeniah pushed the startled guard into her former prison. As the guard stumbled into the cell, she slammed the door shut and slid the bolt into place. A muffled yell of outrage sounded from the other side of the door.

Jeniah paused, listening. There was no noise other than the progressively more desperate sounds from the cell she had recently occupied. She crept cautiously down the hallway, passing moans and cries from behind doors to other cells, before she came to an outer door.

Remembering the commander's chains around her neck, she removed them and let them fall. She attempted to blur, but pain shot through her body, and she paused to gather her strength. Had her injuries weakened her so much that she could not tap into her powers?

Unwilling to concede, Jeniah eased the bolt, cringing at the noise. She held her breath, opened the door, and peered cautiously out, listening for sound of alert. A portly Hanoran sat nearby, noisily drinking from a horn that had once belonged to a great animal. The guard sat next to a lone candle, but the rest of the room was steeped in shadows. Jeniah hugged the walls, keeping to the shadows as she stole to the outer door. A steady stream of warmth trickled down her hands. Her wrists throbbed in an agonizing pulse. Barely daring to breathe, she kept moving, stepping softly. She'd almost slipped around the guard when he lowered his horn and held it out without looking at her.

"Finish your rounds already? Come, boy, have a drink. It helps pass the night."

She froze. He glanced her way and then took a double take. Surprise registered on his face. For a moment, panic threatened to overwhelm her.

Praying the gloom and his drunkenness would prevent him from noticing her bloody gown, she sauntered toward him slowly, languidly, with a seductive sway to her body. "I'm here to help you pass the night another way," she said suggestively.

His surprise was replaced by open lust, but then he hesitated. "I thought wenches weren't supposed to come in here anymore."

"Do you want me to leave?" she asked, keeping her voice low.

He considered. "No. But the boy might be back any minute." He glanced toward the door through which she had come.

"Go see if he's in sight yet," she suggested. "Then get rid of him so we can be alone."

The guard lurched to his feet and staggered to the door. When he stepped through, looking for his fellow guard, she gave a mighty push. As he tottered inward, she hurled her body against the door and threw the latch, locking him inside the prison hallway. His cries of fury were much more venomous than those of the younger guard. Jeniah paled at the terms of profanity he voiced.

On the floor she spied his sword. She picked it up, knowing that her skill would be pitifully inadequate if she were forced to fight anyone with even basic skills, but at least she wouldn't be completely unarmed. Her wrists sent searing pain shooting up her arms, and she coughed again. Her weakness was gaining on her. She crept down the flights of stairs separating the prison towers from the rest of the castle. Coughing stopped her several times, but she pressed on. She reached the main floor and had almost passed the servants' quarters when voices neared.

Jeniah opened the nearest door and took refuge inside the room. She leaned heavily against the door, praying they would pass by without stopping.

A small cry of alarm sounded from behind her and she whirled to find three women staring at her in fear. They clung to one another, whimpering.

"Quiet!" she ordered with a low voice. "If you make a sound, I will kill you." She brandished her sword with more bravado than she owned. One of the women fell into a swoon at her display of bravery and force. Or it might have been her blood-spattered arms and gown. She probably looked like a ghoul. The other two women wrapped their arms more tightly about each other, nodding, wide-eyed in fear.

One of the women put a hand to her enlarged belly. "Please don't hurt me or my baby," she pled.

"Who are you?" Jeniah asked, softening.

"The king's concubines."

"Cooperate, and I won't harm you. Call for help and—" she wiggled the sword at them "—I assure you I'm quite capable of using this." She didn't confess that she'd only had a few lessons and probably wouldn't be able to defeat a child with a stick.

Their eyes moved to the sword and the concubines nodded meekly.

"Tie her up." Jeniah used the sword to point to the woman who had swooned and lay motionless on the floor.

The pregnant woman gasped.

"You. Sit down here." Jeniah ordered the mother-to-be as she indicated a nearby chair. "You." She pointed her sword at the other women and then indicated the prostrate form. "I said tie her up. And gag her."

They both obeyed. The pregnant woman sat in a chair and watched fearfully while her companion used veils to tie and gag their unconscious friend.

"Now, tie her up, too." Jeniah ordered. After her instructions were carried out and the mother was trussed, Jeniah motioned to a remaining chair. "Sit."

When the woman obeyed, Jeniah stood behind her, veils in hand. "If you make any move, I will kill you and your friends," she warned menacingly.

The woman stifled a sob and nodded. Watching for any resistance or tricks, Jeniah cautiously lowered her sword and looped the veil around her, first tying her to the chair, then binding her hands so they could not move. Before she gagged the terrified woman, Jeniah moved to face her.

"I need Hanoran clothing. Where can I find some?"

The woman moistened her lips, fear mirrored in her eyes. "There is a chest of clothing against the far wall." She motioned toward it with her eyes.

Jeniah gagged her and went to the chest. Cautiously, she opened it, wary that she might have been deceived. Inside lay clothing made up of mostly filmy veils. She stripped off her torn and bloodied gown and stepped out of it. After glancing back at her captives several times, she managed to duplicate the way the veils were worn enough to make a passable imitation. She made one last appraisal of her bound victims.

Jeniah washed her face in a basin of water. The water refreshed her, cleared her mind, and removed the dirt, grime, and sweat a courtier or concubine would not have. The water in the basin turned nearly black. Partly to protect her wrists and partly to avoid being noticed, she washed and then wrapped them with strips of cloth, gasping at the pain. Then she wrapped the blade of her sword with several more veils in an attempt to make it appear a women's bundle instead of a weapon.

Perhaps with her dark hair, and dressed in the clothing of the Hanorans, she would blend in with the conquerors, especially under cover of night.

She listened at the door and then slipped out, nearly running into a guard coming down the corridor.

"My lady," he greeted her in surprise as he snapped to attention. "You aren't permitted to leave the rooms after dark . . ."

He broke off as he scrutinized her face.

Jeniah bestowed a dazzling smile upon the guard. He blinked in confusion.

Taking advantage of his bewilderment, she placed her finger

to her lips. "I'll be right back, never fear. And I would be most grateful for your discretion. Most grateful."

He glanced around and then nodded, still wearing a puzzled expression. His eyes fell to her package of veils, but he did not question her further.

She moved down the corridor. She had been so focused on escaping that she wasn't sure where to go. She knew that Captain Tarvok and a few Ardeene loyalists were somewhere in Arden, but had no idea how to find them. First, she must get out of the castle.

So far, she'd had the benefit of surprise and a lack of resistance by her opponents, but she needed surprise and stealth if she hoped to escape. What awaited her beyond the castle gates, Jeniah could not think about at the moment. One adversity at a time. If only she could blur. If only she could call her chayim.

She made her way up to the main part of the castle, staying near less-frequented common rooms. Each person she encountered was Hanoran, but none gave her more than a passing glance. Where were all her countrymen?

From nearby came the scent of food cooking, sending Jeniah's stomach into unhappy grumbling. The next turn brought her to a corridor teaming with people, all carrying large platters of food. She was tempted to steal some food and drink, but a cry of alarm rang out, caught up by several voices.

The guards had been found.

Jeniah swallowed and forced her weak limbs to keep moving. She tried to blur. Again, pain exploded in her head. She slipped in among the servants, hoping she would blend long enough to find a way out. Weak with pain and loss of blood, she stumbled along with the hurrying people.

One group of armed men ran past without noticing her, but when a second set of guards came from the opposite direction, her luck ran out. She found herself face to face with a full complement of soldiers led by Commander Lalen. Prince Aragaëth.

Aragaëth appeared both relieved and angry. "At last. You have no idea what trouble you've caused me."

"I apologize for having inconvenienced you," she snapped.

Knowing it was futile, she released the veils around her weapon and let them flutter to the ground. She held her sword poised and ready in the defensive stance that Kai had taught her. Those times with him seemed long ago.

"You cannot win. Surrender."

She tightened her grip on the hilt. "Kill me here if you must, but I will not suffer your king's ceremony."

"The ceremony must take place." He took a step forward, his sword drawn and his expression determined.

Jeniah glared at him unflinchingly. To die here by his hand did not frighten her; it would spare her the death to which King Rheged had condemned her.

"I had almost begun to believe you were different," she said bitterly. "I should have known there was no honor among savages."

His eyes narrowed. With a quick lunge, Aragaëth stripped her of her sword, swept her feet out from beneath her and pushed her face-down on the floor, catching her arms behind her, all before her sword clattered to the ground.

Jeniah screamed in rage.

Aragaëth kneeled over her with one knee on either side of her, then sheathed his sword. He lifted one of her arms and stripped off the veils she had used as bandages. Turning her arm slightly, he examined her ruined wrists.

"That's how you did it," he said with both awe and pity.

She shrieked and twisted, bucking her body, trying to get at him, to claw out his eyes, but he had her effectively pinned. "If you allow me to be sacrificed in your father's evil ceremony, you are as much a monster as he is. Don't you see what you are doing? His magic is dark. Evil. The very thing you hate."

"The sacrificial ceremony will take place," the prince said coldly.

Distress swallowed her anger. Too numb to cry, she lay helpless on the floor.

Aragaëth hauled her up by her elbows. Surrounded by guards and with Aragaëth still holding her arms, Jeniah was taken through the narrow, dim, and winding corridors back up the stairs to the tower. When she stumbled, coughing, Aragaëth shoved her forward without mercy.

Aragaëth did not bother to chain her inside her cell. "It's almost time." He glanced back at the guards behind him and lowered his voice. "If you resist, they will hurt you worse. Cooperate, and this will all be over soon."

"Over soon? An all-night torture?"

He turned to leave.

Desperation opened her mouth. "Prince Aragaëth, please help me. I know you oppose your father. Oppose him now. This magic you hate so much must be stopped."

Something flickered in his eyes. Compassion? Hope? His face hardened. "The ceremony will take place, and the king will use you as he sees fit." He exited the cell, his movements stiff and jerky.

Jeniah sank to the floor.

Moments later, the door opened again. Two sword tips crossed the threshold. Guards entered, followed by a woman dressed in silvery blue veils.

Tall and slender, she possessed an ageless, icy beauty, suggesting an age much older than she appeared. She had ghostly white skin and eyes that glittered deep and black. Such evil lurked in her eyes that Jeniah could not meet her gaze. A pervading sense of malevolence surrounded her, and Jeniah knew instinctively she was the most sinister kind of sorceress.

She spoke words Jeniah could not understand, her voice silky, frightening. The words hung, twisting and black, in the air. A dark presence invaded Jeniah's mind, and unspeakable horror rose in her throat.

Chapter Twenty-Five

Inside Captain Tarvok's tent, Kai laid down the missive and stared through the tent flap at Arden's once-verdant hills. The sea lay out of view beyond a rise. Most of the snow had melted, but spring had not yet arrived. The countryside looked dull and barren.

The Ardeenes had set up camp a few leagues from the castle in a hollow deep in the forest. Sentries patrolled the perimeter. Tarvok had managed to raid enough supply huts to provide the rebels with plenty of weapons and food. They had built a formidable force.

Kai and the other Darborian knights had arrived at midday. His men immediately sank into an exhausted slumber, but Kai went into conference with Tarvok.

The Ardeene captain pressed a steaming cup into his hand. "Don't you ever sleep?"

"Occasionally." Kai took a drink of the brew.

A messenger entered the tent, nodded at Kai, and saluted Tarvok. "Sir, our spy reported that the princess was brought in this morning by a regiment of twenty-five Hanorans, all wearing white leather cloaks."

Kai swore and began pacing. He'd missed her by a matter of hours. And now she was in King Rheged's clutches. Kai could only imagine what the king would do to her. His hands curled into fists.

"Dismissed." Tarvok turned to Kai as the messenger left. "All right. She's here, as we'd suspected." He paused and eyed him narrowly. "All is not lost, Darkwood."

Kai reined in his frustration, hoping the captain hadn't seen right through him. "It would have been too easy to intercept them before they arrived."

"Nothing's been that easy. Now we implement our plan."

Kai nodded. "The castle fell before. It will fall again. Is the sea strike enough of a diversion?"

Captain Tarvok grimaced. "It appears to be at least attracting the Hanorans' attention."

"And the Govians are in position?"

"They only await our signal."

The sun set as they ate a cold dinner, reviewed their plans, and then briefed the warriors. Then, dressed in full chain mail, Kai lifted the tent flap and went out into the night.

"Light the signal," Tarvok ordered.

The bonfire leaped to life, and excitement rippled through the air as the remnants of the decimated Ardeene army assembled. Captain Tarvok mounted, saluted, and led his Ardeenes to join with the Govians in a frontal assault on the main gates. Kai and his Darborian knights followed at the rear of the company.

With the anticipation of battle coursing through his veins, Kai waited in the rear of the company as the Govians' battering rams pounded on the gates. Catapults threw boulders, doused in oil and burning, at the walls. The bright moons lent enough light to illuminate nearby obstacles, but all Kai could see of the assault were the fiery projectiles.

When the first breech appeared, Tarvok let out a battle cry. The Govians and the Ardeenes charged through the crumbled hole in the outer city wall, and Kai took his men in with them. Once inside the city wall, Kai led his knights around the side of the castle, while Tarvok's men engaged the Hanoran guards and fought their way to the main castle gates.

As they approached, Kai reined. "Listen." He held up his hand as his ears strained.

A large feline materialized out of the darkness and loped to Kai. "Wait," he said to his archer.

The feline slowed and stopped a few hand spans in front of Braygo. Its form shimmered and grew into Zayla.

She fixed a sober gaze on Kai. "The princess is being taken from the tower to the main courtyard. You have only until the moons join to get her out or they will torture and kill her in a ceremonial sacrifice."

Kai turned cold. Behind him, urgency rippled through his team as they rechecked their weapons, anxious to do battle. But as he opened his mouth to give the command to move forward, his gaze returned to Zayla. She looked up at him with thinly disguised hurt and longing.

Regretting that he'd hurt her, yet knowing there was no way to soothe her, he slid off Braygo and went to her. "Thank you, Zayla."

Her words came out stiff and cold. "I'm only doing my duty."

"Still, I consider this a personal favor."

Her eyes flashed. "I do it out of loyalty to King Farai. No other reason." She turned away, then stopped and turned back, a faint, self-mocking smile touching her lips. "A princess." She shook her head and melted back into her feline shape before disappearing into the shadows.

Kai let her go, gratified to see her pride intact.

Anxiously, he looked up. The moons had moved closer together, the halos around the glowing orbs already blending into one. Stealthily, he led the team to the far side of the castle, opposite Tarvok's diversion, to the base of the castle. A sewer drain, protected by a metal grate, emptied into a ditch that led away from the castle. Kai eyed the filthy, sluggish water.

Garhren slapped him on the shoulder. "Nothing but adventure and glamour, eh?"

Kai tried to smile but it came out as a grimace. He took a breath, dismounted, and led the way through knee-deep water to the grate. He glanced at Garhren, who smirked and withdrew two large, metal files, which the two knights used to begin sawing through the bars. With each screech of the files, Kai expected to see a regiment of Hanorans upon them, but Tarvok's diversion appeared to be effective.

The files broke through, and Kai and Garhren removed the grate. Kai glared at the mouth of a tunnel. It was dark and narrow, definitely not wide enough to walk upright in.

"What are you waiting for? Let's go." Garhren plunged into the tunnel.

Kai clenched his teeth and climbed in after him. The other members of the team followed. Kai dragged in his breath but suddenly couldn't make any air enter his lungs. Within a few hand spans of the entrance, total darkness overcame him. He couldn't even see Garhren. It took all his will to refrain from shrieking in a cowardly flight out of the sewer and back to the safety of open air and light. The tunnel grew smaller and tighter, shrinking as they moved further in. If the water had made any less noise, the others would have heard Kai's labored breathing as Kai struggled to force himself to keep moving.

Cold sweat poured off his body and his weak knees could hardly support his weight. Every muscle in his body shook. He felt as if he were falling, though his fingers dug into the unyielding sides of the tunnel.

Someone bumped into him from behind, and he clawed his way back to life.

"Sorry, sir," came a mumble, the voice echoing dully off the walls.

The terror receded, not completely, but enough to make Kai aware he was holding up the team. He managed to keep moving. He had the presence of mind to begin a Sauraii mind-clearing exercise. Closing off his thoughts, he pushed them roughly into an empty place and locked the door. He concentrated on controlling his breath, his heartbeat.

First his breathing evened. Then his pulse slowed and his muscles unclenched. The fear hadn't left, but it pulled back. He felt it there, lurking like a deadly predator waiting for him to lose control. But it was manageable, and for now, it was enough.

The expedition moved slowly through the darkness, carefully feeling their way along the slippery rocks. Although the water was never deeper than waist-high, it was icy, and the steady current taxed their strength. How far they traveled was impossible to tell in the endless blackness. Kai could only rely on his groping hands to guide him.

Garhren stopped and Kai ran into him. "Gar—"

"Do you see it? Light!"

Kai lifted his head and peered into the darkness. Far ahead, there did seem to be a faint glimmer of light. His spirits lifted and the team pushed ahead more quickly now. Soon he saw Garhren's faint outline.

Another grid barred their way, but Kai and Garhren sawed quickly through it. One by one, the determined rescue party emerged triumphantly from the sewer and climbed up into the castle proper. Kai never wanted to see the inside of a cave or a tunnel again. He lurched to his feet, consumed with the thought that they might be too late to save Jeniah.

Ceremonial drums beat to the rhythm of a human heartbeat. Torches and candles illuminated the courtyard, sending eerie shadows flickering over the faces of the people jammed in the courtyard. The smell of incense permeated the air. Voices chanted softly, rhythmically.

Jeniah followed the dark sorceress the Hanorans called the Lamia, the sorceress who invited demons to the ritual, a monster who fed on the death of mortals to fortify her immortality.

The waiting crowd parted, clearing a path. In the eyes of the people, Jeniah saw both fear and a fanatical sense of reverence. Many in the crowd were Ardeene. By the furtive looks they cast toward the Hanoran guards, she knew they had been dragged here against their will to witness their queen's execution.

The dark, invasive spell the Lamia had cast over Jeniah took away her ability to control her body. With no will of her own, Jeniah did exactly as the Lamia commanded, despite her own mind screaming in protest. When Jeniah had no power to resist, the Lamia's men beat her until she could barely stand. The Lamia had told Jeniah in an arrogantly cruel voice that the spell would keep her alive—and conscious—through the ritual, which was far beyond normal mortal endurance. Jeniah would only be released to death after her spirit was devoured. The pain would be excruciating beyond human comprehension.

Jeniah retreated behind a shield of numbness, refusing to think beyond putting one foot in front of the other. Bruised and aching, she tried not to stagger as she carefully placed her bare feet on the cold stones of the courtyard.

They neared the platform and climbed the wooden steps. On the platform lay an altar carved with hundreds of symbols similar to the figures carved into Thenisis's chambers, but these symbols were vastly different. They positively oozed evil. Jeniah looked away, feeling tainted. At either end of the altar stood a tall pillar, also covered with runes.

The drums beat faster and the chanting grew louder. King Rheged approached the platform, dressed in black robes and carrying a globe that flickered and glowed while smoke poured profusely from the top. He set it on the altar and turned to Jeniah, towering over her. Lust and hunger burned in his eyes—not the lust and hunger of a man for a woman, but of a starving man looking at a feast.

He grabbed her gown by the neckline and tore it apart. The fragile fabric shredded and fluttered down to the floor. Jeniah's breath caught.

The Lamia pointed to the altar. In her disturbingly musical voice she said, "Lie down and remain still."

Jeniah shook with the desire to defy the sorceress, but the Lamia's power over her was too great and she was forced to obey. The Lamia picked up a pouch of dust and sprinkled it over Jeniah's body before raising both hands high above her head. The moment the dust touched her skin, Jeniah felt the forces of light and darkness converge upon her.

The Lamia chanted while her eyes rolled back into their sockets. She spoke in an unknown language, but that it sprang from sinister origin Jeniah had no doubt. The strange words chilled her.

Jeniah called feebly to her chayim but felt nothing in response. The moons began to melt into one. The Lamia continued to chant.

Fear clawed Jeniah's chest, her breath coming in sharp gasps.

This was the end. She would die here, painfully. She had never felt such pure terror. Betrayed by her own body, she waited for the nightmare to begin.

An image of her mother and father came into her mind. The perfect examples of decorum and duty, they were the rulers all Ardeenes expected. Jeniah pulled together her courage. As their daughter, she would not die cringing. She would face her death with the dignity her people deserved from their last surviving monarch. Regardless of how the king took her life, she would choose how she would die. She chose to die with courage.

Peace gently stole over her.

The king placed the smoking globe on the altar near Jeniah's head, then sprinkled dust from the pouch over her body. Again, Jeniah felt as if all life and light, all death and darkness, converged in one point inside her.

The Lamia picked up an ornately carved dagger and held it over the smoking globe until blue sparks burst out of the globe, then presented the dagger to the king. He cut a long line in his own hand and let the blood drip on Jeniah's forehead, her chest, her abdomen, and then upon his own tongue.

The Hanoran king looked up toward the two moons that had nearly melted into one. The chanting voices rose in pitch and volume. The drums beat louder, faster. The moons joined into a single, perfectly round, cold orb. King Rheged raised the dagger high above his head, poised over Jeniah's abdomen. The drums beat one final time and the chanting ceased. Jeniah closed her eyes.

At the edge of her consciousness, she felt the soothing presence of her chayim. Another presence, more fleeting, but strong and familiar, touched her mind. From both of them, she experienced an infusion of power flowing into her, fortifying her.

An explosion erupted, and Jeniah opened her eyes. The king frowned at something behind her. Another blast rocked the ground.

"Sir! We're under attack!" shouted a guard.

The king cursed and looked to the Lamia.

Impassively, she replied, "I can continue without you, but you will not feed unless you actively participate. And if you shorten the ceremony, you reduce the power you consume."

Another explosion shook the ground. The king steadied himself on the altar and he looked up at the moons, perfectly joined overhead. He shouted orders to nearby soldiers, then turned back to Jeniah. Once again, he raised the dagger.

A third explosion rocked the platform. A faint whistling noise sounded, followed by a soft thud. The king grunted. Jeniah blinked, wondering if she imagined the shaft of an arrow protruding from his shoulder. Cursing, the king shouted for his sword and pulled the arrow out as if it were a mere annoyance.

In the courtyard, pandemonium erupted.

The crowd became a churning mob of panic as soldiers poured into the square. Hanoran soldiers trampled civilians in their effort to fight off the invaders who stormed the courtyard, yelling and brandishing weapons. Jeniah thought she heard someone call her name, but there was so much noise and confusion that she could not be certain.

The king swore again and emitted a battle cry. The Lamia looked at him with mild annoyance before turning her gaze to Jeniah. Pure, undisguised evil radiated from the Lamia.

Approaching the altar, the Lamia said, "You are nothing."

Jeniah met her gaze. "I'm the daughter of Darvae and Ellorian, king and queen of Arden. I'm chayim-bonded. And I'm the rightful queen of Arden."

She struggled against the power that held her captive like chains controlling her body. Suddenly, the power seemed to bend. Jeniah threw all her strength against it, and it bent further. She sat up. The spell wavered and for an instant, Jeniah thought she saw surprise and fear flicker in the Lamia's eyes.

Jeniah pushed harder against the bonds that struggled to contain her. The spell cracked and then fell away like shattered glass. She was free! She stood. The Lamia stumbled backward, raising her hands and murmuring an incantation.

"You have no power over me," Jeniah's voice rang out.

The Lamia's dark words bounced off Jeniah and fell back, scattering like smoke in the wind, powerless. The Lamia faltered.

Jeniah projected a mass of metal chains around the Lamia's neck. The Lamia screamed as real chains formed around her. Jeniah reached toward her. Backing away, the Lamia screamed.

In that moment, Jeniah understood with perfect clarity how the Hanoran king had become so twisted. This Lamia, with her dreadful rituals, was the real enemy; the king was only an apprentice. The power, the sheer evil radiating from this woman far overshadowed that of the king. But it was hollow.

"You are nothing but illusion," Jeniah said. "Your life has been extended by stealing from others, but it is not real. It is only a manifestation of your will."

"You know nothing!" the Lamia screamed.

Jeniah touched the Lamia's shoulder. It was cold and damp, like mist. The Lamia shrieked, clawing at Jeniah's hand, but her flesh passed through Jeniah's like a ghostly image.

The image changed, fading until it became nearly transparent. The Lamia's face visibly aged in seconds. Her skin crumpled, shriveled like dried leaves, and fell off her skeletal form. Her bones crumbled as well, yet the Lamia's screams continued. A moment later, all that was left of her was a pile of rags, dust, and gold chains. Finally, the last of her screams faded away.

"Jeniah!"

She turned, seeking the voice calling her. It sounded like—"Kai?"

Kai Darkwood fought his way through the battle, his foes falling with every stroke of his sword. He was deadly, but a light shone around him as he charged up the stairs to her side. Not a killer, but a savior. Gathering Jeniah into his arms, he held her in a crushing embrace and buried his face in her hair.

"You came!" she sobbed as her arms went around his neck. "You came."

He shuddered. "I nearly lost you . . . " his voice broke and he held her breathlessly.

Below them, the battle raged.

Chapter Twenty-Six

In the Ardeene camp, Kai paced outside a tent while the doctor examined Jeniah. Moonlight cast shadows behind every rock and stump. The Ardeenes and Govians had retreated from their attack on the castle an hour before, as soon as the princess was secure, but the lingering energy that follows a battle kept the camp lively.

Ignoring the others drinking toasts to their success, Kai continued pacing, his fists clenched. They'd arrived in time to stop the horrific ceremony, but they'd been too late to protect Jeniah from harm. The Hanorans had beaten and starved her. She was ill, and her wrists were an almost indistinguishable mass of torn flesh. What else they had done to her he could only imagine.

Helplessness and terror threatened to drive him mad.

"I need to train. Garhren!"

"Oh, moons, you're going to grind me into dust," Garhren moaned.

To two knights, Kai made a quick gesture toward the tent housing Jeniah. "Sanchen, Duvall, stand guard. No one enters that tent."

They snapped to attention and moved to obey his command. Other knights shot Garhren a look of sympathy as he withdrew his sword, looking as if he were about to get a beating he knew he deserved. They went to a clearing and faced each other in the bright moonlight.

Kai pressed him hard, knowing Garhren could take it better than anyone else in Darbor. Sometimes he wished he could find someone who was truly his match and let loose without holding back. The brief melee at the castle should have tired him enough to cool his fury, but it didn't. Garhren withstood Kai's onslaught surprisingly well. Kai grinned darkly. Garhren was getting very good but would have some interesting bruises in the morning.

Kai gave vent to his anger, falling into a battle state where he saw every detail with perfect clarity, every twitch of his opponent revealing his intentions a second before he moved. Kai went deeper into a state of semi-consciousness where all that remained was his need to destroy.

Kai pressed his adversary until he stripped him of his sword. His foe stumbled and went down, and Kai drove his sword tip down toward his opponent's throat.

"Kai! Peace! By the moons, I said peace!"

Kai blinked.

From the ground, Garhren looked up at him with shock and something resembling true fear. Cursing himself, Kai re-sheathed his sword and pulled Garhren to his feet. Then he retrieved Garhren's sword and offered it to him.

Garhren wiped the perspiration off his face with his sleeve and eyed Kai before taking the sword. "For a second, I thought you were really going to kill me."

"Sorry, Gar." Sick with the thought he might have actually harmed or killed his best friend, Kai held out his hand.

"Don't ever do that again."

Kai shook his head and made an attempt at levity. "If you spent as much time training as you spend chasing women, you'd be able to best me."

Humor returned to Garhren's face as he took Kai's arm in the warrior's grip. He clapped him on the shoulder. "Go spar with Duvall next time you're worried about her. And send a woman to my tent to soothe me."

Kai felt his lips twitch and shook off his guilt. Garhren was unharmed. They returned to camp as the doctor emerged from Jeniah's tent. Kai hurried to him and braced himself.

The doctor grimly rubbed his hand over his face. "She's been beaten. She's completely exhausted, and her lungs are filling with fluid. I've given her a tea from the best herbs available, but she'll need them every two hours day and night. The worst of it is her wrists. She literally tore off the flesh. I had to clean out bits of metal embedded in the bone. I fear she'll develop infection."

Kai put a hand to his face. "She did that getting free of shackles."

The doctor nodded soberly. "She told me."

Kai ducked inside Jeniah's tent, followed closely by the doctor. Wearing a man's tunic and a borrowed cloak, she sat on a bed devouring a piece of bread. Though her face was pale, bruised, and twisted in pain, she offered Kai a smile, her eyes soft. She coughed, the sound tearing from deep inside her chest. The doctor frowned and handed her a steaming cup of tea. She smiled her thanks and emptied her cup before finishing the remainder of the food, her manners still perfect. Kai almost smiled.

"How do you feel?" He sat beside her.

"I desperately need a bath, but I feel better now."

The tent flap opened and an Ardeene knight stepped inside. As his gaze fell on Jeniah, he bowed. "Your Highness." He turned to Kai. "Captain Darkwood, Captain Tarvok said to inform you that there's a peace flag approaching."

"I'll be out momentarily. Escort the messenger to the main tent."

The knight saluted, bowed to Jeniah, and left the tent.

Jeniah finished eating, and after drinking deeply from her goblet, she stood. "Let's go see what the Hanoran messenger has to say."

The doctor eyed her with disapproval. "You need rest, Highness."

She fixed a patient but firm gaze on him. "My country is at war."

He backed down and grumbled, "I'll see you when you've concluded your business."

She nodded. The doctor left and Kai moved closer to Jeniah. He looked searchingly at her, dread forming a hard knot in his chest at the thought of what else she had suffered at the hands of the Hanorans. The raped and murdered bodies of the women and children the night the Hanorans invaded Arden still haunted him.

Jeniah laid a hand on his cheek. "I'm all right."

He probed for any sign of deeper hurt but did not find the shattered, hollowed look he feared he would. Relieved more than he could have expressed, Kai put his arms around her and held her carefully, afraid to hurt her battered body.

"The Hanoran messenger is at the perimeter, Captain," called a voice from outside the tent.

Kai frowned at the interruption. Still holding Jeniah's hand, he left the tent. Garhren grinned at them both as he and Duvall, another Darborian knight, moved to walk beside them outside.

"Garhren!" Jeniah threw her arms around Kai's friend.

Garhren returned her embrace, and Jeniah flinched. He instantly released her and fixed a searching gaze upon her. When he saw her bruised and cut face, he shot a look of horror at Kai. His face darkened in rage and Kai knew the war had just become personal for Garhren.

Jeniah held both of Garhren's hands, smiling affectionately at him. "I never thanked you for helping Kai rescue me tonight. I'm glad you're here."

Garhren's righteous anger softened. "I'm in your service, Your Highness," he replied deferentially. But a mischievous glint came into his eyes and he raised her hand to his lips. He glanced at Kai, clearly enjoying making him squirm.

"All right," Kai barked. He'd have to take Gahren to task for that one.

Kai took Jeniah's hand out of Garhren's and placed it possessively on his own arm. She exchanged a conspiratorial smile with Garhren, but then turned and looked up at Kai with such adoration that he instantly forgot his irritation.

Garhren fell into step behind them while Duvall swept the area in front, both fulfilling their duties as Jeniah's personal guards. Kai never planned on willingly leaving her side, but he might be needed elsewhere. He'd take no chance with her safety. At the moment, he began to rethink his choice of Garhren as one of her guards. He looked over his shoulder at Garhren, who winked. Kai fixed him with a fearsome scowl that would have left a lesser man quaking in his boots. Garhren only chuckled. Oh, yes, Garhren would definitely pay, and Kai would show no mercy next time. Perhaps he'd even draw a little blood.

A gentle breeze stirred the tents and fluttered the flames of the torches and campfires as Jeniah and her escorts stood at the edge of the rise. A single messenger carrying a torch rode through camp, cantering his beast steadily, unflinching as Darborian and Ardeene guards surrounded him and escorted him into the main tent.

Captain Tarvok appeared at Kai's side, warily watching the Hanoran rider as he dismounted and spoke to one of the Darborian knights under Kai's command.

An Ardeene runner arrived. "He says he's under orders to speak to no one but the princess."

Kai looked in alarm at Jeniah. "Are you too tired for this?"

She nodded serenely at the messenger. "I'm on my way." She turned to Kai. "I'm fine. I must hear the messenger."

Kai instinctively checked to ensure all his weapons were in place. They moved to the largest tent, where the planning meetings took place. Jeniah sank down in a seat. Her pallor alarmed him, but her expression remained calm. Tarvok cleared the table of its maps and scrolls before he sat next to her. Kai and the guards remained standing, their hands resting on their weapons. Expectant tension rippled the air.

A servant handed Jeniah a goblet, from which she drank deeply. The tent flap opened and a Hanoran soldier was escorted inside by four Darborians knights.

Jeniah blinked at the Hanoran. "I know you. You're Prince Aragaëth's first lieutenant. Dayel, correct?"

The Hanoran went down on both knees at her feet and bowed his head. "Yes, Your Highness."

Kai tensed, watching for any sign of hostility. He knew the guards would have searched the Hanoran for weapons, and the lesser mage who had accompanied the Darborians to Arden would have checked him for dark magic, but Kai remained alert. Without looking at Garhren or Duvall, he knew they were as watchful.

His voice and posture perfectly respectful, the Hanoran said, "Thank you for seeing me, Your Highness. Prince Aragaëth wishes to discuss an alliance to help overthrow King Rheged."

Kai stiffened and opened his mouth to demand what the Hanorans wanted in exchange, but Jeniah asked quietly, "And in return he wants . . . ?"

"Only to be king of Hanore."

"And what of Arden?" Jeniah continued, poised and calm.

Kai watched her, amazed at her confident, commanding air. He sat in the presence of a queen.

The messenger looked steadily at her. "Arden will be yours, Your Highness, with Prince Aragaëth's blessing, and his hope for a peaceful alliance."

Captain Tarvok snorted. "And we should trust a Hanoran?"

The messenger glanced at Tarvok and then returned his gaze to Jeniah. "The Hanorans who follow Rheged are your enemies. Those who follow Aragaëth are your friends."

Captain Tarvok stood. "I think we're finished here."

Jeniah placed a hand on his arm. "No. We're not finished." She turned to the messenger as a surprised Tarvok sat back down, watching her. "Tell Prince Aragaëth if he comes alone, he will be granted safe passage into our camp and I will listen to his offer. And I will grant him safe passage out."

Kai stared at Jeniah. She actually considered joining forces with the barbarians who destroyed her home and murdered her family, and nearly slaughtered her in a brutal ceremony?

The messenger paused. "He requests that we meet in the middle of the field, Your Highness. You and he each bring two trusted advisors. No more. No less. And all come unarmed."

"Agreed. Light a ring of torches at sunrise, and we will come. Only three of us. No weapons." She gave the messenger a meaningful look. "I will have archers trained upon them, in case there is any duplicity, Lieutenant Dayel."

He nodded, bowed, and left, flanked by the guards.

Tarvok turned to her. "Princess, do you think this is wise?"

"King Farai told me that Prince Aragaëth has been planning an uprising. He did treat me well when I was his prisoner. And he clearly hates his father. I believe Aragaëth to be trustworthy."

Kai stared. "Treated you well? You've been beaten!"

She took his hand. "That happened at the hands of Rheged's men after we arrived in Arden. Aragaëth never harmed me, nor did any of his men."

"And if he plans to simply kill you the moment you arrive at his meeting place?" Tarvok demanded.

"He won't. I'm sure."

Captain Tarvok blinked, then stared at Jeniah as if he'd never seen her before. He looked wary, but reluctantly conceded. "As you said, archers will be ready, as will the rest of us. If he even thinks of harming you—"

Jeniah smiled gently and Tarvok faltered, clearly undone. "I will never forget your loyalty, Captain. And do not fear. If I must, I'm quite capable of defending myself."

Kai remembered her defeating the king's sorceress with a mere touch of her hand. What other powers had she discovered in his absence? She wore quiet confidence like a mantle, and she almost glowed with latent power.

She also looked exhausted. "In the meantime, I need a bath. And more food."

A servant hovering nearby snapped to attention. "It's already prepared in your tent, Your Highness."

Kai made sure Jeniah was safely in her tent, with Garhren and Duvall standing guard outside. Then Kai looked down and realized other men's blood still spattered his hands and armor from the earlier battle. "I need a bath as well."

"Your squire has already prepared that, sir," replied a servant.

When Kai entered his tent, there sat his Ardeene squire, beaming.

Kai grinned. "Romand."

"I heard you were here, sir."

Kai resisted the urge to hug the lad and instead allowed Romand to help him out of his armor. An hour later, bathed, shaven, and changed, Kai waited impatiently for Jeniah. When she appeared, he simply stared. Vaguely, he wondered where a gown for her had been found. It was too long and too loose, but clean and well-made, the gown of a courtier. Her hair flowed freely around her slender body like a dark cloud. Even bruised, her face glowed with beauty. She looked up at him with such love that Kai had to swallow hard. Then she smiled, and Kai nearly fell to his knees.

Garhren and Duvall backed out. Garhren winked as he closed the tent flap behind him.

Jeniah glanced about, noticing the table set only for two. "No one else is joining us?"

Kai shook his head slowly. "I didn't invite anyone else."

Her mouth made an "oh" and her smile broadened. He reached for her and she willingly came into him. He wrapped his arms around her very gently, acutely aware of her injured body, and held her close. The doctor had assured him that none of her bones were broken, but he did not forget the way she winced when Garhren had hugged her.

Kai caressed her face and lightly kissed her cut and swollen lips, keeping the pressure gentle.

She responded without hesitation, completely opening up to his kiss with all the tenderness of her guileless heart. She followed his lead, her unpracticed kiss deepening with his. Astonished at the depth of her innocent passion, Kai tightened his arms around her and basked in the warmth and softness of her mouth. He kissed her until he feared he would lose his powers of resistance. Shaking with the effort, he dragged his lips away from hers and held her.

She lifted her head. "I felt your presence in the courtyard—it gave me the strength to cast off the spell the Lamia placed on me. The bits of metal in my arms dampened my magic, so without you there strengthening me, I would not have been able to defeat the sorceress."

Kai tightened his arms around her. "I should have come sooner, before they put you in the tower. Before they hurt you. I should never have let them get to you in the first place. I should have kept you safe in Darbor." He had to stop then or his emotions would get the better of him.

"Oh, Kai," she breathed. "I hold you blameless."

"I love you, Jeniah. No matter what, I love you. I don't know what lays in store for us. I only know that it's wrong not to love you."

Saying the words renewed his conviction. Her arms tightened around him, and he basked in the feel of her body against his.

A small sob shook her frame. "I've longed to hear that. I've loved you since before Darbor, even knowing I may never earn your love in return."

It had been plain the way she looked at him, though she resisted telling him, but somehow hearing her speak those words shook Kai to the core. He was undeserving of such devotion, such love.

"I'm so sorry I didn't keep you safe in Darbor." He swallowed hard. "I'll never leave your side again." He tightened his arms around her, loving the feel of her in his arms. She nestled against him without speaking.

A feminine voice cleared her throat. "Dinner, Your Highness?" A servant stood at the opened tent flap, holding a tray laden with dishes and cups.

Kai reluctantly released Jeniah. She smiled as he held out her seat for her. The food was served Ardeene style, with individual plates arriving one course at a time.

Jeniah coughed into her napkin then waved away his alarm.

"It's nothing. A mere cold."

They ate in comfortable companionship as the courses arrived, but her color continued to fade, and Kai grew concerned. "You need rest. Dawn is only a few hours away."

"Perhaps." She pushed away from the table, not able to touch the last course.

"Jeniah?"

She tried to stand, but her legs buckled. Kai shouted for help as she crumpled into his arms. Garhren tore inside, looking terrified, while Duvall ran for the doctor. Kai carried her to her tent and laid her down on the bed, while a concerned Ardeene servant fluttered about nervously. The doctor soon arrived.

Kai turned to Garhren and Duvall. "Go rest. I want you on watch tomorrow when she meets with the Hanoran prince."

Jeniah lay on the bed, looking so still that Kai's heart nearly stopped. He fell on his knees by the bed and caressed her face and hands. Fever radiated from her body.

The doctor gave her another cup of steaming herbs and spoke in a hushed voice. "The infection has set in already. It will probably be several days before she's out of danger."

Captain Tarvok entered then, wearing a look of fear and wonder. "There appears to be a chayim approaching."

"She came," Jeniah whispered. "I called for her."

Tarvok leveled a steady gaze upon her. "I ordered a wide berth to be made. It's coming straight for the tent." He paused. "Are you chayim-bonded?"

A faint smile touched Jeniah's lips, but she lacked the strength to keep her eyes open.

Kai answered, "She has been since before the invasion."

Tarvok looked thunderstruck.

Kai stood at the tent opening and watched, along with every eye in the encampment, as the mythical beast padded silently into their midst. The large creature walked straight into the tent as if it knew exactly where to find its goal.

Kai and the others backed away slowly. The chayim turned and looked at Kai, great, dark eyes conveying a depth of wisdom. Kai blinked, astonished at the realization that this animal was not only sentient, but eternally wise. Kai had the impression he was in the presence of a sort of deity. He went down on one knee. Renewed remorse that he had killed such a creature swept over him. And this magnificent creature had saved his life many times.

The chayim moved to Jeniah. Those alarmingly sharp teeth carefully bit through the bandages on her wrists, and then a large, pink tongue licked the open sores. Kai stared in disbelief as flesh regenerated over the wounds until the skin looked as if it had never been damaged. The chayim nosed the princess, breathed into her face and licked her cheek. The cuts on her face healed and the bruises faded, leaving her skin creamy and flawless. Color flooded into Jeniah's skin—a healthy, natural glow. Jeniah sat up and plunged her hands into the animal's thick mane, an expression of rapture replacing the pain that had tightened her features only seconds ago.

Kai's relief left him weak.

The chayim nosed Jeniah again before she moved to Kai. He bowed his head, wishing he could communicate both his regret for his actions and his gratitude for the chayim's.

Ooomph. The chayim blew a great gust of air at him before she turned and padded silently out of the room, leaving a breathless hush in her wake.

Jeniah smiled steadily at Kai, her eyes clear. "She likes you."

Chapter Twenty-Seven

tanding on the rocky outcropping that served as their lookout point, Jeniah watched as the three riders came into the middle of the field.

"That's Prince Aragaëth in the middle," Jeniah said to Kai and Captain Tarvok. "His lieutenant, Dayel, is on his left. I do not recognize the other soldier."

The Hanorans were still far enough away that their features were difficult to determine in the first rays of dawn, but Prince Aragaëth's form had become familiar to Jeniah.

She glanced at the man she loved, standing next to her. Smiling, she took his hand. Kai responded readily, twining his fingers with hers, and when he looked at her, his frown of concern and concentration softened. She wanted the world to go away so she could fling herself into his arms and kiss him senseless.

Captain Tarvok stood rigidly at her other side. He'd aged visibly since she left Arden with Kai, and a new, very ragged scar ran the length of his cheek. Tarvok looked at the Hanorans with narrowed eyes, his expression mirroring his mistrust.

The riders dismounted, spread several thick blankets on the ground, and sat to await them.

Flanked by Kai and Captain Tarvok, Jeniah climbed down the rock formation to three waiting duocorns. In between Kai's

Braygo and Tarvok's mount stood a shining white duocorn.

A servant bowed as he handed her the reins. "A gift from the duke of Nortean. A queenly, mount, do you not think?"

Touched by the gesture, Jeniah stroked the beast's neck and rubbed the velvety nose. "Indeed, he is."

The white duocorn stood almost twice the size of her childhood duocorn, Egan, nearly rivaling Kai's Braygo. The beast looked her over and then nuzzled her hand. All around her, people whispered that she was chayim-bonded and destined for greatness. Jeniah felt the heavy weight of responsibility for her people. She prayed she would not fail them.

Kai lifted her into the saddle and she settled upon the back of the duocorn. She stifled a smile as two ladies-in-waiting rushed forward to arrange her skirts and cloak until they draped grandly. Riding between Kai and Captain Tarvok, she walked her mount through the camp.

People paused in their tasks and bowed as Jeniah passed them. Word had spread of her return, and Ardeenes from all trades and professions were flocking to her banner, offering their willingness to fight. Jeniah was shocked at the sheer numbers that arrived. Between midnight and dawn, the Ardeene army had already swelled to almost twice its previous size, leaving the Darborian knights a staggering number of unskilled recruits clamoring to be taught how to fight. For Arden. For the queen. The realization was humbling.

Kai had arisen long before dawn and efficiently organized the new soldiers under the skilled Darborian knights, who began to oversee their training. Jeniah knew he would help train them himself after he returned from the meeting with Prince Aragaëth.

His tension palpable, Kai glanced about continuously. Captain Tarvok sat no less alert. Jeniah knew the archers waited, arrows nocked, in case of danger. She also knew with calm assurance that Prince Aragaëth would not harm her.

Under a low fog, they rode out to the center of the field. The snow had melted, leaving thin drifts in some places, but mostly bare ground in others. A wind gusted and Jeniah pulled her cloak more tightly around her.

Three figures awaited in the field in the ring of torches. Aragaëth bowed. "Princess Jeniah."

He, too, had bathed. His black hair shone smooth and glossy in the morning sunlight and his clothes were clean, but he still dressed in the leathers of warrior. He'd discarded the white cloak distinguishing him as a leader of the Hanoran king's special forces.

Jeniah dismounted and took Aragaëth's offered hand. His dark eyes searched her face and she thought she saw relief there. He seemed on the verge of asking her something, but instead released her and introduced his aides next to him.

Jeniah also indicated the men at her side. "Captain Darkwood, Sauraii master, trainer of the knights of Arden, liaison, and commander of the Darborian forces." She resisted the urge to smile, knowing she sounded just like her father with his grand titles and ceremonies.

Aragaëth's eyes flicked back to Kai, clearly aware of the meaning of Kai's title of Sauraii master. He inclined his head warily.

Jeniah indicted Tarvok. "Captain Tarvok, general of the Ardeene army." As soon as she held the power, she would make his title official.

Aragaëth's eyes moved over both men, his gaze resting a moment longer on Kai. Kai's expression was perfectly impassive, but Jeniah recognized the glint of anger at the far edge of his control. Tarvok exuded undisguised hatred. Aragaëth's aides looked back mildly, seemingly unperturbed by the open hostility displayed on their counterparts' faces.

Kai shifted, moving his hand to his hip, where his sword would normally have rested. Jeniah briefly wondered if he had truly come unarmed, or if he still carried enough weapons secreted about his person to arm a small garrison.

"Prince Aragaëth," she said, completing the introductions.

Kai scowled and eyed Aragaëth as the two men stood face to face.

Jeniah's gaze flew back to Kai. His shirt was opened at the throat, revealing his collarbone. The braid of hair he had always worn on a thin leather strip no longer hung from his neck.

Before she could consider further, Prince Aragaëth spoke. "May we sit?" He indicated the cushions laid out on the blanket.

Pulling her gaze away from Kai, Jeniah sat on the nearest cushion, folding her legs underneath her. Kai and Captain Tarvok waited until she had settled herself to take their places beside and slightly behind her.

When they were all seated, Aragaëth looked at her closely. "Thank you for agreeing to speak with me, Your Highness."

She inclined her head. "You treated me fairly when I was your prisoner. I'm willing to hear you now."

"Are you well?" He dropped his air of formality and spoke quietly, still searching her face.

"I'm recovered."

He hesitated. "You were not badly hurt?"

"No thanks to you," snarled Tarvok.

Without removing her focus from Aragaëth, Jeniah reached back and laid a hand on Tarvok's arm. He stilled under her touch.

Aragaëth nodded patiently. "We should address that first." He took a deep breath. Behind him, the sunrise spread glorious rays over the land, tingeing the clouds with pink and scattering the shadows. "We have been facing civil war for years. The people are divided. Some are loyal to the king, but many hate and fear him and his magic. He invaded Arden because he craves blood and he needed the plunder, but mostly because he wanted to win the loyalty of the people by reminding them that he's a great war hero as well as a dark sorcerer. Warriors are more likely to win loyalty. Instead, they saw how his evil grew. More joined the dissenters and the rift between my people widened."

Jeniah nodded slowly, her gaze never leaving his face. "Then why did you take me from Darbor if you oppose him?"

"To protect you from Rheged's loyalists."

"Then why didn't you let me go when I escaped the tower?"

"I couldn't yet. I was counting on Rheged wanting to sacrifice you when I brought you to him. That's why we rode so hard, so we could get back in time for the eclipse. It was the only way I could defeat him."

"What do you mean the only way?"

"Rheged is immortal."

Jeniah felt Kai's and Tarvok's reactions—the subtle shifting, the increased tension. "How is that possible?"

"He and the Lamia are only vulnerable to death during the ceremony in the few seconds between the time his dagger is bathed in moonlight and the time his victim's first drop of blood is shed. Otherwise, it is impossible to kill either of them. I needed the king to begin the sacrifice. It was my only opportunity to strike."

"I wish you had told me," she whispered, remembering her dark terror, the desperation of her escape, the agony of wrenching her hands from the shackles.

Pain entered his eyes. "I wanted to. I really did. But I didn't dare risk someone overhearing me. The king's spies are everywhere."

Still locked in those too-recent memories, Jeniah swallowed against a painful lump. She had truly thought, despite his acts of kindness, that Aragaëth was going to allow her be tortured and killed.

He added, "And really, would you have trusted me?"

She hesitated. "I'm not certain."

"When the moment was right during the ceremony, I shot the king with an arrow. But at the last second he turned, and I only hit him in the shoulder rather than the heart. I had a second arrow nocked, but he moved out of range, and I lost my only chance."

"You should have found a way to tell me, given me some hope."

Aragaëth regarded her quietly. "I didn't entirely trust you, either. I couldn't imagine how anyone as pure and good as you could possibly possess magic, but I was convinced all magic was evil. I almost told you in the tower, but the Lamia seems to hear everything. Then I saw you facing the Lamia. She was so dark, and you were so light. I knew you were not only her match, but her perfect opposite."

Jeniah nodded slowly. "She was pure evil personified."

Aragaëth spoke again. "Ridding our country of the king's magic will help all of my people. But he cannot be killed until the next ceremony."

Jeniah shook her head. "Your king is not a sorcerer. The only magic he possessed came directly from the Lamia. Once she died, the king was left with none. He's as any man now."

Aragaëth rocked back. "He's mortal?"

"You pierced him with an arrow. Does he bleed?"

He frowned. "I will find out." He nodded to one of the men at his side, who got up and sprinted to his mount. "If he's truly only mortal now, he can be defeated. That will give great hope to my men. My spies will know soon enough." He grew earnest. "I can never make up for your losses in Arden, Princess, but please let me do what I can. Join with me. Let's defeat him together."

"I need a moment to consult with my advisors," Jeniah said, then stood and motioned for Kai and Captain Tarvok to follow her. Once they were out of earshot of the prince and his two men, Jeniah turned to look at Kai. He trembled in restrained fury, and she was impressed that he had remained silent. He spoke the moment she made eye contact with him.

"He seems sincere, but he's lying. He has to be. No one can do what they did to your family, your country, and have any honor."

Tarvok nodded. "I don't think we should trust him either. This might all be an elaborate ruse to discover our plans."

Jeniah studied them both carefully, then turned at looked at Aragaëth. Feeling her gaze, he looked up. When her eyes met his, she knew that the responsibility of his people weighed heavily upon him, and that he desperately wanted to free them from Rheged. He truly was a man of honor; she had known it even when she was his captive.

Jeniah turned back to Kai and Tarvok. "I trust Aragaëth. We will form an alliance with him to defeat Rheged."

"You can't be seriously considering this," Kai said.

Tarvok looked earnest. "Princess, we have enough aid to defeat them on our own. The Govians are here, the Darborians—"

"We have a ragged army of untrained men," Jeniah broke in, "plus two hundred Govians, three hundred Tiraians, and fourteen Darborian knights. We cannot possibly defeat Rheged's warriors on our own."

Tarvok's tone turned patronizing. "We won't lay siege on them tomorrow."

"We can if we join with Prince Aragaëth," Jeniah explained. "His army will double ours. He's genuine. He needs us and we need him."

Kai shook his head. "I don't like this."

"Every day we delay, another child dies on Rheged's altar."

Her advisors had nothing to say to that.

She fixed a stern look on them one at a time and called on their sense of duty. "I am the rightful queen. I need your support and your loyalty."

Kai closed his eyes briefly. When he opened his eyes, his gaze was steady. "You have my loyalty. I will follow your command." He bowed his head, placed his fist first on his chest and then on his forehead in the same gesture of respect she'd seen him give both her father and the Darborian king.

Tarvok looked grieved, but said, "I trust you in this, Your Highness. You are chayim-bonded. How can I dispute you?" He dropped to his knee. "I, Shaen Tarvok, pledge my hand, my sword, my loyalty to you, Your Highness, all my life, to my death, or until you release me." The Ardeene oath rolled off his tongue unquestioningly.

Touched by his devotion, Jeniah raised her hand. "Rise, General Tarvok. Let us free our people."

She turned to Kai, who nodded. They went back to the Hanorans, who rose to their feet, clearly apprehensive.

She offered the prince her hand. "We are agreed. Let us be allies. Come back to camp with us, and we will formulate a new plan to defeat Rheged and free Arden."

Relief and joy overcame Aragaëth's face. He took her hand. "I vow you will not regret this, Princess. I thank you for your faith in me. We must strike quickly before he comes after us."

They all mounted and rode back to the Ardeene camp. More than a few furtive glances were cast in the direction of the Hanorans, but all bowed to Jeniah like a running wave everywhere she went. Tarvok sent messengers to assemble the council immediately.

Once inside the main tent, they sat at the table and took refreshment while they waited for the others to arrive. With bewildered looks directed at Prince Aragaëth, the leaders of the Govian, Darborian, Ardeene, and Tiraian armies filed in and sat down.

Once they had all assembled and introductions were made, Jeniah stood. "Prince Aragaëth is our new ally. He will help us free Arden."

Stunned silence followed her announcement. Then, one by one, each deferred to the leadership of a girl of nineteen to decide the fate of a kingdom. Whether they did so because she was chayim-bonded, or a white sorceress, or merely the only heir to the throne, Jeniah did not know, but she was gratified by their acceptance. She hoped she would prove worthy of their trust.

eniah drew a deep breath. Except for the guards standing unobtrusively to the side, she was actually alone. The council had adjourned to eat a midday meal and stretch their legs, and Jeniah welcomed a moment of quiet. She circled the hollow, pausing to admire a few tiny, green shoots of grass venturing from their winter's nap. The trees still looked lifeless, but soon they too would awaken. Renewed, Jeniah returned to the tent.

Angry voices reached her as she neared.

"It's so very noble of you to want to help make Jeniah queen of Arden after your people murdered her whole family and destroyed the country." Sarcasm flooded Kai's voice. "But we don't need your help. We don't want your help. We already have a plan in place, and you will not be given the opportunity to discover it and betray us."

Jeniah stood in shock. She had expected something like this from Tarvok, not Kai. She paused inside tent's entrance, not wishing to intrude, but fearing to leave them alone lest they come to blows.

Aragaëth bristled and his words came out clipped. "You need my help. Without it your plan is more likely to fail, and even if you succeed, there will be much more bloodshed. Besides,

Captain, this really isn't your concern, is it?" A triumphant tone touched his voice.

Kai clenched his fists. "I'm her sworn protector. That makes it my concern. I've seen how much your supposed good intentions helped her before I arrived. I don't intend to let you hurt her again."

Aragaëth jumped to his feet. "I haven't hurt her! I'm trying to help, to make restitution."

"Stop." Acid poured from Kai's voice. "I don't know what you're really after, but whatever it is, as long as I'm alive, you will not get it."

Aragaëth shook his head angrily. "I knew it was a mistake to try to reason with you. You're so bitter you won't even listen."

"I don't trust you! You're a liar and a murderer like the rest of your people!"

The two men stood face to face. Jeniah had never seen Kai so angry. His narrowed eyes could have pierced Aragaëth's heart. A lesser man would have backed down.

"Are you challenging me?" Aragaëth asked in a dangerous, quiet voice.

"Yes! I don't believe for one moment that you have Jeniah's best interests at heart. I think this is all some elaborate scheme to win her trust so that you can take her back and execute her. Or worse." He paused and his voice quieted, growing more menacing. "Or that you are trying to trick her into marrying you so you can rule Arden as well as Hanore."

Jeniah burst into the tent. "Kai!"

Aragaëth rocked back as if Kai had struck him. He pressed his mouth together and glanced at Jeniah, with eyes filled with longing.

Jeniah stepped back, shaken by Aragaëth's expression. Despite her highly developed empathy and her clear understanding of people's motives since her chayim bonding, she'd never suspected he'd developed feelings for her. He was a good man, but she did not return his romantic affections.

The prince's voice gained strength as he locked his gaze with hers. "I'm not trying to gain power over Arden. We both need to defeat Rheged. It makes sense to help each other."

Kai made a sound of disgust and turned away.

Aragaëth turned to Jeniah. "I give you my word, I have no designs on your country."

Somewhere in the distance, birdsong filled the silence. Jeniah moved to him. "You proved what manner of man you are by the way you treated me when I was your prisoner. I knew then that you are a man of honor even though I tried to believe otherwise. I trust you. We are allies."

Kai stood woodenly. She knew he wanted to believe her, but trusting a Hanoran ran against his instincts. "That night you and your men attacked Arden—"

"If it means anything, Captain, my men and I weren't involved in the initial attack."

Jeniah was tempted to ask him where he was that night, but she held her tongue.

Aragaëth let out his breath, shaking his head. "I tried to talk him out of it before we left. I believed that we could strike up a trade agreement with Arden peacefully. I still thought that was what this was all about. I was stupid. Rheged laughed at my suggestions and said war would bring glory to our kingdom and reunite our people." Aragaëth's eyes darkened.

"And you didn't have enough support yet to oppose him," Jeniah put in.

"Not yet. He offered me power if I would lead the second line of attack. I hoped I could ultimately use that power to dethrone Rheged. It was the only way I could banish the Lamia and end those gruesome rituals. Then I saw the atrocities that Rheged and his men committed. No declaration of war. No established battlefield. Every plan he formed with me before we left was a lie. By the time my men and I arrived in Arden City a few hours later, the royal family had already been executed. Except you." His gaze flicked to Jeniah. "I knew then that I had to take action. Not only for my country, but for all the kingdoms. And now, what he's doing to the children . . ." Aragaëth looked as if he were about to become ill.

Jeniah kept her gaze steady upon the prince. "I believe you." She looked at Kai, silently pleading with him.

Kai nodded his head once. "I trust you, Jeniah." He turned to the prince. "I'll trust you. For her."

A messenger handed a missive to the prince. After reading it quickly, he nodded and looked up. "It's confirmed. King Rheged is injured. He was pierced by an arrow and the doctors have had to treat him. He's barely recovered from the fever." He smiled. "He's mortal. We can defeat him."

⁂

The night before the allies planned to wage war with the Hanoran king, Aragaëth motioned to Jeniah to join him by one of the outdoor fires. He radiated nervous energy. Kai had gone to oversee the final stages of the recruits' training. Garhren and Devan hovered nearby, taking their role as her guards seriously.

Jeniah sat beside the Hanoran prince. "You're excited."

He nodded, his mouth twitching in pleasure. "I can't wait to see the look on Rheged's face when he realizes what has happened. He taunted me all of my life that I was never going to amount to anything." His eyes glinted. "I do look forward to this. I relish the idea of bringing Rheged down."

"Then this is personal," Jeniah observed quietly.

"In many ways," he replied, his dark eyes intense.

Something in the forest drew her attention. She saw nothing, but her heart told her that her chayim was there. Drawn by the irresistible pull, Jeniah stood. "I must go. Do not follow."

Alarmed, her guards straightened. Three Hanoran spies had already been captured, and the likelihood that others were nearby remained a constant threat.

"It's all right, Garhren, Devan. It's my chayim."

"What's a chayim?" Aragaëth asked.

She left as an Ardeene tried to explain. She felt Garhren's watchful eyes, but he held back to give her some space. Maaragan's gentle guidance drew her into a strand of trees, where the chayim materialized and came to her. Jeniah burrowed into her thick mane as their minds touched, wrapping her in indescribable joy and warmth.

Assurance and comfort flooded through her. She had chosen well in forging an alliance with the Hanoran prince. Her plans were solid. Maaragan approved and saw the shedding of blood as a necessary end to the tyranny. She had been nearby during Jeniah's capture and imprisonment, but she kept back to allow Jeniah to find her own latent strength—the strength necessary to defeat the Lamia.

Renewed, Jeniah returned to camp but halted when she saw Kai and Aragaëth standing alone together. Jeniah blurred and moved closer.

"I'm placing a great deal of trust in you," Kai said.

"I know, Captain," Aragaëth said quietly.

"If anything happens to her—"

Aragaëth held out his hands, looking deadly sober. "I know. You will hunt me down and kill me slowly with your bare hands. And I know you're not only a Darborian knight, but also a Sauraii master, fully capable of doing just that, even if an entire army stood in your way. But I swear to you by all that's dear to me, I won't let her be harmed. I have many reasons to keep her safe. I'll defend her with my life."

Kai studied him. "I hope it's enough."

Chapter Twenty-Nine

Jeniah sat upon a scaly Hanoran beast, while all around her men prepared for battle. Kai vibrated with tension and his fingers shook slightly as he tied her hands loosely in front of her. Jeniah wished she could say something to reassure him.

"Try that," he said.

She twisted and pulled one hand free from the ropes.

"Can you reach your weapons?"

She pulled a long dagger from the sheath strapped inside her sleeve, and a longer one from the sash around her waist.

He looked satisfied but not relieved. Concern etched lines into his face, and his jaw was rigid. "We could use a double. It doesn't have to be you."

She sheathed her daggers and laid a hand on his cheek. "It has to be me."

"I hate using you as bait."

Jeniah put her arms around his neck, almost smiling at the unique feeling of being on eye level with him. He hugged her so tight that she let out a squeak. His chain mail bit into her but she said nothing.

After a moment, she pulled away and looked him in the eye. "This plan is solid. It will succeed."

"I won't fail you." He kissed her with frightening desperation, as if he feared he'd never see her again.

Aragaëth and a dozen of his most loyal men surrounded her. "We're ready, Your Highness."

Kai carefully repositioned the ropes around her wrists and stepped back. Kai and Aragaëth exchanged a weighted look. Then Kai left for his post to await the signal, while Jeniah left camp with Aragaëth and his men. Surrounded by men wearing white cloaks over their armor, she cantered her Hanoran beast down the main highway toward the castle of Arden, rounded the curve, and came within view of the castle. The main gates opened, spilling out a complement of Rheged's men riding hard toward them.

Aragaëth glanced back at Jeniah, nodding in reassurance. It was time.

She swallowed her apprehension. She trusted him. Maaragan trusted him.

Aragaëth pulled his hood over his face and fell back to let another man act as the leader. The acting leader reined and held up his arm for the rest to follow suit. The soft talking of the other warriors trailed off as they were completely surrounded by King Rheged's men, about fifty in all. Jeniah's heart began pounding and her hands grew sweaty. She resisted the urge to look back toward the woods where she knew Kai and his men waited.

The acting leader called out to Rheged's man. They spoke animatedly and she caught the words "recaptured the princess."

Jeniah sat with her hands tied, her hair unbound and disheveled, trying to look defeated as the Hanoran's gaze raked over her. Next to her, Aragaëth's lieutenant, Dayel, slouched in an attempt to appear inconspicuous.

Satisfied, the Hanoran leader motioned his men to circle Jeniah and Aragaëth's men to escort them back to the castle. She let out a breath she didn't realize she'd been holding. At least the first phase of the ruse appeared to be working.

At the sight of the castle, Jeniah shuddered as she remembered the nightmare she had lived there only days before. Cold sweat ran down her back and she tested the ropes. She glanced back at Aragaëth. He met her gaze and nodded. Reassured, she returned her gaze to the ground.

They had traveled only a league when a battle cry suddenly rang out. Out of the forest charged a hundred Ardeene knights. In their forefront rode Kai, yelling and brandishing his sword, flanked by Garhren and the rest of the Darborians, all wearing Ardeene colors.

The Hanorans gave battle. Aragaëth's men made the appearance of fighting the Ardeenes, each carefully placing his strokes as if in a sparring tournament. Rheged's men fought with savage force against the Darborians who rushed to meet them. Kai ruthlessly cut down more of Rheged's men than the rest of the Darborians combined, and Jeniah almost pitied those foolish enough to face him.

The battle was terrifying. Deafened by the clashing of weapons and cries of pain, Jeniah watched in horror as Hanorans fell from their saddles. The smell of death laced the air.

A single Hanoran rider raced back to the castle to call for reinforcements. Their battle however, had already been witnessed from the castle watchtower, just as Jeniah had planned, and before he reached the outer wall, the Hanoran messenger was met by a full regiment of soldiers pouring out of the main gates. The Hanoran soldier conferred with the leader.

"That's Rheged's captain of the guard leading them," Aragaëth said to Jeniah under his breath as he sparred with a Darborian.

Rheged's captain and two hundred men thundered toward the melee. Kai fought his way to Jeniah's side, plowing between

Aragaëth and Dayel, who flanked her. She knew he was only making an appearance of fighting them, but at first glance, he looked fully willing to kill them both. Either way, they fell back under his onslaught with convincing alarm. Kai let them withdraw and refrained from delivering a fatal blow. His steely gaze ran up and down Jeniah as he assured himself she was unharmed.

Hoping her fear wasn't showing, she said, "I'm all right."

He acknowledged her with a nod and continued to destroy with calm dispatch until a startling number of Rheged's men littered the highway. A new understanding of Kai dawned in Jeniah's heart. He was efficient and deadly, but he was not a killer. He fought out of necessity, not because he embraced violence. She had thought she understood that before, but she realized it fully now. She also realized with sobering clarity that each time he took a life, he lost a part of his soul, and he suffered for it privately. A part of her shrank from the thought that he was killing—and losing another part of himself—for her sake.

When the soldiers from the castle neared the site of the battle, Kai grabbed Jeniah around the waist and pulled her onto Braygo with him. She glanced back at him, her brows raised. This was not part of the plan.

Kai looked back at the regiment charging at them from the castle. "Go!" He shouted to his men.

He and his knights and the rest of the Ardeene rescue party spurred their mounts. Aragaëth's men appeared to give chase. Few of Rheged's soldiers had survived the ambush, but those that did, rode in pursuit. No one seemed to notice that the Hanorans who had originally captured the princess still lived and only Rheged's men had died.

"The Ardeene rebels have the princess!" Aragaëth shouted.

The captain of Rheged's army spurred his men to pursue the rebel Ardeenes. The Ardeenes led them on a grueling chase over rocky hills and through deep forests, Aragaëth and his men following as well. Jeniah glanced back. The prince met her gaze with a determined, triumphant grin as he appeared to make every attempt to catch up to them. Their plan appeared to be working.

Jeniah knew that while the chase took place, an army made up of the remainder of the Ardeene army, along with Darborian, Lariathan, and Govian forces, was descending upon the castle with a vengeance. With a portion of Rheged's army led away from the castle to recapture her, the allies would easily overpower the remainder of the Rheged's men. That is, if all went as planned.

When the Hanoran flag lowered and Arden's flag rose in the castle parapets, Jeniah knew that the castle was secure. Kai and his men led Rheged's regiment to an open field.

"Garhren!" Kai shouted.

Garhren appeared next to him and scooped Jeniah into his arms. He settled her in front of him astride his duocorn. Garhren and Kai exchanged a nod before Garhren wheeled his beast around. Surrounded by five other Darborian knights who would act as her guard during the battle, Garhren raced his mount up to the bluff where their camp lay. His arms encircled her protectively and she knew he would keep her safe, not only out of duty, but out of loyalty to Kai.

"Are you all right?" he asked, eyeing her with concern.

"Of course. Kai took no chances."

Garhren nodded and glanced back at the other members of her guard to be sure they had fallen into position. They ringed her. She looked up at Garhren, remembering what he had done for Kai, how he had helped him when Ariana died. A surge of gratitude for this man overcame her. Friends with that kind of fierce loyalty were rare.

"You're a good man, Garhren Ravenwing."

Clearly taken aback, he glanced down at her. Then his sardonic exterior fell into place. "Don't tell anyone or you'll ruin my reputation."

She smiled faintly, then turned her attention to the field. Kai and his men engaged the enemy, while the less-experienced recruits fell back. Rheged's men were obviously astonished when many of the Ardeenes threw off their Hanoran cloaks and revealed themselves to be Darborian knights—the best-trained, most formidable warriors in all the kingdoms. Then Aragaëth lowered his hood and led his men in a charge against Rheged's men, fighting alongside the Darborians and Ardeenes, with whom he had clearly allied himself. Clearly enraged by the treachery, Rheged's soldiers fought ruthlessly.

Breathless, Jeniah waited in the trees, still on Garhren's mount, encircled by her five guards, her eyes upon Kai. He fought with such ferocity and skill that she never feared for him. He was magnificent. Every stroke of his flashing sword brought down enemy soldiers. The Sauraii cut down a wide space around him, quickly, gracefully, his movements absolutely effortless, as if he only sparred with children.

Jeniah hated the death, the bloodshed. Suddenly, all alliances fell away and she saw only men, killing and dying. No wonder Arden's history and culture abhorred fighting. But because of men like Rheged, Kai and other warriors had to live this way.

Nearby, Aragaëth fought against his countrymen with as much fierceness as the Ardeenes. The Hanorans he killed were loyal to Rheged, which made them his enemy. Some of Rheged's men recognized him and threw down their weapons, but others singled him out. Once, he took a hard blow and was knocked from his mount. Jeniah gasped.

Kai fought his way there in an instant, battling off those who tried to finish Aragaëth while he was down. With Kai shielding him, the Hanoran prince remounted, holding his arm protectively in front of him.

Allied reinforcements of Govians and Tiraians arrived, led by Tarvok and the remaining Ardeene knights. They surrounded the battlefield and the tide quickly turned.

A messenger rode in breathlessly. "Your Highness!" He shouted as he raced to Jeniah. "King Rheged himself is leading a full company this way!"

Alarmed, Jeniah cupped her hands. "Kai!"

He paused, alarm leaping into his face, until he saw that she still sat safely within Garhren's arms, the other Darborian knights carefully circling them.

Jeniah shouted, "Rheged is coming."

Kai nodded and called out commands to his men. Moments later, a column of Hanorans appeared on the highway, riding hard. Jeniah's heart fell to her stomach.

They were hopelessly outnumbered.

Kai regrouped his men, formed a new line, and with a battle cry, led them in a full charge. Her pulse throbbing, Jeniah watched as they came together in a terrible clash. For a few heart-stopping moments, she could not see Kai in the turmoil.

"I have to do something," she breathed. "I have to help them."

Garhren's tension and helplessness rippled off his body, and she knew he ached to be with his comrades instead of standing safely on the outskirts.

He spoke grimly. "There's nothing you can do. You need to stay here where it's safe. You are their standard. If anything happens to you, their fight would be lost."

"I know, Garhren, but—" Frustrated and helpless, she watched as brave men died by the dozen. Kai still battled, nothing touching him. But so many others perished.

She wanted to help them, shield them. She stilled. Perhaps she could.

She straightened and sent out a screen to protect all of the allied forces combined to free Arden. Using her senses, she reached out, seeking all Ardeenes, all Darborians, all of Prince Aragaëth's men. Separating them from Rheged's men proved difficult, but she probed their minds, seeking their loyalties. Using every bit of strength she possessed, she concentrated on protecting them, shielding them. Soon it became apparent that the blows delivered by the Hanorans had no effect on the allies, even when their aim was sure. The allied warriors retaliated, and each man was able to slay the Hanorans he faced.

It took a tremendous amount of energy to create such large shield. Jeniah quickly weakened and grew lightheaded. Though she did not see her chayim, she felt Maaragan's presence as the creature lent her strength. Their combined energy created the power to protect her people from harm.

Hanorans began to fall by the hundreds, pressed by the inexperienced Ardeenes, who should not have been able to defeat them. The allies broke through the Hanorans' line of defense.

Jeniah's eyes moved to the center of the field, where two men faced each other in a battle that made the fighting around them look like play. Kai and King Rheged battled with terrifying ferocity.

Jeniah wanted to shield Kai, but knew he would resent her interference. Still bearing a self-imposed guilt for failing during the first battle in Arden, Kai needed to do this on his own. She sat alert, ready to shield him if the need arose.

There was no need. Kai slammed through Rheged's defenses and cut him down. The king fell off his mount, bleeding and beaten. Kai dismounted and stood over him.

Even from a distance, Jeniah could feel the glare Rheged focused on Kai. Aragaëth came then and also dismounted, standing shoulder to shoulder with Kai. The hatred Rheged directed at his son made Jeniah's blood turn cold. With his dying breath, the king spit on Aragaëth. Then he died.

A cry rose up. "The king is dead. King Rheged is dead."

Men stopped fighting, and an eerie hush fell over the field.

Aragaëth stood over King Rheged for a moment, then removed his helmet and kneeled. Gently, he slid off his father's helmet. With his hands on either side of the king's head, Aragaëth closed his own eyes and lifted his head. His voice raised in a death song. It was caught up by the other Hanorans as they honored the passing of their king.

When the last notes of the death song faded away, Aragaëth stood and turned to an alert Kai, who poised to fight him if the need arose. Jeniah knew Kai worried that Aragaëth would turn on them once his purpose had been served. That Kai had still chosen to save the prince's life during the battle in spite of his misgivings spoke volumes of Kai's character. He would make a great king.

At that moment, Jeniah realized Arden needed him as badly as she did. Determination burned within her more brightly than before to marry Kai. She would find a way.

Aragaëth bent over, retrieved his sword, and turned to stand near Kai. He raised his sword, his other arm hanging useless and bleeding at his side.

"Brave warriors of Hanore! You are outnumbered, but you do not need to die. If you renounce Rheged and pledge your loyalty to me, your lives will be spared."

After a brief hesitation, as one, the Hanorans dropped their weapons and went down on bended knee, pounding their hearts with their fists and bowing their heads.

"Long live King Aragaëth!" Dayel shouted.

The cry gained strength as it was repeated by the Hanoran army. As Aragaëth turned to face Kai, Jeniah held her breath.

While the shouts of acclaim continued, Kai bowed his head, then placed his fist first on his chest and then on his forehead. Jeniah smiled. Solemnly, Aragaëth offered his arm and Kai took it in the warrior's grip.

Jeniah slid off of Garhren's duocorn and, followed closely by her guards, moved toward Kai and Aragaëth.

Aragaëth met her halfway. His face streaked with dirt and sweat, his clothing stained from the battle. "This changes nothing. We are still allies." He went down on one knee with bowed head.

She sank into a deep curtsy. "Long live King Aragaëth of Hanore."

"Long live Queen Jeniah of Arden."

Someone lying on the battlefield called weakly. As Jeniah listened, she heard the young tenor voice of a man barely out of boyhood, calling for his mother. Sickened by the carnage, she stepped carefully over bodies, following the sounds. Out of a tangle of bodies on the ground, a hand reached toward the sky. She moved to it.

"Mother." A young Hanoran soldier with a wound that had nearly cloven his head in two lay crushed under the weight of his dead mount. He was only minutes from death.

Moved by compassion, Jeniah kneeled beside him and took his flailing hand. "I'm here, my son," she said softly.

His blood-stained fingers gripped her hand desperately. "I'm afraid, Mother," he whispered.

Jeniah pressed his hand in between both of hers. "It's all right, my son, I'm watching over you. You'll be home soon."

Instantly, fear on the young soldier's face changed to relief. The youth smiled, his battered face becoming peaceful. His hand fell limp and his eyes closed in eternal sleep. She placed his hand on his chest, feeling fully the horror of war.

Jeniah stood looking down at the Hanoran soldier and wept for a boy too young to have died in battle, and for the loss of life all around her. Kai pulled her into a comforting embrace.

The sun sent long shadows over the land when Jeniah remounted. Escorted into Arden City by a full regiment of Ardeenes and Darborians, she rode between Kai and Prince Aragaëth toward the castle, the colors of the former king of Arden proudly flying on the tops of the towers.

Captain Tarvok and his men galloped up to Jeniah. His arm was bound with bandages, but he looked steady. A wolfish grin crossed his face. "We gave them the beating they deserved."

Jeniah did not share his enthusiasm for the carnage around her. "You did well, General."

He turned and rode alongside her and her entourage as they entered the main thoroughfare of the capital city of Arden. There, lining the streets and kept in order by vigilant Ardeene guards, gathered Jeniah's subjects, the people of Arden. They were starved, battered, and beaten, but not defeated. Hope glimmered in their eyes.

When Jeniah was spotted, a shout rang out and a deafening cheer rose up. It continued as the procession followed the ruins of the main thoroughfare. Men threw their hats. Women and children waved scarves and ribbons. Some had tears in their eyes.

These were her people. Tears ran unchecked down her cheeks as understanding dawned on her how much the Ardeenes looked to her with hope for the future.

At the square in the middle of town, Jeniah dismounted and made her way to the top of a heap of rubble, flanked protectively by her soldiers. She held her arms out toward the throng. The crowd pressed forward and hushed.

"My people," her voice rang out clearly, "we have all suffered terrible losses. You have endured great evil. Crimes have been heaped upon you. But there is still good in the world, in each of you. Together, we will rebuild our homes, our land, and our lives. Together, we will again make Arden a safe place to raise our children. We will again have peace and prosperity. We will not let the suffering of our fellow Ardeenes go uncomforted. My beloved people" —she had to stop to compose herself, hearing the emotions of the crowd— "I vow to rule with equity and honor. I'm both your queen and your servant."

As she bowed a thunderous cheer arose. Then a ripple of excitement followed by a hush made her straighten. The crowd parted as her shaggy, golden chayim padded noiselessly toward her. Not even a bird song broke the silence. Jeniah and her chayim stood nose to nose before her chayim turned to flank her, face out, as if to declare to all of Arden that Jeniah was bonded to her. In unison, the people fell to their knees in homage to their new queen and to her bonded chayim.

Chapter Thirty

When Jeniah failed to return home from her ride, Kai cantered Braygo to the shoreline to check on her. He had seen her wandering like a lost child through the gardens and knew she must be deeply grieving her family. Now that she was home, their presence would be sorely missed.

At the break in the trees, he spotted Jeniah sitting on the rocks at the shore. As Kai neared, he came upon Aragaëth, who sat watching her.

Kai dismounted and approached the future king of Hanore. Three Ardeene guards saluted Kai and continued sweeping the area, keeping Jeniah in sight.

Aragaëth turned with a start. "I hate it when you sneak up on me like that," he grumbled.

"You were looking so hard that you wouldn't have heard a stampede." Jealousy colored Kai's voice.

Aragaëth appraised him. "Why so hostile, Captain?"

"Stay away from her."

Aragaëth faced him fully. "Are you threatening me?"

"Consider it a warning."

First anger, then puzzlement crossed the young king's face. "What's the matter, Captain? I thought we had gone past this."

"I know you desire her."

Aragaëth met his gaze unflinchingly. "Of course I do. I'd be a fool not to."

"Go back to Hanore. She has no need for you now."

The king raised his eyebrows, but then understanding shone in his eyes. "You aren't royalty. She is, as am I. Is that what concerns you?"

Kai took a menacing step toward him.

Aragaëth held up his hands. "Captain, I've no quarrel with you. In fact, I owe you my life. It's clear you love each other. I'm not going to try to win her from you." His eyes grew thoughtful. "But you do have a problem. If her family were alive and in power you might have a chance, since you are a Sauraii master and a celebrated war hero. But she's the queen. That complicates things. Her people need her to keep to their traditions. She has a duty to them. This is bigger than the two of you."

Kai turned away, not wanting to hear all his thoughts expressed by another.

"What choice do you have? Stay here and torture yourself trying to resist her? Or be her lover and bring dishonor to you both? Ardeene morality is legendary."

Kai's gaze never wavered. "I don't need you to tell me to keep her pure. But I also swore to her that I would never leave her."

Gently, as if aware of the depth of Kai's emotions, Aragaëth said, "Captain, Jeniah is young. A young girl's heart is a fickle thing. She will learn to love someone else."

"Someone like you?" Kai shot back.

After a moment, Aragaëth replied, "Perhaps. In time."

Kai gave a short, terse laugh. "Her duty does not include marrying the king of a country that invaded hers, massacred her people, and executed her entire family. Feelings are still very strong toward Hanore despite your new, fragile alliance. She would never marry you."

Aragaëth appeared to swallow an angry retort and turned to watch the princess, who still sat at the water's edge, her shoulders shaking. "She needs you. At least until after she's crowned queen. After that . . ." He looked back at Kai. "You are a man of honor. I believe you'll do the right thing." He gave Kai a long, searching look, then turned and strode away.

For several minutes, Kai stood unmoving. Aragaëth was right, of course, and had voiced the very fears that had tortured Kai all along—even more so now that they had defeated Rheged. Jeniah would be crowned queen the next day. They had no hope of a future together. What Kai would do, he did not know.

He went to her where she sat on the rocks, hugging her knees. At his approach, she raised her tear-streaked face and held her hand out to him. Kai sat down and pulled her against him. They sat quietly together. He loved the feel of her in his arms, the way she snuggled into his chest, the scent of her hair, the softness of her body. This was real. This was as it should be. How could this not be right?

Jeniah lifted her head and carefully studied his face. He felt as if his soul was being laid out to her.

"What's wrong?" she asked.

He took a steadying breath. "You will be queen tomorrow. I will have no place in your life."

Alarm widened her eyes. "Do you really think I care about that? I love you."

He hugged her to him fiercely, a weight pressing on his chest. "I love you. That will never change, but your people need a strong ruler and a sense of stability. They need their customs and traditions to help unify them. Only you can help them heal. Having a commoner for a king is against everything they believe in. No matter how much we want to, we cannot change the facts."

She clung fiercely to him. "Everyone knows that if it weren't for you, I wouldn't be alive. The minstrels are already singing about your heroic deeds. There would be no queen without you, and Arden would still be under Rheged's tyranny. Do you really think anyone would be surprised if we married? It's common knowledge how we feel about each other."

Kai pulled on his stoic façade. "Duty must dictate our actions."

She pushed him away. "Don't you recall what you said to me? You said that it didn't matter what lay in store for us, only that you knew that it was wrong not to love me. You swore that you would never, ever leave me. You gave me your word. Don't you remember?"

"Of course I remember. I meant every word. I will always love you, Jeniah. I will love you until I die. I—" He raked his hands through his hair. The old familiar fear arose, fear that these intense feelings were cracking his armor, making him vulnerable. His shoulders slumped in defeat. "Consider the future we really have."

She laid her hand on his cheek. "I do think about it, constantly. Trust me. I'll find a way." She searched his face carefully. "New recruits pour in daily. I realize the oath you pledged to my father does not necessarily apply to me, but I need you to train them. We have no army of any significance. We're helpless. Will you stay?"

The weight in his chest turned to searing pain as he considered life without her.

"Kai? You're not leaving, are you?" Panic touched her voice.

He fortified his emotional armor. He couldn't cave in now. "I'll remain as long as my king allows it." But he knew it wouldn't be long now before he'd be recalled into service, before he'd have to leave her.

It was better that way.

At Jeniah's coronation, every rule of etiquette was rigidly followed. All of the neighboring kings and queens attended in support. There were endless speeches and priceless gifts.

The feasting, dancing, and celebrating went on until dawn. Kai stayed nearby throughout, his presence lending Jeniah strength, but he remained shielded and distant. Her coronation had only emphasized the hopelessness of their future together. She knew she was running out of time. Jeniah spent much of the next day conferring with lawmakers and historians. When they stopped for a break, she went into the gardens, following its winding paths in solitude.

Spring had arrived, awakening a few of the hardier trees and shrubs. Vines and stalks tentatively opened their blooms. Jeniah stood still, breathing it all in before going to a part of the garden where there was a view of the shore. How she longed to ride down to the beach and lose herself there for a time.

Aragaëth found her then.

She smiled. "Please join me. I love the gardens. I feel so alive here."

"They are beautiful," he agreed as he sat beside her. "Nothing in Hanore is so lush. But I tire of the damp, and I long to return home to Hanore."

"There's something on your mind."

His mouth curved. "I came to tell you that I'm leaving in the morning."

Jeniah nodded. "You are needed in Hanore. You have helped heal the rift between our people. I'm grateful to you for all you have done for Arden. And for me. It will be a long, slow process, but I hope that someday our people will become friends as we are."

"That is my wish as well."

She waited, knowing there was more.

He seemed to be searching for the right words. "Jeniah, I . . . I find that I'm reluctant to be away from you." He rushed on. "And I know how you feel about Captain Darkwood, but Jeniah, I love you. And I wish for our alliance to go beyond the political arena."

"Aragaëth—"

"Look me in the eye and tell me that you feel absolutely nothing for me."

Jeniah dropped her eyes and took a steadying breath.

He lifted her chin, forcing her to see the genuine love shining in his dark eyes. His finger ran along her cheek and he smiled softly. "I've wanted to do that for a very long time."

She swallowed hard and opened her mouth to speak, but before she could utter a word, he leaned in and kissed her. His arms went around her and he pulled her close, his mouth insistent upon hers.

She pushed him away. "No!" she whispered tersely.

"Tell me that you felt nothing then, that you didn't want me even a little."

Her voice was stern. "I love Kai Darkwood."

"You didn't answer me."

Anger and remorse battled in her heart. "You've done a great deal for me, for all of Arden. You are a wonderful man, and you will go down in history as a brave and wise king. But I don't love you. I feel affection for you, but it is esteem, not love. I love Kai. Nothing will ever change that." Aragaëth's hurt, so clear on his face, tore at her heart, but she continued, "And no matter who his parents are, he's my one true love."

"Are you sure? Couldn't your feelings be gratitude for him saving your life and protecting you? What about your people? Are you willing to turn your back on everything you hold dear so you can be with him?"

"I loved him before he became my protector. I've always loved him. And yes, I would dry up the ocean if it meant keeping him with me."

Defeated, Aragaëth dropped his eyes and stepped back from her. "Very well, Your Majesty, I understand."

"Aragaëth." She waited until he made eye contact. "You are a man of honor and courage, a credit to your people. And you will lead them into a new age. I'm honored that you find me worthy of your affection. I realize you do not give it on a whim. I wish I could return it."

If her father's plan had been carried out, she would have married this man. Now that she knew the prince, that thought was no longer terrifying. Perhaps her father had been more wise and careful than she realized at the time. But because she loved Kai so deeply, she felt no temptation to choose another over him.

Aragaëth nodded sadly. "I knew my suit was probably in vain." A ghost of a smile flitted over his mouth. "You can't really blame me for being so bold as to make an attempt. I'd hoped you'd see all of my fine qualities: my charm and good looks and the fact that I'm now going to be king. And I'm sure there are many more, but I can't think of any at the moment." He made a wry face but the disappointment behind his jest was obvious.

Jeniah smiled sadly.

He pressed her hand to his lips. "An alliance between our countries was not based upon your acceptance of a personal alliance, you know."

"I know." She leaned up and kissed his cheek.

He closed his eyes as if the gesture hurt him. "Shade and sweet water to you and your house, Your Majesty." He bowed and left her alone in the gardens.

Jeniah returned to the library and her work with the historians and searched with greater fervor. Very late that night, she found what she sought. Elated, she ran to share the news with Kai, but when she found him in his room, he looked stricken.

She felt as if the wind had been knocked out of her. Had he seen her with Aragaëth? No, something else was wrong. "What is it?"

He lowered his arm and let a missive flutter to the floor. "I've received my orders. I'm to go to Govia. The northerners are burning villages along the border."

Jeniah sank down in the nearest chair. "No," she whispered.

Kai dropped to his knees in front of her and took her by the hands. "I'm sorry. I must report back immediately."

"Get someone else to go."

"You know I cannot refuse an order."

As Jeniah tried to blink back her tears, Kai lifted her chin. "Perhaps this is better."

"No, Kai. No." She lost the battle over her tears.

"I'll leave a contingent of knights to help train your army. They are good men, good fighters. You will not be left defenseless." Kai's hands were on her face, his thumbs wiping her cheeks.

His gentle touch filled her with unexplained fury. "They told me in Darbor you always do this. You leave every woman who gets too close. You refuse to let anyone inside, to let anyone near your heart."

Kai stared at her, his face paling. "You think that's what this is?"

"At the time, I thought it would be different with me. Now I know I'm no different than the others."

Aghast, he stared at her. "I'm not lying."

"I believe your orders are genuine, but you have been searching for a way out, and now here it is. You can leave me without guilt and go find your next lady, someone who won't threaten your heart."

"You don't really believe that."

"If it weren't true, you'd find a way to be with me. You would stay. You would trust me."

Clearly anguished, he stared. But he did not deny it. And he did not appear to entertain thoughts of refusing to leave her. She ground her teeth. So much for finding a way to make him king.

She snatched her hands out of Kai's and arose, her anger giving her fortitude. "Go, then."

Jeniah's heart broke as she walked away from the man she loved more than her own life.

Chapter Thirty-One

The Govians and their allies won the border war, defeating the wild men from the north, but the casualties on both sides were catastrophic. Even so, the Govian king had proclaimed the battle a great victory. After receiving commendations and expressions of gratitude from the Govian king, General Kai Darkwood began leading the survivors of his army home to Darbor.

Kai looked back at the weary column of warriors behind him and paused at the top of a low rise before descending into a valley. They should be home in another day or two. Winter was upon them, making the landscape lifeless and barren. Kai felt the same way inside.

His eyes were drawn to the gray sky. A few snow flurries drifted down intermittently, swirling in the wind, but melted before they hit the ground. Jeniah's face haunted him, and her words wounded him each time he recalled them. Lately, he had wondered if she were right. Had he taken this set of orders as the honorable escape from a hopeless situation? Was he wrong to leave? It certainly seemed so. He hadn't felt so lost since he buried Ariana.

When they stopped for the night, Kai checked on the wagon of wounded men. Garhren lay among them, pale and grim, but alive.

"We're almost home, my friend," Kai said.

Garhren opened his eyes. "Good. Then you can tell the king you've decided to leave his service and live in Arden."

Kai stared at him. "I can't quit."

"No. You can't. That's why you need to go back to her."

Kai shook his head and a hint of a smile touched his mouth. "You would have me walk out on our king, show up at her doorstep, tell her I've been a fool, and ask her to marry me."

"It's what every woman wants."

Kai snorted. "Advice coming from the worst womanizer that ever lived."

Garhren's gaze was steady. "If I found a woman like her, I would cross the whole world to be with her, get down on my knees, and beg her to marry me."

"And if I arrive and find her in King Aragaëth's arms?" Kai muttered darkly, his stomach clenching at the thought.

"Challenge him to a duel," his friend replied without hesitation.

Kai chuckled, relieved that Garhren was feeling well enough to jest. "That would be well received in a land that frowns on violence," he replied dryly. Then he grinned, thinking it might be fun watching Aragaëth squirm. Or die. Especially if he had touched Jeniah. "I think I'm starting to like your idea."

"When are you going to admit that all of my ideas are good?" Garhren said, sounding like himself. "And when your competition is dead, or at least humiliated, proclaim your love and beg her to marry you."

"You keep using the word 'beg,'" Kai pointed out.

Garhren shifted, groaning in pain. "Kai, you are the finest man I've ever known, but you've got a weak sense of what women want. You have to fight for her. Overcome any obstacle. Smash every barrier."

"Oh? And you are the expert?"

"Just because I haven't found anyone to give my heart to, doesn't mean I don't know how to go about doing it properly when I do." Garhren's gaze was steady.

Kai stared unseeing, the dull ache in his chest sharpening into pain. He missed Jeniah. He was incomplete without her. Empty.

"Kai, do you or do you not want to spend the rest of your life with her?"

Soberly, Kai looked out over the darkening horizon. "I do."

"Then make her see she would be foolish to turn you down."

Agitated, Kai started pacing. "And simply turn my back on everything else—King Farai, her royalty and my common blood?"

Garhren scowled at him. "I never realized you had a cowardly streak in you."

Kai stared at him as if Garhren had punched him in the face. "If you weren't already wounded, I'd thrash you for that."

"If you hadn't spent the last six moons acting like a man who had nothing to live for, I would have thrashed you ages ago," Garhren growled.

They stared at each other, anger crackling between them, before Kai turned and stalked away.

He spent a sleepless night. Cowardly? Hadn't he proved his courage countless times? Hadn't he faced everything that had ever frightened him and defeated it? Cowardly! Garhren was obviously delirious.

Jeniah had accused Kai of looking for an excuse to leave her. That was ridiculous. He wanted to be with her. He wanted to marry her and love her freely every day of his life. He wanted to have children with her and grow old with her. But that wasn't possible, was it?

Should he have rejected every rule and asked her to marry

him? He wouldn't have had to beg. She would have married him gladly. Then. But now? Had her feelings changed?

Since he had left Jeniah and Arden, he had been a shell. He should never have left her. He thought he was being strong in denying himself and keeping her elevated in her position, by not making her condescend to marry a commoner. Perhaps it would have taken more strength to smash the social barriers between them and follow his heart. Was he too late?

Kai didn't know, but he had to find out. He quickly scribbled a missive to King Farai, handed it to one of his men, and jumped on Braygo. He wasn't sure, but as he rode away, he thought he heard Garhren laughing.

⌘ ⌘

When Queen Jeniah emerged from her council chambers followed by her chief advisors, she nearly fell over with shock. Standing before her, looking as if he hadn't slept in a moon cycle, stood Kai Darkwood. His handsome face was haggard, he appeared to not have shaven in several weeks, his hair was too long, and his blue eyes were shadowed. In fact, his scruffy appearance reminded her of how he had looked the first time her gaze had fallen upon him almost two years before.

The Darborian Sauraii looked at her as a man dying of thirst looks at a cup of water. He swallowed hard and visibly restrained himself from moving.

Her pulse throbbed in her ears and elation raced through her nerves. Her first impulse was to throw her arms around him and kiss him until she grew gray hair. Her second thought was to slap him and have him thrown in the tower. She settled for folding her shaking hands in front of her and staring at him with controlled coldness. "Captain Darkwood, it is customary to request an audience with the queen in writing." With distain, she pointedly looked over his armor and traveling clothes. "It is also common practice to bathe and change one's clothes before presenting oneself to royalty."

Those who were nearby discreetly left them alone. Even the guards eased back to give Jeniah and Kai privacy.

For the briefest moment, Kai hesitated. Her reception appeared to have thrown him off balance. Then his determination shone.

"Common practices be hanged," he replied with uncharacteristic vehemence. He stepped to her and swept her into his arms, his mouth descending on hers with breathtaking passion. "I love you, Jeniah," he breathed before his mouth captured hers again. "Marry me. Marry me, and I will spend the rest of my life begging your forgiveness. I never should have left you."

His kisses prevented her reply, but she wouldn't have been able to form thought enough to give him one anyway. She leaned into him and wrapped her arms around him, savoring his kiss and the feel of his arms about her. Her heart, neatly back inside her chest, began to beat again.

Kai was back. He loved her. He wanted to marry her. She succumbed to him, immersed in warmth and wholeness.

But he had left her once. What was to stop him from leaving her again?

She tore her mouth away from his and pushed against his chest. He was slow to loosen his embrace. One of his hands caressed her face. The love that shone in his beautiful blue eyes nearly undid her.

"I have not been whole since I left you. Marry me."

When she pushed him again, he released her, a touch of fear showing in his eyes. She had not sensed it before, but suddenly she knew he was afraid she would reject him, that she would choose tradition over him, or that she no longer loved him. In a manner very unlike him, he lowered his carefully mastered shields and stood before her, his eyes devouring her, looking as desperate and battered as she felt. His visible anguish and longing stunned her. Her heart nearly broke at the thought of Kai consciously allowing her to see inside his shields.

"How do I know you won't leave me again when it suits you?" she asked him with as much bitterness as she could muster.

The hurt on his face deepened at her words and tone of voice, but he remained open. "I won't leave. I resigned my position of service to King Farai of Darbor."

"I could have you thrown out," she threatened.

He blinked. "I'll lay siege on the castle until you let me back in," he said with determination.

She folded her arms and eyed him doubtfully. "How many men are with you?"

"Just me."

She clamped down on the smile that threatened to curve her mouth. "A siege of one?"

"I'll make a nuisance of myself."

"I'm sure you are more than capable of that," she remarked dryly. "And if I throw you in the tower?"

"I'm a Sauraii. No prison wall can hold me." Smugness touched his voice.

Perhaps he was ready after all. But she had to be sure. She would not risk another heartbreak at his hands. "Go away, Kai. You don't belong here." It took all the willpower she possessed to turn her back on him and walk away.

He grabbed her by the arm and turned her toward him. "You never were one to play games, Jeniah. What is this you are doing?"

She poured all of her tear-filled nights and empty days

during his absence into her answer. "You left me to go fight a war with barely a by-your-leave. You were gone for nearly eight moon cycles. You never sent me word. Now you show up here, unannounced, tell me what you think I want to hear, and expect me to fall at your feet in gratitude that you have chosen to grace me with your presence. I've no assurance you will even stay." Though aghast at the cruel words that tumbled from her own mouth, Jeniah continued to pour out her frustrations. "You are arrogant and cruel, Kai Darkwood. Go find a wench to keep your bed warm, and leave me be."

His hands tightened on her arm, the intensity of his eyes burning. "There has been no one since I met you. And there will be no one except you. Not ever."

If her heart had been as icy as she portrayed, that fierce declaration would have melted it. Using all her practiced decorum, she gave no indication how much his words moved her.

"How terrible that must be for a man like you," she replied sarcastically. "Please, feel free to resume your normal indiscretions, for I will not stand in your way." She twisted her arm out of his grasp.

He stared in astonishment. "Do you really think I would have traveled this far, left my service to my king, if I weren't sincere?"

Jeniah moistened her lips. If Kai had truly left his king's service, that act alone confirmed his dedication to her. She fully understood how difficult that sacrifice had been. Yet she wondered if she could truly trust Kai. "I don't care why you've come, Captain. Go back to Darbor." It nearly tore her heart out to say the words.

Kai flinched as if she had struck him. When he replied, his voice was subdued but his eyes remained intense. "I will go for now, but not to Darbor. I've been given quarters inside the castle.

Come talk to me when you've had time to think about it. Don't decide rashly. Please."

The "please" nearly crumpled her resolve. She turned away.

"Jeniah."

How delicious her name sounded in his voice. She froze. Oh, how her heart ached!

"I do love you."

All her willpower engaged, she walked away from him without looking back. If she had, he would have seen the tears in her eyes. She began walking without direction.

He loved her! He had come back to her! It had taken him nearly a year to do it, but he was back, professing his love and willing to break every rule to marry her. He meant it. Of that she had no doubt. But would he be true?

⁂

Kai's weariness found no relief that night. Jeniah was hurt and angry. He didn't blame her for her reaction, and he knew he was the cause. At least it proved that she had missed him, and that somewhere underneath all that bitterness, she must still care. If he had met apathy, he would have known he had lost.

How could he prove to her that he loved her and was willing to do anything she asked of him? Leaving his king and country and coming here was not enough—he knew that now—but what would be enough?

At dawn, Kai sought out Tarvok. The castle had been rebuilt in a vague imitation of Darbor's castle, the outer walls three times as thick as the original walls. Guard towers stood at each of the four corners, and a wide moat lined the walls, both of the castle and of the city surrounding it. It looked impenetrable.

He found Tarvok leaning against the bailey wall with a frown almost fearsome enough to look unfriendly. Tarvok pushed off and drew his sword.

"General Tarvok," Kai greeted as he drew his own sword.

Tarvok's eyes glittered and he grinned darkly. "The man without a country."

"Your future king, I hope."

Tarvok laughed. "You poor, lovesick fool."

Their swords came together. Kai pushed him mercilessly, pouring out all of his frustration upon Tarvok, who was as near his match as he'd ever found. Except possibly Garhren.

"She's not betrothed, is she?"

"Her advisors suggested that the queen needs to find a husband soon. Duty to marry and produce an heir, you know."

"Any prospects you know of, Hanoran or otherwise?"

Tarvok took so long to reply that Kai feared the answer. He parried and countered, sickened that he truly might have lost her.

"No. She's rejected all of her advisors' recommendations." Tarvok's eyes glittered. "She appears to be in love with some Darborian Sauraii. However, she's only now passed her twentieth year. I suppose there's time for her to get over that lout and chose an appropriate husband."

Kai thrust his blade deeply, but Tarvok threw him off.

"You're slow today, Captain," Tarvok taunted.

"It's General, by the way. Or at least, it was before I resigned."

"If you weren't trying to kill me, I'd salute."

Kai gave a short, terse laugh. "If I were trying to kill you, you'd be dead."

"Your moves have never been so predictable. What's wrong?" Tarvok teased. "Haven't you slept well? In a few moons?"

Kai glared at him.

Tarvok laughed. "She loves you, Darkwood. But she needs to

decide if she really wants to put up with you all her life." He put down his sword and rested upon it.

Kai lowered his arm. "What can I do to prove myself to her?"

"You've already done it. She's not the child she once was. She's a woman, and she has a woman's mind. When she's ready, she will send for you. And she will. In the meantime, go get some sleep. If you were one of my men I'd give you a leave of absence until you started to look human again."

Kai sighed. "I would too."

Tarvok sheathed his sword, clapped him on the shoulder, and walked away.

Kai's weariness settled over him so deeply that he barely made it to the room he'd been given inside the castle before he fell onto the bed fully clothed and went to sleep.

⟡

Knowing Kai was in the castle gave Jeniah a long-absent peace. She slept better than she had in ages. In the morning she awoke feeling whole. She forced herself to patiently hold court, have her meals, and attend the usual meetings before she went to see Kai. He had made her wait nearly a year; it wouldn't hurt him to wait one day. That afternoon, she could not resist any longer.

There was no response to her soft knock. One of the guards said the captain had sparred with Tarvok the previous evening and then had gone inside his room without emerging or requesting meals.

Jeniah pushed the door open. The late-afternoon sun slanted through the leaded windows on a motionless form lying crosswise on the bed. She quietly went inside.

Kai lay in his chain mail on his stomach as if he had simply collapsed and not moved. His booted feet hung off the side of the bed and his head was turned to one side. Remembering the first time she had seen him sleep, Jeniah gazed down upon his stunning face. A strand of hair fell over his eyes and his lashes lay close to his cheeks. He looked serene. And beautiful in a raw, masculine way.

She resisted the urge to touch him. She knew his habit of denying himself sleep when he was troubled or had pressing responsibilities. If he were finally sleeping after days or weeks without rest, she would not disturb him.

She could deny it no longer. She still loved him as much as ever, and she could not bear the thought of living without him another day.

Jeniah tiptoed out of the room and activated a plan she had devised before Kai left her.

⟡⟡⟡

An aggravatingly persistent knock on the door woke Kai. He sat up blearily and rubbed his eyes. A faint light glimmered through the leaded window. It was too pink for dusk. Was it dawn? His stomach rumbled loudly enough to convince him he had skipped far too many meals. The knock continued. With a groan, Kai rose and pulled the door open with a scowl. A messenger stood there.

"Good morning, sir," he said brightly, annoyingly oblivious to Kai's fearsome glare. He handed Kai a missive with the queen's seal on it. After another cheeky grin, the servant left.

Inside the room, Kai leaned against the door. With less than steady hands, he broke the seal and read. By royal command, he was to appear before the queen that evening to receive a Medal of Honor. His heart began to beat faster. It was possible that this was nothing more than royal courtesy, but knowing Jeniah, there was more to it than that.

After devouring enough food to feed a small army and then spending a few hours training in the arena, Kai bathed, shaved, and changed into full dress uniform. Ardeene uniform.

As he entered the throne room, Kai remembered the day he had arrived in Arden so long ago to be greeted by the king. Today, the throne room was full of people, many more than Kai thought could possibly fit inside. After he was announced and the trumpets played a fanfare, he strode to the throne, where Queen Jeniah sat in stunning, glorious beauty.

His heart pounded. She wore a mysterious smile, confirming that something was happening besides recognition and a Medal of Honor. In homage to the queen, Kai kneeled on the floor before the steps leading to the dais. He bowed his head, placing his fist first on his chest and then on his forehead.

Queen Jeniah stood. "Rise, Kai Darkwood."

He mounted the first few steps until their eyes were at the same level. Mischievous joy twinkled in hers.

"For courage and valor far beyond the call of duty during a time of terrible loss, and for personally protecting and helping to restore upon the throne the only living member of the royal family, I award you, Kai Darkwood, this Medal of Honor." She held up a beautiful, intricate medallion hanging from a braided cord.

"This medal has been awarded only once before in the history of Arden. My great-great-great-grandfather awarded this medal to a young soldier in his army who, very much like you, found himself in difficult circumstances and who also rose above them to protect the royal family from certain death.

"In gratitude for your bravery and heroism far above your sworn duty, I now bestow this upon you."

Jeniah leaned forward, and Kai bowed his head so she could

place the medallion around his neck. Her nearness sent his senses spiraling.

"When this medal was awarded by the king, he also offered to the young man—who was a commoner without any royal blood, and not even a knight—the hand of his one and only child, his daughter, in marriage. They did marry, and upon the death of the old king, he and the princess ruled Arden as king and queen. That commoner-turned-king was my great-great grandfather."

Kai held his breath as he filled in the blanks.

"Therefore, in keeping with the tradition attached to the awarding of this medal, I offer to you the same—" she paused dramatically, her face shining "—my own hand in marriage, to rule by my side as king of Arden."

Kai's pounding heart nearly leaped from his chest. Could this be true? Cheering filled the room to an almost deafening roar. Jeniah's smile widened. For a moment, Kai was so overwhelmed that he could only stand mutely staring. Finally, trying to think of an appropriate response, he dropped to one knee. Then he stood. Tossing aside all rules of decorum, he swept Jeniah into his arms as the cheering increased tenfold.

"Does this mean you accept?" she asked breathlessly between kisses.

"How long do I have to think about it?"

"I think you'd better decide before you assault the queen again, if you want to keep your head on your shoulders."

"In that case, I guess my answer had better be yes."

Kai sealed their agreement with another kiss.

Never before in the history of Arden had a more widely anticipated wedding taken place. The love story of Kai and Jeniah was told repeatedly in homes and taverns across the country. Minstrels sang of it in every hall. Women dabbed their eyes at each retelling, and every young girl dreamed that a handsome man would save her life and give her his heart.

Extensive preparations commenced and every tradition was honored. The new queen would have the very best, whether or not she cared, which, for the most part, she didn't. She and Kai would be together. That was all that mattered to her.

Queen Jeniah's only request was that all the necessary supplies and food needed for the wedding, banquet, and ball be purchased from her own people. Much of the royal treasury had dwindled in the construction efforts to rebuild after the war and consequent siege, and what was left was used to buy from local farmers and merchants who in turn, used the money to purchase provisions from neighboring countries in the open-trade agreements that Queen Jeniah established.

At last, the day of the wedding arrived. Every king, queen, prince, and princess in all the kingdoms attended. They brought enough food to feed the country for a year and such priceless gifts as Jeniah had never imagined. The wedding was an even grander affair than the coronation. Jeniah was fussed over by a dozen ladies-in-waiting until, at last, every hair lay in its place and every fold in her gown was carefully arranged. With more splendor than the castle had seen in generations, the royal wedding finally took place.

Jeniah felt as though her heart would stop when her hand was placed in Kai's. As they gazed at each other, she drank deeply of his beautiful blue eyes, knowing that at long last, she would be his. She remembered little of what was said or even who was there. They were finally declared husband and wife, and Kai was crowned king of Arden. The room filled with cheers and all the bells in the city rang in celebration.

The banquet was artfully laid out with exquisite dishes of food on tables that groaned with the weight of the bountiful feast. After everyone dined, the dancing began, the new couple leading the first dance. When the first dance ended, Kai led Jeniah from the dance floor. Other couples filled the floor as the next set began.

Garhren Ravenwing clapped Kai on the shoulder. "I'm not sure how I feel about having a king for a best friend. I suppose you will have to be perfectly respectable from now on. I guess that will be easier without me around all the time." He frowned a bit ruefully and Kai gave him a good-natured punch. Then, with more feeling, Garhren added, "I'm happy for you." He turned to Jeniah and drew her attention when he took her hand. "You are getting the finest man I've ever known. Take good care of him."

Jeniah kissed Garhren's cheek. "I'm grateful to you, Garhren. You are always welcome here." Wickedly she added, "But only if you leave your Darborian morality behind."

Garhren looked crestfallen. "Then I fear I will not visit frequently, or for long."

King Farai approached them, bowed, and then heartily clapped Kai on the shoulder. "Congratulations!" He winked at Jeniah.

"Well done, Your Majesty. Kai, I feel I should warn you about the dangers of feisty women. Especially one who can find a perfectly acceptable way to marry the man she wants in spite of everything stacked against them."

"I look forward to all the danger she can bring," Kai replied, pressing his lips to Jeniah's hand. Then he took her hand and led her to an older couple, whom he proudly introduced as his mother and stepfather. His mother had a pretty, heart-shaped face and the same blue eyes as Kai. His stepfather, clearly uncomfortable in his formal attire, bowed low. They both warmly congratulated the couple and wished them joy.

Kai's mother hugged Jeniah and kissed both cheeks. "Welcome to the family. Thank you for making my son whole again."

Jeniah's eyes stung with tears and she returned the hug. "Thank you for raising a wonderful son."

Then Kai's mother turned to him and embraced him. "I'm so proud of you, son."

As he held his mother tight, Jeniah was moved at how much his mother's approval clearly mattered to him. Then he shook hands with his stepfather.

"I know your father would be pleased. Not just at your choice in brides, but at the man you are," Kai's stepfather declared solemnly.

Kai eyed him steadily. "Thank you."

Then King Aragaëth of Hanore found his way to them and bowed low. "Congratulations, Your Majesties." His smile was genuine. "Jeniah, you look even more beautiful than ever." He turned to Kai. Their eyes locked, and Jeniah felt the tension between them.

"I think you already know how much I envy you," Aragaëth said to Kai. Before Kai could respond, Aragaëth added, "Be happy. Be well."

Kai nodded. "Of that you may be sure." He glanced quickly at Jeniah. "Thank you for your aid. And your friendship, King Aragaëth. We are in your debt."

Aragaëth held out a hand, which Kai clasped tightly in the warrior's grip. "Remember, Hanore is your ally. I will always be here if you need me." He bowed respectfully and made a graceful retreat.

There was more dancing, more eating, and several toasts. Then, at dawn and with much ceremony, the bride and groom were escorted to the bridal chamber. As soon as the new couple went inside and the doors closed, the revelers returned to the main hall and the celebration continued.

All alone with Kai, Jeniah felt suddenly shy and nervous.

"You look beautiful, my queen," murmured Kai, taking her hand in his and smiling at her. "I don't think I told you today how much I love you."

She laughed anxiously. "I don't believe love is actually part of the wedding ceremony with all these arranged marriages."

He cupped his hands around her face while undisguised affection shone in his blue eyes.

"Jeniah, queen of Arden, I love you more than any man could possibly have ever loved any woman. I've waited my whole life for this moment."

As he kissed her with infinite tenderness, her apprehension melted and she nestled into his strong arms, feeling a surge of longing rise up within her. As his kiss grew stronger and he drank her deeply, passionately, all their inhibitions dissolved and they discovered exquisite joy that exceeded all of Jeniah's expectations. Kai had banished the shields that stood between them for far too long and willingly gave her his heart. She kept it safe all her life.

Donna Hatch has had a passion for writing since the age of eight when she wrote her first short story. In between caring for six children (seven counting her husband), she manages to carve out time to indulge in her writing obsession, with varying degrees of success, although she writes most often late at night instead of sleeping.

A native of the Southwest desert, Donna writes Regency romance and fantasy, and she thrives on a happy ending. All of her heroes are patterned after her husband of over twenty-two years, who continues to prove that there really is a happily ever after.